# SARAH MAY

# *The Rise and Fall of a Domestic Diva*

**HARPER**

## HARPER

An imprint of HarperCollins*Publishers*
77–85 Fulham Palace Road,
Hammersmith, London W6 8JB

www.harpercollins.co.uk

A paperback original 2008

3

Copyright © Sarah May 2008

Sarah May asserts the moral right to
be identified as the author of this work

This novel is entirely a work of fiction. The names,
characters and incidents portrayed in it are the work
of the author's imagination. Any resemblance to actual
persons, living or dead, events or localities
is entirely coincidental.

ISBN-13 978-0-00-723233-8

Set in Meridien by Palimpsest Book Production Ltd,
Grangemouth, Stirlingshire

Printed and bound in Great Britain by
Clays Ltd, St Ives plc

FSC is a non-profit international organisation established to promote
the responsible management of the world's forests. Products carrying
the FSC label are independently certified to assure consumers that they
come from forests that are managed to meet the social, economic and
ecological needs of present and future generations.

Find out more about HarperCollins and the environment at
**www.harpercollins.co.uk/green**

**Mixed Sources**
Product group from well-managed
forests and other controlled sources
www.fsc.org Cert no. SW-COC-1806
© 1996 Forest Stewardship Council
FSC

This book is dedicated to all women who are either currently attempting – or who have in the past attempted – to raise children and pursue a career ... at the same time. Whatever your bank balance ... whatever your dress size ... whatever the state of your mental health ... you're all DIVAS!

# – THE PRC –

## THE PRENDERGAST ROAD COMMITTEE

### *CONTACTS LIST*

| *Name* | *Address* | *Tel.* |
| --- | --- | --- |
| *Harriet Burgess* | *236 Prendergast Rd* | *020 8369 4435* |
| *Ros Granger* | *188 Prendergast Rd* | *020 8369 2311* |
| *Kate Hunter* | *22 Prendergast Rd* | *020 8369 7866* |
| *Evie McRae* | *112 Prendergast Rd* | *020 8369 4956* |
| *Jessica Palmer* | *283 Prendergast Rd* | *020 8369 4221* |

# Prologue

Deep in a valley in the heart of south London, Kate Hunter woke up suddenly among the kind of rumples only a night-mare's sweat can give black sateen sheets. It was 4.52 a.m. She pulled the sheet up over her head, not wanting to see the early hours' outline of their IKEA wardrobe, IKEA bed, or IKEA chest of drawers – in case she saw something else that wasn't meant to be there; something that didn't feature in the IKEA catalogue – excluding Robert.

The only thing she could remember about the nightmare – and it was a vivid memory – was the feeling of water beneath her. She'd been floating effortlessly until she became aware that the dress she was wearing was beginning to pull her down – was in fact weighted in some way. As soon as she became conscious of the dress, her legs fell down through the water and she started to drown.

She and Robert had argued the night before – or rather, she had argued and he had watched. This was the way they rowed these days. What had the row been about? She didn't know any more – all she remembered was Robert sitting on the edge of the bed, looking sad and slowly undressing.

For a moment she thought it had started to rain, but it

was just a dry April wind brushing through the branches of the rowan tree outside.

Peeling the still-damp sheet from her face, she watched orange streetlight and flat moonlight fall through the broken blinds and compete for space on the bedroom walls. Turning towards the unconscious hump of Robert's back, she curled into his warmth, her fringe tickling his spine in a fragile apology as she let her nostrils fill with the scent of his skin – and drifted back to sleep.

On the brink of losing consciousness, she thought she heard a strange, sobbing scream. Her body jerked momentarily awake. One of the children? Robert's mother – Margery – asleep on the sofa bed downstairs? Whoever it was, she wished . . . she wished . . . her right leg slipped out of the side of the bed until her toes were hovering just above the floorboards. So that it looked as though she'd been dancing.

At that moment, Robert Hunter woke up without meaning to, unsure whether it was the scream – which he'd heard in his sleep – or Kate's hair and breath running up his spine that had done it. Rolling carefully onto his back and trying not to trap any of his wife's hair under his shoulder blades, he listened. In his muddled, pre-dawn mind, he became convinced that Kate's breath on his spine and the scream had conspired to wake him.

The scream unsettled him and, not entirely convinced he wasn't still asleep, dreaming, he took himself off to the bathroom and had a perplexed, early morning wank in the shower.

Afterwards, he let his back slide down the tiles until he was crouching, hot water pounding on his bent head.

Today he was teaching Jerome.

On Tuesdays, Thursdays and Fridays, he taught Jerome – and today was a Thursday. He didn't know when exactly it had happened, he was only aware that now he plotted his

2

week mentally around when he did and when he didn't teach Jerome.

There were children who got to you and then there were children who got inside you. Every teacher he knew – apart from himself, up until now – had one, and his was Jerome. When he shut his eyes he could see Jerome's face more clearly than he could see his own son, Findlay's, and what terrified him more than anything was that Jerome was changing him in a way nobody else had; not even Kate, not even his children . . . and he hated Jerome for that. He'd never been afraid of teaching before, but he was afraid now.

The dry April wind carried on making its way up Prendergast Road through the branches of winter-flowering cherries, silver birches, poplars and more rowans, past bay-fronted Victorian terraces whose drawn curtains were meant to conceal nothing more than healthy functioning families coping with life's run-of-the-mill ups and downs. The wind knew better, but didn't have anybody to tell.

As it brushed past No. 112 (which had featured on TV's *Grand Designs* only a fortnight ago), Evie McRae – in the grip of exhaustion-induced insomnia after having scored more than a line of cocaine in her garden office – left the house with her five-month-old daughter, Ingrid, and headed for the 24-hour Sainsbury's where she did the McRae weekly shop.

Ingrid was an abnormal baby.

She slept through the night – often for more than twelve-hour stretches – leaving Evie with very little to talk to other women about. So she'd woken Ingrid up – partly because she hated spending time alone and partly in the hope that by 8.00 a.m. she would have the same shadows under her eyes as everybody else she knew – and was now pushing her, screaming, down empty aisles towards the one open checkout.

At No. 188, Ros Granger woke up in an empty bed. It was only 4.52 a.m. Martin was sleeping on the floor of his office at Curlew & Fokes where they were so stretched on the immigration case that most of the lawyers working on it were only getting a maximum of four hours' sleep a night. After making sure the alarm was set for 6.30, she buried her face in the pillow that still smelt of him and waited to fall back to sleep. 'I deserve to be happy,' she said, through gritted teeth. 'I *do* deserve to be happy.'

At No. 236, Harriet Burgess woke up to eight-week-old Phoebe's still newborn-sounding screams. She had been dreaming that Miles had grown breasts and was feeding their daughter. Probably because her sister had phoned last night to tell her she'd just found out that prehistoric Irish chieftains used to symbolically breastfeed their entire kingdom – men, women and children. What sort of person *knew* this kind of thing? What sort of person thought *other people* wanted to know this kind of thing? Hauling herself out of bed, she went through to Phoebe, the sensory-triggered security camera they'd had installed in the hallway training its lens on her as she plodded past.

At the top end of Prendergast Road – beyond the crossroads with Whateley Road – Arthur Palmer, aged four and three quarters, woke up screaming. His mother, Jessica Palmer – only half awake – stumbled automatically into his room, tripping over a garage and farmyard, until her hand grasped the foot of Arthur's bed where Arthur was sitting screaming, still asleep. He was having a night fright, the extremist form of a nightmare.

Even in the half-light, Jessica could make out the muscles on his neck as his body took the strain of fear. He looked like he did when he was having one of his bad asthma attacks and she grabbed his inhaler off the bookshelves.

As she sat down next to him on the end of the bed, closer than she wanted to, the screaming stopped.

Arthur raised his arms weakly – one hand clutching his favourite Transformer, Burke – before sinking untidily back onto the duvet.

Jessica waited, then yawned and got slowly to her feet, creeping out of the room.

In the hallway, eyes nearly shut again, she walked into her sixteen-year-old daughter, Ellie.

'Everything okay?' Ellie asked.

'Oh – everything's . . . yeah, it was just Arthur, one of his . . . one of his . . . you go back to bed.'

They eyed each other uneasily and, after a moment's hesitation, Ellie walked unsteadily back into her room on her spindle legs.

'See you in the morning,' Jessica called out after her, hoping it sounded natural, then went back to bed herself, thinking she'd fall straight to sleep again; only she didn't. She rolled around in the big empty bed that seemed to get bigger and emptier every night, then listened to the central heating coming on and – realising that she wasn't going to get back to sleep until it got dark again in twelve hours' time – got up.

Downstairs in the kitchen, she stared at her day, plotted out in blue marker pen on the whiteboard next to the fridge.

Her neighbour, Kate Hunter, was picking Arthur up from nursery at 4.30 and taking him to Swim School with Findlay then bringing him home, because Jessica had viewings booked throughout the afternoon. She yawned again as the wind changed direction outside and the fan in the kitchen window started to clack unevenly in its broken frame. When would she get round to mending that? Probably never.

Turning round, she saw the pot of chrysanthemums on the windowsill that she'd bought because she liked the colour pink they'd been in the shop. When she got them home the pink seemed different, and she couldn't work out why she'd bought them when she'd never liked chrysanthemums anyway. Now they were half dead, the leaves and petals shrivelled.

She went over to the sink, filled an empty milk carton, and was about to water the plant when she stopped, suddenly pouring the contents of the milk carton back down the sink and lighting a cigarette instead.

She stood by the windowsill, smoking and staring at the chrysanthemums, not thinking about anything much.

*APRIL*

# 1

When Kate woke up again, an hour later, the edge of her pillow was wet, and for no reason at all her first thought was that Robert had been crying. Only Robert wasn't even in the bed.

'Robert?' she called out, anxious.

'Here,' he mumbled.

Then she saw him, kneeling on the floor in front of the chest of drawers, the bottom drawer open.

'I didn't hear you get up.' She didn't like to think of Robert awake while she was asleep.

'I couldn't sleep,' he said and carried on digging around in the drawer.

Neither of them mentioned last night's row; the sun was shining, a new day was beginning, and there just wasn't room for it.

'You're wet,' she observed.

'Yeah – I showered.'

'Already? I didn't hear the shower.' Kate carried on watching him.

Robert scratched at his armpit then stood up suddenly.

'What is it you're looking for?'

'I don't know – I've forgotten. Christ . . .' he added, ambivalently.

On the other side of the bedroom door they could hear Margery, who was staying with them at the moment while she had her Leicestershire bungalow repainted, irritably attempting to make a pot of tea. Everything about No. 22 Prendergast Road irritated Margery – primarily because she couldn't believe what Robert and Kate had paid for a terraced house with neighbours on one side who weren't even white.

The kettle started shrieking on the hob. The kettle irritated Margery – why didn't they get an electric one? Even the water coming out through the tap irritated her, and the irritation was so intense that Kate, lying upstairs in bed, could feel it as Robert walked towards her through bars of early morning sunlight.

'I heard someone screaming last night,' she heard herself saying as the smashing sounds carried on downstairs. 'I thought it might have been your mum.' Why had she said that? She hadn't meant to say anything about the scream in the night.

Robert, who had been about to sit down on the side of the bed and kiss her, stayed standing instead.

'She used to do that when I was a kid,' he said, suddenly remembering.

Still propped on her elbow, which was sinking deeper and deeper into the pillow, Kate waited for him to carry on, but he didn't. Unexpectedly, at 6.10 on a Thursday morning, the clouds had parted and Robert had given her a picture of a small child standing outside a shut bedroom door on a cold landing in the early hours of the morning, waiting for the woman on the other side to stop screaming; hating himself for not having the courage to open the door and walk in and comfort her when he knew he was all she had.

Kate and him stared at each other, momentarily stunned.

Robert never talked about his childhood. He never talked about it with Margery or other people who had been there, so why talk about it with people who hadn't? For him, it was time that had passed – and anyway, now he was healthily involved in the direct manufacture of his own children's childhoods.

He shrugged uncomfortably at his own transgression, then said cheerfully, 'So – what's on for today?'

'Today's the day.'

'For what?'

'Robert – you can't have forgotten.'

'What?'

'St Anthony's. Today we find out . . . whether Finn's got a place at St Anthony's.' That's what the row had been about last night – now she remembered and, pulling the pillow out suddenly from under her elbow, threw it at him.

Robert ducked and the pillow went crashing into the already broken blind, breaking another three slats.

'God, I hate those fucking blinds.'

Kate was trying to decide whether he was genuinely angry or not when she heard Flo, on the other side of the bedroom wall, starting to cry.

'Princess is up,' Robert said.

Ignoring this, Kate hauled herself automatically out of bed and said, 'Well, let's hope we don't have to sell the house or anything.'

'Why would we need to sell the house?'

'It's the only viable option,' she carried on.

'Viable option for what?'

'Getting Finn into St Anthony's. This end of Prendergast Road isn't guaranteed catchment area.'

'But isn't that why you've been dragging him to bloody church every Sunday since before he could talk, and why you—'

Kate started to speak over him. 'Beulah Hill's guaranteed. Jessica's been telling me about this place that's been on the market for over a month now – and it's a hundred and twenty thousand cheaper than what we'd get for this so we'd actually make some money,' she said, realising as she looked at Robert's face that this was the first time either of them had openly acknowledged that they needed to. 'What d'you think?' she said after a while, over Flo's increasingly loud and peculiar bleating sounds. Even after six months, the bleating still sounded odd to Kate.

She smiled absently at him as he walked over, put his hands on her shoulders, eventually kissed her and said quietly, 'I think that's fucking nuts.'

'But, Robert—'

'If we need to talk about our finances—'

'Our finances?' Kate started to laugh.

The laughter was ambiguous. Now he was anxious and over the past six months, which had been difficult – although the word 'difficult' didn't do justice to their marriage so far, so he'd avoided using the word – anxiety had become the third person in their marriage, making it an unpredictable *ménage à trois*.

There was a scratching at the door and Margery's voice, 'Flo's awake – do you want me to feed her?'

'It's fine,' Kate said, 'I'm just coming.'

How long had Margery been there? It was difficult to tell; she'd perfected the art of creeping soundlessly around the house. Sometimes, when Kate came back from work, she thought the house was empty until Margery appeared at random, framed in a doorway Kate was about to walk through, claiming to have been asleep.

'She's really working herself up.'

'Mum – it's fine,' Robert cut in.

Margery paused. 'Morning, love.'

12

'Morning, Mum,' Robert called back, watching Kate pull on some black pants that had gone threadbare at the back.

'D'you want tea – I've just made some?'

'We're fine.'

'There's plenty in the pot.'

'It's okay – we're coming down now.'

When Kate appeared five minutes later, Margery was still hovering on the landing.

'I didn't like to leave her in case she was choking or something.' Margery paused, as if the fatal choking had already taken place, adding, 'She's only six months.'

Kate disappeared into Flo's room and, as she lifted her daughter – now bleating hysterically – out of her cot, Margery, who was still in the doorway, said again, 'She's only six months.'

Kate stared at the rhinoceros on Flo's safari curtains, pulled over the Gina Forde-recommended blackout blinds, rhythmically stroking her daughter's back, aware of every bump in her unformed animal spine, and didn't say anything.

She didn't know how long she'd been standing like that, but when she at last turned round, Margery was gone and the house was full of the smell of economy bacon frying in the water it had been injected with at the processing plant.

Kate crossed the landing, walking through the toxic bacon fumes with Flo towards Findlay's room. Findlay was up, kneeling intently on the floor. His bed looked as though it had barely been slept in.

'I'm building a world,' he said, without looking up from the piles of Lego he had heaped on the rug in front of him – the Lego obscuring the Calpol stains that raising Findlay for the first four and a half years of his life had cost her so far.

'We need to get you dressed,' Kate said vaguely, over Flo's body draped across her shoulder.

'Okay,' Findlay agreed, standing up in a manner that was efficient rather than obedient, and that already lured her into confiding in him things about the world and the people in it that she wasn't convinced he was ready to hear yet.

'Should I wear my Spiderman suit?'

'Oh, Finn . . .'

'I should,' he insisted.

'But you've worn that nearly every day this week – it's filthy.'

He thought about this for a fraction of a second. 'But I should,' he said again. Then, 'Is it okay?'

Kate felt as though Findlay was prompting her, and when she finally nodded at him, he smiled back at her as if they'd just consented to take a huge leap forward in cross-cultural understanding.

Unnerved, Kate made a show of efficiency, opening curtains, making the bed – all with one hand. 'But not the mask – they won't let you wear the mask to nursery.'

Findlay watched approvingly as she helped him into the Spiderman suit while listening to what was going on downstairs. Had Robert, who didn't mind the economy bacon sandwiches as much as he pretended, finished making his way through the rashers leaking white residue, layered between Blue Ribbon margarine and two slices of Mighty White? She hadn't heard him come back upstairs and he hadn't brought her a cup of tea yet – a ritual observed every morning since the first time they woke up together.

Downstairs, Margery, who had been outraged when she'd discovered that Robert was expected to help himself to a bowl of cereal – when there was any – at breakfast, before a full day's work, was overwhelmed with pride that now she was here she could send him out into the world with meat in his stomach as well as a greasy chin and cuffs. That was one wrong in this marriage she'd been determined to set to rights.

She trailed after him now to the front door, in a grey tracksuit she'd been given by American Airlines on one of her Florida trips when her luggage got lost, and waved frantically as he cycled off down the street – until he turned the corner, out of sight. Then she sighed involuntarily, stared threateningly at the innocent commuters passing No. 22 on their way to the station, and shut the front door quickly before the Jamaican next door saw her standing there and decided to rape her. According to the free paper they got at home, *The New Shopper*, these things happened in BROAD DAYLIGHT in London, and nobody lifted a finger to help.

When she turned round, Kate was standing at the foot of the stairs, watching her.

'He's gone,' Margery said, fairly certain from the look on Kate's face that this was the first – or one of the first times, anyway – that Robert had left the house in the morning without saying goodbye. Had the Hunter marriage entered a new phase, and would she – as she'd always hoped – live long enough to witness her son rising like a phoenix from the ashes of a passion gone cold?

Kate hid her face in her daughter's back again, briefly shutting her eyes so that Margery couldn't read in them the last two minutes spent at the bedroom window, watching Robert cycle off down Prendergast Road without so much as turning to look up at the house; without so much as even saying goodbye.

When she opened them again, Margery had disappeared into the kitchen.

'You're never wearing that to nursery,' her voice exclaimed, outraged at the perversity of Findlay's fancy dress when there was no occasion.

'Mum said I could.'

'You'll get your eczema back if you wear that nylon suit in this heat.'

'What's nylon? I'm not hot anyway.'

'You wear it day in, day out – it needs washing.'

This had been Kate's point upstairs. Is that what she sounded like to Findlay? God.

Findlay didn't respond to this.

'You'll be covered in eczema by this afternoon.'

'I'm not hot,' Findlay said again, beginning to sound tearful.

At this, Kate went into the kitchen.

'The eczema's got nothing to do with the heat, it's stress related.'

'Stress related?' Margery stared at Findlay. 'He's five years old.'

'I'm four and a half,' Findlay said. 'Can I have some fruit?'

Unable to bear it in the kitchen any longer and feeling suddenly displaced, Kate prepared Flo's baby rice and took it upstairs, balancing Flo on their unmade bed among the pillows, and feeding her what she could. She got her dressed and was just getting into a pair of trousers when she heard Findlay, yelling distinctly, 'I DON'T LIKE PINEAPPLE.'

Leaving Flo floundering on the bed, Kate ran back downstairs into the kitchen.

'What's going on down here?'

'She's giving me pineapple,' Findlay said, pushing his face into his hands.

'You like pineapple,' Margery said petulantly.

'I don't,' Findlay started to sob.

'He drinks pineapple juice,' Margery appealed to Kate.

'I like pineapple juice, but I don't like pineapple,' Findlay sobbed.

'It's okay,' Kate said, going up to him and stroking the back of his neck just beneath the hairline.

'I've opened it now,' Margery grunted. 'It'll go to waste.'

'Opened what?' Kate said, losing patience.

16

'The can.'

'Can of what?'

'Pineapple.'

'But we don't have any cans of pineapple.'

'I bought this yesterday.' Margery held up the can with the can opener still clamped to the top, slamming it back down so that the syrup ran down the side over her fingers, which she started sucking on. 'He said he wanted some fruit.'

Kate watched her, suddenly revolted.

'He meant fresh fruit.' She gestured aggressively towards the basket on the surface near the coffee machine, adding, 'It's not like we're on rations or anything.' She tried to laugh, but it didn't work. She'd been waiting to say that for too long.

'I know we're not on rations,' Margery said, thinking suddenly of a cousin of hers who'd fought in the war and been taken prisoner in Burma by the Japanese, 'But real fruit's expensive and it goes off in this weather – doesn't keep.'

'It doesn't need to keep, it just gets eaten – and it's only April,' Kate said, her hand gripping tightly now onto Findlay's neck.

Margery licked the last of the pineapple syrup off her fingers. She was drifting now, more concerned with the memory of her POW cousin than the preservative quality of tinned fruit.

She stared at Kate, trying to remember what on earth they'd been talking about, but in the end gave up and turned away from her, starting to wash the frying pan instead.

'You're sure you'll be okay today?' Kate said, finally letting Findlay go.

Findlay ran upstairs.

'I'll be fine,' Margery responded, without turning round.

Kate wasn't convinced. 'You're sure you're going to be

okay?' she said again, feeling a sudden, unaccountable remorse at the sight of Margery's swollen feet, bound purple with varicose veins, emerging from a pair of mauve slippers they'd bought her at Christmas.

'I was thinking about doing some cleaning,' Margery said after a while.

'Cleaning?'

Margery tore off the rubber gloves she was wearing and strode purposefully to the kitchen door, standing on tiptoe and running her finger along the top of the frame. 'Look.'

Kate stared at her.

'Dust!' Margery said and, as she said it, Kate had a sudden memory of Margery filling the indoor drying rack with baby vests and sleep suits after Findlay was born, saying, 'You'll be washing at least twice a day from now on.' Stumbling blearily around the postnatal void and trying to come to terms with the fact that she had become two people, Kate had nothing at her disposal with which to defend herself against Margery's prediction of infinite domestic drudgery.

'I never knew you were meant to clean the top of door-frames.'

'I had an electrical engineer round once, who complimented me on the top of my doorframes,' Margery said, as if this settled the matter.

'Well, Martina's coming today.'

'Who's Martina?'

'The cleaner.'

Margery digested this rapidly, staring at the dust on her fingertip. 'I never heard Robert talking about a cleaner; he's never mentioned a cleaner to me.'

For a moment, Kate thought Margery was going to cry – it looked like her eyes were starting to water.

'She's a friend's au pair.'

'Where's she from?'

'Bratislava.'

'Have you given her keys?'

'Of course she's got keys.'

'Oh, I couldn't . . . I just couldn't.'

Margery was about to predict something apocalyptic when there was a banging sound from upstairs, followed by screaming.

'What's that?' Margery yelped, her nerves shattered under the duress of the newfound information about the cleaner who'd infiltrated her son's household.

'Shit – Flo.'

Was somebody breaking into the house to kidnap Flo? When she was a child and her mother lost her temper she used to say she was putting her out for the gypsies to take, but now it was the Arabs you had to be careful of. As everybody in East Leeke knew, there was a buoyant market for blond children in the Arab world. Were they coming for Flo here – now? The world was a terrifying place Margery thought, her mind full of Arabs scaling drainpipes – too terrifying sometimes.

Ignoring the strange whimpering sound that Margery, immobile, was making, Kate ran upstairs.

Flo was lying on her back on the stained carpet in their room, howling, and Findlay was kneeling beside her. When did Findlay come upstairs? She couldn't even remember him leaving the kitchen.

'I was waving at the face in the other house, then she fell,' he said, waiting.

'The face?' Kate picked Flo up, tentatively feeling her head and looking out of the window. There were no faces at any of the windows in the house opposite, which – local rumour had it – was some sort of Albanian- or Russian-run brothel. 'She's fine,' she tried to reassure him, as Flo started to calm down.

Findlay remained motionless. This wasn't good enough.

He wanted to know why she had permitted such a thing to happen and it dawned on her, standing there cradling Flo, that he was angry with her. The eyes staring at her through the slits in the Spiderman mask, which he must have come upstairs and put on himself, were angry. She'd shattered an illusion he didn't want shattered and now he knew that mothers – in particular, his mother – sometimes left their babies on beds and forgot about them, and sometimes the babies rolled off.

She tried to think of a comforting lie to tell him when she heard the post being pushed aggressively through the letterbox by the postwoman, who had some minor mental-health issues.

From the top of the stairs, she made out the red gas and electric, and the one from Southwark Council that would be their second and final reminder for overdue council tax. Between the recycling bag and piles of shoes that were beginning to look like something a UN forensic scientist might go to work on, was a brown A4 envelope that had to be the letter from Schools Admissions.

'Was it okay to wave at the face?' Findlay called out behind her.

Ignoring him, she stumbled down the stairs towards the letter.

'How is she?' Margery said, watching her.

'Who?' Kate couldn't take her eyes off the brown A4 envelope.

'Flo. What happened?'

'Oh – she rolled off the bed.'

'You left her on the bed?'

Kate swooped down on the letter from Schools Admissions, trying to decide whether to open it now or in the car.

'What's that?'

'The letter from Schools Admissions.'

'Well open it,' Margery said, impatiently. She'd been in on most of the week's conversations leading up to this moment – and the rows; like the one that had resounded through the ceiling last night.

With Flo balanced awkwardly on her shoulder, Kate – now nauseous with anticipation – ripped open the envelope and scanned the lines of the letter over and over again until she became aware of Margery watching her.

'So?'

'What?' she said, stupidly.

'Did he get in?'

Kate carried on staring stupidly at her and it was only when Margery said, 'Well, that's a relief,' that she realised she must have nodded.

'Your face,' Margery said after a while.

'My face – what?'

'It's a picture.'

'It's gone bendy,' Findlay put in from behind her on the stairs.

Margery, still watching her closely, didn't look entirely convinced. 'Don't forget to tell Robert.'

'I won't,' Kate said, automatically, with a sudden awful feeling that Margery was about to ask to see the letter – when the doorbell rang, followed by the sound of keys turning in the lock. 'Martina!'

Pushing the letter quickly into her suit jacket pocket, she ushered in Evie's Slovak au pair who, Kate sensed, much preferred the Hunter family to Evie and the rest of the McRaes at No. 112.

'Hey – it's Spiderman.'

'Tell me about the pig,' Findlay said, running up to her.

'Not right now, Finn,' Kate cut in, 'we're late for nursery.'

'Her grandma made a football out of a pig's head,' Findlay said to the assembled adults.

21

'For my bruvvers – it was Christmas,' Martina said, resorting to the south London colloquialism she found easier to pronounce than the 'th' sound of received pronunciation.

'Fascinating,' Kate said vaguely, beginning to lose the day's thread. 'Finn – come on.' She was about to leave when she remembered Margery, framed ominously in the kitchen doorframe.

'Martina, this is Margery.'

'Hello Margery,' Martina said cheerfully, entirely unaware, Kate thought with pity, of what the next few hours held in store for her.

Margery took in the tall skinny girl with bad skin in the bottle-green leggings and Will Smith T-Shirt, and grunted. Margery didn't know who Will Smith was and wondered if Martina was some sort of activist. She'd always been under the impression that one of the things the Communists had going for them was that they didn't like blacks.

'Martina – your money's in an envelope by the cooker,' Kate called out, starting to make her way down the hallway towards the front door.

'D'you want me to get anything for supper tonight?' Margery called out after her.

Poised on the doorstep, Kate's mind and stomach skittered rapidly over last night's chicken chasseur assembled with the aid of a chicken chasseur sachet and some best-buy chicken goujons. 'It's fine – I'm out tonight.'

'But what about the children?'

'They get hot food at nursery and I'm only doing a half-day so I can get them some tea.'

'And Robert?' Margery tried not to yell. 'What about Robert?'

Kate shrugged. 'I guess there's pasta and stuff in the cupboards – he can dig around and fix you both something.'

Margery was staring at her open-mouthed. She knew

things were bad, but not this bad; not only had Kate been sucking him of potential all these years – his glorious, glorious potential – she'd been starving him as well. Margery felt suddenly, almost crucially short of breath. Her poor, helpless boy.

'I'll shop,' she gasped.

'If you want – but there is stuff in the cupboards.'

The two women stared silently at each other before Kate turned and made her way with the children to the Audi estate parked on the street outside next to an abandoned blue Bedford van that she would have seen on last night's *Crimewatch* in conjunction with an armed robbery at the Woolwich Building Society – if she'd got round to watching any TV.

# 2

Margery carried on standing on the doorstep to No. 22 until the Audi had turned the corner out of sight. She was about to go back inside when a BMW pulled up on the opposite kerb, the doors clicking smoothly open as a smart young woman got out and walked towards the house with the red door and nets (at least somebody on this street had the sense to have nets) – No. 21. The house with faces – that was what Findlay called it. Kate said it was a brothel – Margery wasn't sure whether she was joking or not – and Robert thought Oompa-Loompas lived there because, apart from the smart young woman and short man in a suit now following her, nobody ever went in and nobody ever came out.

As Margery continued to watch, a face did appear at a first-floor window. The smart young woman who was at the front gate looked instinctively up and the nets fell back into place. She turned round and said something to the man, and it occurred to Margery that the man was afraid of the woman, now framed in the doorway to No. 21 and glancing across the street at Margery.

Margery smiled – she wasn't sure what else to do – and

continued to smile as the woman disappeared into No. 21. She looked – Margery decided – like the girlfriend of the landlord at the Fox and Hounds where Margery and her friend Edith had a spritzer on Fridays – and she was Lithuanian. Darren, the landlord, had intimated softly to Margery and Edith that Lithuanian girls really knew how to look after men.

Edith always used to say that Robert would end up with someone like that. A Lithuanian – or worse – a Rastafarian. Margery wasn't even sure if there *were* female Rastafarians, which made the insult even worse. Was Edith implying that Robert was gay? She'd got East Leeke library to order a biography of Haile Selassie in order to get to the bottom of the matter, and had been halfway through it when Edith informed her – through pinched lips – that her son, Andrew, was marrying a girl called Joy, who was Thai.

Up until Joy, Edith and Margery's friendship had a formula. It was understood that Edith had things and people in her life that Margery – bringing up an illegitimate child alone – was expected to envy. That's how their relationship had always worked, and Margery had put up with a lot from Edith over the years because Edith was all she had and her son, Andrew, all Robert had.

Joy changed everything.

Edith had been all the way to Thailand to visit her. Joy lived in a village with no running water, but they'd gone to a restaurant for Edith's birthday where you paid for the glass and could then refill it with Coca-Cola as many times as you liked. Not that Edith liked Coca-Cola, but – as she was quick to point out – that wasn't the point.

Edith said Andrew was going to buy Joy's village and turn it into a tourist destination – the Genuine Thai Experience. She also gave Margery some lurid and unasked-for details about Andrew and Joy's sex life that Margery was unable to fathom how she'd come by. None of this sex and commerce, however, detracted from the fact – as far as Margery was concerned – that Andrew had married a mail-order Thai bride because he couldn't get himself a decent English girl.

Since their sons' respective marriages, the balance of power had shifted in the relationship between Margery and Edith.

While Margery might not exactly get on with Kate, Kate did at least speak English.

'Do you like tea?' a foreign voice called out from some-where in the house behind her.

'Tea?' Martina asked her again, from the kitchen doorway this time.

Margery nodded, shutting the front door tentatively behind her and staying where she was, listening to the clink of china in the kitchen. So the au pair knew how to make her way round the kitchen then; knew how to help herself.

'Please – try this,' Martina said, reappearing in the hallway and handing Margery a cup of scarlet-coloured tea.

'What's this?' Margery asked, sniffing at it.

'Raspberry. I drink it three times a day,' Martina said.

Margery had no intention of drinking the tea. Not after the article she'd read in *CHAT* last week about the cleaner who'd given an elderly woman like her a drink with a paralytic in it that had paralysed her from the neck down. Once the woman was paralysed, the cleaner performed an autopsy on her WHILE SHE WAS STILL ALIVE, filmed the whole thing and put it on the Internet. Nobody was catching Margery out like that – especially not a commun-ist. Nobody was performing an autopsy on Margery without her permission.

She followed Martina back into the kitchen, noting the carrier bag on the bench with the box of tea bags inside that Martina must have brought with her.

'You bought these all the way from Czechoslovakia with you?' she asked, suspiciously

'From Slovakia – yes.'

'You can get hold of that sort of thing there then?'

'Of course,' Martina said, lifting her cup. 'You like?'

Margery didn't respond to this. 'Did you have to queue a long time for the tea?'

'For this tea? I don't know. My mother bought it at the supermarket. There are always queues at the supermarket.'

Margery put her cup of tea down on the kitchen surface. 'You have supermarkets?'

Martina nodded, blowing on her tea. 'I take my mother in the car one time a week.'

'Car?'

'My car – yes.'

'You've got more than one?'

'We have two.'

A two-car family – and there was Robert having to either cycle to work or get the bus because Kate needed the car. Margery glared at Martina, as if her car, the Krasinovic's second car, parked outside their block in Blac, was somehow denying the Hunter family their second car.

At least – as she discovered several minutes later – all the Krasinovic family lived in a flat; unheated, she presumed, until Martina set her straight on this as well, informing her that the Krasinovic apartment in Blac not only had central heating, but double glazing as well.

Margery's eyes skidded, mortified, over the rotting, peeling sash windows in the Hunter's kitchen that Kate refused to replace with new uPVC double glazing – not even after one of Margery's insurance policies came off and she offered to pay for the double glazing herself.

Presuming the conversation over, Martina retrieved the Carry-It-All that Margery had bought Kate at Christmas from the cupboard under the sink. The Carry-It-All was a turquoise plastic container with a handle that you could use to transport your cleaning arsenal round the house.

Margery had a lilac one at home – which she had ordered from the Bettaware catalogue along with Kate's – and it gave her a huge amount of pleasure, on a Monday morning, to make her way round her East Leeke bungalow with it. It was dishwasher proof as well – something she'd pointed out to Kate when Kate hadn't shown quite the right amount of enthusiasm or appreciation of the carefully chosen Carry-It-All. 'It's dishwasher proof,' she'd said, pointedly, and Kate had given her that lopsided grimace she thought passed for a smile, followed by that look she put on – like she was the only person on the planet who'd ever had to forsake their dreams.

Margery found the Carry-It-All at the beginning of this visit, at the back of the cupboard under the sink – where Kate had thrown it – on its side with part of its handle discoloured where bleach had dripped onto it. Its abandonment felt more intentional than careless and this fact had moved her almost to tears when she'd discovered it on her first morning here, in an empty house. She'd since washed it, replenished it with a selection of cleaning products bought with her own money, and left it at the front of the cupboard.

Someone was talking to her. She'd got lost in herself again and hadn't heard; one day she'd get lost in herself and never come back and Robert and Kate and the children would put her in a place that smelt perpetually of food nobody could remember eating – like that place her and Edith went to visit Rose in when Rose came down with Alzheimer's.

'What's that, dear?' she said to Martina. The 'dear' surprised her, had slipped through usually tight lips without her even thinking about it. She said it sometimes, to waitresses when she was out with Edith, or to young cashiers at the Co-op. She only ever said it to strangers, and it always caught her unawares.

Whether Martina understood the endearment or not, her face lost some of its wariness.

'I must clean now,' she said, the Carry-It-All in her hand.

'Yes,' Margery agreed vaguely, suddenly shouting, 'wait!' Martina was going upstairs to clean. What if she'd forgotten to flush the loo? She pushed upstairs ahead of the au pair, breathing heavily, until she was standing, panting while staring down the toilet bowl. She *had* flushed the loo, but flushed it again anyway for good measure. Watching the flush, she thought fondly of the streams of luminescent blue that flooded her toilet at home as the flush passed through her new toilet bloc, clipped to the rim. She thought about how she'd stood in the new ASDA store where the mobility bus dropped her off and debated for at least five minutes over whether to choose the green or blue toilet bloc. There was nothing so colourful about the flush at No. 22 Prendergast Road; nothing to wipe away the memory of necessity.

For a moment Margery forgot what she was doing up in the bathroom, staring down the loo, then at the tread on the stairs, she remembered. They really were going to put her in that place alongside Alzheimer's Rose if this didn't stop.

# 3

Kate pulled up slowly in front of Village Montessori, checking to see if cars belonging to anybody she knew were parked in the nursery's vicinity. Seeing Evie's, she drove round the block slowly twice and after the second lap saw the tail end of the black Chrysler disappear into Hebron Road. It was safe.

Fading out Findlay's monologue on the death of one of the nursery chickens, which were kept in a hut in the playground – bird flu? – she moved swiftly through the security gate with Flo on her and Findlay behind her towards the nursery entrance, past the Welcome to our Nursery sign in French, German, Spanish, Hebrew, Welsh, Gaelic, Arabic, Chinese, and Urdu. On the wall next to this was a montage of photographs taken by Sebastian Salgado of child labourers in South American mines that parents were beginning to complain to the Management Committee about.

'Red rooster's eyes went yellow and mushy when she died, like inside a wasp when you squish it, and Sandy who does music and movement said it wasn't a fox,' Findlay carried on as he hung up his coat, then added, 'Martina's grandma *did* make a football out of a pig's head and it's true. I've seen the film.'

Kate, who'd been on the verge of pushing him gently into the Butterfly Room, stopped. 'Film?'

'She's got a film of it on her phone. Arthur,' he yelled, then, turning back to Kate said, 'is Arthur going to my new school?'

'We don't know what school Arthur's going to – why don't you ask him?'

Findlay ran over to the Home Corner where Arthur was kneeling in front of the oven, removing a large green casserole pot that he'd put a Baby Annabel doll in earlier.

'What school are you going to?'

Kate waited.

Arthur was about to respond when one of the nursery staff went up to Findlay and said loudly, 'Shall we give this to Mummy?' tugging pointedly at the mask on his head.

Sighing, Findlay pulled it off and pushed it into Kate's hand, turning his attention back to Arthur.

'We need knives and forks,' Arthur was saying, efficiently.

'We have a no-masks policy at nursery,' the woman said.

'I forgot,' Kate quickly apologised before virtually running along the corridor with Flo towards the Caterpillar Room, where she handed her over to her primary carer, Mary.

She got back to the car without running into anybody else she knew, and checked her phone. There was an ecstatic message from Evie telling her that Aggie was 'in', an almost identical one from Ros re. Toby Granger, and a message from Harriet telling her in a strangely officious manner that Casper had won a place – won? – and reminding her to bring a food contribution to that night's PRC meeting. Kate hadn't even given it a thought.

She drove the car round the corner to Beulah Hill and parked outside the property Jessica had told her about. The house had nets up at windows painted peach, and a dead laurel in the front garden. She got the letter out of her breast pocket and read it again, just to see if anything had changed since she put it in there. She reached the *Yours sincerely, Jade Jackson – Head of Admissions* at the end. Nothing had changed. She felt, irrationally, that Findlay not being offered a place at St Anthony's had something to do with Jade Jackson being Jamaican.

*We are writing to inform you of the outcome of your application for a Southwark primary school. Your child has been offered a place at Brunton Park. The school will be contacting you with further information shortly . . . .*

She watched a pit-bull urinate against the tree on the other side of the window, then tried phoning the Admissions line, knowing how hopeless it would be trying to get through on the day all the offers had gone out. She listened to the engaged tone until she was automatically disconnected, then tried phoning St Anthony's instead, eventually getting through to a woman who told her the school was once again oversubscribed and how this year more than twenty-five places had gone to siblings.

The woman cut her off before Kate even got round to telling her that they attended St Anthony's Church every Sunday – *every* Sunday – or asking whether the school had definitely received the Reverend Walker's letter confirming this.

She pushed her head back roughly against the car seat and tried phoning Robert, who didn't answer, so sat contemplating No. 8 Beulah Hill instead. She was going to be late for her first appointment, and didn't care.

# 4

At No. 22 Prendergast Road, Margery stood listening to Martina clean the bathrooms, then went back into the kitchen, humming a Max Bygraves song to herself as she started on the pastry for the corned beef and onion pie she'd decided to make for Robert's tea that night. She watched her fingers lightly pull the mixture together in the way she'd been taught as a girl by her grandmother, who went mad playing the organ, and thought of all the different kitchens she'd watched her fingers do this in over the years, and how the fingers had changed – grown lines, knobbles, arthritic twists and turns and finally gone all loose; so loose that the few rings she had would probably have already fallen off if they hadn't got caught in the loose folds of skin round the knuckles.

The litany of industrious sounds coming from upstairs comforted Margery as she rolled the pastry and lined the pie tin – Communists certainly knew how to clean. When she went to wash her hands, she saw the envelope Kate had left for Martina on the surface by the sink. She went into the hallway and listened. Martina had just started hoovering. Margery went into the lounge and took another envelope out of Robert's desk drawer – it wasn't actually Robert's desk, it was Kate's, but Margery always referred to it as Robert's – and went back into the kitchen.

She quickly tore open Martina's pay packet and pulled out a twenty-pound note. She stood there for a moment, brushing flour off her nostrils with the crisp new note and knew that, according to her calculations, there was no way Kate and Robert could stretch to eighty pounds a month on a cleaner. Margery knew the Hunters' finances as well as any accountant because she'd spent the better part of yesterday morning going through their two fiscal files. The Hunters were, in her opinion, in dire straits – she didn't know how they kept the show up and running or why they weren't collapsing under the strain of their imminent financial ruin. She could only surmise that Robert was keeping it from Kate and bearing the burden alone. She didn't understand her son's marriage. It seemed unnatural to her; more important still, it was unsustainable. What was it Robert said to her all those years ago: 'Wait till you meet her, Mum – she's going to change the world – not just mine; everyone's. Kofi Annan beware.'

Well, personal finances were clearly below the likes of Kofi Annan, but Margery knew bailiffs – had had experience of bailiffs throughout her childhood, and she could smell them in the air now. Kofi Annan or not, when it was time they came for you and nothing could keep them from the door. They went where they were sent and didn't discriminate. Margery stuffed the twenty-pound note into the new envelope as the hoover cut out upstairs, put it back on the bench by the cooker and opened two cans of corned beef that she'd bought with her from East Leeke. When she turned round, Ivan the cat was standing motionless on the kitchen floor, watching her, its back arched. She felt immediately nauseous; cats always made her feel nauseous. They brought her underarms out in a rash and gave her vertigo.

Then the phone started to ring in the lounge and she wasn't sure what to do about it because Ivan showed no sign of moving, was in fact now sending out a hissing spit in her general direction. Even without Ivan, the phone alarmed her with its flashing lights and antennae.

'You want me to get?' Martina called out from the upstairs landing.

At the sound of Martina's voice, Ivan relaxed and strolled past Margery towards his bowl, brushing her ankles.

Margery jogged quickly into the lounge and started to wrestle with the still ringing phone, eventually pressing the right button – because it might be Robert; it might always be Robert . . .

It was Beatrice, Kate's mother.

'Margery – how are you? I had no idea you were in town.'

Town? What town? 'The cleaner's here,' Margery said, for no particular reason.

'That's nice,' Beatrice said after a while.

So the cleaner was news to Beatrice as well. Margery relaxed a little. 'She's from Czechoslovakia,' she explained.

On the other end of the phone Beatrice, unsure why they were talking about the cleaner, said briskly, 'There's no such place.'

Margery baulked. 'What?'

'There's the Czech Republic and Slovakia, but no Czechoslovakia.'

'Martina never said,' Margery carried on, more to herself than Beatrice, 'but they were Communists?'

'While the Soviet Union was still in power – yes.'

'I was going to ask her if she had any KGB stories.'

'KGB?'

'You know – the KGB – the secret police.' Margery had withdrawn an abundance of material on the Gestapo and KGB from East Leeke Library's well-stocked history section.

'You must of heard about the KGB, Beatrice – how they used to come in the night while you were asleep,' Margery carried on, breathless. 'The footsteps on the stairs, down the hallway . . . knocking on doors, doors opening . . . people disappearing.' She paused. 'They came in the night,' she said again, insisting on this.

After a while, Beatrice said lightly, 'So does Freddie Kruger.'

'He sounds German – was Czechoslovakia covered by the Stasi?' Margery asked, interested.

'Margery,' Beatrice reined her in. 'How long are you staying for?'

This brought Margery up short. Always sensitive to any hint of expulsion or the fact that she was outstaying her welcome, she said quickly, 'Not long – it's just while I've got the decorators in.'

'What colour?' Beatrice asked. She'd been to Margery's East Leeke bungalow once – when Kate and Robert got married – and the only place she'd ever been to before that bore even the slightest semblance to the bungalow in terms of décor and overall atmosphere was a euthanasia clinic on Denmark's Jutland coast.

'What colour – what?'

'What colour are you having the walls painted?'

Beatrice was shouting – Margery was sure Beatrice was shouting at her, and there was no need to do that; there was nothing partial about her hearing.

'Magnolia,' she said, surprised Beatrice had even asked.

'What colour was it before?'

'Magnolia.'

A pause. 'Margery – is Kate there?'

'She went out,' Margery said, making it sound like she'd gone shopping and not to work as a clinical psychologist.

'I was just phoning to see if Finn got into St Anthony's – Kate said they were meant to hear by today.'

Finn – was Robert Rob or Robbie? 'The letter came.'

'And?'

Margery paused; suddenly thrilled by the notion that she had a small piece of the Hunter family's future in her hands that Beatrice wasn't yet aware of. 'Well . . .' she trailed off, provocatively. She could get Edith to the point sometimes where she was begging, her cheap dentures sliding around inside her mouth across saliva-ridden gums.

'Did he get in?'

'The letter said he did.' What did that mean? Margery wasn't sure, but she felt herself scanning the lounge to see if Kate had left the letter anywhere. She wouldn't mind a look at that letter.

'Thank God,' Beatrice breathed down the phone. 'Kate was talking about home schooling if Finn didn't get in . . . leaving London – the works,' she carried on.

'Leaving London?'

'Well, now she won't need to bother.'

'Leaving London for where?'

'I don't know, Margery, you know those two – Kate was going on about America, and Rob . . .'

She called him Rob.

'. . . was talking about New Zealand. They talked themselves into a taste for bigger things; who knows, maybe they'll end up going anyway,' Beatrice concluded cheerfully.

Margery was shocked. New Zealand? Robert never said anything to her about New Zealand.

'I'll try and catch Kate before she starts work – and you must come down here to see us – get a blast of fresh air.' She paused. 'Come on your own, if you like, I mean if you get sick of family life. I can always come and get you – just give us a bell.'

Margery didn't respond to this; still hadn't responded by the time Beatrice rang off. New Zealand. She tried phoning Edith, but Edith didn't answer.

Martina appeared in the lounge doorway.

Margery stared helplessly at her before blurting out, 'New Zealand's on the other side of the world.'

Martina smiled and moved cautiously into the room with the hoover, watched by Margery. After a while she put the hoover away and disappeared into the kitchen. Margery remained in the lounge, staring at the phone.

'I go now,' Martina called out.

'Already?' Margery responded, involuntarily, walking slowly into the hallway.

Martina was at the front door, the white envelope in her hand. 'Now I have much ironing to do for Mr Catano.'

'Catano?'

'A bit Korean, I think.'

'Korean?' Margery said as Martina opened the front door, thinking briefly of cousin Tom.

Martina pushed her bike past sunflowers that Kate had let Findlay plant and that Margery thought would look ridiculous by July when they reached shoulder-height.

'I see you again next week.'

'Maybe,' Margery called out, unable to think about next week when she could barely keep her mind fixed on what was happening the rest of today – especially after hearing about New Zealand.

'And please – I fed the cat.'

Margery was about to say something about the cat when she heard the door to No. 20 – the Jamaican's door – start to open. She went quickly back inside, slamming the door to No. 22 shut and going into the lounge where she watched carefully, through slatted blinds Martina hadn't forgotten to dust, as Mr Hamilton moved slowly over to his recycling bin and put an empty milk carton in it.

The sun glanced off his gold wristwatch as he turned

round, shaking his head at a private thought before looking up suddenly, straight at her, smiling.

Scowling, Margery backed away from the window, almost running into the hallway where she slid the chain across the front door as quietly as she could, then waited. No sound of movement on the other side. Then, after another minute, the front door to No. 20 was shut.

Scared as well as preoccupied, Margery went into the kitchen to pick up where she'd left off with the corned beef pie. She sliced an onion over the pastry base and went to get the corned beef out the cupboard before remembering that she'd already done that. There it was on the bench. Only the tins were empty. When had she done that? She looked from the empty tins to the empty pie case.

Where was the corned beef?

Slowly her eyes took a downward turn to Ivan's bowl, which was full.

# 5

Robert sat staring about the Ellington Technology College staff room waiting for Kate to call him about St Anthony's – and whether Findlay had got a place.

The seat next to him was blue and covered in cigarette burns from the days when staff were allowed to smoke. A Swiss cheese plant belonging to Les Davies, deputy head – that had been there as long as Les – was on top of a filing cabinet behind him that nobody had opened for years, and that blocked out what little natural light had the heart to try and make its way into the room.

The bell had rung and the dust had resettled. An art teacher with a cold was snivelling in a corner and muttering at a memo Sellotaped to the wall while inadvertently slopping the sleeves of her jumper into her coffee. The memo was from the Metropolitan Police warning staff at the school of a new gang whose initiation ceremony comprised driving a car in the dark without putting the car's headlights on. If another driver on the road flashed the car, the wannabe gang member had to pursue it and shoot the driver. Bettina, the new geography teacher from South Africa, was looking at a property investment magazine's special Romania supplement, which was the only place in Europe on her salary where she could afford to buy.

After staring for another second, transfixed by a ripped corner of carpet tile the same helpless blue as the chairs, Robert hauled himself to his feet. Bettina looked up from the computer-generated image of a Romanian shepherd's hut after modernisation, and stared – distracted – at Robert.

'I'm meant to be teaching now,' he said.

Bettina didn't say anything to this; she just nodded and went back to the modernised shepherd's hut.

The art teacher carried on muttering and Robert left the room, the smell of burnt coffee, frustration and despair replaced immediately by the smell of the next generation – whoever they were.

When he got to his classroom, the door was open and the kids were inside, unaccountably silent, until Robert realised that the squat man in the corridor outside, staring through the window opposite the door, was Les the deputy head. Despite bearing an uncanny resemblance to Goebbels, he was the only incorruptible thing in the school and, because of this, the children were terrified of him. Les was from the Rhondda Valley and used to get heavily involved in school musicals – when they used to have school musicals . . . when they used to have a music department.

Most people found Les aggressive; some of them even found him tyrannical, but Robert and Les shared a mutual, hard-earned respect for each other, and Robert always found him protective.

'Sorry about that,' he said to Les's back, jerking his thumb at the classroom full of children and suddenly aware that he was out of breath even though he hadn't been running. 'I got caught up, and . . . sorry,' he said again.

Les sighed, but didn't turn round.

He carried on standing, motionless, as if he had finally

come to the conclusion that while he didn't have a life, he did have an existence and an existence, if nothing else, did at least provide respite from having to decide whether he was alive or in fact dead.

'What are you doing with them?' he said at last, still without turning round.

'Seamus Heaney,' Robert said, automatically.

'I never did like Seamus Heaney – I think I tried to. Anyway, I unlocked the classroom and got them in for you.'

'Thanks – thanks for that.'

'I was passing and Keisha was banging Shanique's head repetitively against the wall.'

'Yeah, Keisha does that.'

'Ellie Palmer's in this class,' Les said, suddenly changing the subject.

'Ellie's—'

'A brilliant and messy girl,' Les finished quietly for him. It was Les and Robert, jointly, who were behind getting Ellie to apply for the St Paul's sixth-form scholarship. He turned round suddenly, staring at Robert. 'Are her and Jerome Simmons still going out?'

Robert shook his head slowly. 'Don't think so.' He didn't have the perverse interest in the students' love lives that a lot of the staff had.

The two men watched each other, Robert fighting hard against his instinct to tell Les that, for the first time in his professional life, he was terrified of walking through that classroom door because of Jerome Simmons. That up until this moment he'd always felt that the job needed him as much as he needed the job, but now he was starting to believe he was in the wrong place and that somebody else should be doing this. He wasn't sure he wanted Les knowing this because this would make him, Robert, just like every other teacher in Ellington and the kids already knew . . .

were already onto him with the instinct of a pack, systematically rooting out weakness because children can't abide weakness.

'What's he doing?' he said instead to distract Les, pointing at Simba, the caretaker, who was out on the flat roof just below.

'What's that?' Les turned slowly away from him to stare at Simba. 'Oh – pigeons. He's been trying to perfect some sort of acid glue he can paint on the roof to discourage them from landing.' Les let out another sigh. 'The acid in the glue burns their feet off if they do land – apparently.'

Robert didn't comment on this.

The murmur from the classroom behind them was getting louder and interspersed with distinct screams, shrieks and rhythmically choreographed abusive exchanges. Robert recognised Jerome's voice and knew his face had changed and knew that when Les turned round he wouldn't be able to disguise the fear his face was full of.

So he turned quickly to the window again, staring out over Simba's bent back and the edge of the roof to the only piece of green in sight; an inexplicable mound about the same shape as a small Iron-Age fort that was known among staff and students alike simply as 'The Clump'. Beyond The Clump was the Esso garage the council had sold the school's last playing field to and, beyond that, the Elephant and Castle.

Local press abounded with mythical promises of regeneration, but at the moment the panorama on offer was a four-lane super-roundabout with exits leading to some of London's most destitute spinal cords – and a Soviet-era shopping centre, which was quite a feat of urban planning in a country that had never had its own Soviet era.

A couple of boys – possibly students – pushed a moped across the empty playground.

'In the beginning,' Les said suddenly, 'somebody somewhere

had a vision, that's all.' He sounded elegiac – as though he'd decided right then and there that he'd lived one life too many. He clapped Robert warmly, forcefully, on the shoulder. 'You'll be all right.'

Robert nodded.

Then, with Les's footsteps still ringing down the corridor, he walked into the classroom and the crescendoing, unavoidable, 'Yo, sir! Yo, sir!' There in front of him was the mob.

His eyes hit Ellie because she was sitting at the front of the class to the right-hand side of his desk and was the first thing in his line of vision. He hadn't meant to look at her in particular, and certainly never intended to look at Jerome after that. But he did – and saw that Jerome had seen him looking at Ellie.

He'd been caught off guard, but then it had been so long since anybody had looked at him in the way Ellie had when he walked into the room. When was the last time he'd caused anybody so much pleasure, simply by walking through a door?

Her eyes opened so wide he felt he could have just carried on walking straight into them.

He came to a halt behind the desk, pressing his fists down hard into the surface. This was wrong. The wrong way to think and the wrong direction to start walking in – no matter how wide her eyes opened.

# 6

At No. 22 Prendergast Road, Margery was on all fours crying with rage over Ivan's bowl, which was full of corned beef. She'd seen it, smelt it and tasted it – and it was definitely corned beef.

When Ivan came creeping back into the kitchen, his shoulder blades rolling smoothly as he sniffed at the floor around his bowl, Margery screamed at him, still sobbing, 'Bugger off, just bugger off.' She elbowed the white cat away, anger replacing fear, but Ivan came back, nonplussed by the elbow in his flank – and gave the corned beef a few aggressive licks.

Margery staggered to her feet and kicked him across the kitchen.

After bouncing off the fridge, he landed with a whine, paused, licked at a back paw then padded quietly into the hallway where he sat and waited, letting his posture insinuate that *his* dignity, at least, was intact.

Panting, Margery slammed the kitchen door shut, decanted the corned beef from Ivan's bowl into a plastic mixing bowl and, taking a pair of tweezers from her handbag, which she always kept within close range, started to painstakingly pick Ivan's hairs out of the corned beef.

# 7

Jessica Palmer was inside No. 8 Beulah Hill doing a viewing with a young, top-of-the-range couple when her mobile rang. She didn't usually take calls during viewings – not unless it was Ellie or the nursery – but she took this one because it was Kate Hunter, and Kate was meant to be picking Arthur up from nursery and taking him to Swim School. In fact, Kate Hunter was her childcare lifeline.

The top-of-the-range young couple drifted upstairs.

Beulah Hill, like the rest of the streets in the postcode, had gone from destitute to up-and-coming to boom as generations of Irish and Jamaicans started selling up and moving out, and young couples started selling flats in Battersea, Putney and Clapham and moving in; taking out extra-large mortgages in order to pay for the reinstallation of sash windows the Irish and Jamaicans had replaced with uPVC double glazing. Once the sash windows were reinstalled, they moved onto the floors, replacing carpet with solid wood flooring. Sea green and lilac bathroom suites were ripped out, along with any dividing walls – to create living spaces that allowed lifestyles to circulate more freely. Some of the

46

houses – like the McRaes' – got to feature on TV makeover programmes.

No. 8 had yet to be made over.

'Kate?' Jessica whispered into the phone.

'Hi, Jessica?'

'Hi . . .'

'Why are you whispering?'

'I'm doing a viewing on Beulah Hill.'

'What's that?'

'I said, I'm doing a viewing on Beulah Hill.' There was a pause. 'Kate?'

'Beulah Hill? You're there at the moment? Has anyone put an offer in yet?'

'No.' Jessica scanned the green shag-pile carpet and green leather three-piece. The light coming through the double layers of net at the windows made the room seem as though it was under water, and had the effect of making Jesus, with his arms outstretched, executed in oils and framed on the wall above the mantle – look as if he was floating.

'Why were you asking – ?' she joked. Then, before Kate had time to respond to this, said, 'Is it still okay for you to take the boys swimming tonight and pick them up?' She tried not to sound desperate, knowing from experience how off-putting desperation was but, since Peter's death, she seemed to be perpetually desperate, and perpetually having to conceal it was draining.

When Kate didn't respond to this, she prompted her, 'The boys? Swimming?' and waited.

'Swimming?' Kate's voice sounded vague and preoccupied.

'You were going to take the boys to Swim School after nursery and then I was going to pick Arthur up from yours around six?'

Silence, as Kate rapidly processed these facts as if she was hearing them for the first time, which she wasn't. 'Fine – yes, that's fine. Robert's going to pick the boys up from swimming.' She made a mental note to remind Robert.

Jessica, trying not to cry with relief, missed what Kate said next. 'What's that?'

'I said maybe I am interested.'

'In what?'

'Taking a look at Beulah Hill.'

'You're thinking of moving?'

'Possibly.' Kate's only appointment that morning had been a teenage schizophrenic, so she'd spent most of her time after printing off a map of the St Anthony's catchment area, as well as two copies of the appeal form, on Rightmove. By the time she discovered that the only property with at least three bedrooms under seven hundred thousand and within the catchment area was No. 8 Beulah Hill, a dull thumping sensation had started somewhere just behind her left temple, and she knew that at some point that day she would have a migraine.

'But you've got a lovely house.'

In the silence that followed, Kate realised that Jessica was waiting for some sort of explanation. 'We were thinking of buying something abroad,' she lied – another lie. 'Maybe downscaling in London, cashing in on some capital and getting somewhere in France – to take the kids in the holidays.'

'Well, how much were you thinking of spending?' Jessica said, thinking that at least the Hunters would be around in the term-time still. Kate was the only person she knew who ever offered to help with Arthur.

'Around four fifty?'

'This is on for four eighty.'

'I know, I've been looking at it on Rightmove. How long's it been on the market for?'

48

'Over six weeks.'

'So you haven't been able to shift it.'

'Well, I've got a young couple here at the moment . . . you never know: people are unpredictable.'

There was undisguised panic in Kate's voice as she said, 'What about this afternoon? Could I take a look this afternoon?'

'This afternoon?' Jessica laughed. 'I can't – I'm booked through to five thirty. I think everybody in the office is.'

'What about now?'

'Now?'

'I can be there in under ten minutes.'

'I don't know . . .'

'Come on, Jessica.'

'I'll give you ten minutes then I'll have to go – I've got another viewing.'

'I'll be there.'

Jessica was about to call off when Kate said, 'Wait – I meant to ask. Did you get your letter?'

'What letter?'

'The St Anthony's letter?'

'No idea – I left before the post. Did Findlay get in?'

'He did.'

'Well, I hope to God Arthur gets a place then. They're almost like brothers – he'll be distraught if he and Findlay get separated.'

Kate tried to think of something to say – a statement like this warranted something – but she couldn't. Arthur Palmer swore; Arthur Palmer looked malnourished; Arthur Palmer's hair was too short, his clothes inflammatory. Arthur Palmer was all wrong and Kate had done everything she could to separate him and Findlay, but nothing worked. Ros Granger and Harriet Burgess had both commented on this – smugly – but no matter how hard Kate tried to push

Findlay in the direction of Toby and Casper, Findlay refused to have anything to do with either of them.

When Kate failed to respond, Jessica said, 'So it's definitely okay for you to pick Arthur up after nursery?' – getting back to her primary concern.

A moment's hesitation, as Kate fought to remember the complicated logistics involving her own children and Jessica's, then, 'Yes – fine. Okay, I'm leaving now.' Kate called off.

Jessica hadn't heard the young couple come back downstairs, and now they were standing in front of her, and she could tell from the way the man said, 'So how long has it been on the market for?' that he'd already asked her once, maybe even more than once.

'Not long,' Jessica said.

'How long?' he insisted.

'Just over a week,' she lied, 'which is why we haven't got round to printing details yet – and, to be honest, properties like this are going so fast, nine times out of ten we don't even get round to printing details. A lot of the properties don't even make it onto the Internet.'

The man was staring at the oil painting of Jesus on the wall opposite, unconvinced.

Jessica was about to give them the whole spiel on getting the loft converted into a fourth bedroom with en-suite, and how unusual it was to find a seventy-foot garden in this area, when Mr Jackson, the elderly Jamaican vendor, shuffled into his home carrying a blue plastic bag with two cans of Kestrel inside.

'Y'all right?' he smiled awkwardly at them all. 'Sorry – I stayed out; thought you'd be done by now.'

'Don't worry, we're just leaving, Mr Jackson,' Jessica said as brightly as she could.

Mr Jackson carried on staring at them all, confused by the whole process. 'That's my wife,' he said after a while, following the young man's gaze and pointing to the picture of Jesus.

The young man nodded and smiled and tried not to look scared.

'She was the one what had the religion.' Mr Jackson paused. 'She died,' he added, looking hopefully at them all, as if one of them might have heard otherwise.

The young man mumbled, 'Sorry to hear it,' and started to propel his partner towards the hall.

Jessica followed them out.

Mr Jackson stayed where he was. 'Y'all goin?' he said to the empty room.

On the pavement outside No. 8, she shook hands with the young couple as a fleet of motorised scooters raced up the road behind them.

'I'll be in touch,' she called out enthusiastically, watching the couple get into their car and start to argue.

No. 8 Beulah Hill was a bargain – if she had the money, she would have bought it herself. All it needed was thirty to fifty thousand pounds of work done on it and it would be worth over six hundred and fifty, but nobody seemed to have the imagination to see beyond Mr Jackson and the Jackson décor. People these days wanted to walk into ready-made lives. Her phone started ringing again.

It was Kate.

'Still there?'

'Still here.'

'Great – I'm just round the corner. Oh, and Jessica, I meant to say – you're the only person I've told about the whole downscaling/second property in France thing, so . . .'

'Don't worry, I won't say anything.'

'To anyone.'

'To anyone.'

'Great.' A pause. Then again, 'Great.'

By the time she came off the phone, the silver BMW containing the young couple had slid away. She turned and knocked on the door of No. 8 again – to see if it was okay to do the viewing with Kate now.

After a while, she rang a second time, and Mr Jackson appeared in the door, the blue carrier bag still in his hand, staring blankly at her. He looked as though he'd been crying.

'Mr Jackson? It's Jessica, Mr Jackson – Jessica from Lennox Thompson Estate Agents?'

He nodded patiently at her – without any apparent recollection.

She turned and pointed to the Lennox Thompson For Sale sign attached to his gatepost.

'It's Jessica, Mr Jackson,' she said again, glancing at him standing in his doorway staring at the Lennox Thompson For Sale sign as though he'd never seen it in his life before. 'I've got someone who wants to see the property.'

'The property,' he repeated, grinning to himself.

'Yes, the property – your house – now. If that's okay with you?'

'They want to see it now?'

'They want to see it now – is that okay?'

Mr Jackson sighed, shaking his head and disappeared back inside without shutting the front door.

'Mr Jackson?' Jessica called out.

Then the Hunters' Audi estate pulled up and Kate got out panting, as though she'd been running, not driving.

'Jessica – thanks so much.'

'Are you serious about this?'

'I just want to take a look,' Kate said, her eyes once more skimming the peach-coloured window frames and impenetrable layers of net hanging at the windows.

'It needs work doing to it – about thirty grand's worth.

Nothing structural – mostly cosmetic. Sorry, we're going to have to be quick, I'm meant to be somewhere else.'

Jessica gave Kate the tour.

Mr Jackson remained motionless on the sofa watching a Gospel channel.

'I'll be in touch,' Jessica called out to him as they left the house.

There was no reply from Mr Jackson.

'Well, I'm definitely interested,' Kate said on the pavement outside No. 8.

'Have a think about it.'

'I'm definitely interested,' she said again.

'Well, talk to Robert –.'

'I'm going to.' She nodded to herself then swung back to Jessica. 'What are you doing tonight?'

'Tonight? Nothing.'

'Why don't you come to the PRC meeting?'

'I didn't know there was a PRC meeting.'

'Didn't Harriet phone you?'

Harriet hadn't phoned for some time. In fact, Jessica hadn't been to the last three PRC meetings. 'No.'

An awkward silence. Jessica was one of those people it was almost impossible to lie to. 'Harriet's probably just lost your number or something. You know what she's like.'

Jessica didn't respond immediately. 'Look, I'll let you know – I'll see how Ellie's day's been, and if she minds me leaving Arthur with her.' She paused, looking suddenly pleased. 'Are you sure?'

'Course I'm sure. It's an important one tonight – about the street party.'

'What street party?'

'The street party we're having in June.'

'Oh. Okay – well, I'll call you.'

Even though she was late, Jessica stayed on the pavement

waving stupidly at the disappearing Audi before getting into her own car.

Watching her in the rear-view mirror, Kate felt a stab of regret.

What had incited her to invite Jessica to the PRC?

Harriet had an almost pathological hatred of Jessica Palmer, whose misshapen life filled Harriet with horror. She treated her as though tragedy was contagious, because even dull-witted Harriet realised that the grief that comes with tragedy has the ability to shape lives in a way happiness never does.

Sighing, Kate turned the corner onto Lordship Lane.

Jessica sat for a while, listening to a dog barking somewhere close by, then turned the keys in the ignition.

Twenty minutes later, she walked into the newly open-planned offices of Lennox Thompson.

Most of the staff were out on viewings or valuations – apart from Elaine and the manager, Jake, who was almost ten years Jessica's junior, on the Oxford Alumni, and seriously addicted to coke, which gave his skin a grey pallor that was only heightened by being perpetually offset against the white shirts he insisted on wearing.

Jake thought Jessica and him had things in common – primarily their education – which led him to keep up a repartee with her that was at once fraternal and elegiac.

Jessica knew it wasn't Oxford they had in common – it was tragedy.

In Jake's case, the fatal error of perpetually trying to impress parents who had never learnt how to love their children – he once told her his father used to make him weed the borders naked, as a punishment.

In Jessica's, never having made any provision – emotional or material – for Peter's untimely death.

'Guess what?' Jake said, looking up as Jessica walked into the office.

'What?'

'They're opening a branch of Foxtons here.'

'Foxtons?'

He nodded, pulled at his nose and said, 'With a promotional six-month zero per cent commission. It's going to kill us,' he added, starting to chew on his nails before shunting his chair backwards and disappearing, jerkily, towards the loos at the back of the office.

Elaine looked across at her.

Jessica was about to say something when her mobile started to ring.

'Jess?'

It was Lenny – her stepmother.

She didn't feel like speaking to Lenny right then and started to scratch nervously with a drawing pin at the edge of her desk.

'I was just phoning to see if Arthur got into St Anthony's.'

'I don't know – the post hadn't arrived when I left this morning.'

'Oh.' Lenny paused at Jessica's flat tone.

Jessica let herself fall back in her chair, slouching uncomfortably as she started to swing it from side to side.

'Well, give us a ring later.'

'I will. How's Dad?' she said, with an effort.

The line started to break up and Jessica, now swinging aggressively from side to side, hoped they'd lose the reception altogether, but Lenny was still there. It was something she'd been trying to come to terms with since she was fifteen – the fact that Lenny would still be there – always.

'I said – how's Dad?'

'He's fine – engrossed in some new cat-deterrent he got by mail order this morning.'

At the beginning, because of what happened between Joe and Lenny, it had been more necessary for Lenny to get on with Jessica than it was for Jessica to get on with Lenny, and this early imbalance in their relationship had never really been redressed. Lenny had made huge efforts – Jessica could see that now, from the vantage point of being thirty-five – and not only out of necessity. Lenny had genuinely cared, but at the time Jessica felt she was owed too much to bother responding to overtures made by the woman her father had been having an affair with while her mother was still alive, who became the woman he moved in with after she died.

'You keep cutting out – where are you?'

'I don't know – somewhere between Brighton and Birmingham; on a train. How's work?'

'Fine – yeah, it's fine.'

'Well, you know where we are if you need anything – why not bring the kids down and have a weekend to yourself?'

'I don't know – it's busy at the moment.'

'We haven't seen them in ages, and Dad's started on that tree house for Arthur.'

Jessica tried to think of something to say to this, but couldn't.

'And I miss Ellie – I really do.'

'I'll call,' Jessica said, as the line broke up for a third and final time.

As she came off her mobile, the office phones started to ring. 'Lennox Thompson sales department – how can I help you?'

'I'd like to speak to someone about the Beulah Hill house you've got on the market.'

'Well, you're speaking to the right person.'

'Wait a minute – is this Jessica?'

'This is Jessica – Jessica Palmer.'

'Jessica – it's Ros.'

'Ros?'

'Ros Granger from No. 188?'

'Ros . . .' Why was Ros calling? Ros never called her . . . had never called her since she took Toby to McDonald's in Peckham that time for Arthur's fourth birthday. In fact, nobody from the PRC apart from Kate had phoned since Arthur's fourth birthday – and that was nearly a year ago.

'So – how's it all going?'

'Fine.'

Ros let out a long, smooth laugh as though Jessica had just said something funny. 'I was phoning to arrange a viewing –.'

'You're not thinking of moving as well, are you?'

'Who else have you been speaking to?'

'Nobody,' Jessica said quickly.

Ros paused. 'Today would be good.'

# 8

Even late as she was after the impromptu Beulah Hill viewing, Kate still found time to stop at St Anthony's vicarage on the way to Village Montessori. Jolting over a speed bump at the crest of the hill, she was sure she saw someone – the vicar? – in the vicarage garden, and on an impulse decided to stop, parking behind a distinctive black Chrysler just pulling away, which – if she hadn't been so preoccupied – she would have recognised as Evie McRae's.

She got out of the car and started to walk through the dull April drizzle, trying not to slip on the overspill of gravel from the vicar's newly gravelled drive. Ignoring the increasingly invasive smell of wet tarmac, which always made her panic, she emerged from behind a bank of hydrangeas with what she liked to think of as a healthy smile on her face.

'Hi,' she said across the uneven trail of hydrangea cuttings littering the immaculate lawn.

The Reverend Tessa Walker – it *was* the vicar – looked up, a pair of secateurs in her hand. She managed to master her annoyance at the interruption – the second interruption that morning – but it left her face looking glum.

After what felt like a minute's silence, Kate said, 'Sorry – this is a bit impromptu; I should have phoned. Actually, I did phone, but no one was in and then I was driving past and I saw you in your garden and . . .' She inhaled a lungful of wet tarmac and then panic set in as the memory of long wet suburban days fell over her . . . She stared blearily at the Reverend Walker, trying to claw her way back into the present moment. 'I tried to phone, but there was no answer and . . .'

The Reverend Walker lost the grip on her secateurs so that they hung from the band round her wrist. She didn't attempt to speak; she just carried on staring at Kate.

'I'm Kate – Kate Hunter? I come to church here on Sundays. Every Sunday . . . here to St Anthony's every Sunday – well, most Sundays . . .' She paused, letting out a nervous laugh that made her feel like the only child in a roomful of adults.

The Reverend Walker said nothing. She was too busy thinking . . . this woman comes to my church every Sunday and I don't recognise her. It made her feel old.

The drizzle was gaining momentum. There was going to be a downpour, which hadn't started yet, but there was so much moisture in the air that Kate could feel it collecting on her eyelashes.

The sound of children being let out onto a playing field reached them through the dense, moist air and she started to panic again. Nursery – she needed to collect Findlay and Flo from nursery. 'I came here to talk about a child,' she said suddenly. This sounded epic; she hadn't meant to sound epic.

The Reverend Walker said, 'A child?'

'My son – Findlay.'

'You want to talk to me about your son?' the Reverend Walker said, helplessly. Was this the first time the woman had mentioned a child? She didn't know any more. It just seemed as though she'd been standing on her wet lawn among the hydrangea cuttings for weeks, and now wasn't a good time for anybody to be talking to her about their children – because she was undergoing a crisis of faith; a profound crisis of faith. With an effort, she twisted back to Kate. 'You're having concerns about your son?' she said, trying to sound less helpless this time.

'Concerns?' Kate echoed.

'Spiritual concerns?'

'He's five years old,' Kate said, trying not to yell. 'No, it's nothing like that. I just came to check that you wrote the letter to St Anthony's confirming the fact that Findlay comes to church here on Sundays. You needed to write a letter – about Findlay. It was part of our application, and I just wanted to check that it was done because I got a letter this morning saying he didn't get a place.'

A place where? Heaven? Full of a sudden dread, the Reverend Walker wondered whether they were talking about a dead child – the woman's son? Was he dead? Had there been a funeral she'd forgotten to attend? A child she'd forgotten to bury? She started to walk slowly, earnestly, towards Kate.

'We've been coming here to church since he was nine months old and this morning – this morning – I find out that he doesn't have a place at St Anthony's, and nobody seems to know why. Every Sunday – nearly every Sunday – for over four years, and he doesn't get a place.'

The clouds gathered and the moisture thickened until it officially became rain – the steady sort of rain the birds carry on singing through.

Kate tried to breathe in but there was no air anywhere, her nostrils were full of rain and it seemed as though the Reverend Walker was staring at her from the end of a long green tunnel.

'We've been coming to St Anthony's every Sunday,' she said again, before realising that she was repeating herself.

Somebody's voice – a long way off – was saying, 'Only fifty per cent of places are offered on the basis of faith; the other fifty are offered according to catchment area criteria and whether a child has siblings at the school. Do you want to come inside?' the Reverend said at last.

'We've done everything right – everything,' Kate yelled. 'Right down to sitting through sermon after sermon on those fucking Sudanese orphans.' She broke off, vaguely aware that the rain was running so steadily down her face now it was impairing her vision. The right-hand side of her head seemed to be filling with blood, and the weight of it was pulling her down through the rain towards the lawn. She stumbled, but managed to regain her balance. This prompted the Reverend Walker to say, 'Come inside,' again.

Kate stared at her, suddenly intensely aware of the fact that she was, in effect, accosting the vicar in her garden. If she took a look around her, the evidence would be there: her footprints in the gravel on the drive, and across the wet lawn behind her. God. This was exactly the sort of thing her mother would have done. God.

The church bells began ringing and, pushing the vicar's hands away, she turned and ran back across the lawn and gravel drive, her head thumping so badly with migraine now that it was beginning to seriously affect her balance. She staggered towards the Audi. Somewhere beyond the bells there were screaming children and, beyond them, a dog was intermittently whining and yapping.

A workman standing in front of a Portaloo on the drive next door was staring at her. How long had he been standing there?

Ignoring him, she yanked open the driver's door and fell into the car – the sound of the wet afternoon immediately muffled by safety glass as she slammed the door shut.

What was it she'd yelled at the Reverend Walker? Something about Sudanese orphans . . . ?

Afraid, she phoned Robert, but Robert didn't answer his phone.

# 9

She pulled up in front of Village Montessori nearly twenty minutes late – which, following stringent regulations, she'd have to pay for by the minute – with a full-blown migraine; but at least the rain had stopped. She retrieved Flo from the sensory room where she was lying on her back with fifteen other babies – who looked as if they'd just been thrown out of heaven, and landed on a rug of synthetic fur – all jerking their arms and legs towards the ceiling where silver spirals were revolving, overlooked severely by the black and white faces on the Wimmer-Ferguson Mind Shapes mural. There was a CD of rainforest sounds playing.

Mary handed her Flo from among the minute bodies jerking on the floor, and Kate wasn't entirely sure – if it hadn't been for Mary – that she would have recognised her daughter. The lighting in the sensory room was eerily low and Kate wondered how Mary coped, sitting among the parakeets and the jerking, snuffling bodies, with the door shut. Surely Village Montessori was in breach of EU health and safety regulations?

Once in her mother's arms, Flo showed absolutely no sign of recognition. It must have been the same with Findlay at this age, but with Flo, for some reason, Kate felt less able to cope. Flo twisted her head blearily from side to side, blinked her wet eyes at nothing in particular, posited a dribble of something white and curdled on Kate's lapel then concussed herself on her collarbone – and started to cry. Kate felt a wave of violence pass through her that she found difficult to control – because of the migraine.

Her arms started to shake and she experienced an almost vertiginous nausea as she tried to remember the names of familiar sights and sounds. This had been happening to her at least twice a day since Flo was born – the first time, slumped in a hospital bed at King's, she had been staring past the mass of bouquets on the table at newborn Flo, in her Perspex hospital tank, and there, right in front of her, her daughter turned into a piglet.

Findlay, sitting on the end of the hospital bed, pushing a small fire engine with a broken ladder along the railings, became a centipede, and Robert became a bear – a huge bear clumsily trying to pull the blue curtains round the bed for some privacy.

Now, all she wanted to do was hurl Flo over Mary's shoulder through the silver spirals and into the wall behind her, where the impact would no doubt make various bits of Flo burst open and trickle over Wimmer-Ferguson's impervious black and white faces. Then everybody – including Mary – would be able to see that Flo wasn't a human baby after all; she was in fact nothing more than a tiny pig.

Kate stood with her arms shaking, listening to Mary give her a rundown on all Flo's bowel movements since 8.30 a.m.

Then it passed, and after it had passed, she remembered to smile adoringly at Flo – like the woman on the front of the Johnson & Johnson's wet wipes packet – and nod and say 'great' in response to Mary's monologue.

Mary looked surprised, indicating that 'great' wasn't quite right.

'Everything okay?' she asked.

'Everything's fine,' Kate said, hoping she was still smiling.

'I saw Findlay today – he's a big boy now – he'll be leaving us soon?'

Kate was aware of Mary – who had been Findlay's primary carer as well – watching her.

'I know,' she said vaguely.

'Where's he going?'

A pause. 'St Anthony's.'

'That's good – a good school. A lot of my friends – their children, they all went there and now they go to university.'

Mary was smiling at her.

'And Findlay – he told me Flo had an accident this morning. He told me she fell off the bed.'

'I know,' Kate said again, sounding as though she was confirming gossip she'd heard about another person's child. 'She did sort of roll off – onto the duvet, fortunately. Our duvet was on the floor.'

Mary carried on smiling, and carried on watching. 'I think she has a bump, just on her left temple. There's a swelling.'

Mary's finger hovered over the pink and green protrusion.

'But the duvet was on the floor,' Kate insisted, taking in Flo's swollen forehead.

Mary nodded. 'I didn't put her to sleep this morning.'

'She hasn't slept?'

'I didn't want to – not with that swelling. It's not good for them to sleep after a head injury.'

'Head injury?'

'I think she should see the doctor,' Mary said calmly.

Kate watched her take hold of Flo's hand and balance it

on her finger and for a brief moment it became a tiny trotter she saw balanced on Mary's index finger before the tiny trotter became a tiny baby hand again. After reassuring Mary that she would take Flo to the doctor's that afternoon, she finally managed to exit the sensory room with the A4 sheet of paper she was given every day, accounting for Flo's dietary and excretory highs and lows.

Findlay was retrieved from the Butterfly Room and coaxed into his coat. It was all looking normal – no sign of pigs or centipedes. She even managed a breezy smile – in case Mary was still standing in the corridor behind them, watching – and a light-hearted, faux commander's, 'Okay, people, let's move out,' for Findlay.

Ignoring his retort – 'We're not people, I'm Spiderman' – she propelled them across the playground past the nursery's chicken coop, and through the security gate. There, on the pavement by the Audi that they were two instalments behind on, was Ros Granger, mother to Lola and Toby Granger.

'Kate!' Ros called out, dismounting from her Dutch-style bicycle, 'I've been trying you all morning – where've you been? Did you get my message?'

Kate nodded, not trusting herself to speak, and wondered how it was that, despite the rain, Ros didn't look bedraggled. Her skin was tanned and the white T-shirt advertising her company, *Carpe Diem Life Classes*, was still white. Ros was somebody other women wanted not only to emulate, but to *become*, and here she was walking towards Kate, her eyes glistening with an obscene wellbeing she just couldn't keep to herself. The overall effect was pathologically upbeat. She looked as if there wasn't a thing in existence she wouldn't be able take succour from – not even mobile-phone adverts that used Holocaust survivors to imply that global communications had the ability to wash away all tears.

Ros was *the* postcode prototype of a young, successful

mother. Within their group – the PRC – she'd gained herself a reputation for originality that was, if you looked closely, nothing more than a highly evolved form of plagiarism. When Ros dropped her wheat intolerance for lactose intolerance, everybody followed suit because – as Ros pointed out – if you were still wheat intolerant it was because you weren't buying sourdough bread. So then everybody had to buy sourdough bread from the deli and – after the lactose intolerance phase – make sure their fridge was full of soya milk.

'So –.'

'So – what?' Kate managed to say cheerfully back, pretending not to understand while knowing exactly what was coming next, exactly what question she was going to be asked.

Here it was – in Ros's clear, ecstatic diction: 'Did – Findlay – get – in?'

The letter was crackling in the pocket of Kate's suit jacket just above her heart –, as if it was about to start talking. With an effort, she managed a slow up and down nod and the sort of smile somebody recovering from a minor stroke might produce.

Ros couldn't quite work out what was going on.

Kate, who had never seen Ros's eyes darken with doubt before, saw them darken now, and had a sudden apocalyptic vision of just how lonely her future in the postcode would be if she were ever excommunicated from the PRC. She would become Jessica – and nobody wanted to become Jessica. Suddenly terrified, she threw the arm that wasn't holding Flo up into the air and screamed an evangelical, 'YESSSS!', walking for no reason whatsoever into Ros's arms.

The next minute the two women were hugging and Ros was the first to pull away. This unexpected physical contact with a woman she didn't even particularly like provoked an unexpected, almost uncontrollable urge in Kate to cry, and to counteract this she started mumbling, 'I can't tell you how . . . how . . .'

'. . . relieved,' Ros put in, letting out one of her light-hearted laughs.

'Relieved – that's it – I am about the whole St Anthony's thing.'

'And now you've got Findlay in, getting Flo in won't be such a hassle.'

'Exactly,' Kate said heavily, while thinking, who the fuck's Flo? Then remembering, and patting her on the back, hoping this wouldn't make her posit anymore.

'So – everybody's in,' Ros said.

Apart from me, Kate thought, staring at her. 'Everybody?'

'Evie, Harriet, me, you . . . everybody in the PRC.'

'What about Jessica?' Kate asked.

Ros's pause suggested that this question wasn't strictly necessary given that Jessica wasn't a fully acknowledged member of the PRC, but she showed magnanimity by shrugging and responding with, 'I can't get hold of her.'

'Me neither,' Kate lied.

A strobe-like frown flickered over Ros's face, then she was smiling again because life really was unbelievably good – apart from when you had to run past people in mobility aids. Although, in her darker moments, she had to admit that the thought of the cripple's eyes on her honed body as she streaked past, fully functioning legs pounding, did thrill her.

'You wouldn't mind keeping an eye on the bike for a minute, would you? Just while I nip in and get Tobes – saves me locking it up. Bless you,' she said, squeezing Kate's arm and jogging past her through the security gates and into Village Montessori.

Kate put Flo, in her car seat, down on the pavement next

to the railings and got Findlay into the car, pushing on a nursery CD whose tracks she now heard in her sleep. Satisfied that Findlay's head was bobbing in time to the music, and that his laughter wasn't hysterical, merely effusive overflow from some complex childhood game, she scanned the contents of the Sainsbury's Organic Bag bulging out of Ros's bicycle basket, and had just managed to uncover a tub of natural cherries and a bar of Valrhona chocolate, some luxury Jersey cream and a gluten-free swiss roll, when Findlay's window whirred down and Findlay called out, 'That's not yours.'

'I know that, Findlay – I wasn't looking in it, I was looking after it,' Kate explained as Findlay swung his head out the window. 'There's a difference.'

Findlay grinned, nonplussed.

What did that grin mean? Was Findlay being *ironic*?

'My bike's got four wheels,' he said.

'Four?' she said, uninterested, but relieved he'd changed the subject. Her mind swung back to the natural cherries and gluten-free swiss roll . . . she was sure there'd been something heavy at the bottom of the bag as well – potatoes? Keeping her eyes on Findlay, she gave them a quick squeeze. Definitely potatoes. Was Ros making tortilla for the PRC that night as well?

Kate had, she realised – staring into the abyss of perfectly honed merchandise in Ros's bicycle basket – set her heart on tortilla for the PRC that night, and making something else instead just wasn't an option at this stage. She had eggs in the fridge – in fact eggs were about all she had.

Findlay was saying, 'Soon it's only going to have two.'

'Two what?' Kate asked, preoccupied.

Findlay was staring at her and there was a baby whimpering somewhere nearby. 'Wheels,' he said after a pause, still staring.

Did she have time to get up to the allotment this afternoon? If Ros *was* making tortilla as well, wouldn't home-grown potatoes give her tortilla the edge? Kate let out a sharp, involuntary chuckle: a home-grown tortilla.

Behind her, the nursery security gate clanged shut, the sound searing through her cranium as her entire head continued to pulsate with migraine.

'Thanks for that,' Ros called out, and was soon strapping Toby and Lola into the child-carrier attached to the back of her bike.

Toby sat staring blankly through the PVC window at Findlay – who was still hanging out of the car – as if he'd never seen him before. Kate thought Toby Granger might be autistic, but even if he was – or ever turned out to be – Ros would somehow manage to turn her son's autism to her advantage. As Ros always pointed out, whenever she had an audience – even a non-paying audience: everything you do, right down to whether you decide to pick up that piece of litter on the pavement or just walk on past, defines you. So why, with a maxim like that, didn't Ros look more exhausted – surely there were only so many definitive moments one person could sustain in the course of a lifetime, let alone on a daily basis.

'Harriet wants us there by eight tonight,' Ros said, as she tucked in the ends of the Sainsbury's bag that Kate had undone and forgotten to push back down again. 'A Labour councillor's meant to be turning up.'

'Why's that?'

'To talk to us about getting speed bumps on Prendergast Road. It was Evie's idea.' She paused, adjusting the Sainsbury's bag again. 'You know Evie's been campaigning for speed bumps? I mean – I'm thrilled about the speed bumps, it's just the focus of tonight's meeting has to be the street party: it's less than two months away now.'

70

'My digger,' Findlay started to yell, 'I want my digger.'

The digger was in the boot of the car and Kate was about to get it when she remembered that the Pampers extra-value pack she'd picked up in the chemist that morning on the way to work was also in the Audi's boot. Members of the PRC didn't do Pampers or Huggies, and they never did supermarket own brand. They bought Tushies, Nature or the German *Umweltfreundlich* brand, Moltex Öko, which looked as though they'd been made by young offenders as part of some community project. Ros, of course, used non-disposable nappies. Buying Pampers was on a level with buying non-organic food or Nike baby trainers or getting Flo's ears pierced or naming your children after luxury goods. Getting Findlay's digger out of the boot was out of the question because it would give Ros, perched on her ergonomic bike saddle, a bird's-eye view of the Pampers value pack . . . and Ros mustn't see the Pampers value pack.

'My digger,' Findlay carried on yelling. 'I want my digger.'

'Seems like he wants his digger pretty badly,' Ros said with an indulgent smile.

Kate was about to answer when she heard a car door open behind her and, turning round, saw Findlay climb out and make his way towards the boot. 'Findlay . . . Findlay!'

Findlay stopped short in his tracks, his hand on the catch for the boot.

'Get back in the car – now!'

Aware that the request for his digger was entirely reasonable, Findlay – taken aback – didn't move.

Kate tried to say it more calmly, 'Get-back-in-the-car-now.'

Findlay still didn't move so she crouched down in front of him, beside the wheel arch, and grabbed hold of his arm, which was difficult to find inside the Spiderman suit's foam musculature.

Ros was staring at her. Kate saw her glance at the stain on the lapel of her suit jacket as well. 'Everything okay?'

'Fine . . . fine. Just work. Work stress,' Kate said, folding herself up rapidly and getting into the car they were defaulting on. 'See you later.'

'Eight o'clock,' Ros reminded her.

Kate nodded, started up the engine, put the car into gear and pulled away, trying to ignore Findlay who was yelling at her to do up his straps. Her phone started to ring. It was Ros.

Ros?

Looking in her rear-view mirror, she watched Ros put her mobile away and swerve off the pavement onto the road in pursuit of the car.

Despite all precautions, Ros must have somehow seen the Pampers extra-value pack in the boot after all – and now she wanted to lecture Kate on disposable nappies and the death of the world.

Kate accelerated.

At the crossroads the Audi hit a red light and she seriously thought about jumping it, then panicked and ended up slamming on the brakes at the last moment. Findlay thudded into the back of her seat and screamed something sanctimonious about Kate not strapping him in and how he was going to die one day. 'So – die,' she yelled, wrenching up the handbrake and getting out of the car as Ros, shaking, came to a halt beside her.

'Okay – so they were out of Moltex Öko at the chemist's, and I was in a rush. I grabbed the first thing to hand and . . . it wasn't Moltex Öko because they were out,' she said.

'Flo,' Ros grunted, out of breath and still shaking.

'Flo?'

'Flo – she's back there – on the pavement. You left Flo in her car seat on the pavement.' Ros fell over her handlebars, sweating and gasping. 'I tried phoning you.' Toby stared out, expressionless, through the child-carrier's PVC window.

Kate peered around the interior of the car. The passenger seat where she usually put Flo's car seat was empty.

The light changed to green and the cars behind were leaning on their horns as drivers pulled angrily on their steering wheels and tried to circumnavigate the parked Audi and the woman on the bike, inadvertently digesting the slogan on the back of her T-shirt: *You deserve to be happy*.

Kate stared blankly at Ros for another ten seconds before getting into her car, executing a three-point turn into oncoming traffic and driving back down the road to the patch of pavement outside Village Montessori where she'd left Flo.

# 10

By the time they finally got back to Prendergast Road, it was after two and Kate couldn't get the door open because Margery had put the chain across.

'Margery!' she yelled.

Further down the street, the Down's syndrome boy at No. 8 – David – was in his front garden, smiling happily as he hugged the loquat tree growing there. The next minute, he started to sing – a series of loud, prolonged wails that started to make Kate panic.

'Margery,' she yelled again.

'Who is it?'

'Kate. Margery – come on, it's starting to rain again.'

The chain was taken off and the front door opened to reveal Margery standing in the hallway with Robert's old hockey stick raised above her head.

Findlay ran past her without comment.

'I heard someone at the door – wasn't sure who it was,' Margery said, without lowering the stick.

'It's us.' Kate stared at her. 'I work half-days Thursdays – I told you.'

Tripping over the same recycling bag in the hallway that

she'd tripped over earlier, she navigated the unmoving Margery and reached the kitchen, where she was confronted with a row of pies.

'Once I got started, I couldn't stop,' Margery said behind her, the hockey stick still in her hands. 'He's got corned beef and onion, cheese and onion and potato to choose from,' she carried on more to herself than Kate. She'd been keeping up a steady patter of conversation with herself most of the morning since Martina left.

'Potato pie?'

Margery nodded.

Her eyes bouncing off the mound of carbohydrates, Kate said, 'Can you keep an eye on Flo for me while I go up and change?'

'Off out again?'

'I thought I might go up to the allotments.' She paused, and with an effort added, 'Why don't you come with us?'

'It's raining.'

Kate glanced out through the kitchen window but didn't say anything.

'You don't want to take them up there in this weather. Findlay won't want to go,' Margery insisted, raising her voice so that Findlay who was playing in the lounge would hear.

'What are you talking about me?' he called out. 'Where won't I want to go?'

'The allotments,' Margery shouted back.

'I don't want to go to the allotments,' Findlay moaned.

Margery's eyes skittered triumphantly over Kate as Findlay appeared in the kitchen doorway, his shoulders pushed forward and his arms hanging loose – a posture he often assumed to denote despair.

'Half an hour, that's all – I need you to help me dig.'

'Digging stinks.'

'Findlay . . .'

'I don't want to go – my suit'll get wet like it did last time then it won't fit.'

'He can stay here with me,' Margery put in.

'Yes, yes,' Findlay started to shout, gripping onto the door-frame and using it to jump up and down.

'Findlay, calm down – if you stay here there won't be any TV.'

The last time she'd left Findlay with Margery for an afternoon they had watched a documentary on the Milwaukee cannibal.

Findlay stopped jumping.

'He can help me with my Tom Jones jigsaw.'

Findlay remained silent, considering this, as Flo started to cry.

'What's wrong with her?' Margery said, irritably.

'Hungry. Could you heat her up a bottle?'

Margery grunted something Kate chose to ignore as she made her way upstairs, running the rest of the day's schedule through her head. She couldn't stay up at the allotments for more than an hour – she had to leave herself time to pick Arthur up from nursery, take him and Findlay swimming then get back to make the tortilla. Pausing at the top of the stairs, she made another mental note to phone Robert and remind him to pick the boys up, before disappearing into the bathroom and swallowing 400 mg of Nurofen.

She took a quick shower in the Philippe Starck shower room they'd remortgaged the house for – along with the Philippe Starck en-suite – before it finally dawned on her that nobody they knew would know the fixtures and fittings were Philippe Starck . . . unless she told them.

On the way to the bedroom she stuck her head over the banister as the microwave she'd finally capitulated to – which Margery had brought in triumph at Christmas when Flo was barely two months old – let out a resounding bling. The

76

constant bling, bling, bling of the microwave had become one of the signature tunes of Margery's brief Christmas reign at No. 22 Prendergast Road. The entire Christmas, in fact, had been a nonstop triumph for Margery, who found her usually challenging daughter-in-law captive in a postnatal world where sleep deprivation and hormone imbalance sent her careering between vegetative trances and hysterical ranting. For the first time in their relationship, Margery had been able to control Kate. Robert no longer knew how to and, anyway, needed all the help he could get when he realised that the two weeks' paternity leave granted him by the government wasn't nearly long enough to construct the illusion that the Hunter family was a happy, thriving unit.

The Christmas dinner Margery insisted on buying was entirely microwaveable. Everything, including the turkey, was nuked – the bell kept blinging, the door kept opening and shutting and there was so much packaging stacked against the kitchen window that it blocked out entirely the drab, drizzling festive daylight.

Kate only finally came alive to the fact that Margery's self-defined role as douala was a smokescreen for total takeover when Robert started mumbling something about getting the spare room properly fixed up so that Margery could be on hand to give round-the-clock help. Enough was enough. Margery was dispatched swiftly but messily back to Leicestershire. This was the first time since the post-Christmas dispatch that Margery had been to stay at Prendergast Road.

In the bedroom, Kate changed into jeans and her new boutique wellies by Marimekko – black daisies on a white background – that Evie had insisted she had to buy on one of their shopping trips, and that Kate had only been able to afford because the family allowance had just gone into the account. Sometimes it felt as though her libido had been sacrificed to Marimekko, Orla Kiely, Philippe Starck . . . along with the Reverend Walker's Sudanese orphans and other people she didn't know.

Dressed in the postcode's requisite uniform for young mothers, which basically consisted of suggesting rather than revealing your female anatomy, she sat down on the bed and thought about having two minutes' lie-down, but knew if she did that she'd never get up, so straightened out the creases she'd made on the throw and stood up again.

Through the broken blinds, she saw a woman standing at the same window as her in the house opposite. She was wearing a Disneyland Paris T-shirt, but didn't look as if she'd ever been to Disneyland. She was holding back the curtains that were usually drawn and was staring intently at the Hunter house. Kate made out black hair hanging down either side of the woman's face, then she started to flap her right hand.

It took Kate some time to decipher the flapping hand.

The woman was waving at her.

Kate was about to wave back when she remembered the St Anthony's letter, Harriet and Evie's ecstatic voicemails, hugging Ros – and was overcome with a sudden nausea she didn't think she could control. Everybody was in apart from them, and it had something – she was convinced – to do with the woman waving at her from the house opposite. The brothel. Evie, Ros and Harriet didn't live opposite houses whose curtains remained permanently shut. The woman opposite, still waving, was the flaw in their lives.

Kate was about to turn and leave the bedroom when she saw that the woman was now holding up a sign – plees help 02081312263 – written in blue on what looked like the inside of a cereal packet.

Kate, startled, stood back and let the blinds fall.

Forgetting about the discarded suit, still on the bed, she went downstairs.

Margery was nursing Flo awkwardly in the crook of her arm, and Findlay was shuffling the pieces of the Tom Jones jigsaw.

'I don't want to get my suit wet,' he said morosely.

'Well, if you don't come to the allotments, you won't be able to go swimming.' She paused.

That stumped him.

'Why?'

'Because after the allotments we're going to pick Arthur up from nursery and then I'm taking you both swimming. So . . . if you don't want to go swimming with Arthur you can stay here and finish that jigsaw.'

Findlay looked up, flicking his head between his mother and Margery, aware that they were both waiting.

After a while he dropped the piece of jigsaw he was holding and followed Kate out to the car. She pulled the seat belt over his bulging foam abs and pecs, then got into the car herself and was about to start the engine when Margery appeared in the front garden with Flo over her shoulder.

'That's my sister,' Findlay said.

Kate got back out of the car.

'I thought you'd gone without her,' Margery said.

Without commenting on this, Kate retrieved the car seat from the kitchen. 'I'll be home around five,' she called out, making her way back to the car – with Flo this time.

'What time's Robert back?'

'I don't know, he didn't say, but he's picking the boys up from swimming at six.'

Margery nodded, then slammed the front door quickly shut.

Five minutes later, Kate was driving at high speed down Prendergast Road towards the allotments, through rain that wasn't letting up.

# 11

Once Kate had gone, Margery went upstairs to change in Findlay's room – where some space had been cleared for her in the wardrobe and chest of drawers.

She chose carefully.

She was dressing for the meal with Robert that evening.

It took her over fifteen minutes to decide on the easy-fit bottle-green trousers and aubergine silk blouse, and she had just got into the trousers when she heard a drilling sound on the other side of the bedroom wall. Was the Jamaican drilling spyholes? How did he know that this bedroom was the one she used to get dressed in? Her eyes scuttled nervously over the wall as she quickly pulled the aubergine blouse on as carefully as she could – she'd already had to repair one underarm tear. She fumbled with the buttons while eyeing the wall opposite warily, expecting the drill to break through at any minute.

When the drilling stopped, the silence that followed was even worse, and Margery waited for it to start again – at least then she knew what the Jamaican was doing.

But the drill didn't start again and, after a while, Margery found herself staring at the three pairs of shoes she'd managed to fit into her case and bring with her, trying to decide whether or not to christen the blue ones she'd bought with Edith in Leicester. Her shoes never retained their original shape for long – after a while they all ended up acquiring the same bunion-riddled silhouette as her feet.

She decided she *would* wear the blue ones and after this went into the bathroom to put her make-up on and spray her hair.

She smiled at herself in the mirror – the coy leer she always reserved for mirror gazing – and was about to go back downstairs when she saw Kate's suit strewn across the bed. She turned automatically into the bedroom and picked up the suit. She didn't view this as a transgression, although she was aware that her daughter-in-law would. Margery couldn't abide mess, but this wasn't her mess and it wasn't her house. The discarded suit would be the cause of an argument between Robert and Kate – because Kate would see Margery going into their bedroom to hang up *her* suit as a transgression verging on the pathological. Robert would come to her defence and say she was only trying to help out. They would hiss and shout at each other behind the closed bedroom door – a pointless precaution given that Margery would be able to follow it word for word through the ceiling, while lying on the sofa bed downstairs.

In deference to the argument that hanging up the suit would provoke, she stroked the creases out once it was on the hanger – and felt a letter in the jacket pocket.

Again, automatically and with no sense of transgression, she pulled the letter out of the pocket. It was the St Anthony's letter. She read it. Then put the envelope back, but kept the letter and was about to go downstairs when something caught her eye through the blind slats. A woman in the house opposite was holding back the curtains, staring straight at her.

Margery pulled the slats further apart.

She didn't know whether the woman could see her or not until the next minute, she started to wave.

Margery waved quickly back – something she wouldn't usually have done – then let the blind slats drop back into place and went downstairs humming something from an advert she'd seen on TV.

She put the letter in an inside pocket of her suitcase, then, still humming, went into the kitchen and made herself a sandwich out of WeightWatchers' bread, cottage cheese and the tinned pineapple she'd opened that morning, and took this through to the lounge where she settled into the sofa in time for the *Dynasty* rerun she was following. Joan Collins thrilled her – had always thrilled her. If she was truthful, she'd put on her green and aubergine outfit, new blue shoes and make-up as much for Joan as she had for Robert.

Joan Collins and Margaret Thatcher made her proud to be a woman.

# 12

Parking beneath a bank of beech trees – the Hunters' was the only car there – Kate got out and opened the boot, putting on one of Robert's old jackets, the pockets weighed down with conkers he must have gathered months ago – back in the autumn before Flo was born.

Findlay, who was singing, 'Happy birthday to me . . . happy birthday to me,' refused to get out of the car, worried that the rain would shrink his foam musculature.

'Okay, okay, but I want you to stay there in the back,' Kate said. 'I don't want you going in the front or touching any of the controls. Findlay . . . are you listening to me? I said, ARE YOU LISTENING TO ME . . . Findlay?' she yelled.

Ignoring Findlay's stunned face, she slammed the boot shut, picked up Flo – who was chewing on her fist, asleep – and stalked off across the allotments towards the one they'd had their name down on a two-year waiting list for.

Keeping the plot – once assigned to you – was almost as hard as acquiring it in the first place. Letitia Parry, chair of the Allotment Committee, made a formal inspection of all the plots the first Sunday of every month, and if it wasn't up to scratch you were *dispossessed* of it. Not a monthly inspection went by without a dispossession getting chalked up on the board that Letitia kept hung outside the committee's old Nissen hut – a board that Giles Parry had spent a fortnight making a waterproof hatch for so that not even rain could wash away the incriminating evidence. Letitia was so harsh that families and individuals – once dispossessed – preferred to forsake tools and anything else they'd bought for their plots rather than face Letitia and get formally drummed out into the wilderness of the rest of the world where there were no allotments.

A man named Gordon, who used to have one of the full plots two down but was unable to keep it up due to the onset of Parkinson's, tried to come back for tools given him by his dead wife on their last wedding anniversary. He left his car down by the golf club at around midnight and crept, shaking, through the orange London dark, past the old scout hut to the top of the hill where the allotments were. He'd brought his torch, but he didn't want to use it – just in case. So he skirted the fringes of the allotments, winding his way through the halo of beech trees – all that remained of the prehistoric Great North Woods – until he reached his plot.

He'd been worried – all day – that the padlock on his shed might have been changed, but it hadn't, and he hissed with relief when the key fitted. So he opened the shed door with difficulty because the key was so small . . . and there was Letitia, sitting on one of his deckchairs, pointing a torch with its beam on full at him. Before he was allowed his tools back, he had to stand there, shaking – at 12.22 a.m. – and listen to the whole lecture on neglect as a form of vandalism, and the impact it had on the ongoing battle the committee was waging trying to keep the land out of the hands of the local council – and all the time he was standing there in the shed, his arm held shakily across his eyes to shield them from Letitia's beam, which she kept on full throughout, he was thinking . . . how did she manage to lock the bloody padlock FROM THE INSIDE?

Months of mental torment passed before Gordon found out that Letitia had asked Giles to lock her in – and not just the night Gordon turned up at midnight either, but every night since the dispossession notice had been chalked up on the committee board.

The Grangers used to have a plot, but Ros fell out with Letitia over ideas she had about permaculture and was finally *dispossessed* when she covered the entire plot in old carpet they'd had ripped up from their study floor – with the idea of replenishing the soil's nutrients by leaving the plot fallow for six months. The carpet had Letitia yelping at Ros from inside the huge body warmer she wore, summer and winter, which was covered in manure stains long since gone shiny – not only because it desecrated the plot, but because Letitia and Giles had just had exactly the same carpet put down in their sitting room.

Kate put Flo inside the Little Tikes house they'd brought up to the allotment for Findlay to play in, which doubled as a shed. She waited to see if the rain drumming on the red plastic roof tiles was going to wake up Flo, who was sleeping soundly, then took the fork balanced against the cooker and went back out into the April storm. Descending into the mud, she started to dig. Others – Ros – might be making tortilla as well, but was anybody making it with *home-grown* potatoes? Before having Flo, her dinner parties had acquired quite a reputation on Prendergast Road and now people had expectations of her.

She was unable to stand for more than a minute in one place without her feet sinking into the now liquid mud, and the potatoes weren't as far on as she thought they were when she checked on Sunday. The earth yielded nothing she could transform into tortilla – the four potatoes she pulled up looked as if they'd been manhandled by O. J. Simpson – so she hauled herself out of the mud and onto the grass pathway, staring bleakly into the rain for some sort of inspiration, and trying to ignore the sound of a dog whining somewhere nearby.

Inspiration came to her, at last, in the shape of Letitia's plot. Letitia's plot had the best potatoes in a 2,000-mile radius, and she only needed three medium-sized ones. There were no lights on in the Nissen hut and still no cars other than the Audi in the car park. Stumbling along the grass verge, she slid behind the old metal Conway container just to the side of Letitia's plot and checked the Nissen hut and the car park again, peered warily into the forest and even up at the sky – after all, Letitia had been waiting for Gordon five nights in a row ON THE INSIDE of a padlocked shed.

She waited another minute before making a dash for Letitia's potatoes, slipping on a Savoy cabbage, thinking she heard a car, freezing, realising it wasn't a car, only the rain battering the roof of the old scout hut five hundred yards or so away, then pulled up three of the best-looking plants, her hands shaking.

Without even checking them, she broke into a lopsided run, still shaking, tripped over some stones in the car park, threw the potatoes in the boot, slammed it shut, then got into the car. She sat, panting, staring at the misted windscreen, the water streaming off Robert's coat down over her wrists and hands, filling the creases in the leather covering the gear box.

In the back, Findlay was concentrating hard on trying to block out his mother's frantic breathing and the way the rain was running off her, out of her – as if it had somehow got inside her.

With her hands slipping over everything she touched – the ignition, gear stick, steering wheel – Kate finally got the car into gear and reversed almost into the Nissen hut before swinging the wheel round and pushing the gear stick violently into first. The wheels spun and skidded in the mud before they pulled away, shooting past the scout hut and the entrance to the golf club.

'Mum!' Findlay said.

Kate was about to respond when she was confronted with Letitia's Volvo coming towards them, doing what it had been manufactured to do: course smoothly through rain and mud. The headlights flashed on and off in an improbable Morse code and the horn sounded. Letitia had seen them.

Knowing she didn't have a choice, Kate skidded to a halt and slid the window down.

Letitia was smiling the smile of a fanatic, her face – her whole head, in fact – looked as if it had been involved in some intense physical activity, like driving a herd of cattle across a flooded river in Brazil's Pantanal.

'Undeterred,' she hollered at Kate, through the rain, ecstatic at the thought of people maintaining their plots during storms. 'That's what I like to see,' she carried on, swallowing gallons of water as her mouth opened wide. 'UNDETERRED,' she hollered again before banging on the steering wheel and accelerating up the hill towards the allotments.

After Letitia had accelerated out of sight, Kate sat there listening to the Audi's frenetically capable wipers dealing with the flood on the windscreen. She ran her wet hands over the wet steering wheel, trying to find a grip, and didn't even notice the rain coming in through the still-open window, soaking the upholstery and what was left of her to be soaked.

'Mum!' Findlay said again. 'You forgot Flo.'

Slamming the gear stick into reverse, she drove the car at high speed back up the hill, got out, opened the boot and clicked the back shelf into place to hide the potatoes; then started to slip and stumble her way back towards their plot, past Letitia's Volvo, which was already parked, and the wet, hulking figure of Letitia herself, crouched at the edge of her plot, the rain hammering onto the resinous back of her body warmer.

Letitia was grunting and didn't seem to notice Kate slipping and sliding across the soaked grass behind her until she skidded to a halt outside the Little Tikes house.

Kate wrenched open the door and stuck her head inside.

There was Flo in her car seat, awake now, giving her the same wet, blank look she'd given her earlier when Kate picked her up from Village Montessori.

With difficulty – much more difficulty than she'd had when putting her in – Kate hauled the car seat, with Flo inside, out into the rain. This time, no longer asleep, Flo started to cry as soon as the drops as big as her fists started hitting her face.

Kate tried holding the bottom of Robert's coat over her, but there was as much water coming off this as there was out of the sky, so in the end she just decided to make a run for it, only now Letitia was standing, watching her – waiting for her?

'Where did you get that?' Letitia said, jerking her rain-sodden head at screaming Flo, suspended from Kate's arm in the uncomfortably heavy car seat.

'This?' Kate laughed, staring down at her daughter. 'Just over there – in the Little Tikes playhouse.'

'Oh, I thought I saw you heading downhill in your car.'

'I was – then I remembered I'd left Flo up here.' Kate laughed again.

They both stared at the screaming Flo, then Letitia turned away, back to her plot.

'Some bugger's been up here – ransacked my plot.'

'Ransacked it?'

'There!' Letitia cried impatiently, oblivious now to Flo's wailing. 'And there – and there – whoever it was got away with three prize potatoes.' She shot Kate a quick look then stalked off round the boundary of the plot. 'No other damage, far as I can see.'

'That's terrible,' Kate said, over roaring rain and Flo's hysterical tears: a traitor's commiseration.

'It's bloody sacrilege, that's what it is – didn't see anything when you were up here earlier?'

Kate shook her head slowly, the rain running in rivers off the end of her chin.

'Can't remember – I think I was the only one up here.'

'Didn't notice anything amiss?'

'I can't say I was looking,' Kate said.

Letitia grunted. 'I'm not having this. I'm not having it,' she yelled into the rain. 'I'm going straight to the police.' She walked heavily off in the direction of the Nissen hut and Kate managed to get back to the car.

'Where was Flo?' Findlay said, leaning forwards in his seat, guilty he hadn't thought about this earlier before they'd started driving down the hill.

'Over there – in the Little Tikes house,' Kate said.

'Does she like the playhouse?' Findlay asked.

'I don't know – why don't you ask her?' Kate threw her head back into the rain and laughed, suddenly.

Findlay, worried, stayed silent.

Through the window of the Nissen hut, Kate saw Letitia on the phone, her body jerking as though somebody was trying to jumpstart her as she attempted to interest the Brixton police – most of them fresh from another fatal shooting in McDonald's – in her three missing potatoes, currently in the boot of the Hunters' car as it slid past the illuminated hut back down the hill, towards the South Circular.

# 13

Half an hour later – after picking up Arthur Palmer from
Village Montessori and dropping both boys at the leisure
centre – Kate, exhausted and soaked to the skin, tripped
over the recycling bag in the hallway for the third time that
day as she made her way towards the kitchen with Letitia's
potatoes in her left hand and Flo, still in her car seat, swinging
from the right arm. Leaving the potatoes on the surface next
to Margery's pie line-up, she went into the lounge with Flo.

The TV was on loud – she'd heard it from the front garden
before even getting round to opening the front door – and
Margery was asleep on the sofa. She was leaning rigidly over
to one side with her hands pushed between her thighs and
her chin tucked neatly down. As Kate stood there, she let out
a shuddering whimper and slipped another inch sideways, but
didn't wake up. For a moment, Kate felt uncharacteristically
protective towards Margery; then the moment passed.

Before losing consciousness, Margery had been watching
Bid-TV and a man on screen was trying to shift 200 CD
players shaped like electric guitars priced at £49.50 each.
Kate watched the number of remaining CD players go down
to 195, momentarily fascinated, and it took her a while to

realise that the persistent dripping sound she could hear was in fact excess rainwater running off the coat she was still wearing onto the carpet.

Leaving Flo in her car seat down on the floor by Margery's feet, Kate hung her coat up in the hallway and went into the kitchen. She'd gone into the kitchen for a reason and now couldn't remember why . . . until she saw the potatoes on the bench. Tortilla – for tonight's PRC.

Over the next twenty minutes she made a small, immaculate amount of tortilla. This was a tried-and-tested PRC trick, given that plates were expected to be empty by the end of the evening or – better still – the middle.

She moved quickly and efficiently round the kitchen, not doing anything that would sidetrack her or break up her rhythm. This was how most food preparation took place at No. 22 Prendergast Road – on borrowed time, and borrowed time wasn't something she had any control over, so thirst and the need to urinate were compartmentalised because at the moment Margery was having an afternoon nap and Flo was quiet and this was the only way she was going to get the tortilla made and not suffer the shame of turning up empty-handed, which basically amounted to a public declaration of *not being able to cope*.

She was just pouring the eggs into the pan when the phone rang. It was Jessica.

'Hello,' she said, distracted, as she slid the dish under the grill and the sound of scraping metal drowned Jessica out. 'What's that?'

'I said I was just phoning to make sure that Arthur was okay after nursery.'

Kate, preoccupied by the tortilla, had barely any memory of leaving two small children at the crumbling leisure centre the Lib Dem council was forever promising to regenerate.

'He seemed fine.'

'Fine?'

What sort of details was Jessica prompting her for?

'He didn't seem quiet or anything? I mean, like, too quiet?'

Kate slid the tortilla out, satisfied herself that it was bubbling in all the right places, then slid it in again.

'Jessica, he was fine.'

'He seems to have become quiet lately – and he's started biting his nails. I noticed that the other day.'

In the silence that followed, Kate turned off the grill.

'Did he have everything he needed? I kept thinking I might have forgotten something. So Robert's picking the boys up from swimming still?'

Kate had completely forgotten to phone Robert and remind him. 'Of course.'

'Brilliant,' Jessica breathed out, relieved.

'And don't forget about the PRC meeting tonight.'

'I'll see . . . it depends on—'

'Ellie. I know.'

Kate rang off, passing her face over the tortilla and inhaling. She was about to phone Robert when she heard Flo in the lounge.

Margery was still asleep and the man on screen had sold nearly all 200 CD players. Trying to imagine the sort of people who were buying them – then giving up – she took Flo upstairs into her bedroom. Once there, she stared absently out through the window at a eucalyptus they'd planted two years ago that was already over fourteen feet tall, thrashing about in the wind and rain. The house the Hunters backed onto was being painted white, but they'd only got half of it done before the rain must have started.

She watched Ivan make his way unevenly along the fence that separated their gardens and jump onto the shed roof, certain he was limping. Lying Flo under her baby gym, she pulled up the sash window, which was difficult because the wooden frame was swollen with rot at the bottom and got stuck after about four inches, and called out Ivan's name.

He stopped, settled onto his haunches and looked up at her. After a while he licked at one of his front paws and looked away, distracted.

Sighing, Kate watched Flo pull off one of her socks.

A cloud must have shifted then, as late afternoon sunshine broke through into the room, the trees still blowing outside, making it move restlessly round the walls and ceiling. Even though it was only April, the sun had warmth in it and, where it fell on her, Kate felt warm. When the sun vanished the room was suddenly much colder and darker.

Overcome with exhaustion, she went through to their bedroom and, without thinking, rolled under the duvet – pulling it up over her head and curling her body round her clenched fists. There was something she needed to do that she kept forgetting to do. What was it?

In less than a minute, she was fast asleep.

# 14

When she woke up just over an hour later she couldn't even remember falling asleep. The house was silent and dark and, lying there, Kate wasn't entirely convinced she *was* awake. It was too quiet – as though the entire city had been evacuated while she slept. Rolling onto her side, the events of the morning came slowly back to her. The St Anthony's letter. She sat up in a sudden panic. Where *was* the St Anthony's letter? Her hands groped instinctively around the bed, remembering the suit jacket she'd worn to work and left on the bed – was almost certain she'd left on the bed – before going to the allotments.

She threw the duvet off and slid awkwardly out of bed without bothering to put the light on. A vague trace of migraine remained and it felt as though blood wasn't being pumped evenly round her head, so that she kept losing her balance and falling suddenly into things as she staggered over to the wardrobe it had taken Robert and her five nights to build, and that they both hated, ignoring her mobile, which had started to ring. There was the jacket – hanging up. She felt the envelope in the inside pocket and pulled it out. The envelope was empty. Had she taken it out at work and left it there? Maybe it was in the car – or downstairs somewhere.

She ran downstairs into the kitchen, walking into just about everything there was to walk into on the way, including Flo, who was there on the floor in her bouncy chair, reaching out excitedly for the furry stars hanging from the bar above.

And there was Robert, standing at the bench by the cooker with a screwdriver in his hand and the motor from the old Morphy Richards blender in pieces beside him.

He was wearing his favourite T-shirt, which said he'd run the New York Marathon in 1998 – only he hadn't – and smiling.

'Kate' he said, sounding pleased to see her. 'I heard you stumbling around up there – don't worry, she's down here with us.'

'Who is?' she said, distracted, her eyes scanning the kitchen surfaces. No letter.

'Flo.' He paused. 'She's got some kind of bruise on her forehead.'

Kate stared down at Flo, then back at Robert. 'Nursery. When did you get home?'

'About forty-five minutes ago.'

'What's the time now?'

'Almost six.'

'I didn't hear you come in.' She yawned.

'You were out cold so I just left you.'

Upstairs, her mobile started to ring again. Kate yawned and took in the scene in the kitchen. The light was falling strangely on Robert, making him look guilty, as though he was trying to make amends for a crime he hadn't committed yet.

'Was my suit jacket on the bed when you went up earlier?'

He shook his head. 'Haven't a clue. Hey – where are you

going?' he said as she grabbed the car keys from the rack below the cupboard.

'I left something in the car,' she called out, disappearing through the front door.

Outside, the rain hammered on her back as she searched the car with forensic precision – and failed to find the letter.

She went back indoors. It had to be somewhere.

In the kitchen, Robert was standing with the screwdriver still in his hand and the abstract, easy-to-please look on his face that he assumed when he was concentrating intently on something his future didn't depend on. 'Find it?'

'Robert – what are you doing?' she said, irritably.

'Just mending this.' He nodded at the motor on the bench, nonchalant, pleased with himself. Something was wrong – carrying out impromptu repairs, midweek, just wasn't something Robert did. Ever.

'But that broke over two years ago.'

'Did it?' He looked at the motor again, less confident now, but still enthusiastic. 'Oh.' He started smiling again.

'Why now? Why tonight – when I've been going on to you about that blender for over two years?'

Robert shrugged. 'I thought I'd have a go at mending it.'

'I don't even use it any more – we bought the red KitchenAid instead because I got sick of waiting for that one to be mended.'

He stared blankly at her as she walked over to the units and opened the cupboard door, and he carried on staring blankly – at the red KitchenAid this time – on the shelf inside. 'I didn't know we had that.'

She slammed the door shut. 'We've had it over two years.'

'I haven't seen you use it.' He realised as he was saying this that it was the wrong thing to say – that it could even be classified a criticism – but he was getting himself lost; he couldn't remember what it was they'd been talking about or why he was holding a screwdriver in his hands. He stared at the disembodied motor unit on the bench in front of him, wondering when exactly he'd had the idea of trying to fix it – when exactly he'd felt enthusiastic enough to take on the motor.

'What's brought this on?' Kate demanded.

'What?'

'This . . . fixation with repairs.'

'Fixation? I'm not fixated – I just found it in the cupboard when I was looking for tea bags and I thought—'

'Why now?' She insisted.

'Kate – I don't know.'

'I wake up and find you mending a motor that's been waiting to be mended for over two years – for a machine that no longer exists. Why?'

'Why does it have to bother you so much?'

'It doesn't – I just need to know why.'

He mumbled, 'There is no why,' before starting to collect the parts together, putting them back in the box next to the teapot with the broken spout Sellotaped to it, as Kate's mobile started to ring again.

They stared at each other.

'You want me to get that?'

She shook her head.

Making an effort, Robert said, 'Smells nice.' He nodded at the tortilla on the hob.

'It's for the PRC meeting tonight.'

'Tonight?'

'I did tell you,' she warned him.

'Okay, okay. I forgot, I'm sorry.'

'You've got pie.'

'Pie?'

She moved her hand across the panorama of carbohydrates filling the bench opposite. 'Corned beef, cheese and onion – and I think the last one's potato.'

Robert didn't say anything as his elbow slipped off the bench and he lurched forward into the middle of the kitchen, regaining his balance and wobbling back towards the bench.

Kate heard herself saying, 'You're drunk,' before she even realised it.

That's why he looked strange earlier – his movements had been slower and more deliberate than usual.

'I'm not drunk.'

She stared at him in silence, trying not to panic, waiting for an explanation and at the same time not wanting to hear it. 'Christ, Robert,' she said at last.

'So I had a few drinks with Les after work,' he blurted out, aggressive with guilt.

'How many's a few?

It was getting darker in the kitchen and Flo was blowing raspberries at the star that squeaked.

Robert had been working in the light from the cooker hood, which cast itself unevenly round the rest of the kitchen, not quite reaching everything and bouncing off the surfaces it did reach, making them look fragile. It hadn't occurred to either of them to switch the overhead lights on.

'Did something happen today?' Kate said, looking at him properly for the first time since she came in.

'Today?' Robert said slowly. 'Today something did happen – yes.'

This was unusually cryptic for Robert. 'Jerome?'

The name had a visible effect on him, but he didn't say anything.

'Jerome's a problem, isn't he? Why do we never talk about Jerome?'

'Because you're not always the easiest person to talk to . . . at the moment. It's like you're never here.'

'Well, in case you hadn't noticed, I'm trying to bring up a five-year-old and a six-month-old baby – of course I'm never here. I'm nowhere close to being bloody here. You've got no idea – sometimes it takes all I've got just to get up in the morning.'

'Kate . . .'

He watched her yelling at him, suddenly wanting to touch her somewhere, to try and contain her in some way before she disappeared in front of his eyes.

'Are you going to say anything? Robert?'

'I want to kill him.'

'Who?'

'Jerome. I want to kill him. I think about killing him – all the time. He gets to me.'

'They all get to you.'

Idly, Robert picked up the broken motor from the blender again. 'Not like this – never like this,' he said, tired, suddenly aware of just how much he didn't want to talk to Kate about this right now. Then, before she had time to start up again, he said, 'I saw a job advertised in the *TES* today.'

'You did?' She didn't even try to sound interested.

'Botswana.'

'Stop it,' she said sharply.

'What?'

'The motor – whatever it is you're about to start doing to the motor.'

Unable to bear his tinkering any longer, she crossed the kitchen, grabbed the box out of his hands, then walked over to the bin and threw it in.

As the lid clattered shut, Robert was aware that, within the last three seconds, he had become angry.

'What was all that about?'

'What?' She turned on him.

'That . . . just now.'

'Nothing.' She walked out of the kitchen and down the hallway – away from him and his day.

'Kate,' he yelled, 'are we going to talk about this? What is this? What's this all about? I know you've been stressed lately . . .'

Peering at Flo, whose arms jerked towards him as he side-stepped the bouncy chair, he followed Kate out into the hallway.

She was about four paces in front of him, moving slowly, silently, away from him towards the stairs. There was something intractable about her posture – as though she was taking something away from him she had no intention of ever giving back – and he hated her for that, hated her so much he could have killed her right then.

He caught up with her at the first landing, grabbing hold of her wrist. If he didn't stop her now it felt as though she would just carry on climbing flight after flight of stairs, willing them into existence, and he'd be fated to walk four paces behind her – in perpetuity.

'I haven't got time for this,' she said, against a backdrop of hall wall that needed painting, but that they couldn't agree on a colour for.

She didn't try to pull her wrist away.

'For what?'

She paused. Up close, even in his own clothes, Robert smelt of other people's children, and poverty – other people's poverty. She hadn't started out afraid of poverty, but she was now. 'This,' she said, suddenly unsure.

'Listen, I know you've been stressed lately,' he said again. 'About St Anthony's and stuff.'

'You should be saying *we've* been stressed, but you're right – *I've* been stressed. Throughout the whole thing it's felt like me and my stress, we're over here somewhere and you . . . fuck knows where you've been.'

'It's Jerome, he . . .'

'. . . Probably went to Brunton Park before going to

Ellington. Ellington's biggest intake comes from Brunton Park. They have children there who were child soldiers in the Congo, Robert.'

'I know – I've got most of them sitting in the back row of my English class.'

'And would you want to see Findlay sitting in the back row of one of your English classes?'

'Well, they wouldn't timetable it so that—'

'Robert!'

'Okay – okay.'

'How would you feel about Findlay ending up at Ellington?'

'What, like me?'

'For fuck's sake, Robert – that's exactly what I'm talking about when I say I've been stressed. This is what it's been like for months now – since before Flo was born.'

'But, Kate,' he moved his hands up to her shoulders. 'Findlay's not going to Oliver Goldsmith's – he's going to St Anthony's. You can relax – Findlay's in now.' This had no visible effect on Kate, who was watching him strangely, with a look that veered between blank and suspicious.

'Kate, look at me – will you just look at me. Kate –.'

He saw the effort on her face: she tried, she really did. Their eyes met and he was startled – suddenly, unexpectedly – by an overwhelming memory of the gloriously filthy sex they used to have. 'No,' he said, instinctively, as Kate's eyes slid away from him, towards the stairs. 'We have to do this now.'

'What?'

'This – whatever we're doing that's . . . that's . . .' The anger had gone, passing through him so quickly it had left him feeling bereft, tearful even. He could feel the tears collecting now somewhere in his belly, getting mixed up with the desire he felt at the sight of the curls the rain had given Kate's hair at the nape of her neck as she twisted away from him – curls he hadn't noticed for months, maybe even years. 'That's . . . keeping us standing here together.'

Kate couldn't move her head any further without hitting wall, so she looked up instead, through the skylight at the top of the stairs to an evening full, suddenly, of starlings.

'Kate . . .'

The way he said it made so many things feel possible again.

Robert saw her face change and could feel himself beginning to unravel. He wanted to kiss her more than anything. The tears were rising up from his belly; he was going to start crying and Kate didn't want to see him cry. Kate wanted . . . what *did* Kate want? Did she feel as lonely as he did right then? Was loneliness what they had in common – the profound loneliness of people bereft of themselves? If Kate had lost Kate and Robert had lost Robert – how on earth were they meant to set about finding each other?

'Kate . . .'

She was looking directly at him now. If he said her name like that once more, she was going to end up telling him everything and she wasn't entirely sure where everything would lead them. 'Stop it! Stop saying that,' she yelled suddenly.

The tears, which had been on the verge of breaking, fell back down into his belly as she vanished before his eyes.

'Please, Kate.'

'Stop it – just stop it.' She was almost screaming now.

The air between them was vibrating wildly, gravity had been shot to pieces and there was no way of holding anything down any more. Who started this, anyway?

Robert let his back slump against the wall and gave in to feeling drunk and exhausted. 'We just need a break, Kate, a clean break.' He paused. 'What about it?'

They looked at each other, and a brief spark of recognition – complicity – passed between them.

Then Kate broke away, unconvinced. 'A clean break, where?'

He was staring wildly at her, thinking anywhere . . . anywhere other than here. 'Botswana?'

'You've already mentioned Botswana. I don't want to go to Botswana.'

'Sierra Leone?'

'Let's just leave Africa out of it.'

Then Margery's voice croaked up the stairs, 'You're not talking about New Zealand are you?'

Kate and Robert pushed their heads in unison round the turn in the stairs and saw Margery standing at the bottom of them, her hand on the banister. The hair on the left-hand side of her head was flat from where she'd been sleeping on it and there was a red patch on her face where she'd dribbled over the sofa and the wet fabric had irritated her skin.

'She's awake,' Kate hissed at Robert. 'How long has she been awake for?'

Robert shrugged. 'What's that, Mum?'

'You're home,' she said, then carried on with, 'When I was talking to Beatrice earlier, she said you were thinking about going to New Zealand.'

'There was never any talk of New Zealand, Mum.'

'Well Beatrice said there was.'

'In passing, maybe . . . nothing more.'

'New Zealand's on the other side of the world.'

'Mum!' Robert said more forcefully than he'd meant to, 'nobody's going to New Zealand – nobody.'

He turned desperately back to Kate, his eyes sliding down her throat, whose veins were still shaking, and felt an almost uncontrollable wave of desire.

'Beatrice really upset me,' Margery persisted.

Robert reeled towards Kate, wanting to make love to her here on the stairs, regardless of Margery standing at the bottom of them.

'She really did.'

Kate was watching him, afraid.

Robert paused, saw her face, then pulled himself aggressively away and went heavily downstairs.

Kate stayed where she was, staring at the sets of handprints big and small on the grey wall. She heard Margery say, 'I'll make some tea.' Then her phone started ringing again and this time she carried on upstairs into their bedroom and retrieved it from her handbag.

It was HSBC – she'd spoken to them earlier about increasing their overdraft limit – phoning again. There were four other missed calls – one from an unknown number and three from Jessica. Three?

Then she remembered.

'Where's Findlay?' she yelled, running downstairs and into the kitchen.

Robert, who was emptying the teapot into the sink, turned slowly round. 'What?'

'I said – where's Findlay?'

'Findlay?'

'Yes, Findlay – where's Findlay? He's meant to be here – you were meant to be picking him and Arthur up from Swim Club.'

'Swim Club?'

'Shit, Robert – what's the time now?'

'Twenty past six,' Margery's voice called out from the lounge.

'Shit!'

Kate was aware of a mauve and green blur suddenly surrounding Robert as she screamed, 'You forgot to pick up the boys!'

Robert continued to stare blankly at her. 'So I'll go now.'

'You can't go – you're drunk.'

'Drunk?' Margery said, outraged at the accusation.

'Tell her you went to the pub after school,' Kate demanded.

'I went to the pub after school.'

'And that you're drunk.'

'And that I'm drunk.'

'You're not drunk,' Margery said, ignoring the confession.

'Robert – I don't have time for this. I'm-going-to-get-our-son-Findlay.' And with that, Kate hauled Flo, now screaming, out of her bouncy chair and into her car seat.

'You can leave Flo here – with me,' Robert said.

'You're drunk,' Kate hissed. 'I'm not leaving her with you.' Grunting, she swung the car seat up into the crook of her arm.

'I'm here,' Margery said from the kitchen doorway.

Kate stared at her, then, without another word, walked out of the house, slamming the front door shut.

Robert and Margery stood in the kitchen listening to the footsteps disappear, the screech of the un-oiled gate and a car engine starting up soon drowned by the sound of other traffic on the road. Robert drifted through to the lounge and Margery, with a contented sigh, got the tea tray ready.

'Come on, love,' she said a few minutes later, walking through to the lounge and putting the tray down on the coffee table. 'We won't be having supper till late, so I thought I'd put us some bits out.' Her eyes scanned the plates full of Battenburg cake, Mr Kipling's Bakewell tart and Nice biscuits. 'You don't mind supper late?'

When Robert didn't respond to this, Margery said, 'Don't beat yourself up about the boys – you've been at work all day.'

'I completely forgot.'

'Did Kate even tell you?'

'Last week.'

'But did she remind you this morning about picking the boys up – or phone you?'

'Mum, that's not the point.'

Unsure what the point was, Margery started to make her way contentedly through a slice of Battenburg. 'Her saying you're drunk.' She shook her head.

'What's that?'

'Kate . . . saying you're drunk.'

'Maybe I am.'

'You're not drunk.'

'I did go to the pub after school.'

'Well, you're entitled to it – and you're home now. She needs to calm down,' Margery added, trying to keep the bits of Battenburg in her mouth. Another minute passed with Robert slumped inert, making no effort to help himself to the contents of the tea tray. Suddenly irritated, Margery said, 'Beatrice really did upset me – saying what she did earlier about New Zealand.'

Robert stood up suddenly and left the room.

'Where are you going? Margery shouted, her mouth full again. 'Your tea's all poured – we've got biscuits.'

'I don't want tea,' Robert said, blinking into the light of the fridge while banging his head repeatedly against the door.

'What's that?'

'Nothing,' he yelled back, louder than he'd meant to.

# 15

The smell of chlorine filled the stairwell leading up to Jessica's maisonette at No. 283 Prendergast Road – chlorine and onions frying. Kate climbed the stairs, banging Flo's car seat off walls covered in intricate biro drawings of spiders – a legacy from the previous owner's children. The door at the top of the stairs was open and she could hear Arthur and Findlay yelling at each other as she walked up the last few steps and into the Palmers' maisonette.

Jessica appeared in the kitchen doorway, still dressed in her suit and drying her hands on a tea towel.

'Jessica, I'm so – so sorry. Robert got held up at work and—'

Jessica cut in with, 'I didn't know what was going on when the leisure centre rang. They said nobody had come to collect the boys and they couldn't get hold of you. Then I tried to get hold of you and couldn't—'

'It was Robert, he—'

'So I thought I'd better go and collect them myself and . . .'

For a moment Kate thought Jessica was going to cry, but she held tightly onto the side of the kitchen bench and the moment passed.

'Jessica, I'm so sorry. I don't know what to say.'

'I had to get Jake to cover my two valuations.'

'I'm sorry.'

Jessica sighed. 'Come in – I'm making hot dogs.'

Unable to bear the way Jessica was looking at her any longer – she didn't think she'd ever seen Jessica angry before – Kate went through to the lounge where Findlay and Arthur were practising karate on the patch of carpet not taken up by Arthur's Transformers collection. The maisonette always felt messy – no, disorganised was a better word. Arthur's eyes briefly scanned her from behind a pair of science goggles then switched back to Findlay.

Findlay looked up, saw his mother, then shot his left foot out, catching Arthur just below the knee. 'Why didn't Dad come?' he asked. Then, before she had time to answer. 'Where's Flo?'

'Flo? She's here with me.'

Findlay relaxed and gave Arthur another kick.

Kate put the car seat down by the dining table – still obscured by breakfast cereals and a copy of *A Choice of Ethical Careers*.

Arthur dropped onto the floor, panting, staring with bloodshot chlorine eyes at the gas-effect fire, which was on.

'Thinking of a change in career?' Kate called out, wanting to smooth things over.

Jessica reappeared in the kitchen doorway, the water from a pack of Hertz frankfurters she was holding leaking over her suit jacket.

Kate held up *A Choice of Ethical Careers*, which Jessica peered at while sucking her fingers.

'Oh, that's Ellie's,' she said coldly.

Kate was about to put the book back on the dining table when she saw the St Anthony's letter, covered in a trail of milk. She scanned through it twice. 'Oh, my God – Jessica!'

Getting her foot caught round one of the table legs, she tripped then made her way over to the kitchen. 'Jessica . . .'

Jessica, who was dropping frankfurters into a pan of water, didn't turn round. 'What?'

'Arthur got in.'

'What's that?'

'I saw the letter just now on the table. ARTHUR GOT IN.'

'Oh – yeah.'

Jessica was staring strangely at her. Kate let out a solitary, hysterical laugh. 'You must be *so* pleased.'

'Yeah – I didn't think he'd get in. At least him and Findlay will be together,' Jessica said, smiling for the first time since Kate's arrival.

Kate continued to stare stupidly at her, trying to think of something to say.

'This is fucking hopeless,' Jessica muttered, trying to scoop the frankfurters out of the pan. 'It was Peter who used to do all the cooking. God, I miss borscht,' she sighed.

Kate smiled awkwardly. She'd never heard Jessica refer to Peter before.

'Does Findlay want one before he goes?' Jessica said, dropping them into hot-dog rolls, which became immediately saturated with the boiling water still running off the frankfurters.

'No, it's fine,' Kate said quickly. 'We've got to get going.'

The smell of burnt onions was rapidly filling not only the kitchen but the entire maisonette, and somewhere in the background a baby started crying just as the burnt onions finally got round to triggering the maisonette's decades-old, fugged-up smoke alarm.

'Fuck,' Jessica said, taking the pan off the heat and opening the kitchen window.

Findlay and Arthur appeared in the doorway, the skin around their eyes puffed up from overexposure to chlorine – and excitement at the smoke alarm.

Jessica took a swipe at the alarm with the tea towel until it stopped ringing and was left hanging from the ceiling by two wires.

'Mum—' Findlay started.

Then Jessica cut in with, 'D'you want me to get her?'

'Who?'

'Well, Flo, she's . . .'

'Oh.' Now the smoke alarm had stopped, Kate became aware that her daughter was crying – screaming in fact.

'I'll get her,' Jessica said when Kate showed no sign of movement.

She reappeared a minute later holding Flo against her chest. 'You're sure you don't want to stay for tea?'

'Sorry – we've got to run.'

'Maybe another time,' Jessica said, suddenly desperate. Then, 'She's gorgeous, Kate,' staring down at Flo and running her forefinger down the length of the tiny nose.

Without responding to this, Kate yelled, 'Findlay – we need to get home.'

Findlay appeared in the doorway, pushing his damp fringe off his face as he started to slowly pull on his shoes.

Flo immediately started to cry again as soon as Kate took her from Jessica, who followed them downstairs.

Findlay was singing loudly, 'Who let the dogs out? Who – who – who . . . ?'

Kate thought she was going to explode.

At last, Findlay was buckled in and Flo was staring with fretful, wet-eyed wonder at the felt carousel dangling about twenty centimetres directly above her that Kate now activated to calm herself, before getting into the driver's seat to the chiming melody of '*Au Clair de la Lune*'.

Jessica tapped on the window. 'Are you still on for the PRC tonight?'

'Are you coming?'

'Probably. I've spoken to Ellie.'

'See you around eight.'

Before Jessica had time to say anything else, Kate gave a wave and the car slid out from under the streetlight, executing a fraught U-turn before driving at high speed back down to the lower end of Prendergast Road.

# 16

Jessica watched the Audi until it disappeared downhill by the Pentecostal church where some information about Christ's Second Coming was written in black marker pen – in such large letters she could read it from where she was standing on the pavement. When Kate's car had gone, she looked up at the windows of the maisonette she'd bought six months ago – that she was going to have to put a lot of effort into calling home – and instinctively sniffed her hands, which smelt of Flo. Her insides lurched as they had done when she'd first picked up Flo. Up until then she had never thought of wanting more children.

Ellie appeared like a ghost at an upstairs window.

Jessica waved, but Ellie didn't wave back.

Ellie shut the curtains.

Looking up the street in either direction as if waiting for somebody long overdue, Jessica sighed and went back indoors, walking over some stray rose stalks and chrysan- themum leaves that must have blown under the florist's door into her hallway. After six months, she was almost imper- vious to the scent of the flowers – all except the lilies, which gave off a carnivorously humid smell that unsettled her.

The maisonette needed painting but paint charts didn't feature large in the life of the Palmers. Paint charts – like a lot of things – were for other people.

Pushing hair that hadn't been cut for over a year out of her eyes – and catching the smell of Flo on her hands again – Jessica looked down the street one last time, watched two cars pass the junction with Harlow Road, then shut the door.

Upstairs, Arthur was on the sofa watching TV, his hair damp with sweat.

She gave him two wet hot dogs smeared in ketchup, which he accepted with the comment, 'One in every four people on the planet's Chinese.'

'I'll be back in five minutes,' Jessica said to him in response to this. 'I'm just going to check on Ellie.'

Checking on Ellie was something Arthur was so used to her doing that he barely noticed as she left the room and headed towards Ellie's bedroom with a second plate of wet hot dogs smeared in ketchup.

Ellie was sitting at her desk and the computer was on. The only part of her daughter that Jessica could see from behind the huge Mastermind chair was her crepuscular left hand, moving the mouse backwards and forwards.

Ellie's room was immaculate, the tidiest in the house – as if she was biding her time until a better alternative came along and keeping the room tidy so as not to leave any traces behind when she'd gone.

'What are you doing?' Jessica asked

'What does it look like?'

She walked over and stared at Ellie's hair; so fine it was bristling in the screen light. She had to put a lot of energy into overcoming the urge to put her hands on her daughter's shoulders and say, 'Ellie, you do love me, don't you?'

'Looks violent,' she said, casually balancing the plate of hot dogs on the edge of the desk.

Ellie looked sharply at them. 'What's that?'

'Tea,' Jessica ventured. Then, to change the subject, nodded at the screen. 'And what's that?'

'That?' Ellie turned back to the screen. 'That's Baghdad after the American ceasefire.'

'But they're still fighting,' Jessica said, making a show of peering at the screen while trying not to actually look.

Ellie groaned. 'That's the point.'

'What's the point?'

'There *was* no ceasefire. This is footage from unembedded *Al-Jazeera* reporters.'

Jessica tried to think of something to say to this that wouldn't irritate Ellie. 'How was school today?'

'Shit, actually. Apart from Mr Hunter. I thought he wasn't in today because he wasn't there at the beginning of the lesson and I hadn't seen him around school. Then he did come in and everything . . .' Ellie stopped, suddenly aware of Jessica standing there. 'We learnt how to make a nuclear bomb in chemistry.'

'You did?' Jessica tried not to sound distracted – sounding distracted when you talked to Ellie was something that triggered her anger.

Ellie nodded, not noting the distraction. 'According to Mr Edmonds, it's not nuclear bombs we should be worried about, it's plutonium; plutonium in the hands of the wrong people – say an amateur terrorist. Getting your hands on Grade A plutonium is far easier than getting your hands on a nuclear bomb.' Ellie paused.

Nervous, Jessica picked up one of the china fairies from the collection on Ellie's desk; she had had them since she was five years old.

'He mentioned your book – *How To Survive A Nuclear War*.'

'He did? I thought it was out of print.'

'God, you're so negative. Anyway . . . he called it a

114

post-Apocalyptic etiquette guide.' Ellie chuckled. 'I thought that was pretty good.'

Unable to decide whether Ellie was being cruel or not, Jessica pulled Ellie's copy of *How To Survive A Nuclear War* towards her. The copy was well read and had a stamp inside from London Borough of Hackney Libraries: withdrawn for sale.

'Put it down,' Ellie said, fractious.

Ignoring her, Jessica flicked through the book until she got to the author's photograph on the back flap. She'd forgotten about the photograph.

There she was – the same age as Ellie now – standing beneath a cherry tree in a suburban back garden with co-author, Lieutenant Browne and Peter's mother, Mrs Kluszynski, flanking her on either side. 'That's me,' she said, sounding shy and unsure, inadvertently holding it out to Ellie for verification.

'You look happy – in the picture,' Ellie observed, hoping it sounded like an accusation rather than a compliment.

'I do, don't I?'

'That's Grandma . . .'

'D'you remember her?'

'Not really. I was – what – four or something when she died?' Ellie paused, looking more closely at the photograph. 'I remember going to Poland to visit her that time, though – just before she died. There were all those ski lifts running up through the meadows past her house. They scared me for some reason. I don't know why. I didn't mind them in the daytime when they were working and people used them to take picnics and stuff up the mountain, but I hated it when they shut the machinery off at night and the lifts just used to hang there, swaying. They made this awful squealing noise.' Ellie shuddered.

'It was a big deal for Grandma, going back to Poland when

the wall came down. She left there when she was only your age. The house she bought right on the edge of town belonged to a cousin she'd kept in touch with. I think she was happy – in the end. Second time round she got to do Poland on her terms.' Jessica paused. 'It's funny, that time you remember going over to visit her: we were half thinking of moving there ourselves.'

'What – you and Dad? To Poland?'

'All of us – yes.'

'Whose idea was that?'

'I don't know, it was just this idea we had at the time – moving to Poland.'

'So why didn't you?'

'I think we got overwhelmed by the idea of learning Polish.'

'Didn't Dad speak Polish?'

'Some . . . badly.'

Jessica put the book down, aware that Ellie was watching her hands as they attempted to restore it to its original position on the desk – its exact original position. Ellie was very particular about things like that.

In the silence that followed, Jessica heard herself saying, 'Just imagine . . . if that had happened. If we'd all moved to Poland. Everything would have been different.' She realised, too late, what she'd just said.

'Yeah, we'd all be speaking Polish.' Ellie paused. 'And Dad would still be here.'

Now Ellie was being cruel, and cruelty towards Jessica – since Peter's death – was something they had both subconsciously decided was permissible. But this was too much. She stared at her daughter, rendered suddenly helpless by a memory of Peter turning to look at her in the car as they were driving. 'Ellie . . .'

Ellie swung away from her, back to face the screen.

'What you said – that wasn't fair,' Jessica said.

'Well, maybe if you'd loved him more, it would never have happened anyway.'

'If I'd loved him more? I loved him—'

'But not enough. If you'd loved him enough—'

'Stop it! Stop it, Ellie – you don't know what you're saying.'

Ellie spun round suddenly and they stared at each other. 'I do know what I'm saying, and I know love.'

'You don't know love.'

'I do – I do know love.'

Relieved, Jessica heard Arthur's bare feet slapping at high speed up the stairs.

'Mum,' he said from the bedroom doorway, breathless, his eyes wide open. 'There's some naked animals downstairs and they're doing stuff to each other.'

'Downstairs?' Jessica looked quickly at Ellie – who was looking at Arthur as if she was trying to weigh up the collateral damage her five-year-old brother was likely to cause with access to Grade A plutonium – then back to Arthur.

'On the TV,' he added, worried that he was responsible for the weird looks on his mum and sister's faces and the fact that they'd been shouting. He wasn't allowed to do or say anything that made weird looks happen to his sister's face.

'Okay – I'll be down in a second,' Jessica said.

Arthur, reassured, went back downstairs.

'I've got nothing more to say to you,' Ellie announced.

'But you can't just say things like that. There isn't the space in our life together for you to say those things.'

'What life?'

'It's never going to work – if you harbour those sorts of thoughts towards me.'

'I'm not harbouring them, I'm saying them, and now I've got nothing more to say.'

117

It's true, Jessica thought, staring at her daughter in horror. The things we give birth to have the power to annihilate us. 'Ellie—'

'And you can take that with you,' Ellie said, elbowing the plate with the hot dogs on it that Jessica had put down on the edge of the desk.

'I'll leave it up here in case you change your mind and want them later.'

'I won't want them later.'

'You might.'

'I won't,' Ellie snapped.

'Okay . . . okay,' Jessica heard herself saying, as if a long way away, helpless, suddenly exhausted and close to tears. 'Okay,' she said again, picking up the plate.

She went downstairs and watched from the lounge doorway as two polar bears finished mating to David Attenborough's voice-over. 'Don't worry – they're just loving each other,' she said to Arthur, who still had Ellie's old science goggles on.

Arthur stared blankly at her then back at the screen. 'That's love?'

# 17

'I was about to send out a search party,' Margery said as Kate walked through the front door. 'I thought you were only going up the road – aren't you meant to be going out at eight? It's gone seven now.'

Without responding to this, Kate said to Findlay, 'Go upstairs and start running the bath.' Then, turning to Margery. 'Why are you whispering?'

'Robert's asleep.'

'Where?'

'The lounge.'

As the sound of running water started coming from upstairs, Kate went through to the lounge where the curtains had been drawn, the gas fire put on and the lights dimmed.

'He's asleep,' Margery hissed, following her in.

The TV was on – with the sound off – and Kate watched, distracted, as two polar bears finished mating – did animals orgasm? – and started killing a seal instead. The huge white bears collaborated with far more grace and ease over death than they had just a second ago when copulating.

Sighing, she turned the volume up and put the lights back on full.

'What are you doing?' Margery carried on hissing – loudly now, to make herself heard above the TV. 'He's only just gone to sleep, bless him.'

Ignoring this, Kate put Flo, in her car seat, on the floor by Robert's feet and, sweeping past Margery, went to retrieve a bottle from the fridge.

In the lounge, Margery grappled with the TV controls, finally managing to turn the volume down again. She was about to start tampering with the dimmer switches when Kate walked back into the lounge.

Without commenting on the TV's diminished volume, she knelt down and unstrapped Flo, depositing her viciously in Robert's lap.

Robert tried to pull himself up, knocking the bottle of milk off the arm of the sofa and onto the floor. 'Shit, what was that?' he said, blearily.

'Here, give her to me,' Margery said, nudging herself onto the sofa beside him and hauling Flo, who was frowning, out of his lap. 'I told her you were asleep,' she added.

'I'm going upstairs to give Findlay his bath,' Kate said, yelling, 'Finn, you can turn that off now.'

Robert sat up, still stunned with sleep, and watched her leave the room before getting slowly to his feet and stumbling after her. 'Kate—'

Margery listened to him walk unsteadily upstairs, slip on a tread, then carry on, calling out, 'I'll do Finn, you go and get yourself ready.'

She heard footsteps go through to the bedroom above her.

'Kate – I'm so sorry about the boys. I just totally forgot.'

Kate didn't respond.

Then, after a while, Margery heard Kate's voice saying, 'I think there's something wrong with the cat. He's limping. Robert? Come and take a look.'

# 18

At eight o'clock, Kate drove to No. 236 Prendergast Road because of the rain – with the tortilla on the seat next to her – and parked behind the Burgesses' new Range Rover that they had bought with the disappointingly small amount of money they'd made out of Miles's mother dying.

She rang the doorbell under the taut gaze of the CCTV camera positioned in the corner of the porch, and Harriet's husband Miles answered – all five foot eight of him, wearing a stained rugby shirt and old deck shoes. He had a small watering can in his hand and stared at her, smiling, his eyes shining behind the sort of spectacles that looked good on a German architect but that would never look good on Miles – not unless he got a head transplant. His head, as it currently stood, looked as if it had been dehydrated at some point in late childhood – then rehydrated rapidly. As a consequence the skin on his face – as well as the rest of his body – had the same tonal range as that of a pre-miracle Lazarus. None of which was helped by the fact that Miles had spent most of his life so far trying to become something he had never been designed to become. Miles, like Jessica Palmer, worked for Lennox Thompson Estate Agents, only he was manager of the Forest Hill branch.

'Hi,' he said to Kate's breasts, 'I was just coming out to water these.'

As he stooped over one of two semi-dead bay trees in the front porch, Kate saw Evie appear in the hallway over his back.

Honing in rapidly on Kate, she screamed, 'I loooove your T-shirt!'

'It's one of yours,' Kate managed to scream back, navigating the bulk of Miles blocking the doorway.

'Thought I recognised it – looks gorgeous on you.'

'And you look amazing. Very . . .' Kate took in the pair of cigarette-cut jeans that they'd all worn in their mid-teens throughout the eighties and that they were now expected to wear again in their mid-thirties; the formal sporting jacket, and the Bavarian hat, which cast strange shadows over Evie's face. The overall effect was one of unhinged hysteria. '. . . Eva Braun,' she finished.

Evie ran down the hallway on full throttle, obliterating Miles and grabbing hold of Kate, who just about managed to keep the tortilla balanced in her left hand. 'That's the nicest thing anybody's said to me all day.'

Evie, who used to be a buyer for Top Shop and Oasis before the birth of Aggie, opened her own boutique – 'Boutique' – two years ago in the Bellenden area of Peckham, filling it with samples by graduate designers the High Street stores weren't ready to take a risk on. One of the unwritten PRC rules was that on meeting nights you wore something from 'Boutique'.

During the three seconds she spent nestled forcibly against Evie's thorax, Kate tried to achieve the sort of energy levels being in Evie's company demanded. Evie's husband, Joel – who used to be a triathlon winner in his spare time – now needed an entire pot of Viagra just to take a piss in the morning because Evie never stopped, and Evie on full tilt was as terrifying as seeing a battery-operated toy with its batteries removed – still running.

'It wasn't you who invited Jessica was it?' Evie hissed suddenly while Kate was clamped to her still.

'No,' Kate lied.

'God knows who did then. Harriet's really pissed off about it, but it's hardly like we can ask Jessica to just fuck off.' She stepped back – alarming, energy-sapping dimples in either cheek, her eyes shining. 'Anyway – more importantly – FINDLAY'S IN.'

'In?'

'ST ANTHONY'S. Ros told me earlier. In fact, EVERY-BODY'S IN. Even,' Evie lowered her voice, 'Arthur Palmer.' She executed a strange little movement, which consisted of her shaking both fists in the air before turning on her heels and walking off up the hallway.

Realising that there was no point even trying to match Evie's euphoria, Kate followed her in silence, up the hallway and into the pseudo-Edwardian world of Miles and Harriet's lounge – unable to detect the faint whirr of the sensory camera in the corner, above the DJ Yoda remix of *Final Countdown*.

Every surface in the Burgesses' lounge was covered in tortilla – which Kate had no choice but to add to, because everybody (apart from Jessica who had bought a jar of Sauerkraut) had made the tortilla featured in April's *Waitrose Magazine*, which had come with everybody's Ocado shop – that everybody had so far explicitly avoided referring to . . . until now when Kate walked in and Jessica said, 'Shit, not more of the stuff.'

Ignoring this, Harriet smiled blearily at Kate as she entered the room, her thick, blonde hair pulled back in a schoolgirl ponytail. The light in the room was bouncing off the nipple shield covering her right breast that was supposed to make the pain bearable as Phoebe fed. The velvet on the armchair's left arm had been rubbed bald. Over the past week, having contracted mastitis, she'd resorted to expressing and giving Phoebe bottles, but for tonight's PRC she wanted to be seen actively, successfully, breastfeeding her five-week-old daughter – even if it meant bleeding onto her sleeve as she took the nipple shield off.

Harriet – like Miles – was wearing a stained rugby shirt and old deck shoes, because she hadn't lost the weight she'd gained with Phoebe yet, and Miles's clothes were the only ones that fitted her. She sometimes cried when she looked at photographs of herself taken the summer before she became pregnant with Phoebe when she'd been just about able to get into a pair of low-rise jeans purchased from Boutique; even if the sensation of wearing them hadn't been dissimilar to that of her body performing an involuntary hysterectomy on itself. And she *was* trying, but nothing she did seemed to shift Phoebe's legacy. Not even the prambotics DVD released by her friend Polly, who used to live on Prendergast Road and was fast becoming South London's postnatal exercise guru. So clothes from Boutique were out of the question.

Sitting on the sofa next to Harriet was Ros – looking preoccupied and showing uncharacteristically few signs of life. Her eyes – after an hour's prambotics in the park with Polly, followed by Swim with Baby, followed by two hours in the kitchen making sweet potato tortilla (her own take on the *Waitrose Magazine* recipe), followed by another hour waiting for Martin to fulfil his promise to a) come home at all, and b) come home before midnight for the first time in over two months – had no focus whatsoever.

Jessica was sitting on the sofa opposite and, next to her, an elderly male whom Kate didn't recognise.

Kate took the armchair with the concealed recline function that Miles watched sport in.

'Okay,' Evie's voice exploded into the room, high and loud, 'now everybody's here, I can introduce Labour councillor Derek Stoke, who's kindly agreed to join us here tonight to talk about the proposed speed bumps on Prendergast Road, which – as you all know – we've been campaigning for for nearly two years now.'

Derek, whose wild walrus gaze had been fixed on Harriet's bleeding, lactating 36Ds, started and dropped the remains of his tortilla onto his lap, where he brushed it surreptitiously onto Harriet's cream carpet, his lips sucking emptily at the air in anticipation of speech. He was too old for this – that's what he'd been thinking before he heard the blonde woman who wasn't wearing a bra scream out his name. There was too much noise and these women terrified him. It was always him the local Labour party sent to these community meetings and he just wasn't convinced he was up to it any more. John was too young; too full of mantras rather than ideas, which made two-way conversation limiting; Ruth had never been the same since her Congo trip and the only thing you could get her to talk about with any real clarity was female genital mutilation; Elizabeth was an ambitious Nigerian who only attended high-profile meetings, and Nigel was forever engineering positive publicity for local MP, Tessa Jowell. So there really was only him – even if he was so unashamedly old school he'd only ever thought of faggots as something you ate with gravy.

'Speed bumps!' Evie prompted Derek, turning DJ Yoda down and refilling her glass of wine.

This time, Derek launched automatically into the speech he'd prepared on the proposed speed bumps and 20 m.p.h. limit for Prendergast Road, which would not only increase road safety, but act as a deterrent to gangs of youths looking

125

for quiet side roads on which to race entire fleets of motorised scooters.

On cue, a fleet of motorised scooters made their way up Prendergast Road.

Evie screamed with laughter and turned expectantly to Derek, who – cut off mid-flow – lapsed into a sudden inertia that left him tugging subconsciously on his ear; the one in which he'd been hearing a low-pitched buzzing all evening. Looking up, he noticed a microscopic camera on top of the side cabinet between two china Staffordshire dogs. The camera was moving. Were they recording the meeting? If they were, shouldn't he have been told earlier and asked to sign a disclaimer or something?

'Are we done – with the speed bumps?'

Derek nodded dumbly, his mind entirely taken up with the possibility that he was being filmed without his prior consent.

'We need to move onto the street party,' Ros put in. 'Only eight weeks left to go . . .'

'Eight?' Evie echoed, excited, as though the true properties of the number eight had just been revealed to her.

'Well, so far we've got face painting confirmed – that's Harriet. And Kate's our cake and barbecue lady . . .' Evie paused to draw breath.

Kate smiled dimly at nothing in particular.

'We've also had confirmation from Ethnic Wind Chimes – who did the Goose Green Spring Fayre: they're happy to do a stall . . . . And Ziggy the junk percussionist, who came to nursery at the end of last term. Ros, you're happy to promote Carpe Diem that day and obviously Boutique will have a stall.' Evie broke off to refill everybody's wine glasses. 'We thought about getting a bike surgery along, maybe in conjunction with South London Recumbants, and the council are talking about setting up a compost and recycling awareness stall. I've spoken to the girl who has the jewellery stall on Northcross Road on a Saturday morning and they're all getting back to me. Stalls are being delivered by 8 a.m. on the actual day.'

'When is the actual day?' Harriet asked.

'June fifteenth.'

Nobody said anything for a while until Jessica said, 'June fifteenth's a Monday. It's Parents' Evening on the fifteenth.'

Evie turned to her. 'Parents' Evening?'

'New Parents' Evening at St Anthony's – that's what the letter said.'

There was a fraught pause that filled the entire room.

'Well . . .' Ros exhaled. 'Let's make it Saturday the thirteenth.'

'Saturday the thirteenth,' Evie's voice said, rising about everything else. 'Saturday the thirteenth?' She appealed to Derek Stokes, without knowing why.

Ignoring this appeal, Derek leant forward. 'Is this being recorded?' he asked no one in particular.

# 19

At No. 22 Prendergast Road, Margery would look up from her plate every now and then and smile at Robert through the pair of candles she'd lit, before lowering her head again and letting out a series of small satisfied belches. She'd had trouble finding a tablecloth and in the end had to use the one she'd given them when they first married – which looked as if it had been in the ironing basket since then – and whose edging she'd crocheted as a girl, in anticipation of her own marriage. Only she never had got married.

'Guess who I saw the other week?' she said, suddenly.

'Tell me.'

'Walked right into her coming out the Co-op – nice as anything; recognised me immediately. "Margery," she said.'

'Mum, who was it?'

'Had a beautiful new Range Rover parked just outside the shop on double yellows, but I don't suppose she'd have any trouble with the traffic wardens looking like she did.'

'Mum . . .'

'Amanda Wakefield.'

'Who the hell's Amanda Wakefield?'

'Sorry – that's her married name – Amanda Snaiton. You remember Amanda Snaiton?'

'Yeah – she got married, didn't she?'

Margery nodded. 'Got married, moved down to Surrey somewhere. Anyway, now she's back and she's not "Wakefield" any more. Told me everything – right there on the pavement over her shopping. Looks like she did well out of the settlement, what with the Range Rover and everything . . .' Margery paused. 'She's got two kids – probably moved to be near her mum.' Margery paused again. 'You do remember Amanda, don't you, Robert?'

'Sort of,' he sighed.

'You went out with her for *two* years – two years is a long time.'

'I was seventeen,' Robert said.

'Well, she was asking after *you*.'

Robert tried to say something, but ended up choking.

'Robert?'

'Something . . . in my throat.' He got to his feet, his eyes bulging.

'Where are you going?'

'Water . . .'

He left the room and a few minutes later the choking sounds stopped.

'You all right?' she said as he sat back down.

'A hair got stuck in my throat.' He held the hair up to the light.

'Looks like one of yours,' Margery said, recognising one of Ivan's hairs that she must have overlooked with the tweezers earlier.

'Christ – don't tell me I'm suffering from premature hair loss on top of everything else.'

'What is it now?' Margery said as he got to his feet again. 'Sit down – I'll get you seconds.'

He shook his head. 'It's Flo.'

Margery listened, but couldn't hear anything. 'You sure?'

'I'll be back in a minute.'

'She's probably just dreaming.'

'I'd better go and see. I'm worried about that bruise on her forehead.'

Robert was drunker than he thought and tripped over the bottom step before managing to haul himself the rest of the way upstairs. He pushed Flo's bedroom door open just a fraction – enough for light to find its way immediately into the blacked-out room and pick out a corner of wardrobe and the end of the cot. He couldn't see his daughter from the door – the light didn't penetrate the darkness that far – but he could hear her rapid, busy breathing and that made him smile. The high-pitched moaning had stopped. Margery was right – she must have been dreaming.

He stood staring vacantly at a spot of wood on Flo's door-frame where the gloss had been chipped off, feeling a sudden, almost unbearable amount of tenderness towards his daughter at the thought of her lying unconscious in the dark, dreaming.

Robert had loved both his children effortlessly from the moment they were born. He'd loved Kate when she was pregnant with them, so in fact he'd loved them before they were born even. He knew people who'd brought up two or more children without loving any of them, but this hadn't been his experience of parenthood. It struck him as strange that at some deep-seated level of the social subconscious, love of your children was optional for fathers in a way it wasn't for mothers. The possibility that a mother might not actually love her children was unspeakable . . . unthinkable. Still.

Robert veered away from this thought and went back downstairs.

'Told you she'd be all right,' Margery said as he sat down again. 'Mind you, it's a good job you checked – she took a nasty fall today.' She paused, draining her glass of Liebfraumlich. 'Rolled right off the bed while Kate was downstairs.'

Robert sat down. 'What?'

'I said, she rolled off the bed.'

'Mum – she bumped her head at nursery.'

'Nursery?' Margery snorted and slurped on her empty glass. 'Get us another one, love.'

Roger hesitated then poured her another glass.

Even drunk, Margery was aware she had Robert's attention. 'Who told you that?'

'Well, Kate, she . . .'

'I told Kate she shouldn't leave her on the bed like that when she's starting to turn herself over.'

'Whose bed did she roll off?'

'Yours – Kate left her on your bed. We only realised when she started screaming.'

Ignoring the strange turn Robert's face had taken, she looked down at her plate, surprised to see it empty – then up at him again. 'You want some more?'

'No – no.'

'Another sliver of cheese and onion before pudding?'

Robert shook his head, preoccupied. 'Are you sure?'

'I haven't put on that much weight, have I? Surely I can tuck away another small piece of pie without feeling guilty.'

'I'm talking about Flo,' Robert said.

'Oh . . . that. Of course I'm sure. Ask Findlay.' She smiled at him. 'Aren't you going to ask me what's for pudding?' When Robert didn't say anything, she snapped, 'Well, it's apple.'

'Apple what?'

'Pie.'

'I'll have a bit more salad.'

Margery dug happily into the undressed layers of iceburg lettuce, tomatoes and spring onions.

'She's stressed, that's all,' Robert said watching her but speaking to himself.

'Who's stressed – Flo?'

'Kate!'

A strange sound emitted from Margery's throat. 'Stressed? About what exactly? The kids are in nursery; she doesn't cook – doesn't clean.' Margery broke off. 'You might of mentioned you had a cleaner.'

'Mum . . .'

'Nobody tells me anything. I was surprised, that's all – when that girl turned up this morning. And twenty pounds is a lot of money.' Margery stopped suddenly, aware she wasn't meant to know this. But one look at Robert's face told her the transgression had passed him by. 'I had to take you with me when I got that job cleaning at the old people's home – what else could I do? Then, when you started school, you had to get yourself home.'

'That's the problem though, Mum: Kate doesn't have a job – she has a career.'

'You had to get yourself home,' Margery said again in response to this, 'and you couldn't of been much older than Finn is now.'

'I hated that,' Robert conceded.

'But what else could we do?' Margery appealed to him.

'I hated the empty house – you not being there.' He was aware of sounding childish, but his mind was suddenly full of the kitchen in the house they rented from a local farmer when he was a child, and the old stool he used to sit on by the window, waiting for Margery to come home. 'Sometimes I thought you might never come back and that I'd end up in that children's home at the end of the street. D'you

132

remember that kid there who only had half a head of hair? He terrified me.' Robert's mind ran on to other things he didn't mention; things that seemed less easy to define and therefore less shareable . . . like the rabbits' legs strung from the outhouse door where the goose lived. Part of the agreement they'd had with the farmer was that the goose, who did nothing but spit, got fed by them. Then there was the one-arm bandit machine in the lounge.

Margery said, 'I always came home.'

'I know you did.'

'Always.'

'I know that, but I didn't know that then. And we weren't like everyone else and it made me lonely.'

'Well, you never really know what goes on behind closed doors and anyway, we were better than a lot of people,' Margery concluded.

They eyed each other drunkenly; nervously – as if they'd just hit a clearing in the forest they hadn't really been looking for in the first place and, after being used to shadow for so long, were suddenly able to see more than they'd anticipated. More than they'd ever wanted.

And it wasn't as though either of them was trying to gain the upper hand because there was no upper hand to be gained. The joint, overriding memory they both had of Robert's childhood was one of survival, and right now they just needed to reassure each other that they *had* survived.

Margery looked away at the crumbs on the tablecloth, trying to work them into some sort of pattern while thinking of the looks she used to get from shopkeepers on the High Street when Robert was only months old and she pushed the pram in. They served her, but the looks – she'd never forget the looks.

'The look on their faces,' she said out loud. 'Nothing would break their faces – and you were such a beautiful baby, Rob. And that was the late sixties, for Christ's sake – you'd think people might of lightened up a bit after a world war. Not the bloody English; not bloody likely. I nearly moved to London – once; didn't think I could stand it any more.' She smiled timidly at him. 'Wonder what would of happened to us if I'd of done that?'

When he didn't answer, she got up and started to clear the table.

Robert sat and watched, aware that her hands found it difficult to grip the plates as she tried to pull them towards her. He knew he should help, but he was angry with her – too angry to offer to help – and he didn't know why.

She came back in with the apple pie and a jug of cream, behaving deferentially towards the cream as she did all items she considered a luxury.

'It's off,' Robert said after the first mouthful.

'It can't be off – I just bought it.'

He took another mouthful, more wary this time, wondering whether he'd drunk so much beer it was curdling the cream as soon as it hit his stomach. 'Definitely off.'

Margery smelt the jug, then dug her spoon in and slurped it up. 'It's not off.'

'It tastes funny,' Robert insisted.

Margery shunted her chair back, angry herself now, and came in with the empty cream carton to show him the sell-by date.

Robert stared at her. 'That's why.'

'That's why, what?'

'It's UHT – Mum, you bought long-life cream.'

'It's Elmlea, it's what I always buy.'

'But it's long-life – why d'you buy long-life?'

'It's cream,' Margery insisted.

'Long-life cream.'

'Robert – you're shouting.' She stared at him. 'Are you not eating yours now?'

'It's fine – I'll eat it.'

'Well, don't if you don't want to.'

'I'll eat it,' he said, trying not to raise his voice again.

Robert's voice was impatient, unkind. 'I don't know about Kate – I think you're all stressed – the whole lot of you.' She paused, knowing that now would be the ideal time to bring out the letter – Kate wasn't here; she had Robert to herself – but somehow she wasn't ready to part with it. It was starting to feel like a very valuable insurance policy that she wasn't ready to cash in just yet.

She thought about how she'd come across the letter – in Kate's suit jacket – as though she'd been meant to find it. Somebody *was* looking after her. Maybe she did have a guardian angel. Tom used to believe in angels – thought everybody had one. He used to say he could feel his angel's fingers all over his shoulders and back.

'A woman waved at me today,' Margery said, without thinking.

Robert looked up at her, then carried on eating.

'She was standing at the window in the house opposite. Couldn't of been more than twenty-one.' She paused, but Robert still didn't have anything to say. 'Their nets are nice. It's nice to see a house with nets up at the windows, especially living as close as you all do to each other. In London.'

Robert looked as if he was having trouble swallowing the last mouthful.

'Mum – it's a brothel.'

'A brothel.'

'The house opposite – it's a brothel; got to be.'

'I thought Kate was joking. Are you sure?'

Robert shrugged.

# 20

'We were featured – did you see it? WE WERE FEATURED!' Evie cried out, trying to keep the momentum at the PRC going.

'Featured where?' Ros asked.

'*Time Out* – most happening postcode in the whole of London or something. I couldn't believe it, I just sat there thinking, oh my God, that's us – that's here. I know,' Evie carried on, with an apocalyptic reserve of energy, 'we should start our own magazine.'

Kate, who had her eye on her tortilla – untouched and busy reheating under the sidelight – was about to say something in response to this when Evie's voice carried on, 'Colour, small format, covering everything that's happening in the postcode; a sort of postcode lifestyle magazine . . . handbag size. We could launch it at the street party.'

'That's brilliant,' Ros put in. 'Think of the advertising space we could offer.'

'We could cover *What's On*,' Evie said, appealing to everyone.

'Shopping and events update,' Kate shouted suddenly.

'I could take care of that,' Evie responded, pleased. 'You'd be good at Agony Aunt. Ros could do some sort of lifestyle page. Harriet – you could do a mums and babes info section.'

'What . . . me?' Harriet flicked her head up, nervously. So far that day she'd already committed to being a home rep for the Natural Nappy Company and to sitting on the nursery's Management Committee.

'Yes – you,' Evie insisted; her eyes started to flicker round the room again until they fixed on Jessica. 'Jessica . . .' Her voice was full of pity, a pity she reserved for the badly dressed; and tonight Jessica was so badly dressed it was verging on the confrontational. 'Jessica . . .'

Jessica looked across the acre of cream carpet at Evie, about to say something when her phone started to ring.

It was Ellie.

For a moment, Jessica thought she might be phoning to apologise.

'Mum? It's Arthur – he's been screaming.'

'Is he asleep now?'

'I don't know, he's making this whimpering noise. Should I go in and check on him?'

'No, I'm on my way back – don't worry.'

'Okay . . .' Ellie sounded relieved. 'I'll see you in a minute.'

Jessica came off the phone. 'I'm going to have to leave – Arthur's having one of his nightmares.'

The women in the room murmured briefly, sympathetically, a murmur that seemed to say Jessica had the sort of life anybody – let alone a child – would have nightmares about.

Her left thigh caught the edge of the coffee table as she stood up, but it wasn't until her right shoulder bounced off the doorframe that it occurred to her she might be drunk.

As she left the room, she heard Ros bringing up the issue of the brothel at No. 21 with Derek Stokes, then her phone rang again.

She headed instinctively to the downstairs loo.

'Mum?'

Staring at the photo of Miles Burgess shaking Prince Charles's hand at last year's Business and Enterprise Awards, she said, 'Has he started screaming again?'

'No, he's stopped. Everything's fine.' Ellie yawned. 'He seems fine now. Stay a bit longer if you want.'

'No, I'm making my way home.' Jessica's eyes gazed downwards to an aerial photo of the Burgesses' Spanish villa and a pile of Harriet's books – mostly on lactational rescue: *I Eat at Mommy's*, etc., as well as one entitled, *How to Make Your Child Brighter*.

'Mum, you don't need to do that, he's fine now.'

'Ellie, I'm coming home.'

Jessica had rung off.

Ellie rolled onto her side.

Her pillow smelt faintly of the Guerlain Vetiver she'd stolen from the men's perfume counter at Selfridges. Keisha knew the boy at the counter and kept him talking while Ellie put the sample bottle – out on the corner of the counter – in her bag.

It didn't have a lid and leaked on the bus home, but she didn't care.

She'd been tracking down the scent, which she'd first smelt on a book of Gerard Manley Hopkins's poems that Mr Hunter had lent her for two months, and had at last found it.

She got the sock she kept the perfume in out of the chest of drawers, gave the underside of her pillow another light spray then got back into bed, burying her face into it.

It wasn't until she came off the phone that Jessica realised how dehydrated she was. Making her way down the

Burgesses' white and beige hallway towards the kitchen, she kept veering over to one side until she eventually banged into the sink.

She watched her reflection in the kitchen window as she drank tumbler after tumbler of water. Behind her was the Burgesses' kitchen; a normal family kitchen, which was in itself fascinating to Jessica. Normality in all its guises had become fascinating to her since Peter's death; she had taken to staring – she knew she stared – at families when they came into Lennox Thompson, on the street . . . anywhere. Because *they* weren't a family any more. They might all be called Palmer, but they weren't 'The Palmers'. They were Jessica, Ellie and Arthur.

And what made it worse was no longer being certain that it was sharing her life with Peter she missed, or just sharing her life. Was there much point trying to disentangle one from the other now he was gone? They'd grown up together. Towards the end they were more like brother and sister than lovers. So why – since his death – *had* she become so obsessed with classifying what they had as love, or not. It was as if Ellie – in saying what she said earlier – somehow knew.

There was another burst of hysterical laughter from the lounge as Miles came up on her before she even had a chance to turn round.

'Jes-si-ca.'

He always said her name like that – ever since last Christmas when he'd walked her home late, under his golf umbrella, and tried to invite her into No. 236 while Harriet and Casper were staying in Berkshire.

That was after the Lennox Thompson Christmas party.

They'd been standing on the pavement together; she'd managed to laugh the invitation off before walking through the rain home. She didn't even like Miles, but walking away – and turning down some temporary relief from a loneliness so severe it was close to becoming a medical condition – was one of the hardest things she'd ever done.

She finished the glass of water and put it unsteadily down on the draining board.

'They been giving you a hard time?'

She turned round.

'In there,' he said, jerking his head towards the lounge.

Jessica shook her head as he took a step closer, put his thumb gently under her chin and tilted her face towards him. Why did he do that? He didn't look entirely sure himself.

'You've been crying.'

'No.' She touched her cheeks, which were wet, and tried to breathe in deeply, but all she got was a lungful of the fabric conditioner that Miles's rugby top had been washed in.

Now she really was crying.

She was about to collapse on him; about to collapse on Harriet's husband in Harriet's kitchen in Harriet's house. Behind them the lounge door started to open and she jerked suddenly away.

It was Kate.

Jessica stopped in front of her.

The two women stared at each other.

'My bag – and coat,' Jessica whispered.

Kate disappeared into the lounge

Miles was standing behind the kitchen table still, watching her.

She looked away as the lounge door opened and Kate reappeared, instinctively shutting it behind her, Jessica's coat and bag in her hand.

'I'm sorry,' Kate said as Jessica struggled into her coat, carefully pulling out her hair as it got trapped beneath the collar.

'About what?'

'I don't know,' Kate said, suddenly confused.

140

Jessica left and Kate turned to look at Miles, who seemed a long way away and who was staring back at her either hopefully or helplessly, she couldn't decide which, but it didn't much matter because the two amounted to pretty much the same thing on Prendergast Road.

Slamming the Burgesses' front door shut behind her, Jessica ran through rain that was bouncing heavily off the wet shapes of houses, cars, bins . . . straight past the florist at No. 283 until she realised. Then she stopped, turned and walked slowly back towards the maisonette. Things couldn't carry on like this indefinitely; she couldn't carry on feeling like this forever; something somewhere had to give . . . surely.

# 21

Wiping the rain from her face with one hand while trying to fit the key in the lock with the other, she finally managed to let herself into No. 283. She climbed the stairs unsteadily, the lino on the treads continually looming and receding.

'It's me – I'm home,' she said reassuringly into the void of silence that was the maisonette.

In the kitchen, she opened a bottle of wine and poured a glass, took a long sip then went upstairs.

Ellie was lying on her bed, listening to an audio book on Peter's old Walkman. Her hair was spread out on the pillow and she looked as if she was drowning. Other than this, she seemed okay. The body lying on the bed was the anatomically retarded one Jessica had grown used to: no breasts, and hip bones that jutted out obscenely – made more pronounced by the fact that Ellie had inherited Peter's height.

Ellie frowned at Jessica as she walked into her bedroom, irritated by the fact that Jessica was still wearing her soaking wet coat, irritated by the way the rain had matted her hair and made it greasy; irritated at how all this combined, conspired to make her look so incapable. Irritated, most of all, because her mother could have been so beautiful if she wanted to . . . so beautiful.

'What's that you're listening to?'

Ellie turned the Walkman off. 'What?'

'I said, what's that you're listening to?'

'*Carrie* – Stephen King.'

Jessica nodded – a memory of having seen *Carrie* at the cinema with Peter when they were first going out tugging briefly at her consciousness.

'How's Arthur?'

'He's fine now – you should have stayed.'

Jessica went upstairs to Arthur's room and pushed the door open. He was lying on his back, his arms flung out to either side as though he had just fallen from a great height. She went in closer, close enough to smell the deep sleep he was in – and check on his breathing. Then she carefully retreated, shut the door and went back downstairs to Ellie. 'He's okay.'

'I said he was.'

'I know – I know.'

'So, how did it go tonight?'

Ellie was doing a good impression, lying on her bed asking all the right questions, of being a daughter, so Jessica decided to return the favour and do the best impression she could of being a mother.

'It was good to get out; it was good, yeah.'

'No it wasn't', Ellie said. 'I can tell. I don't know why you bother with them, they're all so . . . so utterly pointless.'

Jessica pulled herself away from the doorframe. 'You should turn off – go to bed.' She was about to leave when Ellie said,' You're drunk.'

After a while Jessica said, 'So? One of us has got to be.'

'I'm fifteen years old. Grandad said you were virtually a recluse at fifteen.'

'I had my reasons,' she concluded, her eyes fixed on Ellie. 'But there's nothing stopping you going out.'

'Where would I go?'

'We live in London, for Christ sake – try growing up in Littlehaven. And where's Keisha these days? I never see Keisha round here any more.'

'We're not talking.'

'Why?'

Ellie shrugged. 'I'm not talking about this now – you're drunk,' she said again.

After a moment's pause, she got out of bed and turned off her light, then got back in again.

'And what about Jerome? He seemed nice.'

'Okay,' Ellie shouted suddenly, sitting up on her elbow. 'You want to know about Jerome?'

Jessica nodded, no longer convinced she did.

'Keisha says he was just being nice because he wanted me to give him a blow job and then he was going to film it on his mobile and send it to EVERYONE.'

'I need to speak to the school about this.'

'Since when d'you speak to the school about anything? What's the point anyway? Nothing happened.'

A shaft of light from the hallway cast a long shadow of Jessica across the bedroom floor, reaching the bed where Ellie had turned to face the wall. Suddenly afraid of herself, Jessica was about to leave when she became aware of a scratching sound in the doorway and, turning round, saw Arthur standing behind her, Burke clenched in his hand and the science goggles pushed up on his forehead. How long had he been standing there?

'Couldn't sleep, honey?' she said, starting up the concerned mother patter, but the words sounded too far away to be coming from her mouth.

Arthur stared up at her. 'I'm thirsty.'

144

'I'll get you a drink,' Ellie said, getting suddenly out of bed and pushing past Jessica.

Jessica thought about following them, but in the end took two steps across the floor and ended up falling onto the bed, letting her eyes shut almost immediately.

When she opened them again, she had virtually no memory of having fallen asleep, and no idea what time it was.

She thought she could hear talking, but maybe it was only the mice that came up from the florist's, which she'd given up setting traps for. There was something digging into her left hip and, pulling the Walkman out from under her, she rolled over and fell back to sleep.

When she woke up a second time to the sound of a dog barking somewhere close by, her left arm was numb with pins and needles and she could smell faint traces of some sort of perfume on the pillow her face was pressed into. Disorientated, she didn't have a clue where she was and for a moment wondered if she'd even made it back to the maisonette on Prendergast Road.

She sat up slowly, her head thumping. The alarm clock on the bedside table said 4.10. She didn't have an alarm clock.

Sinking back onto the bed, she turned to face the wall and thought she saw Ellie floating beside her before realising it was the Ophelia poster Ellie had insisted on putting up.

She was in Ellie's room and had been out cold for over five hours.

Once she caught up with this fact, she tried sitting up again. Then she tried getting up, but her head was so bad she was barely able to walk unaided and had to use furniture and the walls to claw her way to the bathroom.

Sticking her head in the sink, she drank from the tap until

it felt as though her belly couldn't take any more liquid. The rapid intake of tap water made her feel grey all over so she hung her head over the toilet bowl, thinking she was going to throw up.

She gagged three times and, as she stood up straight, caught sight of herself in the mirror and looked immediately away.

She took two Nurofen then shuffled across the hallway to Arthur's room.

Arthur and Ellie were lying in Arthur's narrow bed together.

Arthur was lying on his back near the wall, his arm out straight over the duvet.

Ellie was curled precariously on the edge.

Outside, a dog had started to bark.

It sounded like the same dog that had kept her awake the night before. Peering through the curtains at the bedroom window, she saw what looked like a dachshund streaking round the snatch of garden at the back of the florist's, in circles. Whose was the dachshund – and how was it getting into the garden?

Jessica turned away from the window and stood watching her children sleep.

She hated herself.

# 22

The PRC had disbanded for the night and everybody had left No. 236 Prendergast Road – apart from Harriet and Miles, who couldn't because they lived there.

Harriet was standing in front of the fridge looking for the bottle of milk she'd expressed that afternoon. 'Miles? Miles?' Shutting the fridge door, she moved into the hallway.

Miles appeared, leaning over the banister on the landing.

'There was a bottle of milk in the fridge I wanted to give Phoebe at her twelve o'clock feed?'

'Isn't it there?'

'Not that I can see.'

Miles, sighing, plodded his way downstairs past her and into the kitchen, where he took up her stance in front of the fridge.

'Can you see it?' she asked.

'Definitely no bottle of milk – you're sure you put it in the fridge?'

'Sure.'

'Sure?' he asked again.

'Sure – not sure – oh, I don't know,' she said, giving up.

The fridge started to hum and Harriet continued to stare

into its well-lit interior, certain she'd expressed at least nine ounces of milk that afternoon and put it in the fridge – she could picture it on the shelf between the tuna steaks and Rachel's organic yoghurt.

She felt uncertainty course through her, and uncertainty – along with doubt and suspicion – was the sort of thing that made her blotchy and, in extreme cases, brought on one of her sporadic bouts of eczema.

She shut the fridge door but stayed where she was, waiting for some sort of reassurance from Miles.

But nothing came, and after a while she said, 'I'll have to do the feed,' already feeling sick at the thought of the pain.

Miles didn't say anything to this.

He was staring, distracted, at his reflection in the window. This unnerved Harriet – Miles wasn't a vain man – unnerved her as much as his newfound need to spend time alone; a latent hankering after solitude that she found inexplicably strange. Miles had never to date hankered after solitude. Miles was changing, and change and contradiction were, for Harriet, two of the least redeeming features of human exist-ence; ones she categorically avoided, which was why up until now she had felt so safe with Miles.

To those looking in on them, Miles and Harriet – as a couple – had an edgy dullness to them that had its origins in the fact that they had decided to commit to each other before actually falling in love; without knowing whether they *would* ever fall in love.

They met through friends, on line. When they actually met for the first time, face to face, Harriet realised immedi-ately that Miles fulfilled all the criteria on her subconscious checklist for life partner. Miles gave her life structure and pattern. Maybe this was enough for Harriet; maybe – for Harriet – this was love.

Who knows?

148

Harriet didn't.

Harriet and Miles – apart from obvious gender differences – looked very similar. They were at their happiest – or had been up until now, anyway – spread out on the sofa watching Jane Austen adaptations. Nothing unfortunate, accidental or tragic had either shaped or misshaped their lives. Life had – so far – no dark side, and the world they inhabited had no behind-the-scenes; was, in many respects, as palatable as any created by Disney, apart from the moderate sexual references and absence of talking, singing, dancing animals.

The only thing that they differed on was sex.

It came as a shock to Miles to discover that Harriet didn't really like sex all that much – if at all. Probably because she'd never yet achieved orgasm, although Miles didn't know this.

Now, watching the tension across Miles's back, Harriet realised she was afraid; afraid for the first time since they'd been married.

'Where's the letter?' he asked suddenly.

'What letter?' She walked over to the biscuit barrel and dug around for some chocolate animal biscuits. 'Want one?'

He shook his head. 'They taste of cheese.'

'What these?' She sniffed at the elephant she'd started to eat, then took another mouthful. 'They taste of chocolate.'

Miles shrugged.

'Nothing cheesy about them.' She ate the rest of the handful slowly, then started to make a cup of tea.

'Harriet!' he said sharply. 'Where's the St Anthony's letter?'

'Well, I don't know what you've done with it. You must have put it somewhere after I showed you when you came home from work.'

'You never showed me the letter.'

'I did. Miles . . .' She shook her head, smiling, but there was panic in her eyes. Desperately changing the subject, she said, 'Did you see Evie tonight? I never noticed before – but

149

she had dandruff; quite badly.' She got the milk out the fridge; the recollection of Evie's dandruff making her feel suddenly happy . . . anchored to something definite again. 'It was everywhere – completely covered her shoulders.'

'Don't know how I could have missed it . . .'

'No . . .' She stopped short. Was Miles being ironic? It reminded her of the practical jokes he used to play on her when they first met. The practical jokes had taken her by surprise. She changed the subject again.

'And I can't think what possessed Jessica Palmer to turn up – or how she even found out it was happening.'

'Loneliness,' Miles said.

Harriet laughed, instinctively, then realised Miles hadn't meant it to be funny.

Feeling suddenly tearful, she said, 'And I can't believe Arthur got a place at St Anthony's. He had his fourth birthday party at McDonald's – in Peckham.'

'Harriet – I found the letter upstairs.'

'You did?'

'It was in that bag you keep your tights and the passports in.'

Harriet, standing by the fridge with the milk in her hand, burst into tears.

Miles waited.

They stayed where they were. Miles by the sink, waiting, and Harriet by the fridge, sobbing.

'You phoned me at work this morning and told me Casper had got into St Anthony's.'

'I know,' Harriet bellowed through tears, distraught. 'I didn't know what else to say. The letter came and . . . and I was scared.' She ran her hand up the fridge door. 'I didn't know what to do. He didn't get in, Miles. He didn't get in.'

Miles cut in with, 'If you'd told me earlier, I could have done something about it.'

'But you still can, can't you?'

'I don't know.' He watched her waddle towards him.

'We must only be about ten houses out of the catchment area.'

'So, where is the catchment area?'

'Well, given that everybody except us got a place, the lower half of Prendergast Road, Nielson Road, Beulah Hill.'

Miles stared at her with a precision that made her hold her breath. 'Beulah Hill.'

Harriet nodded, still not daring to breathe.

'We're going to write a letter,' he said.

'To St Anthony's?'

'To St Anthony's,' he agreed, almost soothingly, 'and the admissions authority. You're going to tell them that I'm beating you. That I'm beating you to a pulp.'

Harriet smiled enthusiastically at him.

'That you've had to move in with a friend living at Number eight Beulah Hill and that Beulah Hill will, to all intents and purposes, be your new address. The address must remain confidential, for your sake, and for the sake of the children. All correspondence regarding the school should in future be addressed to you at Number eight Beulah Hill. Obviously, this is an extremely stressful time for Casper, and it is essential that he suffers as little upheaval as possible and remains with the friends he made at nursery, all of whom are going to St Anthony's. We'll write it tomorrow.' He broke off. 'I presume you told everybody else what you told me – that Casper got in?'

'Of course I did.'

'Well, you keep it like that – I'll sort it.'

Harriet nodded, relieved but still terrified, and went upstairs.

Miles stood with a whisky in his hand and watched – on the kitchen monitor – as Harriet sat hunched on the side of their bed, scratching at her left hand. Then she broke off scratching and curled her hand protectively round her neck instead as she looked up suddenly at the camera, staring straight at him.

# 23

Evie left No. 236 Prendergast Road not long after Jessica, walking through the same rain in the opposite direction – under the protection of one of the new Orla Kiely umbrellas she had just reordered for 'Boutique' because they'd already sold out. In Evie's opinion, the retreat to vintage in fashion and interiors was an unsurprising reaction to 9/11 – after which people lost their appetite for ethnic, for things from far away with an unfamiliar heritage. But the peak had been and gone; instinct told her that the exodus back to vintage was beginning to thin out.

Looking up, she was surprised to see that she was almost at No. 112. She stopped and tried to make a call on her mobile, but the person she wanted – whom she'd been trying all evening – didn't answer. Standing on the pavement, she could hear screaming coming from somewhere – No. 110, the house next door to them.

The houses at this end of Prendergast Road were semi-detached with fifty-foot gardens and were now fetching well over seven hundred thousand, which wasn't bad considering that the McRaes had bought their house five years ago for just under three hundred. The houses around them were still mixed – a lot of flats, and a lot of social housing . . . like the one next door, No.110, where the shouting and screaming was coming from and where Evie was heading now.

No. 110 Prendergast Road was a parallel universe, where windows stayed open and tattered nets flapped wetly against outside sills.

Evie picked her way round some burst Blue Circle cement bags, a cylinder of gas and a broken dining chair, and banged on the slab of wood that was the front door.

The rain carried on beating down on the Orla Kiely umbrella, louder and faster, and her shoes were now soaked through.

She banged again and was about to give up when a black face appeared at an upstairs window.

The boy looked down, half smiling, and dropped his cigarette – which she had to sidestep in order to avoid it landing on her umbrella – then disappeared.

She waited in the dreary orange light that shone out from the pane of glass above the front door, thinking that the boy was coming down – but the door didn't open. As the woman's screaming on the other side got louder, Evie turned away, getting as far as the pavement when a motorised scooter pulled up – the sort that had incited local residents like the McRaes to campaign for speed bumps through the PRC.

A white teenager in a T-shirt and wet tracksuit bottoms – whom Evie knew as Jack – got off, keeping his helmet on. Pushing his visor up, he stared at her then made his way to the front door.

Evie followed him.

'I told you to phone if you want stuff,' he said, angry.

'I tried phoning – I've been phoning all night, but you never fucking answer,' she hissed back.

There was the sound of a woman's heels passing on the pavement behind her and the muffled giggling of a young couple heading home to have sex in a flat. Evie and Joel had started off having sex in a one-bedroom flat and over the years Evie had come to the conclusion that the smaller the living space, the better the sex.

The front door to No. 110 opened.

Inside the house another door opened and a woman was flung out into the hallway. She rebounded off a rusting radiator and fell onto the floor where she remained motionless for a few seconds, before starting to stir, and trying to get onto all fours.

Evie couldn't take her eyes off the woman's socks, which were white and covered in blue hearts.

Without turning round Jack said, 'I'll push it under the fence at the back. Put the cash through first, and don't ever come knocking again.'

The door to No. 110 was shut in her face.

Within seconds, Evie was putting keys in her own front door – with shaking hands – and opening it to the sound of the TV and Joel's wide, throaty laughter. She could hear the screaming starting up again next door, coming through their hall wall.

Joel didn't turn round when Evie walked into the lounge.

On TV there was a woman in an exercise pool no bigger than an oversized bathtub, swimming against the current.

Joel threw his head back and laughed.

Lately, he'd become obsessed with the shopping channels and claimed to be overexposing himself to the cultural trash can – Westlife CDs, the X-Factor, etc. – on purpose. For his thirty-eighth birthday, he'd taken ten friends to the Take That concert.

'Sorry it's so loud,' he shouted, 'I'm trying to drown out next door. They've been at it for hours. I wasn't sure about phoning the police.'

'Did you?'

'D'you think we should?' He looked up at her, waiting.

'Maybe we should.'

'Um – maybe.' His eyes strayed back to the TV again. 'Only thing is, we could wind up with a brick through our window while Ingrid's playing in here or something – can you imagine?'

'Joel—' Evie started.

Jerking suddenly forwards, he cut in with, 'Is that Cher? My God, it looks like Cher.'

'It can't be Cher,' Evie said, taking in the woman sitting on the edge of the exercise pool, reciting a list of vital statistics only achievable on purchase of one of the pools.

'It's Cher,' Joel insisted.

Uninterested, Evie said, 'Surely she doesn't need the money that badly.'

'Stranger things have happened,' Joel responded cheerfully.

'You coming to bed?' Evie asked, distracted.

'In about twenty minutes. I promised to help Martina revise for her Life in the UK test.'

'Where is she?'

'In her room.'

'I'm just going out to the office.'

'What, now?' he said, turning round again, taking in the fact that Evie was still in her coat with her handbag on her shoulder.

'We were talking tonight about setting up a local magazine – I thought I might just make a few notes before turning in.'

'Great idea,' Joel said, enthusiastic, his face relaxing. 'How long will you be – half an hour or something?'

'About that,' Evie said vaguely, walking through the house and into the back garden without turning on any outside lights.

Something scuttled across her feet and up a nearby tree.

The air smelt inexplicably different in the back garden as she made her way through the grasses they had planted, which gave way to black bamboo twice her height. She wasn't entirely convinced by the bamboo; wasn't sure whether it was okay to still have bamboo, but didn't really have an idea about what to replace it with.

Once she was behind the bamboo, she squatted and pulled the lower panel off the fencing. The scuffed white Reeboks were already there on the other side and the smell of dog shit was overwhelming – Evie only hoped it was in Jack's garden and not theirs.

'Same stuff?' Evie whispered.

A plastic sandwich bag was pushed under the fence then pulled back.

Her hands shaking again, Evie took three hundred pounds out of the yellow and brown Orla Kiely purse that matched her handbag and umbrella and poked it through the fence, her wrist sliding over something wet.

After an unbearable pause the sandwich bag reappeared. She grabbed at it and thumped the panel back into place.

As she stood up again she glanced up at the back of the house – just about visible through the bamboo – but there was no sign of life there, apart from a light in Martina's room.

She made her way quickly towards the mossy hump of her ergonomic garden office, which had featured so prominently in *Grand Designs*. It took her a while to find the right key, but eventually she did, making her way precariously past the outline of desk and computer towards the tiny loo they'd had installed – with a view to the garden office doubling up as guest annexe. Once inside the loo, she finally turned the light on. There was barely room to stand between the loo and the door, and she just about managed to pull the loose tile off the wall behind the loo.

Taking the sandwich bag out of her coat pocket, with water running off her, she shook a generous line of Jack's cocaine out onto the tile and got quickly and efficiently down to business before putting the sandwich bag behind the tile and the tile back on the wall. Then she went into the office and slumped into the chair, jerking it absently from side to side and staring out at the rain-soaked night.

She didn't know how she'd got through tonight, having to sit there listening to how everybody had got into St Anthony's: Toby Granger, Casper Burgess, Findlay Hunter – even bloody Arthur Palmer.

She had seriously thought about not going when the St Anthony's rejection letter arrived that morning. At 7.52, an overriding despair resulted in her dialing 999. After informing emergency services – in an incoherent, tear-stained babble – that Aggie hadn't got her place at St Anthony's and that they had to contact the school for her – had to . . . or she didn't know what she'd do, she had hung up and collapsed on the kitchen floor where she'd lain banging her head repetitively against the reclaimed French limestone they'd finally managed to track down in southwest France that summer. It was only when Aggie – who'd been slowly making her way through a bowl of cocoa pops – came over to tell her she couldn't put her bowl in the dishwasher because it was full (had she forgotten to put it on the night before, again?) that she finally came to her senses. As a precaution, she'd phoned round everybody soon after this – apart from Jessica Palmer, but nobody ever phoned Jessica Palmer – to tell them Aggie was in. Then she'd phoned Joel at work – to tell him Aggie was in. Joel's reaction made it clear that Aggie getting in was a foregone conclusion and that he had never for a moment doubted otherwise.

After phoning Joel, she'd got in the car, dropped Aggie and Ingrid off at Village Montessori and driven round to

St Anthony's vicarage to plead with the Reverend Tessa Walker, begging her to intercede. All the Reverend Walker could say was that they'd had two sets of triplets applying that academic year. So what – Aggie had suffered because of somebody else's successful IVF treatment? It didn't seem fair – and with conception through IVF and resulting multiple births on the rise, if the local council and the Church of England didn't do something to address the issue, soon St Anthony's was going to have no more than five families being offered all fifty places between them.

Restless, she got up from the chair, locked the office and headed back out into the rain. Once in the house, she hung up her dripping coat, aware that the TV had been switched off. She checked herself in the mirror in the downstairs loo then went upstairs.

Joel was lying across the bed, *A Guide to British Citizenship* in his hand.

'Shit, I could barely answer half of these questions myself. Listen to this . . . according to the 2001 Census, what percentage of the UK population reported that they had a religion?'

'No idea.' Evie went over to the bed and started to undress.

'Okay – what about this then . . . . Name three countries that Jewish people migrated to the UK from to escape persecution during Eighteen eighty to Nineteen ten?'

She sat down on the edge of the bed. 'When's she sitting the test?'

'Some time soon. She wants to do a travel and tourism course when she's got her Cambridge English.' Joel clearly approved of all this, Evie thought, watching him. Some men had hobbies . . . affairs . . . played football . . . drank too much. Joel had causes, and his latest cause was clearly Martina, their au pair.

Their marriage was – what was the word she came up

with the other day? – pockmarked with them. Up until the birth of Agnes five years ago. After Agnes, their marriage became a cause in itself – one that Joel was determined to champion. Which was a good thing because, if it hadn't been for this, Evie was fairly certain they wouldn't have made it as far as Ingrid. What lay ahead of them now, she had no idea.

They met when they were well on the road to their respective peaks . . . when *she* was a fashion buyer, forever hopping on and off planes to Tokyo, and *he* was making twenty thousand a shoot as a photographer in advertising. That was pre-digital: things were much tougher now. They were the sort of people things went right for and this didn't change when they became a couple. In fact, Agnes was the first wrong thing that ever happened to them – and neither of them had anticipated it.

The easy pregnancy was seen as yet another success in a long line of successes. Conception had been quick – possibly not passionate, but satisfying: no fertility clinics or IVF for them. The pregnancy was happy and healthy and baby Agnes – despite Joel's recurrent nightmares during the pregnancy – had all her arms and legs, no deformities.

The first disappointment was the unexpected Caesarean.

The last trimester of pregnancy they'd had more of a nightlife than they'd had pre-pregnancy, going to every local antenatal support group for natural births. Joel had the whole thing planned to music – having DJed in advance the entire birth. He had three discs with twelve hours' worth of compilation music on them, starting with The Who to see them through those early contractions, followed by some Prodigy and eighties remixes for when things started to get fast and furious, then . . . the birth itself. He wanted the child – his child – to emerge into the world to Handel's *Zadok the Priest*.

Only it had gone on and on and after the first twelve

hours he'd had to come to terms with the fact that there was nothing photogenic about pain. During the following six hours Evie became some sort of pastiche of Linda from *The Exorcist* only to be delivered as Aggie herself was finally delivered . . . by Caesarean section. Something they quickly mumbled to everyone who came to visit them on the ward, to get it over and done with, lingering on the fact that *Zadok the Priest* had been playing as planned, and that the surgeon who delivered Aggie knew all the words and had sung along. In fact, in those early days, Joel spent a lot more time talking about the surgeon who sang along to *Zadok the Priest* than he did about Baby Aggie.

He told visitors that the surgeon was Croatian and came to the UK during the Balkan conflict. Then he paused, trying to work out the meaning of what he had just said – because it had to mean *something*; had to be currency *somewhere*. 'Our daughter was delivered by a war criminal,' he said to the reflection in the mirror on the bathroom wall in the empty Clapham flat. Would it work – at dinner parties and social gatherings? Was it currency in the marketplace of making yourself interesting – not just to others, but to yourself?

Unconvinced – by this and a lot of other, more general stuff – he invited an old assistant of his, Lucia, round to supper while Evie was in hospital, in order to gauge whether he was still the most sought-after man in the developed world. After only half an hour in Lucia's company – checking to see that the twenty-six year old's northern Italian pupils were dilating in the appropriate manner – he was once more assured that all he had to do was click his fingers and Lucia would fuck an armadillo on his command.

After the operation Evie couldn't do anything for herself and found it difficult feeding Aggie. Joel told her not to give up because nobody they knew used bottles. Shit – even the *Daily Mail* was promoting breastfeeding.

Joel had anticipated Evie being as successful at mother-hood as she was doing business in Tokyo, and was therefore entirely unprepared for the Evie who sat sobbing in her hospital bed with a screaming, abandoned-looking baby sprawled in her lap.

When he ran out of visitors to tell the *Zadok the Priest* story to, it got to the stage where he could no longer bear to visit her himself and so sent his parents instead.

Following the birth of Aggie, neither Joel nor Evie ever really recovered from the depression and despair that came creeping, seeping into all that intact vitality both of them had thought so impregnable. The hardest part of all was losing the envy of their friends. For the first time ever, Joel had to deal with the fact that right then not only did nobody want to spend time with them, but people had stopped wanting to *be* them, and that was hard. Ever since he could remember, everybody he'd ever come into contact with had wanted to be him in some shape or form, and suddenly that stopped. The glowing, bouncing, enviable Evie he had known up to this point became nothing more than one of the variations on offer.

So, after six months, Aggie was in full-time childcare and Evie was hopping on and off planes to Tokyo again. Joel was only able to take on assignments that didn't conflict with the Tokyo trips. The Clapham flat was exchanged for a semi-detached house in SE22, bought cheap because the house they were semi-detached to was social housing and the young kid living there – Joel had lately become convinced – was dealing in drugs, because even younger kids on scooters were forever dropping off packages there.

On one of the Tokyo trips, Evie had some sort of break-down. Joel got a phone call from a frightened assistant who'd lost all plot of time differences and phoned at 3.00 a.m. to tell him Evie had locked herself in her hotel room with the chambermaid's bucket of cleaning fluids and refused to leave until she'd cleaned it herself, it was so filthy.

In the end he had to go to Tokyo to fetch her, telling everyone – including himself – that she had acute glandular fever. Once they got back to London, Evie barely left the house. Joel turned down assignments and took over Aggie, who he was determined would be walking and talking before his brother's daughter – his niece.

Evie was prescribed Seniton to help her – and Joel – sleep at night. Often during this time, he would wake during the early hours of the morning and know, as he watched her sleeping, that the part of Evie he'd never known existed – the part that frightened him most; the part he was actively medicating – was also the part, if he hadn't been so afraid, he somehow knew he loved the most.

Eventually Evie went back to work part-time, but no longer had the inclination or will to make things buzz around her. It came as no surprise to either of them when she was finally laid off.

Joel didn't know what to do. He liked things to work . . . function. Somehow he pulled himself back from the brink. Their marriage . . . children (Evie was pregnant with Ingrid) . . . *were* going to be a success; happiness didn't have to come into it if it didn't want to.

He spent her redundancy on a lease and told everybody Evie was going into business, launching her own label, employing a team of young designers. So Boutique was born.

Things slumped a bit around Ingrid's birth, which was elected Caesarean, but now the shop was really taking off. He was even thinking of a franchise – opening another branch in maybe Barnes or Wandsworth and getting Evie to put in for Best Independent Retailer of the Year award. They had childcare sorted, and he was moving out of commercial photography and trying to cajole his agent onto getting together a studio retrospective of his work at Tate Modern. Then there was that stroke of genius: getting the house onto *Grand Designs*. The McRaes were happening again. Wherever he turned, he could see it in people's faces . . . everybody wanted their lives to be as fulfilled as the McRaes. He was even thinking of contacting that toy manufacturer in Beijing that could make lifestyle dolls from photos. 'Evie' and 'Joel' dolls would make fantastic Christmas gifts.

Evie's energy levels were certainly back up, he thought approvingly, watching her pace aimlessly between bed and wall. Okay, she did look kind of fidgety, but there were no signs of exhaustion or, worse still, inertia – i.e. depression. He'd gone downstairs that morning at 6.00 a.m. to find her unpacking a Sainsbury's shop: that had to be a good sign.

It occurred to him, watching her, that she was semi-naked. He leered pleasantly, meaningfully across the bed at her, thinking that really tonight they should . . . it had been ten days and it would be a good way for her to burn off some of that excess energy she seemed to have at the moment. Their marriage had to function on all levels. They were the couple who did everything – including sex – together. Still.

Evie got into bed and he rolled up close, trying not to acknowledge the smell of drink on her.

She smiled absently at him as he started to nibble at her neck.

If not exactly forthcoming, she seemed amenable; but he took things slowly, cautiously. He never would get over those times they'd tried to have sex after Aggie was born when Evie would just burst into tears. It wasn't that he'd never seen her cry before – when they first started dating they'd cried a lot together at European films; only these tears had been wild, without subtitles or explanation.

Tonight his wife's body felt warm, supple and familiar. He started to consider actually enjoying himself.

Evie, watching him now, gave the same jerky, preoccupied smile she had done earlier, showing no objection but no outright consent either. Joel waited, unsure, until the next minute she rolled compliantly onto her back. Misjudging how close she already was to the edge of the bed, she fell onto the floor.

The hysterical laughter started almost immediately.

Joel peered over the side of the bed at her curled up naked, shaking with laughter.

Laughter in bed needed to be complicit, but there was nothing complicit about this laughter.

Suddenly scared, he said, 'Get up.'

Laughter.

'Evie – get up.'

Continued laughter. Was she ever going to stop?

'What are you – dyspraxic or something?' he yelled. Was that the right word? He didn't know, but it had the right effect on her because she stopped laughing and rolled over to stare up at him.

'You're forever walking into things or falling over stuff – you're worse than Aggie.'

Now her whole face was gaping up at him. 'My God, that's it.'

'What?' Joel said from the bed.

'That's it,' Evie said again, excited.

Why hadn't she thought of it earlier? St Anthony's had a special needs unit specialising in dyspraxia and dyslexia. All she needed to do was get Aggie statemented . . .

# 24

Ros stood inside the en-suite bathroom at No. 188 Prendergast Road, slowly taking out her earrings and inadvertently smiling at her reflection in the mirror.

Martin was home.

That hadn't happened in a long time.

'How were the kids?' she called out.

Martin's voice, coming from the bedroom, sounded as though he was on the verge of sleep. 'Toby was fine – Lola took a bit of settling.'

She went and stood in the bedroom doorway as she rubbed in some face cream, aware that they hadn't spoken face to face – without the aid of a telephone – for weeks.

Martin was sprawled across the bed, dressed in casual wear he'd last worn at Christmas, staring at the wall opposite.

He started when she appeared in the doorway, as if he'd been caught out – and this momentarily unnerved Ros, who stopped rubbing cream into her face and started to watch him more closely as he tried to smile at her.

'Tired?'

He nodded apologetically. 'Boring, isn't it?'

She disappeared back into the bathroom without responding to this.

A minute later he joined her, standing close behind her at the sink and stretching over her shoulder towards the medicine cabinet.

They watched each other in the mirror until Ros leant suddenly forwards and washed her hands. Her back was warm from where the length of him pressed against her as he reached for the Seniton.

'Seniton?'

Martin laughed cheerfully.

'When did you start taking those again?'

'Three weeks ago or something?' he asked his own reflection in the mirror. Then, shrugging at himself, 'I don't know.'

'But, Martin – those aren't the herbal ones we agreed you *could* take.'

'The herbal ones are shit useless,' he said, still sounding cheerful. 'Kind of like the difference between a cigarette and a Nicorette.'

'You're not smoking again as well?'

'Course not.'

Not entirely sure she believed this, she said, 'But what about that article we read connecting Seniton to male infertility?'

'Ros – we've got two children.'

'But what if we want more?'

'Lola is only seven months old.'

'Later . . . later we might want more.'

'Well that's something we can think about . . . later.'

He turned away from her, taking the pack of Seniton into the bedroom.

There was no point talking about it. Martin clearly didn't want to – she wasn't even sure she was all that interested herself. But she knew – suddenly – that she wasn't going to sleep that night until they reached some sort of resolution as to whether or not a third child was a possibility at some stage.

Martin was lying on the bed again and Martin lying on the bed was something she no longer took for granted, she realised. His presence tonight made the familiar landscape of the bedroom seem suddenly precipitous.

'Later when?' she said, pressing her point

He stared at her for a moment, and gave his nose a quick scratch as a tiny feather poked its way through the pillowcase.

'Ros – I don't know.'

She moved away from the doorway and sat on the edge of the bed, giving his chest a playful prod. 'Later – when?' she insisted, trying to get her voice to do provocative, but it just came out sounding irate.

For a moment he looked angry, almost revolted by her. 'I don't know – we'll talk about it after the case.'

'This case?'

'This case.' He tried to roll away, but she'd pinned the duvet down so that he couldn't move. Up close, she smelt of mouthwash and the smell irritated him; irritated him in quite a profound way.

'After this case there'll be another one . . . there'll always be another case,' she added.

'I suppose,' he said, watching her now.

'So my point still stands – later when?'

He sighed and said loudly, 'I don't know. Why are we even talking about this now? I'm getting on average four hours' sleep a night at the moment—'

Ros cut in with, 'So why the pills?'

'What pills?

'The sleeping pills.'

'I'm not sleeping. Over-exhaustion. My mind won't stop

so I just have to shut it down.' He paused. 'It's because I'm terrified – all the time at the moment – of missing something.'

'Missing something?'

'Missing the point; something vital that will swing this for us.'

'The point?'

'The point.'

'Of the case.'

'Of the case – right.' He paused again, 'And I haven't been home in over a week or something.'

'Ten days – you haven't been home in ten days.'

'That's a long time,' he conceded, ambiguously. 'So now isn't the time to talk about big stuff.'

'There's never a time to talk about big stuff – the big stuff's the stuff you have to *make* the time for.'

'But not right now, not tonight. I really am fucking knackered, Ros.'

That was the second time Martin had sworn – Martin never swore.

'I just need to know that there will be a time, that's all.'

He didn't say anything.

'That a third child's on the cards . . . at some point.'

'But, Ros – d'you even want another one?'

'Not right now, but maybe at some point I will – I just need to know that it's a possibility.'

'Or what?' he said.

'And I was thinking,' she carried on, 'if a third child *is* on the cards, we'd have to think about moving – at some point.'

'Moving?'

'Maybe out of London.'

'Ros . . .'

'Just think what we'd get if we sold this – what we'd get for our money in, I don't know, Kent or something. You could commute.'

'Commute.' He groaned.

'Okay, okay. But we will talk about it?'

'Another kid, or moving?'

'Well, they're sort of interconnected.'

'Look, Ros – at the moment, we just need a break.' He paused. Ros was looking at him, terrified. 'I mean, Tobes has got into St Anthony's so we've got nothing to worry about until he's eleven. We just need to relax.'

'But what if Toby hadn't got into St Anthony's?'

'Ros – he did get in, so . . .'

'What if he hadn't?' she insisted. 'Would you have considered moving out then?'

'I don't know.'

'What – you would have been happy for him to go to Brunton Park?' Ros yelled in disbelief.

'Ros, this is too . . . too hypothetical for me right now.'

Martin finally managed to turn away as Ros got up, slipped off her dressing gown and left it in a silky pile on the floor before getting into bed. This was something she never did – she always hung things up.

It was cold and she instinctively curled herself against Martin's spine.

Martin flinched.

Thinking he might be in the process of falling asleep – he often made jerking movements as he started to lose consciousness – she kissed the top of his arm.

Martin flinched again.

She thought he might be asleep, but he wasn't and as he rolled onto his back, she started to move her hand across his chest – the fingers spread out, feeling their way. She wanted to kiss him and touch him; she was entitled to – and was beginning to feel almost tearful as she thought about all the things she was entitled to that never seemed to happen any more.

Then, at just the wrong moment, she flicked her eyes up the length of his chest and caught him staring, transfixed, at the ceiling, his hand curled back on his forehead. A million miles away.

She rolled quickly away from him onto her back, subconsciously adopting the same pose.

'Listen, Ros . . .'

She felt herself start to blush at the sound of his voice. She always blushed before she cried – she'd been doing it ever since she was a child. 'Martin,' she cut him short, then hesitated. She didn't know what to say. All she knew was that she had to stop him speaking because he was about to say something that was going to change all their lives forever and she wasn't about to let him do that – not now, not tonight. 'You're tired,' she said, 'tired, that's all.'

Martin tried to speak again, but the Seniton caught up with him and a minute later there was a snapping sound not unlike a spring being released as his head fell to one side, a thin line of saliva running across his cheek.

Ros lay awake for a long time after this.

She had surprised herself with that comment about moving out of London; wasn't aware until she'd said it that she had consciously thought of it as a solution to the whole disaster of Toby not getting into St Anthony's. Martin *could* commute from Kent. She *could* start up Carpe Diem Life Classes in Kent. She tried to picture them all living somewhere in rural Kent . . . embarking on a new beginning among oast houses, apple orchards and hop fields. To start with it might be exciting, but after that . . . when they'd settled down? It might occur to them that they'd had their last new beginning and all that was left to them was to grow old – or apart.

If only Toby had got into St Anthony's then none of this would be happening. If only her nose wasn't so big – if only her breasts *were* – then none of this would be happening.

She pulled herself up short. What was it exactly that she thought *was* happening? And anyway, she was an educated woman. St Anthony's, her nose, her breasts: these were all things she was more than capable of coping with . . . dealing with . . . rectifying.

She became aware of her shoulder blades digging into the mattress they'd had since their first flat together in Finsbury; that had moved with them three times now and that needed replacing, but that she couldn't bring herself to replace.

This mattress had absorbed as much of their life together as they had. It used to absorb a lot of laughter, but Martin didn't laugh so much any more. He smiled, but his smiles had the effect of disconnecting rather than connecting her to him. Martin's smiles just weren't right and now, alone in bed with him, she was beginning to doubt whether his laughter ever had been either.

One of them had lost the will – and it wasn't her.

# 25

As Kate drove between No. 236 Prendergast Road and No. 22, she was unable to get the image of Miles and Jessica standing together in the Burgesses' kitchen out of her mind and was suddenly desperate to see Robert in a way she hadn't been for a long time – longer than she could remember.

Her post-PRC migraine vanished; even the fact that Findlay hadn't got into St Anthony's became nothing more than a dimly lit feature at the back of her mind as she accelerated down the badly lit street, past the front garden where a schoolboy had been raped in August the year before.

Parking badly outside their house, she ran through the rain to the front door, a sense of urgency making it difficult to get the right key in the lock.

The hall light had been left on.

She made her way upstairs and as she passed the lounge door heard Margery, who must have been dreaming, mumbling, 'Not now Tom.' Then Margery started giggling. It was unsettling, this unconscious stream of giggles coming from an elderly woman.

Kate carried on upstairs and into their bedroom.

Robert was slumped awkwardly against the pillows, his

head flopping over a book Ros had given her – *How to Eliminate Life's Toxins*.

She sat down and gently pulled the book away from him and a few seconds later he jerked suddenly awake, snorting loudly before lying down and pulling the duvet up over him.

Smiling, Kate kicked off her shoes and curled up next to him, stroking his ears. She carried on stroking them, absently, unconsciously inhaling the familiar smells rising from his warm body – and was on the verge of falling asleep herself, fully clothed, when he turned round suddenly, his eyes wide open, large and helpless, staring at her.

'Hey,' he said sleepily, 'it's you.'

He eased himself contentedly onto his back, then turned his head to look at her.

'Where've you been?' He moved his head from side to side on the pillow and yawned. 'I haven't seen you in ages,' he said, pulling the duvet back and propping himself up on his elbow. 'You just sort of vanished some time back and since then I've been living with the other Kate.'

'I did?'

He nodded with mock seriousness. 'Where did you go?'

'I don't know.'

'Where do you go when you vanish like that?' He leant down and kissed her suddenly.

'I don't know,' she said again, running her hand over his chest. She looked up at him. 'What do you do – when I vanish like that?'

'I wait – and hope that each time you come back to me, you stay a little longer.'

He brushed her hair from her face and ran his finger round the edges of it.

After a while, she said, 'Do you ever get scared that I won't come back?'

'I get scared that . . .' He paused. 'I get scared. But in the end you always come back.'

'What if I don't?' she insisted. 'What if one time . . . I just don't.'

'You will.'

'What if I vanish and never come back?'

This time there was no response; they just stared at each other in silence.

'What if – what if you stop caring whether I come back or not?' She could hear the panic in her voice now and her hands were on the top of his arms. 'What if you decide that you've had enough?'

'I won't.'

'What if I'm just all wrong for you?'

He sighed. 'I don't know the answer to that any more, Kate.' He broke off, putting his hand on her forehead. 'You've got a temperature – you're shaking.'

'It's all the rain today. I don't care. Robert . . .'

She hadn't sought comfort like this for a lot of years. She hadn't let him comfort her for even longer; she hadn't admitted to needing his comfort for even longer than that; and they hadn't made love – made love properly – for even longer than that again. An absurd thought passed briefly through her mind – this was the last time they were ever going to make love – then it passed.

Afterwards he started to fall asleep on top of her, and was pushed gently off.

She felt for his hand under the duvet and kept hold of it, squeezing tightly until at last her grip loosened, her breathing changed and she fell into a deep sleep.

*MAY*

# 26

Robert walked into the kitchen and there was Kate in a pair of Marigolds, scrubbing furiously at something on the fridge door.

There were eight cakes, all different sizes, lined up along the bench.

Then he noticed the flashcards. Everything in the kitchen that could be labelled, was labelled.

'Kate?'

Kate stood up straight and stared at him, distant. She followed his eyes round the room. 'Oh – yeah, I did that just now. Findlay needs to improve on his word recognition.' She went back to the FRIDGE door, mumbling, 'Fucking thing won't come out.'

'How did you sleep?'

'I didn't.'

'Bad dreams?'

She shrugged, and carried on scrubbing.

'What time were you up?'

'I don't know . . . four?'

'Four?'

'I told you – I couldn't sleep.'

'So, what have you been doing since four?'

'Baking. Cakes.'

His eyes ran nervously over the line-up on the bench again.

'It's for the street party – I have to start now. I'm meant to be supplying the entire stall's worth in less than six weeks.'

He got himself a bowl of cereal and stood eating it, watching her. From the lounge, he heard Findlay and Margery arguing.

'Here,' he said, picking a cloth out of the SINK, 'Let me have a go.'

Frustrated, Kate went into the lounge to see what all the noise was about.

There was nothing on the FRIDGE door apart from an early morning patch of sunlight. Robert stared at it for a while then followed Kate through to the lounge.

'Did it come off?' she said.

He nodded, 'You okay, Finn?'

Findlay nodded morosely.

'He's bleeding all over the sofa . . .'

'I said it doesn't matter,' Kate said.

'It's his eczema,' Margery carried on. 'He sits there picking at it, then it bleeds. If he put the cream on, it would stop itching.'

'The cream stings me.'

'It's that Spiderman suit – I told you it would bring on his eczema.'

'I've got to go,' Robert said.

'At least you've got somewhere else to go to,' Kate called out after him.

Ignoring this, he left the house, banging the DOOR shut behind him.

She listened to him leave the house then went into the kitchen, trying to remember what she'd gone in there for.

She went over to the WINDOW, looking out at the tattered leaves of a date palm planted by the previous owners of No. 22 Prendergast Road. She hated the date palm; hated the entire garden, in fact.

A bumblebee grazed the WINDOW, trying to get in.

Then the phone started to ring.

'Kate? Kate – you *are* a dark horse.' Evie's voice came jabbering down the line accompanied by low, rapid breathing. 'Putting your house on the market and not saying anything to anybody.'

Evie's was the first of many phone calls Kate had been anticipating that morning. 'I know,' she said.

'But you haven't said anything—'

'I know.'

'To anybody—'

'I know.'

'Not a thing.'

'I know – I know.' Kate coughed.

'So – WHAT'S GOING ON?'

'Well, we're thinking of moving.'

'Thinking? Your house is on the market.'

'Well, we've seen this place . . .' Kate paused. 'Near Lot in France?' She'd been rehearsing this all weekend, but Evie was the first person she'd actually tried it out on.

'You're emigrating?' Evie screamed.

'Not emigrating – it would be more of a second home. Robert gets so much holiday being a teacher . . .'

'So?'

'So, we were thinking of downscaling here in London – releasing a bit of capital and putting it towards a second home.'

'But why didn't you say?'

'I don't know – we've only just started talking about it to each other. It still seems strange.'

'Well, Ros phoned me—'

'How did Ros find out about it?'

'She saw it on the Internet and whoever took the pictures has made it look HUGE . . .' Evie broke off.

'Why didn't Ros phone me?'

'I'm not meant to say anything, but Ros has just put her house on the market as well. What's going on with everybody?'

'Ros has?' Kate didn't know what to say.

'With Foxtons. They reckon they can get over eight hundred and twenty-five thousand for it.' When Kate didn't respond to this, Evie said, 'So – you're not leaving us altogether, then? I mean, you're looking locally.'

'Locally?'

'Because of school?'

'School?' Kate tried not to panic. Did Evie *know*?

'You don't want to lose Findlay's place at St Anthony's.'

'No, I've been looking in the catchment area – at that place on Beulah Hill, actually.'

'Beulah Hill? Well, you'll need to start looking – yours will go in no time, Kate. I had a friend on Derwent Street who put hers on the market on a Friday morning; by the afternoon she had three offers and it went out to bids. She got sixty more than the asking.'

Kate didn't respond to this; she was too busy wondering why Ros had phoned Evie – rather than her – when she saw the house on the Internet.

'Have you had anybody round yet?'

'We've got some people coming this afternoon.'

'Well, keep me updated, and listen – another reason I phoned is . . . I'm having a chickenpox party. I've been stuck in for four days and now Ingrid's gone and got it, which means more quarantine . . . . I'm going completely bloody stir crazy. Come on, Kate, everybody's coming. I've made gallons of Pimms . . . I mean, it's not like we haven't done our bit lately.'

The primary reason for the chickenpox party wasn't in fact chickenpox. Chickenpox was the excuse to gather together as large an audience as possible in order to break the news that Aggie had been diagnosed dyspraxic.

'But Jessica's taking Findlay and Margery down to the coast with her today – and Flo hasn't got chickenpox.'

'Well, it's much better if they have it young – my mother put me in the bath with my sister when she had it.' Evie broke off. 'God, is Margery still there? How many weeks is it now?'

'Don't talk about it.'

'Well, Jessica owes you: you're forever having Arthur for her.'

The idea that Jessica was abusing Kate's generosity was a very popular one among PRC members.

In the lounge, Findlay and Margery were still arguing.

She went through the back door and up the side passage into the garden, drawing level with the back of the house, where a *Hydrangea petiolaris* she'd been told would do amazing things to her north-facing wall was struggling to take hold.

The garden was devoid of life, but at least Margery wasn't there.

She stood staring at the balding lawn Findlay wasn't allowed to play football on that culminated, beyond the eucalyptus and date palm, in a shed they'd lost the key to, and a climbing frame with a tent on the top that local cats urinated in. Before they'd moved to No. 22, they'd talked about how Findlay would at last have somewhere to play; how they'd be able to barbecue. But when they'd moved in, the garden had seemed much smaller than they'd remembered from the two viewings. After one broken window and countless balls over neighbours' fences, they'd decided to prohibit ball games.

Robert had admitted that he found barbecues depressing; that the last thing he felt like doing at the weekend was barbecuing meat for semi-strangers.

With an effort, Kate remembered that she was still on the phone to Evie. 'Listen, I've got to go—'

'Well, don't forget to keep me updated on the house, and if you change your mind about the chickenpox party just drop in – it's open house.'

Kate started to walk slowly back towards the house.

As she went indoors, she heard Margery's voice shouting at Findlay to stop scratching his eczema, and was about to say something when the doorbell started to ring.

Findlay ran to answer it and there were Jessica and Arthur on the doorstep.

'Margery!' Kate yelled, surveying Jessica's strange attire. Jessica was as much an indicator of what not to wear as Ros was of what *to* wear. 'I think you've seriously saved her life by taking her off my hands today,' Kate hissed, leaning forwards. 'And listen – I just found out from Evie that Ros put her house on the market as well. I had no idea Ros was thinking of moving.'

'She rang me Friday – she's put it on with Foxtons.'

'Friday? She hasn't said anything to me.'

'Well, from what she said, they're doing pretty much what you're doing – downscaling in London and buying some-where either in Kent or . . . I can't remember where else she said. Anyway, she's keen to stay in the catchment area for St Anthony's because she doesn't want Toby to lose his place.' Jessica smiled. 'Hi, Margery,' she said as Margery appeared in the hallway behind Kate. 'You've changed your hair.'

Margery's hands went to her hair, self-conscious. Then she smiled.

'The parting's on the other side and the colour – no, it's not the colour that's changed. You've got curls.'

'Natural curls,' Margery said, proudly.

'I never knew you had curls. Lovely,' Jessica added.

Kate and Margery, now standing side by side, paused awkwardly, aware that they had never and would never have a conversation like that.

'Findlay!' Kate called out, suddenly nervous.

Findlay came rushing through the women and past them into the outside world, a Spiderman rucksack on his back, already wearing his goggles and with a bucket shaped like a castle in his hand, yelling 'Arthur!', with no thoughts of anything but what was ahead.

Kate, unsure of herself under Jessica's frank, smiling gaze, let him go and didn't insist on the usual parting rituals. 'Got everything?' she said to Margery.

Margery nodded, patting the handbag that rarely left her side.

'We should be back about five – I'll give you a ring when we set off. Oh, Kate, I meant to say – we've had another offer made on the Beulah Hill house . . .' Jessica hesitated. 'It's Ros, actually.'

'Ros?' Kate yelled.

Jessica paused awkwardly. 'Ros's house has only just gone on the market as well. Mr Jackson's considering both offers.'

'How much was Ros's offer?'

'I can't say – it's confidential.'

'Jessica . . .'

Jessica was turning to leave with Margery when she stopped suddenly. 'You don't know if anybody's got a dachshund that's gone missing . . . ?

'A dachshund?' Kate said, vaguely.

'I saw one in the garden last night.'

Kate shook her head. 'A dog kept me awake a few nights ago, but . . . a dachshund?'

'What else would it be?'

185

'A fox?' Margery said suddenly. 'I've seen foxes in the garden. The other night I thought I heard something – opened the curtains and there was this pair of eyes staring in at me through the patio windows. Nearly died, I did.' Margery paused, going back to the night before and the eyes at the window. At the time, she'd thought it was the rapist next door, Mr Hamilton; that had been her first thought.

Jessica shook her head. 'It's much smaller than a fox.'

'Maybe you've got rats then.'

'It's not a rat.'

'You want to watch it's not rats – I'm sure I saw something near the bins here the other day. Rats can be big – bigger than you think. And this *is* London. I'd get someone to come and have a look,' she said to Jessica. 'You might have rats.'

# 27

Ros was at the printers in Bellenden trying to get the Carpe Diem merchandise ready for the street party. She'd stopped using the printers on Lordship Lane when the 'No Buggies' sign went up.

The printer – who was bipolar – tucked his longish grey hair behind his ears and leant forward, peering at Ros's printout. 'Carpe Diem,' he said, sounding pleased.

Ros gave a quick smile and maintained her impatient posture. 'I'm going to need five hundred postcards, two hundred A-five leaflets – and twenty posters initially. I was thinking about T-shirts as well – I don't know, twenty or something?'

The printer nodded, as if he was thinking about this.

Ros paused. 'Does that sound okay?'

'Carpe Diem,' he said again, grinning suddenly at her this time and showing two rows of teeth that looked as though they'd suffered subsidence and had been left hanging from what remained of his gums.

Ros tried not to look. Dentists were happy to arrange instalment payments for care plans these days. Why couldn't people just look after themselves?

The printer was still leaning over the counter, waiting for

her to respond to his persistent repetition of the words 'carpe diem', and this was having a strange effect on Ros. She felt increasingly violent towards him and wasn't entirely sure she'd be able to stop herself grabbing hold of his hair and smashing his face against the counter if he repeated the words 'carpe diem' one more time. She'd never experienced such a surge of violence before.

'I want everything two-tone,' she said tersely. 'Black and pink.'

The printer – fortunately – gave up then, slumping over his counter as though his world had just died and he was trying to come to terms with it. 'Black on pink or pink on black?'

'Black on pink. I want the pink matt and the black typeface glossy.'

'Raised on the postcards?'

She shook her head.

'What sort of typeface?' He pushed the book towards her and she scanned it efficiently, relieved to feel the violence subsiding.

'Nothing too rounded.'

'Okay, well I'll do a mock-up and you can take a look at it, let me know if you're happy and we'll go from there.'

'You had some A-five leaflets for me to collect as well.'

'What's the name?'

'Granger.'

He rifled, distracted, through the wire tray on the counter and handed her an envelope with the street party flyers inside.

'Should I pay for these now?'

He waved the idea of payment aside, as though he was too depressed to consider making a living right then. 'Later . . .'

Ros shrugged, then stepped out of the printers into the mid-morning heat.

Bellenden had been regenerated, which meant there were more white homeowners living there than black tenants. Mr Walsh, the glazier, had taken an unprecedented number of calls from new homeowners over the past two years, all wanting the same thing – the panels above the front door glazed with the house number, and fleur-de-lys panels put in the front door itself. A dog's grooming parlour had recently opened, and Antony Gormley – who used to live in the area before making enough money to move to north London – had designed the balustrades on the pavements. Despite Antony Gormley's presence and the fleur-de-lys glazing in the majority of front doors, Ros still didn't feel safe, and her eyes skittered nervously over two youths now making their way towards her.

They aren't making their way towards me, she reminded herself, they're making their way down the street. Soon we're going to pass. She walked into the damp shade beneath the railway bridge. The youths' eyes looked flatly into hers.

Their pit-bull strained on its leash, froth trickling from the corners of its mouth.

'Fuck it Tyrone,' one of the youths said, in a high-pitched voice.

A girl's voice. They were girls, Ros realised, elated with relief. Girls immersed in genderless street gear. Then she remembered reading somewhere that girl gangs were on the rise and that some even used gang rape as an initiation ceremony. The dog looked as if it had been trained to rape – maybe the 'fuck it Tyrone' was a command.

They were drawing level, the girls, and Tyrone, spread across the pavement. Ros's left shoulder was scraping along the inside of the railway arch. The moment had arrived. They were going to close in on her.

Her heart thumping, they carried on walking, the flat stares shifting to someone or something else. Only Tyrone gave her a froth-ridden backwards glance.

She carried on walking towards the sunlight, aware that she was actually shaking, and didn't feel herself again until she'd finished distributing street party leaflets to all the shops on Lordship Lane. All the shops, that is, apart from William Hill, the Co-operative funeral parlour, Favourite chicken bar – and Starbucks, which the PRC had made a point of boycotting since it opened a year ago.

Once this was done, she got back in the car, aware that she had to be at Evie's in under ten minutes. She drove to Prendergast Road via Beulah Hill. As she passed No. 8, she saw someone she recognised by the front gate. Ignoring the refuse lorry behind her, Ros stopped the car and leant over the passenger seat. The day had looked suddenly dull through the lenses of her wraparounds.

'Harriet?'

Harriet hadn't anticipated this.

The encounter with Ros was so unanticipated, in fact, that she could do nothing but stand and stare.

Ten minutes ago she'd parked her car outside No. 8 Beulah Hill and rung on the peach-coloured door. It was the first time she'd gone round since they'd written the letter and sent it to Admissions.

No answer.

She tried again and, this time, Mr Jackson's face appeared in the bay window.

The front door opened.

He didn't seem surprised to see a woman he didn't recognise standing on his doorstep with a child in a car seat hanging from her right arm.

'I'm sorry to bother you . . . ,' Harriet started.

Mr Jackson cut in with, 'You come to see the house?'

Harriet paused. 'Actually . . . no. We've just moved to the

area and I've got a feeling our post is being sent to your address by mistake.'

Mr Jackson considered this.

In the house behind him, a gospel choir was singing.

'The name's Burgess. Have you had any mail for Burgess?'

'I don't know what comes through the door. Nothing but rubbish most of the time.' He paused – and forgot what they'd been talking about.

'So, nothing for Burgess then?' Harriet prompted him.

He stared back at her, confused. 'You want to come in?'

'Well . . .'

'Come on – come in.' He walked down the hallway away from her, towards the kitchen.

Harriet checked the street behind her then followed him in.

It was dark inside and it took her a while to get used to the light. The house smelt as though the bath was rarely used and the decor was pre-credit. Threadbare carpets, scratched, chipped and stained G-Plan furniture, which a woman's pride had covered in crocheted runners in order to conceal the more obvious defects.

Mr Jackson stopped in the middle of the kitchen and smiled expectantly at her.

It occurred to Harriet that he had no memory of just having spoken to her on the front doorstep. Did he think she was Meals on Wheels?

'We were talking – just now.'

He nodded, the first sign of worry creeping over his face.

'Some of our post might have been delivered to your house by mistake?'

In the background, the choir on TV were in a state of exultation.

'I throw so much stuff away,' he muttered to himself, then caught sight of a pile of letters by the cooker.

He picked these up and handed them to Harriet.

191

She rifled uncomfortably through the unopened bills, Iceland promotions and half-completed scratch cards. Nothing for the Burgesses.

'Nothing?'

She shook her head. 'D'you mind if I pop round again? I've contacted the post office, but—'

'Nobody wants to work these days,' Mr Jackson put in. 'No, they don't want to work. You see them around, they don't want to work. They're all the same – want something for nothing.'

Harriet wasn't listening. She wanted to get back to her car. 'I'd better get going.'

She made her way back up the hallway towards the front door, glancing into the synthetic opulence of the lounge as she passed – at a glistening sewing machine on a well cared-for sideboard.

'D'you sew?' Mr Jackson asked suddenly.

'Do I sew?'

'You look like you might sew. My wife used to sew. That's her machine over there. She used to be a dressmaker. Maybe you want to take the machine – none of my children sews.'

'I couldn't . . .'

'But you sew.'

'I used to . . .'

'Well – take it.'

Harriet was about to respond when the doorbell rang.

Mr Jackson shuffled past her and stood staring at the woman filling the doorway.

'Uncle Alex? It's me, Jade – come to check up on you.'

Mr Jackson continued to stare at his niece, until suddenly, 'Jade!'

She stepped, smiling, into the hallway – then she saw Harriet backed against the wall with Phoebe hanging from her right arm. She stared expectantly at her.

Mr Jackson seemed as surprised as his niece to see Harriet in his hallway – despite having just offered her his wife's sewing machine.

'I came to see the house,' Harriet lied.

Jade nodded slowly.

Mr Jackson smiled at the two women. 'Who wants a drink?'

'Didn't the estate agent come?'

'No. They phoned your uncle – he was happy for me to come on my own.'

'I told them not to do that – he's got slight Alzheimer's. Somebody should be here with him to do the viewing.'

'I'm sorry – they said it was okay. Anyway . . .' Harriet started to move towards the front door, which was still open.

'I should tell you . . .'

Harriet stopped, suddenly alarmed.

'We're thinking of taking the house off the market.'

'Whose house?' Mr Jackson asked.

'Oh – that's a shame.'

'I meant to contact the agent this morning.'

Harriet nodded, and held her left hand out to Mr Jackson. 'Well, thank you anyway.'

Mr Jackson shook it warmly, pressing a Fox's glacier mint into her hand. 'For the baby.'

She hesitated a moment, then quickly left. The front door shut behind her and she made her way, with relief, back to the car.

She got as far as the gate – and there was Ros parked in the middle of the road, staring at her.

'Harriet?'

Harriet stopped.

This was almost as bad as the time just after Phoebe was born when Ros had seen her through the window at Starbucks even though she'd managed to get a seat at the back near the toilets. PRC members were meant to go to the small local café across the road, even though there was no pushchair access and no baby change. Harriet had wheeled the newborn Phoebe into Starbucks and collapsed with relief into a crumb-ridden club chair. Ros had just come up on her and then – as now – she didn't have an answer.

'Not thinking of moving house, are you?' Ros joked, omitting to mention that she was.

'No,' Harriet said flatly, unable to think of anything else to say – or even begin to offer an explanation.

Ros continued to watch her. Harriet, she decided, wasn't to be relied on. Evie – despite her often hysterical unpredictability – could be relied on to stick her neck out for you. Harriet's 'no' was insurmountable.

'Are you going to Evie's?'

'In about half an hour.'

'See you there.' Ros paused, put the car into gear then headed on to Prendergast Road.

As she drove, she phoned Jessica. 'Jessica?'

'I can't talk – I'm driving.'

'Harriet hasn't said anything to you about moving house, has she?'

'No, why?'

'I've just seen her outside Number eight Beulah Hill.'

'No idea. And Ros? I had to tell Kate you'd put an offer in as well.' Silence. 'Maybe you should phone her.'

'Maybe,' Ros agreed. 'But what I want to know is – why was Harriet at Number eight Beulah Hill . . . ?'

'Ros, I don't know – I'm on the M-twenty-three – I've got to go.'

Five minutes later, Ros was knocking on the door to No. 112 Prendergast Road.

Evie answered, holding a jug of Pimms in one hand, and sucking on a piece of cucumber. She said, 'Hi!' Then, 'Aggie's dyspraxic.'

# 28

'Ros, I don't know – I'm on the M23 – I've got to go.'

Jessica rang off. It wasn't just warm, it was hot – unseasonably hot. The air was barely moving and it was more like a day in mid-August than early May.

After forty-five minutes on the M23 they turned onto the A27 towards Shoreham and the house on Marine Drive that Jessica's dad, Joe, had bought nearly twenty years ago, after selling his company – Quantum Kitchens.

'Hope you don't mind her offloading me on you,' Margery said.

'Course not,' Jessica laughed, a warm complicity passing between the two women.

Margery's eyes noted with approval the conifers and rock garden at the front of the house as they pulled onto the drive – and the double-glazed rose in the front door when they rang the bell.

'He's not in,' Arthur said. 'He's not in,' he said again, his voice breaking this time.

Just then the sound of a mower starting up filled the air.

'That's him,' Arthur shouted, pushing open the side gate and disappearing into the back garden, closely followed by Findlay.

There was Joe driving his new sit-on mower, Toro, towards them, crashing through the buddleia and waving happily.

Joe was happy. Today. Most days. Generically happy.

The impression was overwhelming and unavoidable.

Waving back, Jessica looked out over the garden vibrant with unfashionable, seasonal colour and felt a strange, unnerving sense of comfort. The lawn was early summer soft: a bright, vibrant, fledgling green. The borders were packed with perennials and annuals – the guardians of suburban dreams, bringing the men and women who culti-vated them to their knees when there was nothing else left to.

Joe came to a stop where the crazy paving patio began and, leaving Toro's engine running, jumped down and held Jessica tightly in a hug that was primal in its reassurance.

After being introduced, he hugged Margery just as tightly, making her gasp, before swinging Arthur up into the air and rubbing Findlay's head.

Then, squinting at the boys, he said, 'Who wants a ride?'

Arthur squealed with excitement and Findlay silently conceded as Joe hauled them both up onto the mower. Turning Toro round, they accelerated back up the garden, Joe letting Arthur take the wheel and not caring when they drove into the wigwam of sweet peas.

'Your sweet peas,' Margery said.

Joe either didn't hear or chose to ignore this.

Margery and Jessica stood silently observing the demise of the sweet-pea wigwams as Joe helped the boys off Toro and went over to the barbecue he'd built himself – based on one him and Lenny, Jessica's step-mother, used at their time-share villa in Portugal.

Margery could almost smell the parties and gatherings that had taken place here in the back garden on Marine Drive. She rarely bought anything other than mince, liver, pork fillet and – occasionally – a small chicken if Edith was coming to lunch. She wondered what it would be like to order enough meat for twenty people or more. During what she considered her long life so far, Margery had hosted very little – not even her mother's funeral; not even Tom's. They hadn't let her anywhere near Tom's. Wherever she went, she was the guest grudgingly invited, grudgingly welcomed. Margery had experienced every nuance of social abandonment among family, friends and strangers.

The air filled with the smell of barbecue.

She heard Joe Palmer's voice coming from somewhere close by. 'You stay where you are – this is your day off. Sangria?'

Then Jessica's, 'Dad, I'm driving.'

'It's weak – loads of lemonade in it. I'll make you a coffee after.'

Why couldn't Robert have married into a family like this? Not that barrage of dogs, Wellingtons, loud echoing voices and flat smiling faces that concealed cruelties Margery didn't understand. The few times she'd been to visit Beatrice and Marcus in Gloucestershire it had been like Bluebeard's Castle. There wasn't a door in that Georgian house she hadn't been afraid of opening.

And the lack of warmth and intimacy that pervaded every peeling, rotting nook and cranny of that house had been grafted, by Robert's bride, onto Robert himself, and now Robert was trying to live his life without love and fool Margery, of all people, that he didn't even need hers. Her thoughts turned to Robert himself – what a beautiful, healthy baby he'd been. And the joy – the joy she'd taken in him, despite the way they'd looked at her on that maternity ward, despite the lack of flowers and visitors. The other women on the ward didn't know her, didn't know of her, but her story was clear as day and they kept their distance.

You wouldn't think that the distance between hospital beds varied much, but it did. To the eye it might look the same ... if you were to measure the distance between beds it would have been the same – especially in that place with *that* Sister – but the distance wasn't the same. There was her bed, then there was everybody else's bed.

'Margery?'

For a moment she thought it was visiting time in the ward; that somebody had come for her after all. She squinted up through bright sunshine at a familiar face she couldn't place.

'Margery? Sangria?'

She smiled at Joe, utterly terrified. She had no idea where she was.

'Margery,' Joe said again, then broke off. 'You all right, love?'

'Joe,' she said at last. 'Joe.'

He crouched down, a jug of sangria in his hand, raising it into the air between them. 'Or d'you want water?'

'I want that.'

Joe chuckled warmly and poured her a glass.

Margery took a sip, aware that her heart was racing.

Joe disappeared back into the house.

'Not too close,' Jessica yelled at Arthur, who was running towards the barbecue in pursuit of a football.

Robert never got a chance to play with anybody like that, Margery thought. Never got any invitations anywhere. For a moment, watching Findlay kick the ball back to Arthur, she couldn't think where she was. Who were these people? Did they mean anything to her at all? She watched a ladybird crawling across the back of her hand, then took another sip of sangria and looked away.

Jessica was staring at the cedar tree at the end of the garden, where Joe had started to build a tree house for Arthur.

Beyond the cedar tree there was a line of Scotch pines, bent crooked by sea winds. When smoke from the barbecue blew the other way, there was the scent of pine needles baking in the sun against the cracked, bald patches of lawn under the trees. Jessica thought she could smell creosote as well – faintly – and turned back to the barbecue and the smell of cooking meat instead.

Then Joe reappeared, carrying two salads.

Margery got laboriously to her feet. She had to be useful; that was her role in life. 'Need some help there, Joe? Don't worry . . .'

Joe wasn't worried – until Margery tried to wrestle the salads from his hands.

'I'm fine – Margery, I'm fine.'

'You can't do everything, Joe.'

'Let me just get these to the table.'

'You go and sort out the barbecue.'

Margery pulled the salad dish out of Joe's hands and, failing to grasp it in her own, had no choice but to watch it fall onto the crazy paving where it smashed, the broken pieces mingling with the salad.

Arthur and Findlay stopped their game and came running over. 'What's happened?' Findlay yelled then, embarrassed, 'Grandma—'

'Stay on the grass,' Jessica shouted, 'There are pieces every-where.'

Margery still hadn't said anything.

Joe crouched down.

'Oh, Dad.' Jessica scraped up orange, olives and mint leaves, glancing up at Margery, whose shoes were covered in pomegranate seeds.

'How did that happen?' Margery said at last.

Joe, who'd just cut his hand, disappeared into the house.

'I don't know how it happened,' Margery said to Jessica.

'Margery – it's fine – just an accident. Come on. Boys – away from the barbecue,' she yelled at Findlay and Arthur who, bored, had drifted back over to the fire.

The smell of barbecue was sending a neighbour's dog into paroxysms and the constant yapping was beginning to make Jessica panic.

'It's all ruined – completely ruined. I ruined it,' Margery carried on, watching Jessica scrape the salad and remains of the bowl into a pile. 'He must have spent ages on this.'

'The meat's ready,' Findlay called out. 'I SAID THE MEAT'S READY.'

They all stopped.

Joe opened the kitchen window and poked his head out. 'What's all the noise about?'

'It's all ruined,' Margery said again as Joe reappeared on the patio with dustpan and brush.

'It's only salad.' He scraped it into the bag he was holding. 'I'll make another one.'

'You can't make another one,' Margery insisted, tearful.

'I think I've got enough of everything – apart from olives. We're almost out of those.' He stood up, wincing again.

'You all right?' Jessica asked, watching him.

'I will be if I stop bending down like that,' he said.

'He can't make another salad,' Margery said to Jessica as Joe made his way back to the kitchen.

'Dad loves cooking, Margery – it's fine. Come here.' She put her arms round Margery, who sniffed a couple of times.

Unsure what else to do as Jessica hosed down the patio, Margery drained her cup of sangria then stalked unevenly up the garden to where Arthur and Findlay were playing.

'Who *are* you?' Arthur asked as she bent down to peer at them through the branches of the cedar tree.

'I'm Findlay's grandma,' she said.

Findlay didn't back her up and Arthur didn't respond to this.

After lunch, Joe got Margery into the lounge where he switched the TV on for her. Once he'd left the room, Margery's eyes scanned the walls full of brightly coloured photos of Lenny and Joe taken in global locations: cruise ships . . . winter breaks in Barbados . . . the villa in Portugal . . . snorkelling among coral . . . riding camels in the desert. Margery felt disorientated to the point of nausea. It wasn't the places that bothered her – she had never really dreamt of travel although she had always said she wouldn't mind a trip down the Nile before she died – it was the overwhelming sense of life lived. She had tried to live, but every time she'd tried, something had been taken away from her, and every time that happened she was left with that feeling of waiting again; forever waiting for something . . . anything to happen. So much time to fill in, always; so much time.

'She's asleep,' Joe said, emerging from the house with a tray and sitting down at the wrought-iron table. 'Have the boys got sun cream on?'

'Course they've got sun cream on.'

'It burns quicker down here on the coast – it's the salt in the air.'

'Dad – they've got sun cream on.'

They sat in silence, drinking their coffee, happy to observe a dragonfly that had landed on the table near the sugar bowl.

'Arthur's getting big,' Joe said after a while. 'My mum used to always say that you lose them when they start school.'

'I'll be happy for any childcare I can get my hands on – however it comes – and if it's free, all the better.'

'How's it going – work?'

'It's not,' Jessica said, listlessly.

'And Ellie?'

'Ellie's . . . God, she's difficult.'

'Understatement,' Joe chuckled. 'I know you don't want to hear it, but you're too similar, that's what it is.' Then, suddenly serious, 'If it all gets too much, you know you've got a home here – all of you. I've always said that.'

'I know.'

'Me and Lenny aren't going to just stand by and watch you—'

'Dad,' she cut him off, 'I just need to make this moment work – however rudimentary my attempts look to the outside world.' She sighed, her eyes on the dragonfly. 'I mean having Ellie so young and then losing Peter – Peter was one thing,' she said with difficulty, 'but then, Ellie – there's just never any let-up . . .' She broke off. 'Is it this hard for everyone?'

'No – you've had it harder than most.' He gave her leg a squeeze. 'You're doing brilliant, Jess – brilliant.'

Jessica nodded, not wanting to cry.

'I need to make this work to get beyond it.'

'I know you need to make it work, I just don't want you thinking you've got to do it all by yourself. Come and make it work down here – with us.'

'Don't ask me again, Dad – I might just say yes.'

'You know how much Lenny loves the kids.'

'Dad!' Jessica warned him.

'Calm down, love,' Joe said, taking hold of her hand. 'Just calm down.'

The dragonfly took off.

'Why didn't you and Lenny ever have kids?' Jessica said suddenly. She'd said it without even thinking. Watching Joe, she realised for the first time that Joe must only have been in his mid-thirties – the age she was now – when he'd met Lenny.

Joe looked at her.

'Sorry,' she said quickly, 'it's none of my—'

'We tried.' He shrugged.

202

'You wanted kids?'

'More than anything,' he said with difficulty. 'The things we tried . . . the doctors we saw . . . and then it got to the stage where the longer it went on, the more it felt like – I don't know, it's difficult to explain – but like that was something that wasn't going to happen to us.'

Jessica, listening, was trying to work out when this had happened, chronologically – how old must she have been: twenty?

'Anyway,' Joe said, looking at her, 'People weren't so keyed up on the whole infertility thing or IVF or anything like that – not that it was infertility. More like an inexplicable genetic incompatibility. Did I say that right?'

Jessica nodded.

'I could have children with any woman other than Lenny. Lenny could have children with any man other than me.'

Jessica tried to process the full implication of the choice they had both clearly made, and realised suddenly that if she had known this about Lenny sooner, it might have changed everything between them – because she had never trusted Lenny; had always presumed Lenny and Joe wouldn't last.

To be fair, the relationship between Lenny and Jessica never had the best of beginnings. The year she was fifteen, the year she lost her mother – Jessica realised her dad was having an affair. A year after that, the woman her dad had been having an affair with while her mother was still alive – Lenny – moved in with them and became her stepmother. It was obvious – even to an emotionally decimated sixteen-year-old – that Joe was uncontrollably in love with Lenny. Now, for the first time, Jessica realised just how much Lenny must have been in love with Joe, and how – far from taking anything away from her at that time – Lenny had in fact given her a man who wouldn't otherwise have been up to being a father.

'I have a feeling she might have gone up to London and seen someone – at the time. But she never said anything to me. Anyway, nothing came of it.' Joe smiled, unsure why.

'How is she?'

'Lenny? She's well – works too much, but I can't get her to stop. She's in Birmingham today.'

'Birmingham?'

'A lot of soldiers in hospitals in Birmingham – Scottish soldiers with partners in Scotland who can't visit because they haven't got any childcare and the MOD won't issue rail passes . . . . We should get these boys to the beach soon – there's a haze coming in; might rain.' Joe got to his feet.

'What about you and Mum?' Jessica asked.

'Me and Mum, what?' Joe said, staring at her, surprised. They never talked about Linda; rarely ever had done.

Jessica was as surprised as him at the question. Only lately, she had begun to feel haunted by the failure of her parents' marriage, and wondered, increasingly, whether her real struggle lay not in trying to be herself, but in trying not to be her mother.

'Why didn't you and Mum have any more children? Why was there only me?'

Joe was silent for a moment. 'Things were difficult after you were born – with Linda. I think we both sort of knew we couldn't go through that again.'

'How difficult?'

'Well, you know how it is – only with Linda it was worse. She was put back in hospital when you were six months old – on a general psychiatric ward.'

'A psychiatric ward?'

'I thought you knew.'

'I never knew that.'

'She just couldn't cope – the shock of responsibility, I suppose. But it never got any better. I didn't want her in hospital, but I ran out of ideas and nothing I did made anything any better; didn't even make things bearable. But . . .'

'But what?'

'When they started the electric shock treatment, I wished I hadn't taken her.'

'You never told me Mum had to have electric shock treatment after I was born,' Jessica said, unnerved.

'That's what they did then – people didn't use the expression "postnatal depression". They said she was depressed and that's the treatment they advised and I'd sort of gone under myself and suddenly we were in this place neither of us had any control over.' He paused, staring unseeing up the length of the garden. 'I don't think we ever got over it, and we both knew we couldn't go through that again.' He broke off. 'You all right? You did ask.'

'I know – I know.' She looked at him. 'Have you got any notes or medical records or anything?'

'What – of Mum's? No.'

After another minute's silence, Jessica said, 'What's the time?'

'The time? Around two.'

'We should take the boys onto the beach.'

Neither of them moved.

'I did love her at the start.'

Jessica watched him, unconvinced. 'You don't have to say that.'

'I did love her at the start,' he insisted. 'I mean – not being able to get your keys in the front door your hands are so busy shaking with excitement – love.'

'I don't think I ever loved her. She didn't seem to get anything out of being around me and I never got anything out of being around her. Most of the time, I just couldn't work out the point of her. I don't think a single day of my childhood went by when I didn't wish her dead.'

205

'Jess,' Joe said, 'that's a terrible thing to say.'

'Then when she did die . . .'

'What?'

Jessica shrugged, her eyes fixed on the cedar tree at the end of the garden that Findlay and Arthur had been attempting to climb for the past thirty minutes. 'I don't know . . .'

She forgot what she was about to say. There, on the baked mud beneath the cedar, was a small dog.

She shielded her eyes from the sun and stared. It was digging for something. 'Whose dog is that?' She pointed.

'What dog?' Joe, distracted still by their conversation, briefly scanned the garden.

'That one there – looks like a dachshund.'

This time he looked properly. 'I don't see no dog, Jess.'

The dachshund had gone.

# 29

By the time they got to the beach there was a sea haze beginning to drift in, muffling the sun.

Jessica stayed up in the beach hut Joe and Lenny had bought while Joe took the boys out in the dinghy. She stood outside the hut, her hand raised over her eyes because of the glare coming off the sea, and watched Joe tow the dinghy out while Arthur and Findlay attempted to coordinate the oars. The unnerving flat of a dead calm was taking its toll on people and, as Jessica stood there, at least six groups of women with young children started to leave. Even the emaciated teenager who had been running down the rocks screaming when they'd first arrived, trying to dodge the empty beer cans that a group of friends was hurling at him, stopped suddenly and slid off the rocks.

The group left soon after this and their departure left the beach feeling strangely silent. Jessica went back into the hut and made tea on the gas stove, her eyes scanning the hut as she waited for the kettle to boil. The hut felt much more like Lenny and Joe's than the house on Marine Drive. The house on Marine Drive – Jessica realised now for the first time – felt too big. The house on Marine Drive had been bought after they'd sold their respective businesses, in anticipation of a family of their own. She wondered why they stayed.

There wasn't much in the hut – a shelf full of shells and smaller bits of driftwood, with seagull feathers stuck in the cracks, like trophies; a pair of binoculars hanging from a nail by the door and a collection of buckets, spades, kites and fishing nets bought for Arthur from the beach shop that backed onto the hut, and a series of photographs on the back wall of the Grand after the Brighton bomb in '84.

As the kettle boiled, a woman in white espadrilles and white T-shirt dress with gold tassels stuck her head round the door.

'Oh,' she said, surprised to see Jessica. 'Joe around?'

'He's in the sea.'

'Oh,' the woman said, exhaling smoke into the interior of the beach hut and smiling vacantly through it at her.

'I'm Jessica.'

'Jessica?'

'His daughter.'

The woman picked something out carefully from between her teeth. 'Lovely.' She smiled awkwardly. 'I thought so.'

She stood on the threshold of the hut, swaying slightly, the hand that wasn't holding the cigarette clasped tightly round her waist as she stared out to sea, looking for any sign of Joe.

Jessica, pouring herself a cup of tea, had the impression that the woman spent a lot of time hanging round the hut in carefully contrived outfits, waiting for sightings of Joe. She found herself smiling and the woman, turning round, caught the smile.

'I'd better go.'

Jessica nodded.

'Tell him I called by, will you? Tell him I called by about Sunday.'

'Who called by?'

'Oh – Alexa. Alexa did.'

Jessica nodded again and watched her leave. There was a definite resonance of Linda in Alexa – she wondered if Joe had noticed.

A cup of tea in her hand, she went outside again.

In the hut next door, Alexa's legs lay dark and glistening with a glittery oil that defied the absence of any real sun. Alexa's legs, stretched out on a plantation lounger that was half in, half out of the beach hut, was all that was visible of Alexa, whose toenails, Jessica noted, were painted gold to match the tassels on her T-shirt dress.

The snack hut behind them was playing a local radio station, and she heard the DJ advertising a hot-air balloon show and the fact that the Shoreham Theatre was staging Basil Brush and the Pirates of the Caribbean that summer.

There were people in the water still, and she could hear the bang and drone of a motorboat crossing the bay westwards. Beyond this, she made out a small dog, yapping. She thought it might be coming from Alexa's hut – Alexa looked as if she might keep small dogs. Then the sound vanished.

She went back inside to check on the time – it was 3.30: they should be getting back. Sipping at the rest of her tea, she took in the picture of the Grand. Joe had been in Brighton with Lenny the night the Grand went up. The night the Grand went up was the night Linda died.

Jessica swung away from the Grand collapsing in on itself, in black and white, back towards the sea.

There were three dinghies out on the water now – one of them was making its way back to the shore. She walked slowly down the beach towards the water's edge, letting herself slip down the banks of pebbles marking the year's high tides.

The tide had turned and was going out now, leaving a

strip of wet sand on an otherwise pebble beach for her feet to sink into as she watched the waves wash the blue and yellow dinghy up on the shore. Arthur was climbing over the side, yelling at no one and nothing in particular as he flung himself belly first into the cold water and came up gasping. Joe, laughing, started to splash him.

Jessica shouted, 'Dad,' but Arthur came up again, laughing and swallowing mouthfuls of water, trying to speak then giving up.

The three of them made their way reluctantly out of the water, with Findlay pulling the dinghy as the day lost the last of its brightness and the mist turned to a fine, hot drizzle.

Jessica followed the boys and the dinghy listlessly back to the beach hut where Joe had already changed.

As they walked back to Marine Drive, the tarmac on the pavement was still soft with the heat as the drizzle turned finally to rain.

# 30

Margery woke up.

She didn't know where she was. It felt strange and smelt strange.

It wasn't East Leeke and it wasn't Prendergast Road – the two places most of her life happened in.

To make matters worse, there was somebody padding around in the green and beige area just beyond her peripheral vision. After a while she made out a pair of grey leggings and a shape- less pink sweatshirt. It might be Edith – Edith cleaned in an outfit not dissimilar to that, but Edith wore mauve, never pink. Pink, she said, clashed with her varicose veins and the burst blood vessels on her face. And it wasn't Kate. The pink and grey shape was shifting towards her, talking.

'Margery? It is Margery, isn't it? I didn't wake you, did I?'

Margery made an effort to haul herself up in the sofa until she was sitting right back in it and her feet had left the ground.

'It's coming up to four,' the woman's voice carried on. Then, 'I'm Joe's wife – Lenny. I bet Joe made his sangria, didn't he? He says he puts loads of lemonade in it, but he doesn't.'

At last Lenny came into focus, and what a bloody mess she was – her hair was wet, and she wasn't wearing any make-up. Margery couldn't even conceive of dying in a state like that, let alone receiving visitors.

Lenny must have read her face because the next minute she said, 'I only came in about forty minutes ago and went straight upstairs to shower.' She paused. 'Can I get you a tea or anything?'

Margery nodded, distracted.

'Sorry I wasn't here earlier – I had to go to Birmingham to see one of our soldiers and their family.'

'Birmingham?'

Lenny nodded. 'I run a charity for ex-soldiers – Walking Wounded.'

'Does Joe mind?' Margery asked.

Lenny laughed. 'Does Joe mind what?'

'You out and about all the time?'

'No idea,' Lenny said, disappearing into the kitchen. 'Anyway,' she called out a few minutes later, 'we'd go nuts cooped up in this house together, day in day out.'

Margery didn't respond to this. She couldn't imagine anything nicer than being cooped up with someone day in, day out – and what was the point, anyway, in finding the perfect mate only to lead separate lives. She didn't understand it, she really didn't.

She sat in silence as the first few drops of rain fell gently against the window. The corners of the room had gone dark, and the conifers outside had started blowing over to one side – it was strange to think that they had eaten lunch outside.

'Anyway,' Lenny's voice came through from the kitchen, 'Joe's got his garden and allotment.' She appeared in the lounge doorway, wiping her hands on a towel with a map of Devon on it. 'It was the first time – today – that some of those soldiers had seen their wives since getting back from

Iraq. It's difficult when there's no homecoming – public or private.'

'Terrible, isn't it?' Margery said, watching the rain get steadier through the window, her mind drifting to other wars, other soldiers . . . other homecomings.

'It wasn't much different after the Falklands.'

Margery stared at her drying her hands, the rolled-back sleeves of the sweatshirt a darker pink in places where they'd got wet. 'They'll be wet,' she said.

'What's that?'

'It's raining – they'll be wet.'

'Is it?' Lenny stared through the window.

'That your kettle?'

She jerked away from the doorframe she'd been leaning against and ran through to the kitchen.

Margery continued to watch the conifers blow over to one side and the rain spit against the window, but her nostrils were suddenly full of the smell of paint; a soft rosy paint that her mother and aunt had repainted most of the house in, in time for Tom's homecoming. They'd been going through the motions of celebration ever since they'd got the letter giving them a date – an exact date – when they could expect to see Tom again because Tom was alive. Tom had survived when others hadn't and that was reason enough to celebrate, to repaint the house a soft rosy pink when they still thought – before the car pulled up – that there was some part of Tom intact enough to appreciate being surrounded by soft rosy pink. How old had she been? Five? She remembered kneeling at a window for what seemed like ages; she remembered the pins and needles and not daring to get up and stretch her legs in case she missed the car pulling up. It was the car she was waiting for, not Tom. They didn't get many cars up their street. Then the car did pull up and she started shouting and everybody was suddenly frantic – all the women desperately pulling aprons off and tearing at the scarves on their heads. She wondered what it must have looked like to Tom with all those faces at the downstairs window. He probably hadn't seen any of them – although he said later, much later, that he'd seen hers.

Then Tom had got out of the car.

Someone had helped him.

And at that moment, everyone had known that the new rosy pink walls probably wouldn't mean all that much to Tom. Sam, who'd been hanging streamers and couldn't even see out the window, left off and jumped down from the chair she'd been standing on, shoving the rest of the streamers in the cutlery drawer.

They weren't excited any more, just afraid.

The man who brought Tom in didn't take his hat off and spent barely five minutes on the doorstep with Aunt Teresa, explaining what they should do and what they shouldn't do – for Tom, to Tom.

'You're thinking of someone,' Lenny said, putting two cups of tea on the coffee table that had a basket on it with some wrinkled apples in it.

'My cousin Tom – he was taken prisoner in Burma during the Second World War. He came to live with us after.' Margery stared at the steam rising from the cup of tea, hearing her aunt Teresa's voice saying over and over again, 'What they did to him was terrible; it was terrible,' until the rest of them had had enough and told her to shut up. 'Everybody realised,' Margery said out loud, 'that it would have been better if he hadn't survived.'

Lenny nodded. 'That happens a lot. It's an awful moment. When families realise that the person they've been hoping against hope comes back alive, does come back alive, and that their life is going to be more of a burden to them than their death would have been.' She paused. 'If you see what I mean.'

214

'I do see.' Margery watched Lenny lean forward and pick up her cup of tea. 'Somehow he survived, came home – and there was us lot wishing he was dead. Especially Teresa – his mother – she wished him dead more than any of us. I wished him dead as well, in the beginning, just because everyone else did, but then I was only five or something. After a time, though, I got used to him. The only person he didn't bother was his dad – Uncle Ted – and nobody had expected that. Ted did everything for him – everything – because his mum wouldn't go near him. We just had to teach ourselves about Tom because we never heard from the authorities again . . .'

Margery picked up her tea and took a few sips, not caring when she burnt her mouth, wondering why she'd said what she'd just said to Lenny. It was the first time she had talked to anybody about Tom. She looked around her, stunned, as though she had been talking in her sleep and somebody had just told her what she'd been talking about.

'Walking Wounded – my charity – do more grief coun-selling with families whose relatives come back alive than they do with families who have lost people in action. It's just not something people think about.'

Margery nodded, but wasn't really listening any more.

Then Lenny stood up suddenly. 'They're home.'

Margery watched her leave the room then stood up herself, half expecting to see the black Ford pull up and Tom step out. It took her a while – even with her face pressed up to the glass, staring straight at them – to make out Joe, Jessica and the children, wet from the sea and the rain, filing one by one into the porch.

Even after the front door was shut and the house became suddenly full of voices, Margery carried on standing at the window, waiting.

# 31

'When did you get home?' Joe asked Lenny, coming in from the rain.

'About an hour ago.'

'You all right, love?' he said, shaking the water off himself in the hallway.

Lenny nodded. 'Come on in – you're soaked, the lot of you.'

Jessica moved to kiss her, but then hesitated.

They drew away from each other, smiling awkwardly.

As Jessica disappeared with the children upstairs to the bathroom to dry them off, Joe grabbed hold of Lenny's wrist and pulled her towards him, kissing her quickly, instinctively.

Lenny pushed him away. 'You're wet.'

'So?' Joe pulled her towards him again, harder this time.

'Joe . . .'

He let her go, wiping at his face with his arm. 'So – what's up?'

'Nothing's up,' she said, turning her back on him and disappearing into the kitchen.

Jessica came back downstairs. 'Are the boys all right with

that old tin garage of yours up in the spare room?' she asked Joe.

'They're fine,' Joe said, putting the teapot on the table.

'Where's Margery?'

'In the lounge,' he said, turning round suddenly to Lenny. 'Will you just sit down – relax.'

He pulled out a chair and waited for Lenny to sit down.

'I'll get the cake out – you made cake, didn't you?'

'Just stay where you are – I can get the cake,' Joe ordered, irritable.

The next minute Lenny was up and already at the cupboard.

'Lenny . . .'

'You know I can't sit still, so what's the point?'

'We should go,' Jessica put in. 'I've got to get Margery and Findlay back, and IKEA are delivering that desk we bought for Ellie between six and eight.'

There was the sound of feet running down the stairs and Arthur calling out, 'Mum – can we have some cake?'

The kitchen was suddenly full of people and the sound of crockery being put on the table, and chairs being scraped across the floor.

Arthur's happy, Jessica thought, watching him climb up onto the chair and take a slice of cake – he's happy.

The thought of driving back to London in the rain – the thought of the maisonette – was unbearable.

People were staring at her. Had somebody said something she was meant to respond to? This was happening a lot at the moment. She didn't hear when people spoke to her – and she had to do better than this; had to pay attention or they'd think she wasn't coping, and then there'd be no end to anything.

Arthur was saying, 'Mum – can I have another piece?', losing patience with her.

Margery cut in with, 'Joe – you never made this your-self, did you?

And Jessica was about to say something when a dog started barking out in the garden again; only it wasn't barking this time so much as howling.

'Mum – can I have another piece? Mum?'

There was a pause in the air.

Ignoring Arthur, Jessica stood up suddenly. Crossing the kitchen, she opened the back door. Outside it was still raining, and the sky was orange-grey and full of storm.

The next minute Joe was beside her. 'Jess?'

'There's a dog out there – in all that rain.'

'Maybe one of the neighbour's,' Joe said without looking, putting his arm around her and trying to guide her back into the kitchen. 'Come on.'

She carried on staring out into the garden, thinking she saw movement under the pine trees. The yelping carried on. There was definitely a dog at the end of the garden.

Behind them, in the kitchen, Arthur and Findlay started singing, 'Who let the dogs out – who – who – who? Who let the dogs out?'

'It's getting wet,' Jessica said, 'I think it wants to come in.'

'Here,' Lenny said, pushing a plate of cake in her hand, suddenly standing as close to her as Joe was, flanking her. 'Hope I didn't cut it too big.'

Jessica stared at the cake then up at Lenny, who was staring at Joe.

'I think we should go now,' she said.

# 32

'You're tired,' Ellie said, slowly packing her books away.

'Yeah,' Robert agreed, peering into his bag, which was open on the desk in front of him.

The lights in the classroom were on because of the rain clouds that had been gathering all afternoon and were now breaking dismally against the windows. The lighting throughout the school was a great equaliser – everything looked ugly under it.

Robert even thought his hands looked ugly as he fastened the clasp on his bike saddlebag. He was sure he could smell sweat on himself as well – bad sweat – and wanted to check, but was aware of Ellie standing there.

He never used to sweat in class, but now he sweated like a novice. Or was it an age thing – the male menopause? He'd sweated through today because today was a bad day. He'd taught four minutes of a forty-minute Year 11 English class. The other thirty-six minutes had been spent fruitlessly trying to get Jerome's mobile off him to the rhythmic banality of 'gay wanker'. For some reason most of the students at Ellington felt that having a professional qualification was synonymous with being gay – he'd even heard two Year 9 boys referring to the rain that started when they left as gay. Strangely, the only member of the English department who didn't get called 'gay wanker' was the only member who was, in fact, gay – Les. Something that had always baffled Robert.

'Mr Hunter? I got you this.'

Robert looked up.

Ellie was standing directly in front of the desk holding a brown A5 envelope out towards him. She looked ill, and her mouth must have been dry because he could hear her tongue in it as she spoke.

'What's this?'

'It's for you – because you look so tired all the time.'

She looked as though she was about to run out of the room.

'Wait – stay.'

She paused, unsure. 'You want me to stay?'

He nodded, smiling – and opened the envelope.

Turning it towards the light, he made out some joss sticks at the bottom, something that glittered, and a packet of white stuff. He pulled the packet out.

'Bath salts,' Ellie said. 'They're jasmine scented – they help you unwind. They're really good those ones.'

He didn't know what to say, so just nodded and hoped he was still smiling. All he could now picture, as he continued to stare without seeing into the envelope, was Ellie Palmer in a bath somewhere. To do himself credit, he was aware that he didn't particularly want to picture this, but his mind was working on it anyway. He'd been teaching for over fifteen years and this was a road he'd never gone down before. He'd made himself think about it – especially when he first started teaching – but it never happened. The only time he ever came close was with a girl called Rachel, whom he'd taught the year Findlay was born. She came to every lesson, but he never heard her speak. She wasn't disruptive and the other kids seemed to leave her alone in this strange silence that everybody – for some reason – respected. Even when he asked her a direct question – which he did a lot the first term – she'd just shake her head at him, until he moved on.

He never did hear her speak and sometimes he'd catch himself looking at her in lessons and feel tears pricking uncontrollably at his eyes. He had no idea why. Rachel was the first time he'd ever felt helpless in a classroom.

He never taught her again and afterwards was able to rationalise it as postnatal stress. Kate had depression, and he had an uncontrollable urge to cry every time he laid eyes on a student called Rachel.

Aware now of Ellie's eyes on him, he shook some of the glitter stars into his hands and realised, horrified, that he was about to start crying now – at the sight of the purple, green and gold glitter stars in the palm of his hand. He stared help-lessly at Ellie and tried to choke back the first fast-rising sob, making a strange grunting noise instead.

'Mr Hunter?' Ellie looked frightened.

'I'm fine – fine.'

'D'you need to sit down or something?'

'I'm fine.' He took three deep breaths and tried to empty his mind. 'Thank you. That's very thoughtful of you,' he said, trying to level his voice.

The gift showed a burgeoning sensuality, and had been chosen to express her womanliness – but was essentially a child's gift. Maybe it was this realisation that had moved him to tears. The glitter stars and the joss sticks were chosen with the openness of a child's imagination and had moved him in the way Findlay's gifts of old cereal boxes moved him.

'Thank you,' he said again, calmly this time, tucking the envelope inside the saddlebag and getting into his fluores-cent yellow cycle jacket.

He waited for her to trail, uncertain, to the classroom door after him, then turned out the lights.

The darkness was immediately soothing.

'You shouldn't have spent your money on me.' He wasn't sure why he'd said that – he hadn't intended saying anything other than goodbye.

'It's fine,' she said, pleased, 'I've got a job now.'

'Where's that?'

'Film Nite.'

'The video shop?'

'It's funny, isn't it – people still call it that even though we don't stock videos any more.'

'Different generation,' Robert said, defensively.

'It's not that,' she said quickly, 'I mean – I think of it as a video shop still and I'm, like, sixteen.'

This took them abruptly to a dead end, and Robert was about to say his goodbyes and leave. In the darkened classroom, Ellie had become another child in uniform, one he was fonder of than others, but still a child in uniform passing through his life.

'Only a week left.'

That caught him out. 'A week?'

'Until exam leave starts.' She paused, awkward.

'You're right. I'd completely forgotten.'

She was blushing – even in the darkness he could see her blushes – and looked hurt, but didn't care that she looked hurt.

Kate's face used to look that naked, Robert thought, full of a sudden wonder at the memory of Kate's face ever having been that naked.

It was getting darker; the rain was going to get heavier.

'I think you're a brilliant teacher,' Ellie gulped.

Robert was suddenly overwhelmed with a sense of possibility he hadn't felt for a lot of years. A sense of possibility that – in his darker moments – he thought had gone forever. Whether that was to do with him – or Kate – he didn't know.

His hand strayed inadvertently from the light switch to the crown of Ellie's head. 'You're magnificent,' he mumbled without thinking. He wasn't sure whether he meant Ellie in particular or all children in general.

He moved his hand gently down her hair, aware of the lines of her skull, pronounced beneath the palm of his hand – and was about to kiss the crown of her head, where his hand had just been, when he caught sight of her face.

What had he done?

He jerked open the classroom door.

The corridor outside felt cold.

Ellie was staring at him – he could feel her entire being straining towards him, watching; waiting with the vulnerability of yearning.

How easy it would be, he thought, to slip into this. Adults didn't feel yearning like that – maybe for things past, as they got older, but never for things they didn't yet know.

Ellie wanted the kiss because she thought it would mean everything to her when in fact it would cost her nothing – and him everything – only she wasn't old enough to know this.

He pulled away.

He saw her realise that she wasn't going to get her kiss – and couldn't bear to look at her face.

'Have a good weekend . . .' He walked quickly away from her down the corridor towards the DT lab where he left his bike, and clipped the saddlebag to the pannier – Ellie's face growing clearer instead of diminishing. It wasn't until he started to wheel the bike towards the classroom door that he realised the tyres had been slashed and the front wheel completely buckled.

He sat on the stool and contemplated the bike for a while.

Jerome. The door opened then shut – he didn't see who it was. He left the DT lab and tried looking for Les.

In the main entrance hall, Simba the caretaker was up on some scaffolding with two of the groundsmen, trying to get a widescreen TV up onto the wall. How long was that going to stay up? Laptops walked out of the building on a daily basis – even a whiteboard had gone missing. The widescreen didn't stand a chance.

'Have you seen Les?' Robert called up.

Simba didn't respond. The TV was flickering on. After a few minutes the face of the Ellington Technology College's principal, Sandra Durrant, appeared on the screen. There she was in a canary yellow dress, surrounded by Sudanese orphans from her recent trip to the Sudan – the victims of AIDS and civil war.

Simba stood back, precariously near the edge of the scaffolding, pleased.

'I'm looking for Les,' Robert shouted up again. 'My bike's been vandalised.'

'There she is,' Simba cried ecstatically, ignoring Robert. 'Our prophetess.'

'Prophetess?'

Simba's love knew no bounds and now everyone was going to be exposed to Sandra Durrant's Sudanese crusade every time they walked through the main school entrance.

'Simba,' Robert yelled. 'My bike's totally buggered – some kid – I need to see Les – or the head.'

Simba smiled down warmly at him. 'Mrs Durrant's busy at the moment – she's leading a prayer meeting. We're all praying for you, Mr Hunter.'

'My bike . . .' Robert started to yell again.

'We'll pray for your bike as well. You'll see – everything will be better soon.'

Robert stalked away, so disorientated by the past forty-five minutes that he was almost on the verge of believing Simba – believing him enough to take a second look in the DT lab and make sure his bike hadn't received a miraculous makeover.

It hadn't.

He gave up and in the end found himself walking out of the school gates, past the Esso garage where a green Fiesta was parked, towards Elephant and Castle tube station where there was a cashpoint it was relatively safe to use. He'd have to get the bus home – and only hoped the incident with the bike meant Ellie had got a head start.

He cut his way through the underpass, resurfacing into the backdraught of fumes from the Thai Snack Shack; fumes that were rapidly filling the entrance to the tube station as well.

Feeling increasingly nauseous, he tried to withdraw twenty pounds from the tube station cashpoint, but the machine told him to refer to his bank. At first he thought he'd put the wrong PIN in, so he tried again. Then he checked the balance: £3,300 in debit. Christ, what was their overdraft? Realising he had no idea, he moved away from the cashpoint towards the *Evening Standard* seller and phoned 24-hour banking. After listening to nearly all of Barry Manilow's *Copacabana*, he spoke to a woman who told him that it was £3,000 and that they were £300 over their limit. They were going to incur bank charges. Would he be transferring funds into the account?

Funds from where?

'I thought the overdraft facility was around five hundred.'

'It was extended to three thousand a month ago.'

'A month ago?' He hung up, went back to the cashpoint and withdrew ten pounds using his credit card – then went to the kiosk and topped up his Oyster card.

He got to the bus stop just as the heavy rain started,

relieved at the absence of any Ellington uniforms – especially Ellie's. It was coming on to four o'clock; he should have missed most of the after-school run. The shelter he stood huddled in had been designed to provide as few potential surfaces for vandalism as possible while still staying erect, which meant it had no capacity for providing shelter from the sort of storm that was breaking now over the round-about at Elephant and Castle.

He thought about phoning Kate, but four o'clock in the afternoon wasn't the time to discuss their finances. Had she talked to him about increasing the overdraft and he just couldn't remember? There was so much he couldn't remember at the moment. Three buses pulled up and left. He hadn't been on a bus for ages. Finks, who taught maths and ran after-school football, had been crippled at a bus stop three months ago in a reprisal stabbing by an ex-Year 11 student who had been sacked from the job Finks had organised for him at Evans Cycles.

He eyed the only other people at the bus stop – trying not to do it nervously – a young white boy who was coughing nonstop over his pit-bull, and a middle-aged Jamaican woman in a Nationwide uniform. Distracted by the pit-bull next to him as it started to tense – its ears flattening and its head flicking nervously as it let out a low growl – he didn't hear the car horn, or see the green Fiesta that had been parked at the Esso garage outside school pull up and become semi-submerged in the kerb-side flash floods.

'I think that's for you,' the owner of the pit-bull said to him.

Robert peered through the rain at the green Fiesta he didn't recognise, and approached warily. The windows in the front were steamed up. Through the back window – past a sticker that read FUR COATS ARE WORN BY BEAUTIFUL ANIMALS AND UGLY HUMANS – he made out a child seat and the face of a young girl, maybe ten, staring at him, expressionless. She was wearing a pink anorak and had a McDonald's shake in her drink holder.

Then the Fiesta's front window was cranked down and there was Jerome's over-familiar face bouncing around in the open space where condensation and glass had been. Robert was aware of the little girl in the back staring at him still. He saw a pair of jeans and a ringed hand belonging to the driver, but not his face.

Then Jerome was pointing a gun at him, laughing.

Robert was staring at it, thinking the muzzle looked scratched.

The child in the back started laughing as well, and winding her window down.

The driver said, 'There's a bus coming – you done?' sounding bored, jumped up, irritated.

The gun disappeared from the window and Jerome fell back in his seat in hysterics, 'Your face, man – you get it?' he spluttered to the child in the back seat. The child had a mobile pointed at Robert. There were splats of dark pink on the front of her anorak where rain was falling on her through the open window.

Then the car stalled.

'Shit,' the driver yelled as the bus started to plough through the roadside flood, bearing down on them.

'Shit,' Jerome echoed, leaning forward in his seat, the hand holding the gun resting on the dashboard. 'Come on, man – fuck this,' he yelled, banging on the steering wheel.

'You . . .' the man yelled back as the car came to life and jerked away from the kerb, the girl filming the bus now on the mobile she was holding, until a hand pulled her back into the car.

The only thing Robert was aware of was being covered

in water – suddenly. It was running down over his hands, and his trousers were plastered along the fronts of his legs.

The bus doors opened in front of him.

The woman in the Nationwide uniform pushed past him and he saw the man with the pit-bull get on halfway up the bus so he wouldn't have to pay his fare.

Robert got onto the crowded bus and found a space near the bottom of the stairs where he was in everybody's way. At the next stop the driver let on more wet people and he was shunted up the aisles of the bus by a woman panting, with water steaming off her hair over her face, until he yelled at her, suddenly, 'What the fuck is your problem?' A man's voice, close by said, 'Hey – she's only trying to get home like everybody else.'

A couple of people stared at him for a while then he was forgotten. Jerome had pulled a gun on him. Jerome had vandalised his bicycle and known he would have to get the bus home instead. Jerome had been watching him. He saw East Street Market packing up through windows running with rain, and Charlie Chaplin's birthplace. The bus's wheels slid on tarmac made greasy with rain as the driver swerved to avoid the rush-hour swell of people slopping into the road. Then they got stuck in traffic and somebody close by smelt so stale and helpless that Robert thought he was going to vomit, and the more he thought about how horrific it would be to vomit on a packed rush-hour bus, the more his insides lurched, until he shoved his way to the doors at the next stop, just as they were closing; got temporarily stuck then squeezed himself out, just about managing to keep his balance on the patch of pavement outside Bagel King, where an alcoholic dressed in a suit was swaying carelessly and waving. Was the man waving at him?

He turned away, breathing heavily, his eyes flickering every-where – on the alert for anything resembling a green Fiesta.

The bus slid away and on the roof of a furniture shop on the other side of the road, he saw a sodden wet child hurling rocks at the bus he'd just got off as it pulled away – it was one of the Skinner twins from his tutor group. Without thinking, he started to walk.

Up the rest of Walworth Road to Camberwell, past King's, the Maudsley and the Salvation Army building to the top of Denmark Hill, where he watched the rain raining on the vale of SE22 spread out below. It took him fifty minutes, and every car that passed was a green Fiesta carrying Jerome and the child in the pink anorak. Every car – even when it slid past and turned out to be a silver Mercedes or a white BT van.

He stood in the rain, trying to work out if he'd known – as soon as the green Fiesta pulled up at the kerb – that it would be Jerome. And if that was the case – if he had known instinctively that Jerome would be inside the car – why had he gone ahead and walked right up to it, with something strangely close to relief?

He stood at the traffic lights as they changed three times. He was soaked, and the water running down onto his wrists and hands and face had grit in it from the road. Somewhere down there at the bottom of the hill was his house, his marriage, his children.

A car pulled up beside him.

'It's Robert,' Margery yelled suddenly, from the back of the car.

'What?' Jessica turned her head round as the lights changed to red.

'Robert – there!' Margery paused. 'He's soaked.'

The traffic lights changed to green and Jessica made a right-hand turn she wasn't meant to, pulling up on the kerb beside Robert Hunter, standing motionless in his fluorescent yellow cycle jacket, holding a saddlebag, the rain running off him.

Margery wound her window down, panting with the effort. 'Robert,' she called out. 'Robert?'

Robert turned round slowly, looking scared, the water running over his eyes so that he couldn't open them properly. He had to keep his mouth open in order to breath, his nostrils were so full of water.

He stood on the pavement, staring at them, until Jessica got out of the car.

'Robert,' she said loudly above the roar of the rain and traffic.

He carried on staring at her, not recognising her.

In the back of the car, Findlay and Margery had fallen silent, watching Robert through the window, broken up in the rainwater streaking over the glass.

'Robert,' Jessica said again. 'You didn't have an accident, did you? What happened to your bike?'

This time he looked down at himself then back at her.

She opened the passenger door, took his saddlebag from him and – pulling gently on the sleeve of his sodden cycle jacket – guided him into the seat.

She shut the door on him and stood holding the saddlebag for a moment before putting it in the boot and getting back into the car herself.

She was soaked now as well, but not as soaked as Robert, who was staring at his hands, shaking uncontrollably in his lap.

'We went in a boat,' Findlay said to his dad, suddenly excited at the memory of the hour he'd spent afloat in a dinghy. 'We went in a boat in the sea.'

'Did you?' Margery said, looking worried.

But Findlay didn't want to talk to Margery, it was his father he wanted to talk to because Margery didn't know anything about boats or the sea.

230

'Can we get a boat?' he appealed to Robert.

Robert was still staring at his hands shaking uncontrollably in his lap.

Jessica put the car into gear and they drove down the hill towards Prendergast Road.

# 33

'You want me to come in?' Jessica said when they pulled up outside No. 22.

Margery scanned the road for the Audi, but couldn't see it. 'I don't think Kate's home yet . . .'

'I'll come in,' Jessica said.

Margery nodded, relieved.

She let them all into No. 22, running as fast as she could between car and house, Arthur and Findlay squealing behind her.

Robert didn't move.

So Jessica went round and opened the passenger door and stood in the rain, waiting.

At last, confused, he got slowly out of the car and made his way to the front door, followed by Jessica carrying his saddlebag – and Findlay's rucksack.

Once indoors, he stood with the water running off him onto the hallway's chequered lino so that he slid and squeaked his way aimlessly to the kitchen.

Jessica followed, dropping his saddlebag next to the BIN in the utility room. She watched him move to the middle of the room where he emptied his pockets onto the kitchen TABLE.

This wasn't something he usually did, but he did it tonight. Next, he took off his jacket, letting it drop to the floor. Then he dried his face on a tea towel that had burn marks on it from the gas hob. He stood there for a while with it pressed against his face before flinging it on top of the discarded coat and adding his socks and trousers to the pile.

'Robert, love,' Margery said, mortified.

Robert looked at her slowly. 'I thought he was going to shoot me.'

'Who?' Jessica asked from the doorway.

'Jerome,' he said, suddenly aware of her for the first time.

'Jerome?' Jessica repeated.

Robert nodded.

'Who's Jerome?' Margery asked.

Ignoring this, Robert said, 'He didn't shoot – he just levelled it at me and . . .'

He let out a solitary sob, but no tears came. Instead, his hands began to shake again and he stared at them, fascinated, as he started to undo the buttons on his shirt.

'I need a shower.'

'A shower would be good,' Jessica agreed. Then, gently, 'Have you phoned anybody at the school? The police? D'you want me to phone?'

'I need a shower,' Robert said again.

'Robert,' she insisted, still gentle, 'you have to tell somebody.'

'I'm telling you.' He smiled awkwardly, letting his arms drop to his sides. Staring at a crack on the wall by the FRIDGE, he took a few deep breaths and tried again, but the buttons on his shirt seemed to be getting smaller and smaller until he could barely get hold of them with his fingertips, let alone actually undo them.

'Here,' Jessica said, getting frustrated watching him, and starting to undo the buttons as the doorbell rang.

Jessica's hands fell automatically to her sides as Margery pushed past them both and went to answer the door.

'Jessica!' Margery called out, unsure.

Jessica left Robert and went out into the hallway.

It was the Ocado man, with the Hunter's weekly shop beside him, the rain pounding on the plastic bags.

'Mrs Hunter?' he said, genuinely confused. Then his eyes slid past her, behind her.

Jessica turned round.

Robert had followed her into the hallway.

Margery had shuffled to the coat rack and was searching for something to cover Robert with, mumbling to herself.

Robert followed the Ocado man's eyes and looked down at himself. 'I was about to shower.'

The Ocado man didn't look convinced.

Robert wasn't convinced either. It suddenly struck him that his life was nothing more than a series of explanations – an attempt to make himself more digestible to others, and he was suddenly, profoundly, tired of it.

He didn't – he realised – particularly mind the fact that he was standing semi-naked in his hallway, but he could see from the man's face that he was waiting for an explanation . . . reassurance. Well, he was tired of reassuring people.

He didn't want to reassure this man, who was – for some inexplicable reason – standing on his doorstep.

What Robert wanted – felt a sudden uncontrollable urge to do – was stand there on his doorstep in the rain and masturbate over them.

In fact – if it wasn't for Margery and Jessica in the hallway behind him – he wasn't entirely sure he would have been able to stop himself.

What was happening to him?

The other day at school, he'd only just managed to stop

himself urinating in the drinking fountain.

The Ocado man was focusing intently on Robert's face, terrified of his eyes straying inadvertently downwards.

'What are you doing here?' Robert said at last.

'Delivering your groceries,' the man replied.

'Just put them in the hallway,' Jessica said, coming forwards.

The man hurriedly put the bags inside the front door, by Robert's feet, got Jessica to sign for them – and walked back to the gate, trampling one of the sunflowers.

Robert gave a regal wave, and started to laugh.

He carried on standing there after the van had pulled away – until Findlay came to find him.

'Dad?'

'It's still raining.'

Findlay wasn't that interested in the rain. 'Look,' he said suddenly.

'Where?'

'Up there.'

Robert looked up at the house opposite and there was a woman standing at the window, holding up a sign. Robert tried to read it, but couldn't make out what it said because of the rain.

Findlay waved at her, but she didn't wave back.

'Why isn't she waving?'

For some reason Robert suddenly found it funny – the idea of Findlay waving at the woman standing motionless with the sign – and started to laugh again.

Robert's inane laughter finally enabled Margery and Jessica to take over. With a brief glance up at the woman in the window of No. 21, Jessica got him indoors and Margery got him into a shower.

Ten minutes after that, Jessica and Arthur left No. 22 Prendergast Road.

'What happened to Findlay's dad?' Arthur asked as they got back in the car.

'I don't know – I think he's sad,' Jessica said.

'Um,' Arthur agreed.

# 34

'Robert? Robert?' Kate yelled from the foot of the stairs.

She'd just got back from Swim with Baby to find the house in darkness – Margery would only turn the lights on in the room she was using. There were four switches on the wall and she jabbed each one in rapid succession until she found the one for the upstairs landing – just as Robert stumbled out of their bedroom with his arm over his face.

'Shit – that you, Kate?'

'I could do with some help down here.'

Blinking and yawning, Robert – who had been fast asleep until about twenty seconds ago – slipped downstairs only semi-conscious, and heavily dependent on the banister.

'Jessica just phoned me – said something about a kid at school shooting at you or something.' Her eyes scanned his body.

When Robert didn't respond, she said, 'Have you phoned the police – spoken to the school?' She broke off, distracted by the sound of Margery opening cupboards in the kitchen. 'Robert?' she said, turning back to him.

'What?'

'Well – are you okay – or . . . ?'

'I'm fine.'

'And you're going to sort this out,' she prompted him.

'I'm going to sort this out,' he repeated automatically.

'Jessica sounded really worried.' Kate broke off, now convinced she could hear Margery opening a packet of something. Margery and Findlay were whispering together; she was sure they were whispering, which meant that Margery was giving him something to eat that she shouldn't be.

'I'll sort it out.' Robert yawned.

'And now she's going to have to rearrange the viewing with Ros.' Kate shrugged, suddenly irritable, and – turning her back on him – went into the kitchen.

Margery and Findlay were sitting at the kitchen TABLE together, a box of doughnuts between them. When he saw Kate, he finished licking the jam from his wrist and tried to finish the doughnut as quickly as he could before she tried to take it off him.

'He said he was hungry,' Margery said.

'You could have had some Weetabix,' Kate said to Findlay, ignoring Margery.

'She gave them to me,' he mumbled with difficulty, his cheek distended with doughnut he hadn't got round to swallowing.

'Today's their best-before date,' Margery added. 'It's a waste.'

'Can I have another one?' Findlay asked, his mouth still full.

'No,' Kate shouted, suddenly picking up the box of doughnuts and throwing them in the BIN. 'No you bloody well can't.'

Findlay finished his mouthful awkwardly, looking scared.

'I wouldn't of minded one,' Margery said sullenly. 'And Robert—'

'Robert doesn't like doughnuts.'

'Robert's always liked doughnuts,' Margery insisted.

'Robert hates doughnuts,' Kate yelled.

'But he eats them . . .'

'Because you keep on bloody well buying them.'

'For Christ's sake, Kate,' Robert said, appearing in the kitchen doorway. 'What is this?'

Kate rounded on him, 'Tell her you don't like doughnuts.'

'Fuck the doughnuts,' he shouted suddenly, walking out of the kitchen and heading for the front door.

It had gone quiet in the house behind him and – without thinking – he stepped out into the front garden and looked up, enjoying the sensation of rain on his skin.

A woman coming home from work under a Price Waterhouse Coopers umbrella glanced at him then looked quickly away.

A dog tried to urinate against the trunk of the rowan tree on the pavement outside No. 22, but the owner, after a covert look at Robert, pulled on the lead and carried on walking.

Then Robert heard the muffled sound of a child crying somewhere nearby.

Flo, he thought instinctively, following the sound to where the black Audi was parked, oblivious to the wet pavement beneath his bare feet.

Through the window he saw Flo still strapped in her car seat, hysterical.

'It's okay, it's okay,' he said, his hands on the glass, trying to calm her down.

He ran back to the house. 'The car keys,' he said, breathless.

Kate was carrying the shopping from the hallway to kitchen. 'Why didn't you tell him to bring it through – they're meant to bring it through. You're wet,' she added, looking at him.

'Just give me the fucking car keys.'

'Robert—'

'Flo's in the car, Kate; you left our daughter outside in the fucking car.'

Findlay appeared suddenly in the kitchen doorway, looking at them both, terrified.

Kate stood staring at Robert, who picked up her handbag from the bottom stair and virtually pulled it apart looking for the car keys.

'I'm sorry, Dad – I'm really, really sorry,' Findlay was saying, standing behind Robert.

Ignoring him, Robert ran back outside with the car keys. Findlay followed.

'Dad . . .'

'Go back inside,' Robert said at the gate. 'You haven't got any shoes on.'

'Neither have you.'

The rain was getting heavier again.

Robert opened the back door of the car.

'I'm sorry, Dad,' Findlay started again, shouting this time to make himself heard above Flo's wailing and the torrential rain. 'I didn't check.'

'Finn, it's not for you to check,' Robert shouted back. 'It's okay – just go inside.'

Findlay didn't move.

He stood on the pavement and watched Robert pick up Flo.

'She smells of sick.'

'Yes, she's been a bit sick – probably because she was crying so much.'

'Should we give her a bath?' Findlay yelled.

'Let's just get inside out of the rain – and watch out for glass on the pavement.'

Robert locked up the car again and they made a run for it.

240

As they got to the front door, the rain turned to hail, smashing down on the cars so heavily it triggered off at least two alarms.

'How is she?' Margery said as he pushed past her with Flo in his arms.

'I'll run the bath,' Findlay announced, disappearing upstairs.

'I need a towel,' Robert said to Margery. When Margery didn't move, he said, 'A towel,' again, loudly this time.

Margery shuffled off down the hallway and came back with the hand towel from the downstairs loo.

Robert wiped the rain from Flo's face then handed her to Margery while he dried himself. The towel was wet before he even attempted to dry his hair. He threw it on the floor and took Flo from Margery, holding her close. 'Didn't you realise Flo wasn't here indoors?' Robert said, finally managing to calm his daughter down.

'I just presumed Kate—'

'Well, you presumed wrong – she was in the car.'

'Why's it my fault?' Margery said, upset.

She was right. It wasn't her fault – why take it out on her? 'Mum, I'm sorry.' Robert stared at her through the water still streaming off his hair and over his face, blinking rapidly. 'Where's Kate?' he said at last.

'Upstairs.' Making the most of his apology, Margery caught hold suddenly of his arm. 'You've got to do something about this – she needs to see someone, Robert.'

Robert pulled away, towards the stairs.

'Robert – are you listening to me? Robert—'

'I heard you,' he said to Margery before disappearing upstairs with Flo.

# 35

No. 283 Prendergast Road was empty. Ellie had a shift at
Film Nite and IKEA were meant to be delivering a desk
some time after six. Jessica put Arthur to bed with Burke,
then she phoned Kate, who was just getting into her car at
the leisure centre.

'Kate? It's Jessica – no, we got back almost an hour ago.
Margery was fine – really, she was fine. It's about Robert . . .'

'Robert?' Kate snapped, clipping Flo into her car seat.

'One of the kids at school pulled a gun on him.'

'A gun?'

'He's not in hospital or anything – nothing was fired –
but he's pretty shaken up.'

'Shit – that's all we need.'

Jessica wasn't sure what to say.

'Wait – how do you know all this?'

'We passed him in the car, at the top of Champion Hill.'
Jessica saw Robert again, standing with his saddlebag in the
rain.

'On his bike?'

'No, he was walking.'

'Robert was walking?'

'Something had happened to his bike. I don't know – he was kind of in pieces, Kate.'

'In pieces?'

Kate sounded outraged.

'He was shot at,' Jessica said again.

'I'd better get home – see what's going on.'

After Kate called off, Jessica went upstairs to take a shower. Standing under the jets of water made meagre by the fact that a lot of holes in the shower head had been blocked with lime-scale, she couldn't get the image of Robert standing by the bin in the kitchen at No. 22, soaked through, out of her mind – or the way his hands shook as he tried to undo the buttons on his shirt. Thinking about this, she couldn't shake the feeling that the worst was yet to come. She wanted to phone Kate back and warn her – but what it was she wanted to warn her of, she couldn't say.

She got out of the shower, changed and went downstairs to wait for the IKEA delivery. While waiting, she wandered through the maisonette, picking up stray toys and other daytime debris, redistributing it rather than tidying it away. A remote controlled T-Rex that needed new batteries made it from the floor to the sofa; a pile of ironing was moved from one scuffed dining chair to another scuffed dining chair. It was pointless, but gave her a certain amount of satisfaction. She was whistling as she went through to the kitchen, where she stared for a while at the now almost completely dead chrysanthemum. In a fit of generosity she poured the remains of some old tea over it then dropped the cup – which had been bought by Grandma Belle in Brighton twenty years ago and had JESSICA written across it – into a basin of water now cold and greasy.

She tried phoning Ellie, but Ellie didn't answer, and she was just taking a bottle of wine out of the fridge when the doorbell rang.

'Hey.' The man in IKEA uniform standing in the open

doorway grinned. 'Delivery?' He stared down at her bare feet then up again. 'Jessica Palmer?'

'That's me,' she said automatically.

'You up there?' He nodded at the flight of steps.

'Yes – up there.'

He grinned again then walked back to the lorry.

Another man appeared, older than the first. 'We can't park here – we're blocking the road.'

'Well, this one's down for construction – we're not going to be ready for maybe another half-hour.'

'What's the time now?'

'Coming onto seven.'

Where's the other delivery?'

'About a mile away.'

They hauled a large box out of the back of the lorry and stood it upright on the pavement.

'Look, help me carry this up the stairs,' the younger one said, 'then go deliver the other stuff and come back.'

Jessica followed the two men upstairs.

'Where's this for?'

'Second floor.'

The older man grunted. 'Whereabouts?' he called out, breathless and irritable from the landing.

'Just here on the right,' Jessica said.

'No problem,' the younger one said, backing into Ellie's room.

They put the box in the middle of the floor.

'I'll be back in about forty minutes,' the other man said, ignoring Jessica and running back downstairs, slamming shut the door to the maisonette.

'Sorry about that – work offends him,' the man said as he knelt down on the floor. 'You couldn't flip a light on, could you? Cheers.'

She switched on the spotlight that was on Ellie's desk,

244

and watched it catch the blade of the man's Stanley knife as he started to open the packaging.

'This your daughter's room?' he said, quietly scanning it.

Jessica scanned it as well – and nodded.

'What's she want another desk for?'

'She's about to start her GCSEs.'

He didn't say anything to this, suddenly preoccupied with the construction of the new desk.

'Can I get you something to drink?' she said after a while.

'No, I'm fine.'

She waited a little longer, then swung slowly out the room and went back downstairs and into the kitchen, unsure what to do.

From upstairs there came the odd sound, muffled by carpet.

She went through to the lounge diner and picked up a copy of *CHAT* from the coffee table – how the hell had that got there? Sitting on the edge of the sofa, she skim-read '*So bullied I carved my own face off*' and had just started scanning an article on the next page about paraplegic porn – with pictures – when she heard the IKEA man calling out quietly, 'Hello?'

She went to the foot of the stairs.

'You want to tell me where you want this?'

She went upstairs, tucking her still-wet hair behind her ears, and followed him into Ellie's room. 'That's great,' she said, pleased at the sight of the new MDF desk that she and Ellie had chosen on the trip to IKEA together. That had been a good day. Ellie had been cooperative and they had managed to buy the desk without having a fight. It was the first piece of furniture she'd bought since Peter's death.

They stood contemplating the two desks.

'What about seeing if we can get the old one along that wall there, then we could put the new one in the space between the bed and where the old desk is going.'

'That would work,' Jessica said, pleased.

'It's not part of the service,' the man carried on. 'I'm just offering. No trouble to me.' He eyed her, briefly.

Jessica took the other side of the desk and they spun it round so that it ran along the wall opposite Ellie's bed.

Jessica found herself smiling at him when it was done.

Smiling back, he moved over to the new desk.

'It looks great,' she said with feeling when it was done.

'Yeah,' the man agreed, pleased. 'She's got a sort of L-shaped workstation now.' He paused. 'How old's your daughter?'

'Sixteen.'

He whistled. 'Difficult age, huh?'

'Yeah . . .' Jessica shrugged, aware that the man was watching her. She made a point of trying to look away, but ended up staring at his hands, which were holding the edges of the newly constructed desk.

He stood up, removing his hands, and then she knew what was going to happen next – was suddenly overwhelmed by the feeling that she couldn't stop it even if she wanted to.

'You smell nice.'

'What?' she said, laughing nervously.

'I said, you smell nice.' He was standing next to her, moving his nose over her hair and down her neck. The next minute they were kissing and his hand was sliding down her jeans. Then he pulled her gently down onto the floor.

She tried to push herself up on her elbows to meet him halfway and found herself staring momentarily at the picture of him on his ID badge – but in the end just let herself fall back onto the carpet as random objects crossed her line of vision, uncatalogued: a diary and a pink slipper under Ellie's bed – where was the other one? A Polish dictionary – that was new. Was Ellie teaching herself Polish? The headphones from Peter's old Walkman hanging down the side of the bed . . . then she shut her eyes.

Afterwards they lay staring up at the lumpy contours of a

246

badly plastered ceiling, unconvincingly covered in lining paper, with Jessica wondering what the brown stains were and if water was getting in through the roof – and not caring much. Then it finally dawned on her . . . she had just had unprotected sex with the IKEA delivery man – in Ellie's bedroom.

She turned to face him – he was smiling at her, still smiling. It felt like he'd done nothing but smile at her since she'd answered the door however long ago it was.

'When are your kids home?'

'Kids? How did you know I had more than one?'

'I saw the toys – downstairs.'

'Oh – he's in bed, and the other one – she'll be back soon.'

Neither of them moved.

'What happened to you?' he asked after a while, rolling over to look at her.

Without hesitation, she said, 'My husband died – three years ago.'

'Shit . . . I'm sorry.' He paused. 'You don't want to talk about it.'

'There's nothing to talk about. It's been hell. What happened to you?'

'Nothing.' He sighed. 'I took an arts degree at Manchester and didn't know what to do after graduation so went to Brazil to work for this charity, playing football with street children.'

She watched him, interested. 'And now?'

'Now I'm doing this and just sort of waiting.'

'For what?'

'No idea.' He rolled away from her, staring up at the ceiling again.

'It was a car accident,' she said suddenly. 'We were both in the car at the time, coming down Park Lane from Marble Arch. We'd been Christmas shopping on Oxford Street. I survived.' She paused. 'And I don't know why. One minute you're living your life just like everybody else . . . some days are good; some are bad. Then – BANG – you're on the outside with this life you don't want and you're like nobody else you know.'

'Did you love him?'

She turned onto her side, watching him, then ran her forefinger slowly down his chest. 'I think about that all the time – and I don't know any more.'

'You don't remember – or you don't know?'

'I don't know.' She laid her hand flat on his belly. 'And I don't know how what just happened – happened.'

Propping himself up on his elbow, he looked down at her and said, 'Didn't Home Delivery tell you about the flat-pack fuck?'

'That's horrible.' She pushed him over, laughing.

'It costs extra.'

'Fuck off.'

He sat up, looking around for his shirt.

'How much of a pushover was I – compared to the others?'

Abandoning the search for his shirt, he kissed her suddenly on the forehead. 'You're beautiful.'

'How old are you?' she asked.

'Twenty-eight.'

She sat up on her elbows. 'Shit.'

'What?'

'That's young.'

'So?'

He didn't ask her how old she was.

'Don't . . .'

'What?'

'Get dressed,' she said.

He looked at her for a moment, then crawled across the carpet to where she was still lying. They'd just started kissing again when the buzzer went.

Jessica groaned as he rolled quickly away from her. 'That was getting good.'

The buzzer went again.

'Where are you going?' she said, watching him get to his feet.

'That'll be Dave back with the lorry.'

'Or one of my kids.'

He paused. 'You want to get it, then?'

She shook her head. 'No.'

'You want me to get it?'

'Yeah – I do.'

A second's hesitation then he left the room, buttoning up his shirt and pushing it back into his trousers.

He'd gone. How nice to be summoned by the outside world and for there to be someone else to take the call.

She let go of the moment and started to get dressed herself, able to smell him on her as she pushed legs into jeans and arms into a sweatshirt. She tried to flatten her hair out, which had been wet when they'd started to make love, but had to give up.

Then she heard him running back up the stairs.

'It's Dave.'

She nodded. 'Your feet are bare.'

His face broke suddenly into a smile, but his earlier poise and assurance were gone, and Jessica felt suddenly much older.

She let him go and didn't go down until she heard the door to the maisonette slam shut.

She stood in the doorway, listening to the lorry outside pull away, staring vacantly at a wire hanging from the intercom. She'd just had unprotected sex with the IKEA delivery man. What the hell was going on? And why did she feel like phoning Robert Hunter and telling him?

# 36

At No. 236, Harriet stood at the front window with Phoebe over her shoulder, swaying rhythmically from side to side while rubbing her baby's back. She'd arranged for Evie's au pair, Martina, to baby-sit tonight, and was taking Miles out to The Phoenix. They'd had it planned for weeks.

On the other side of the wall, she heard the dull whine of Casper's remote-control 4x4 and the repetitive thud of it hitting the skirting board prior to the back-flip it was programmed to do.

Outside the rain was getting heavier again, making it dark much earlier than usual. It was barely seven and twilight already, but tonight the rain and the dark didn't make her claustrophobic; tonight they made her feel safe. The cars had their headlights on already and there was a tailback down Prendergast Road, as there was most nights at about this time when it served as a shortcut onto the South Circular. It took her a while to realise that the car at the end of the tailback was their car. There were an increasing number of Range Rovers in the postcode, but the black one at the back of the queue was definitely theirs

– not least because Miles was sitting behind the wheel. She couldn't see him clearly because of the rain on the windows of the house and car, but she knew instinctively it was him.

'Daddy's home,' she mumbled contentedly to Phoebe.

Then she heard Casper's voice behind her and was about to tell him that Daddy was home but Casper was talking to her, asking her why it was so dark in the lounge.

She hadn't realised how dark it was until he mentioned it, and switched on the lights so that the room was suddenly flooded.

'Casper!' she screamed.

Anybody would be able to see in. Terrorists . . . child abductors.

As she hauled the curtains across the windows, she thought Miles turned to look at her. He probably hadn't seen her before – because of the rain and the darkness. She paused for a moment, despite her panic, expecting to see the car reverse into the parking space outside the front of the house – Harriet liked it when there was a space outside the front of the house; took it as a good omen – only he didn't. The Range Rover slid suddenly forwards out of sight and more cars joined the end of the queue. Harriet slowly finished shutting the curtains.

She was sure that was their car; sure it was Miles behind the wheel. Why hadn't he stopped?

'What's that?' Casper was speaking to her. She'd been practising face painting on him ready for the street party and today he was a butterfly. They'd had a fight over it. He didn't mind her doing Spiderman or Batman, but he did mind the butterfly.

'I said,' Casper said, sounding impatient, 'where was I before I was Casper?'

Harriet stared at her son, uncomprehending.

Why did he ask such things? She worried about Casper; had a feeling she'd always worry about Casper.

Staring at his mother, he said, 'Okay – so when will Martina be here?'

'Soon,' she said. 'Soon.'

# 37

Miles had fully intended parking in the space outside the front of the house. He'd seen the traffic on Prendergast Road, come to a halt and – after several seconds – realised he had come to a halt outside *his* house. Excited, he saw that there was a parking space directly in front of the house. He wasn't ashamed of his excitement. Life's small pleasures were something no honest man or woman should be ashamed of. In fact, most people were unaware of just how often small pleasures – such as a parking spot just where you wanted a parking spot – were called upon to act as life's ballast tanks.

Only tonight, for the first time, his excitement over finding a parking space in such close proximity to the house felt wrong. The front of the house was dark, the curtains drawn back. Then the lights went on suddenly, illuminating Harriet standing at the window looking out; looking straight at him, in fact.

This was the moment when he waved and parked the car.

Only tonight he didn't. Tonight, he found himself nudging it into first and carrying on up the road, staying close to the rear lights of the car in front. He followed the flow of traffic right up to the top end of Prendergast Road, where the crossroads were.

He stopped outside the florist's.

He did it without thinking.

He ran his finger round the steering wheel and peered up at Jessica Palmer's maisonette, whose curtains looked as though they'd never been drawn. The lights were on.

Turning off the engine, he got out of the car and went into the florist's.

Once in the shop, he wavered, uncertain. He had never bought flowers like this before. He bought them when occasion demanded it – like the bouquet he had delivered to the hospital after Phoebe was born; or the bouquets he came home with after Harriet agreed to have a bout of biannual sex with him – but never like this.

A young girl with bad skin, wearing an apron, emerged from the back of the shop, bringing marijuana fumes with her.

'Can I help you?'

'Yeah, I need . . . something.' Miles swung round, taking in the buckets of rain-drenched flowers the girl had just bought in. She had been left to shut up shop on her own and was hoping to do it early.

'Something,' Miles said again, nervously. 'A gift.'

'A bouquet?' the girl asked, in a panic.

'No, not a bouquet.'

'Who's it for?'

Miles didn't answer. He was thinking of a book he'd read a lot of years ago. He was no reader; it must have been at school. But he did remember a man in the book who gave a woman he wasn't meant to flowers. Yellow roses. He couldn't remember either of the characters' names, but he remembered the yellow roses – and that they had been just the right thing.

254

The girl was watching him. He made her nervous.

'Yellow roses.'

'What's that?'

'I want yellow roses,' he said, suddenly sure of this.

The girl shuffled round the shop. 'I got yellow freesias,' she said. 'I'll check out the back.'

When she reappeared, she said, 'I've got some – they're not great, but . . .' She sounded excited, the idea of the importance of there being yellow roses in the shop gaining momentum with her. 'How many bunches?'

'Bring what you've got.'

She emerged from the back of the shop with her arms full. 'Six bunches?'

He nodded and watched her wrap them.

Outside on the pavement, away from the shop's orange strip lighting, the yellow roses came into their own.

Behind him, he heard the florist's door being locked. He turned around and the girl was at the door staring at him.

The rain was getting heavier and for some reason this pleased him.

The next minute, before he had time to think about it, he was ringing on Jessica Palmer's old intercom. He rang twice, but there was no reply.

Then he heard feet on the stairs, making the canopy above the florist's shop window rattle.

A light went on behind the frosted glass and the door opened.

Jessica peered out at him as he took in the stained brown carpet and crumpled pile of junk mail behind the door.

'Yellow roses,' he mumbled, suddenly afraid.

Jessica was staring at him as though she'd been expecting somebody else and couldn't quite believe it was him standing there. 'Miles? Did somebody give you those?'

He stared back at her, confused. Maybe somebody had

given them to him. No, he remembered buying them. 'I bought them,' he insisted. 'Just now. For you,' he added, pushing them towards her.

'For me?' Jessica made no attempt to take the flowers. 'But, Miles – why?'

'I had to,' he said, automatically. 'Please take them.'

'I can't take them. I'm sorry, Miles.'

She shook her head awkwardly then shut the door.

Her silhouette vanished from behind the door as he heard her make her way back upstairs.

He waited in the car as the rain turned to hail, loud on the car, forming a ridge along the bottom of the windscreen. The door to No. 283 remained shut and nobody appeared at any of the upstairs windows. He dialled Jessica's mobile number but she didn't answer.

Unsure what it was he had been expecting, he put the car into gear and drove back down Prendergast Road, home – seriously doubting whether he had just bought six bunches of yellow roses for Jessica Palmer or if he had just imagined the whole thing.

Harriet was upstairs running a bath when Miles came in, and she didn't hear him until she turned the taps off.

Casper went running down to see him, but she stayed in the bathroom and finished getting Phoebe undressed.

They came back upstairs together, Casper talking quickly, giving Miles the highlights from his day in no particular chronological order.

Miles didn't comment on the fact that his son's face was painted with a butterfly. Had he even noticed?

Harriet was putting Phoebe in the bath and didn't turn round.

Casper carried on talking about elastic bands.

Miles didn't say anything.

Two of the bulbs in the bathroom had blown that week and Harriet kept forgetting to buy replacements. In the partial lighting, Miles cast a long shadow across the bath and up the tiled wall opposite.

'You're wet,' she said.

'It's hailing out there.'

'Is it?' She wanted to take a look out of the window, but couldn't move because she was supporting Phoebe's head to prevent her from drowning.

'I got caught – running from the car.'

It *was* their car she'd seen driving past the house earlier; she knew it was. If only he'd come back with flowers: flowers would have explained the drive-by.

'Harriet . . .'

She turned round. He was watching her.

'We just don't work. We're all wrong together.'

He was calm as he said it.

Phoebe's eyes were bulging, irate, as she jerked about in the water. Casper was still babbling about the elastic bands.

Harriet had, without being particularly conscious of it, been bracing herself for something like this. As a couple, they never rowed. Miles rarely had explosions of anger or frustration. What he did have were these strange implosions – on average, twice a year – where he said impossible, apocalyptically destructive things. Like just now.

The last time he'd had one of his implosions was when she told him she was pregnant with Phoebe and he told her he wanted her to have an abortion.

She dealt with this one as she dealt with all of them – by smiling blankly at him as though he'd just told her, in Mongolian, that he had herpes. It was a method that had proved effective in the past – as effective as a surgery-free lobotomy could be, anyway.

'We've got a reservation at The Phoenix tonight. Martina's

coming round in about half an hour. Once I've got Phoebe settled, you can sort Casper out for me so I can get ready.' She waited.

Miles, who had been looking at himself in the medicine cabinet's mirror doors, turned to face her again.

A minute later, he sighed. 'Okay.'

'And there's something we need to talk about . . .'

Hope flared up briefly in Miles.

'We can't tell Admissions I'm seeking refuge from you . . . your brutality, at Number eight Beulah Hill.'

'We can't?'

Harriet shook her head. 'Mr Jackson has a niece.'

'A niece?'

'Jade Jackson is Mr Jackson's niece.' Harriet paused. 'Jade Jackson is Head of Admissions for all primary schools in the borough.' She tried to keep her arm steady so that Phoebe remained above the water. 'She was there at the house today, when I went to see if there was any post for us. I'm scared, Miles . . .'

# 38

Robert and Kate were sitting opposite each other over two plates of liver and an empty bottle of white wine.

The Phoenix was one of SE22's best gastro-pubs. Nobody really knew – or cared – how good the food was any more; it was one of those places you were meant to spend your overdraft in.

'It was featured in this month's *Waitrose Magazine*.'

'What was?' Robert said, looking up from the liver he'd ordered. Why had he ordered liver? He used to hate it as a child when Margery cooked it, which was at least twice a week. He came to the conclusion that he'd felt pressurised by the waiter into ordering the liver.

'The Phoenix.'

'Oh.' He looked around him then down at the liver.

'God.'

'What?'

We really need someone to put an offer in, and I thought Ros might—'

The waiter appeared, pulling the empty bottle of wine from the bucket. 'Can I get you another one of these?'

Robert nodded, trying to remember how much the bottle had cost – £28? £38? About one hundred times more than it had cost The Phoenix anyway. Shit.

He pushed the remains of liver to one side.

The second bottle of wine was brought to the table.

'Can I take these?' the waiter said.

'What's that?' Robert, distracted, took a while to realise he was talking about the uneaten liver in front of them. 'Yeah – sure.'

'Things need to move quickly with ours. If someone doesn't put an offer in, we'll lose the place we've put our offer on.'

'*Our* offer?' He stared at her. 'What offer?'

'The offer we put in on the other place.'

'What other place?'

'The Beulah Hill house.'

'What Beulah Hill house?'

'For Christ's sake, Robert,' Kate hissed. 'The Beulah Hill house I put the offer in on.'

'You put an offer in on a house I haven't even seen – don't know anything about?'

'You *do* know about the house. I told you about the house.'

'You never said anything about the house. When did you put the offer in?'

Kate hesitated. 'Wednesday.'

'You're lying.'

'Okay – Monday.'

'You never said anything,' Robert said again.

'I did – you just don't remember. You don't remember anything at the moment. You're somewhere else, Robert.'

'I'm here,' he insisted.

'You're never here – and I had to move quickly. Then today I found out that Ros has got her eye on the Beulah Hill house as well, and now she's gone and put an offer in.

Christ knows why, they could afford Beulah Hill twice over. Shit.' She broke off.

'What?'

'Harriet and Miles – heading this way. I didn't know they were coming here tonight.' She waved as Harriet, wearing something stretchy and made of lace – which only Jessica Palmer would have been able to carry off without implying that something tragic either just had or was just about to happen – made her way towards their table. 'You terrible parents you – abandoning your children like this.'

'I know, it's awful, isn't it?' Kate managed brightly.

Harriet looked not only pleased but relieved to see her. She was speaking loudly, and this wasn't like her – or maybe it wasn't so much that Harriet was speaking loudly as that Miles wasn't speaking at all.

Kate glanced at Miles, who was staring straight over all their heads, smiling blankly at a spot on the wall. The last time she'd seen him, he'd been holding Jessica Palmer in his arms. Now it looked as though Harriet had spent the early part of the evening – before coming out – trepanning him. 'Who's looking after yours?'

'Martina. What about you?'

'Robert's mum.'

At the mention of his name, Robert smiled on cue at nothing in particular.

'I didn't see you at Evie's party earlier,' Harriet chastised her, carrying on before Kate had a chance to explain. 'And you missed out on something very interesting.'

'What?' Kate was curious, despite herself.

'Apparently, Aggie's dyspraxic.'

'Aggie? Who told you that?'

'Evie.'

'No.'

Harriet nodded, pleased to have the information; pleased at the effect the information had on Kate.

Robert and Miles remained silent – sentinels with nothing left to guard.

They didn't get on anyway. The few times they'd collided socially at summer barbecues arranged by the PRC – usually held at Harriet's or Ros's, where the spouses were thrown together and meant to get on in the same way the women already did – they didn't manage to make each other laugh. Miles felt threatened by Robert and dealt with it by convincing himself that Robert was probably a closet queer. Robert, in his turn, was made to feel like a major underachiever by Miles, and dealt with it by telling himself that there was no meaning to Miles's life and that he was in all probability dangerously unhappy.

'Anyway,' Harriet's voice rose again, 'fancy you two putting your house on the market and not saying a thing to anybody. And why France?'

Robert at last came to life. 'France?' he said, looking from Harriet to Kate, confused.

'I thought you'd found somewhere near Lot.' Harriet turned irritably to Kate.

'France?' Robert said again.

Kate continued to smile brightly through the silence that followed, aware that Robert was staring intently – almost violently – at her.

It was Miles – unexpectedly – who came to the rescue. 'We thought about France once,' he said.

'We did,' Harriet agreed, level, but unable to conceal entirely her concern over the glitsch in the program that was Miles. 'Anyway, I'll catch up with you later,' she whispered intimately to Kate.

Kate kept the smile on her face until Harriet and Miles had sat down at their table, Harriet virtually gliding over to

262

it with a spooky serenity that, like the loud, domineering voice, just wasn't her.

'What the fuck was she talking about? France?'

'Stop snarling at me – I'm telling people we're looking for a second place in France.'

'Why?'

'Because the Beulah Hill house only has three bedrooms and everybody will want to know why we're moving to a smaller house. I had to say something. You don't know what it's like for me, Robert. My life – it's tribal, and you've got no idea what it's like living in a tribe day in, day out.

'We've got rules of conduct – no, they're more than that. You know what it feels like sometimes? It feels like we've rewritten the Ten Commandments. You're morally obliged to upgrade continually – house, car, partner, whatever. That's why I'm talking about France. I've got no choice, Robert.' Kate was aware that her voice had risen; that she sounded irate.

Robert leant suddenly forward. 'This isn't living, Kate; it's . . .' He broke off. The steak and kidney pie arrived. 'And you've got to calm down. You're tired. You're just really, really tired. We've spent the last five years bringing up children – Flo's not even sleeping through yet. It's been hard, Kate – it's still hard – and we've been too busy going through it to realise. We're not living at the moment, we're surviving.'

They had both drunk enough now to no longer care how audible their private lives were becoming to the tables around them. The waiter had stopped communicating directly with them; had become a ghostly presence just beyond their elbows.

Kate leant her head in her hand and contemplated the slick, shiny steak and kidney pie. 'Did you order anything without suet in it?'

'What?'

'I said, did you order anything without suet in it?' She let her fork clatter against the side of the plate. 'I can't do this.'

Uncertain whether or not she was referring to the steak and kidney pudding, he said, 'You just need some time alone – you don't get any time to yourself.'

She laughed. 'Time alone? I couldn't be any lonelier.'

She stared at him, watching his mouth slacken and his eyes widen.

'Fuck it,' he said, desperate, 'we don't have to do this. We don't have to do any of this.'

'I didn't choose the restaurant.'

'I'm not talking about the restaurant.'

'I know.' She paused, in order to drink half a glass of wine in one go. 'Are we talking about Botswana again?' She looked away from him, across the restaurant to where Harriet and Miles were sitting, not talking to one another.

Robert saw that her attention had drifted. Her face had assumed that vague look that always made him feel helpless; helpless to the extent of violent. 'For fuck's sake,' he exploded, 'I was shot at today.'

The waiter removed the steak and kidney pies without comment, replacing them with spotted dick.

'I know,' Kate hissed back. 'I took the call – from Jessica Palmer. Have you got any idea what it feels like to have a friend ring you up and tell you your husband's falling to pieces? Have you got any idea what that feels like?'

They stared at each other.

Then, after a while, Kate said, 'This can't go on, Robert. You can't work like this – we can't live like this.'

This was a point – *the* point – they both agreed on. So why did it feel like a disagreement?

The waiter was at Robert's elbow with the bill.

Robert stared blankly at it for a moment before getting out his wallet and dropping a card into the dish.

A minute later, the waiter was at Robert's elbow again. 'Would you mind just coming over here?'

Robert got to his feet with difficulty and tried to follow the waiter as he wound his way fluidly through the linen-clad tables.

Once at the till, the waiter said, 'The card doesn't seem to be working. Do you have a different one you want me to try?'

'Not working?' Robert glanced over at Kate. 'Are the lines busy or something? Here, try this,' he said, handing him his credit card. 'I think that's the number,' he added, punching the machine's digits, suddenly scared. The bill was over two hundred pounds.

'The PIN's okay,' the waiter said, distracted by a colleague shouting at him across the crowded restaurant. 'I'll be right there,' he shouted back as the machine let out a series of irate bleeps. 'Sorry, but that's not going through.'

Robert, desperate, pulled out an old HSBC credit card he hadn't used in ages.

'You want me to try this?'

'I want you to try that.'

'Okay.' The waiter sighed, staring absently through his fringe at a customer's trainers as Robert put the PIN in.

'Wrong PIN,' he said.

'Shit.' Robert was trying to think quickly, but he'd drunk too much to do anything quickly. 'Wait a minute.'

He steered himself unevenly back through the tables to Kate. 'Have you got the chequebook?'

'The chequebook?'

'I've forgotten my PIN – it's written down on the inside of the chequebook cover.'

'But your PIN's six-six-zero-zero.'

'Yeah, but I'm using my HSBC credit card for this.'

'You don't have an HSBC credit card.'

'It's an old one – it's fine, Kate.'

Kate dug blearily around in her bag, then looked up and shook her head.

'Okay,' Robert said, subconsciously scanning the packed restaurant for some sort of resolution.

'Is there a problem?'

'I'll sort it.'

'The card's not going through, is it?' she hissed.

'It's fine – I'll sort it.'

'Shit, Robert.'

'I know – I know. I'll have to ask Mum.'

'Robert, you can't.'

'So what's the alternative – making a run for it or washing the dishes?' He went back over to where the waiter was standing in the corner of the restaurant, cutting up bread. 'I'm just popping out to the cashpoint.'

'I'll have to tell the manager,' he said, aware of the manager over by the bar, staring at them with his small eyes, set in a sunken face.

'Why, it'll be sorted in a few minutes.'

The waiter shrugged, unsure.

'You don't have to look at me like that – I'm a human being,' Robert blurted out.

'No shit,' the waiter said through his fringe, stroppy. His salary didn't cover this kind of hassle from people, especially not people wearing jeans from the last millennium. He turned his back on Robert – who left the restaurant – and went back to the bread.

Kate sat pushing the crumbs on the table into a pile and didn't see Harriet making her way over to the table. She'd forgotten about Harriet.

'Abandoned you, has he?' she said, cheerfully.

'Yeah, we decided to call it quits,' Kate replied.

Unsure of Kate's tone, Harriet forgot what it was she had been about to say.

'Cigarettes,' Kate said after a pause.

'Cigarettes?'

'He's gone to get cigarettes.'

'I didn't know Robert smoked.'

'He did, then he didn't, now he's started again.' She would never, under normal circumstances, have volunteered this information – especially not to Harriet, who she didn't even particularly like. But these weren't normal circumstances; she was semi-drunk and needed to explain Robert's departure somehow.

Even Harriet was aware of this, and was looking strangely at her. 'Well, come and join us till he gets back.'

'I'm fine . . .'

'Please,' Harriet said. 'Please come and join us. It's the first time we've been out – since Phoebe.' She glanced over in the direction of their table.

Kate stared at her.

'I'm exhausted – maybe Miles is as well, I don't know. It just feels . . . unnatural.' The next minute she pulled herself up short. 'That's an awful thing to say – I don't know what I'm saying.'

Surprised, Kate realised that Harriet was about to start crying and, without thinking, gave her hand a tight squeeze. 'It's fine – I'll come over.'

Robert left The Phoenix and ran rapidly through the rain in the direction of Prendergast Road. When he got to the corner he became aware of a slight figure walking ahead of him, shoulders hunched – Ellie. He stopped, assailed by a sudden memory of her telling him she worked at Film Nite. Had he really stood in a cloud-darkened classroom earlier that day and almost kissed her?

He stood in the rain, breathing heavily, waiting for Ellie to pass No. 22. He watched her walk slowly, weightlessly into the distance, and had a sudden premonition that if he didn't call out to her or stop her, he would never see her again. But he couldn't move. He remained on the corner, uncertain now that it had even been Ellie.

A few minutes later, he started to walk again.

'Mum!' he called out hoarsely as he pushed open the front door to No. 22, slipping in his wet shoes across the hallway's wooden floor.

Margery was nowhere to be found downstairs.

'Mum!' he called out again as he started to climb the stairs.

Margery's voice came hissing out of the darkness at him. 'That you, Robert?'

At first he thought she must be in Flo's room – that Flo had woken up and Margery was trying to settle her. But she wasn't.

Margery was standing by the window in their room, in the dark.

'Come and look at this, Robert. Robert?'

He stood next to her by the window and found himself staring at the house opposite. The woman from earlier was staring back at them, dimly lit from behind, holding up the sign again.

'I came up looking for air freshener. I can't find any air freshener anywhere – doesn't Kate keep it?' Margery whispered, irritably.

Robert didn't respond.

'She's been standing there like that for the past five minutes.' Margery paused then, suddenly urgent, said, 'What should we do? Should we try phoning the number? I've made a note of it.' She was clutching one of the scented notelets she used to write Edith letters from London on. 'Does she look Lithuanian to you?'

'Mum, I've got no idea.'

'She definitely looks Slavic to me – maybe Russian. D'you think she might be Russian?'

The woman in the Disneyland Paris T-shirt, and Robert, and Margery all continued to watch each other.

'Maybe it's one of them houses you hear about – run by Russian mafia. She might be a Russian sex slave,' Margery continued to whisper, excited now.

Robert didn't comment on this. His mind was full of Kate left behind at The Phoenix with the unpaid bill, and he didn't have the stamina to turn it in the direction of Russian sex slaves right then.

'Mum—'

'She's being held prisoner. She wants us to help her escape.'

'Mum—'

'I'm scared, Robert.'

The woman disappeared suddenly as the curtain swung back across the window.

'She's gone,' Margery said. 'Maybe we should call the police.'

'Mum!' Robert said, finally losing patience.

Margery turned round. 'Where's Kate?'

'At the restaurant.'

'On her own? What's wrong, love?'

'Mum, we couldn't pay our bill.'

'Your bill?'

'Our bill – at the restaurant. Kate's still there. I don't know – maybe I put in the wrong PIN and the bank automatically put a stop on the card or something.'

'What about Kate?'

'What *about* Kate?'

'Didn't she have any cards on her?'

'She's only got a card for the joint account.'

'So, what are you going to do?'

Robert paused. 'If there's any way you could lend me the money until tomorrow . . .'

'Robert . . .'

'Mum, I hate asking, I really hate asking, but I need to get back to The Phoenix and settle this. Then I can go to the bank first thing in the morning and sort it out, and—'

Margery, who prickled easily around money, cut him short. 'How much?'

Robert heard himself say, 'Two hundred and ten – including the tip.'

'Two hundred and ten?' Margery wheezed. 'I thought it was just the two of you going out to eat?'

'It was just the two of us.'

'But, Robert,' Margery said, more and more agitated. 'What the hell did you have to eat?'

'Liver – steak and kidney pudding – and spotted dick.'

'Spotted dick?' Margery exploded. 'How much was the spotted dick?'

'Six ninety-five.'

'Nearly seven pounds for spotted dick? What is this place?'

'The Phoenix – Kate's been wanting to go for ages.'

'Well she had no business.'

'Mum, I know – but right now, she's . . .'

Without waiting to hear the rest of this, Margery went downstairs into the study and took a small black wallet they'd bought her on their honeymoon out of her handbag, handing it to Robert who'd followed her downstairs – in silence.

'Which card?' he asked.

'I've only got the one. The number's zero-two-one-zero.'

His date of birth.

'I'm helping out because I don't have a choice right now, but you've got to promise me that you're going to sort this money thing out, you and Kate. It can't go on, Robert.'

'We're dealing with it.'

'You are?'

He leant forward to kiss her, but she backed away. 'You've got to sort it.'

Margery watched Robert until he disappeared round the corner.

It had stopped raining.

She was staring at No. 21 opposite, checking to see whether the woman was at the window again, when the door to No. 20 opened and there was Mr Hamilton, smiling at her.

'I got these for you,' he said loudly, holding up a carrier bag.

Margery jumped back into the hallway of No. 22. How did he know she was standing at the front door? He must have been spying on her. He would have seen Robert leave, and now he knew she was alone in the house.

'It's rhubarb from the garden. I got too much of it.' He paused. 'You like rhubarb?'

'Just leave it on the wall,' Margery said, slamming the door shut.

# 39

It was late. Ros was still up, looking at the website of a Ghanaian drummer she was thinking of booking for the street party – on the recommendation of a friend in west London who insisted that Ghanaian drums were the new Tibetan bells. She was in Martin's study – which Martin never used because Martin was never home – flanked by a series of framed photographs of her and Martin diving in the Red Sea before the children were born.

Blu-tacked to the wall above the desk was the stall layout plan for June's street party, which she'd devised with Evie yesterday so that everybody was clear about who was manning which stall and where the stalls were going. The Carpe Diem stall was number six and she'd paid extra for a black awning to complement the pink and black merchandise.

Eventually the phone rang.

'Martin?'

'How did you know it was me?'

'It's ten minutes to eleven.'

Martin's voice sounded shaky and kept coming at her – almost aggressive – before receding again, as if he was short of breath.

'How's it going?' he asked, realising with a jolt that it was his turn to speak.

'Fine – fine.' She paused. 'You're phoning to tell me you're not coming home tonight?'

'I'm phoning to tell you I don't know if I'll be home tonight. So, don't wait up.' He exhaled. 'Okay . . .'

'Martin, wait . . .' There was the sound of laughter down the line – distant, but sudden – then it passed. 'I think we should put an offer in on that Beulah Hill place.'

His voice changed. 'God, Ros – I can't even begin to get my head round this right now.'

'But, Martin, we talked – you *did* get your head round it – to the extent of telling me you thought it would be a good investment buy.'

'I did?'

'Martin . . .'

'Why the hurry anyway?'

'There's no hurry,' Ros said, defensive. 'I just think we should move forward now we've made up our mind.'

Martin exhaled again. 'Ros, we need to talk.'

There was the sound of sirens cutting between them – so loud she couldn't work out whether they were outside on Prendergast Road or being relayed down the line. More sirens followed.

'What's going on over there?'

'No idea.'

Martin's office – where Martin was supposedly phoning from – overlooked a central atrium where a small patch of rainforest grew. The sirens were an impossibility – as impossible as the seagulls she'd heard down the line when he phoned one weekend a month ago.

'Ros, I need to talk to you.'

'See you later,' she said quickly, calling off and turning back to the understanding eyes of Nicholas, the Ghanaian drummer.

A second later she heard, in the distance, the same sirens she'd just heard down the line.

It was happening again.

Martin was having another affair – and she wasn't sure she had the strength right then to listen to his confession or nurse him through the inevitable break-up. The last one left him – this one would as well.

Please, God, don't let it be anybody I know, Ros thought.


Martin put his phone away.

He wasn't in his office in Canary Wharf, overlooking a small patch of rainforest.

He was standing in a phone box outside Metro Tesco, less than a kilometre from No. 188 Prendergast Road.

The laughing couple who had passed him a few minutes before passed again, still laughing.

He left the phone box, crossed Lordship Lane and turned up Prendergast Road, giving his house the cursory sort of glance any commuter might give it as he or she passed twice a day on the way to and from work, because – along with Evie and Joel's at No. 112 – it was one of the nicest houses on the street. Unknown to Martin, his home was the dream home of countless young couples who passed that way every day, the connection between them still vibrant as they walked through the early morning heat before the suck of routine pulled them apart.

Martin walked straight past, and carried on walking until he got to No. 112, where he rang the bell without hesitation.

# 40

Evie was in the garden office, listening to Bonnie Tyler and doing what was left of Jack's coke. The walls were hung with a selection of dresses from the shop, destined for the street party's 'Boutique' stall. She wasn't anticipating selling the dresses; she'd decided to stock the stall with vintage jewellery, accessories and T-shirts. Now the dresses were unsettling her. When her back was turned, she was certain she could feel them moving behind her. When she turned round to check, there wasn't the slightest movement among the dresses. As soon as she turned her back again, she could feel them jostling on their hangers, planning something. What were they planning? They had something up their sleeves for the day of the street party – she just knew they did.

The coke was gone. Unsettled, she left the office without looking at the dresses again and walked across the garden towards the house, resisting the urge to look back and check that the dresses weren't following her.

The back door to the house was open and through it she could see Joel in the kitchen, leaning into the freezer.

The night felt suddenly empty.

She stood in the back doorway, humming and staring at

the white bars covering the back of Joel's Wi-Fi detector T-shirt. 'What are you looking for?'

'Peas – I thought I'd do a pea risotto.'

'Haven't we eaten already?'

Joel stood up, on the alert.

'No, we haven't eaten already,' he said, his eyes quickly scanning her face before he reminded his own to break into a reassuring smile. 'And the reason I know that is because it's my turn to do supper tonight.' He paused, swinging his mind away from Evie and back to the pea risotto.

There was a time when he might have done a risotto for an informal supper with friends, but that was back in the last days of the twentieth century. By the early years of the twenty-first, everywhere you went there was risotto on the menu – each with a different, agonising twist. Buffalo risotto? Fuck me, Joel thought, shaking his head. No wonder risotto had been forced underground – until recently.

He couldn't remember when, exactly, but at some point in the past few months, he'd had a feeling – a big fat hunch, in fact – that it was up for renovation, and the hunch had served him correctly when he opened one of the weekend supplements. There in front of him was a big glossy plate full of pea risotto. The recipe came from the chef's latest book – *Real Honest Food*; the chef blamed the demise of true risotto on the fact that risotto had lost its 'inherent honesty'. While Joel had been in agreement with this – read it over quite a few times, in fact – he still couldn't quite feel the 'rightness' of pea risotto. Maybe it was because he hadn't been able to source any fresh peas – fresh peas were 'absolutely necessary' – and so was forced to use frozen. The risotto had lost its 'inherent honesty' before he'd even begun.

'What d'you think?' he appealed to Evie.

Evie had moved to the other doorway – the one leading into the hallway – and was now standing still again, but in

276

that fraught, restless way that made her look as though external rather than internal forces were pinning her to the spot, and that all you had to do was cut the invisible guy ropes and she'd catapult into outer space.

'About what?'

'About pea risotto.'

'I don't.'

'What – too boring? Too tawdry? God, that's it,' Joel said, feeling suddenly bereft. 'The frozen peas make it too tawdry.' He clutched his head, trying not to panic. 'We just need to forget the whole pea risotto thing.'

'Okay,' Evie agreed, inhaling in the way she used to inhale when she smoked.

'We just need to forget it,' Joel said again, loudly this time.

He quickly picked up the torn-out page with the recipe on it and dropped it into the recycling box under the sink. 'There – it never happened,' he said triumphantly, walking up to Evie and kissing her suddenly.

When he stood back to check that she was okay with the kiss – that some element of communion had been achieved between them – he couldn't help noticing the dusting of dandruff on the black V-neck sweater she was wearing. Now wasn't the time to mention the dandruff, but he made a mental note to bring it up first thing in the morning. If she had a scalp condition, it was her responsibility to rectify it. To Joel, dandruff said self-neglect and there was no excuse for it at the moment, when things were going so well.

He'd taken a call from Tory, his agent, earlier in the evening, after settling Aggie and Ingrid, which had put him in a good mood. After that he'd gone through Aggie's referrals from the speech and language therapist they'd been assigned to, followed by two episodes of *Antiques Roadshow*. He was about to ask Evie if she wanted a takeaway when the doorbell rang.

'You want me to get that?' he said after a moment's hesitation, when it became obvious Evie had no intention of answering it – even though she was closer; even though she was already standing in the hallway. This fact struck him suddenly as immensely irritating. *She* should answer the door.

Evie, blowing on her nails in a way that used to excite him when they first started to date, looked up, uninterested.

'It's probably Martina.'

Joel waited, trying to unpick the logic in the sentence. Why was it his responsibility to answer the door if it was Martina?

'She was out babysitting tonight.'

The doorbell rang again.

After another second's hesitation, he pushed past her into the hallway and went to answer the front door. It wasn't Martina.

There was a man standing outside in the rain. Joel recognised him, but couldn't remember his name. 'Hey,' he said at last, hoping that vague congeniality masked the amnesia.

'I'm looking for Martina?'

'Martina.' Joel repeated the name, and carried on staring.

Then Evie appeared in the hallway behind him. 'Martin,' she said.

This was Martin – of course. Who the fuck was Martin?

'I'm looking for Martina,' he said again.

'Martina?' Evie waited for the explanation, but Martin just kept on smiling at them both.

'She's not picking up,' he said.

'Oh.' Evie was lost. 'Well, she's not in tonight – d'you want me to take a message? Is Ros trying to arrange a babysit?'

'No.' Martin shook his head. 'I just want to speak to her.'

All three of them stood in silence, listening to the hollow tapping of the rain on Martin's mackintosh.

'Is everything okay?' Evie asked at last, trying to conceal a rising panic. Had anybody else noticed that she was short of breath – couldn't draw enough of it – was gasping, in fact. She was sure she was gasping: was she about to have a heart attack.

'I don't know,' Martin said.

Unable to stop himself, Joel let out a short, irreverent laugh.

Martin stared at him.

It was Joel's laugh that made Evie say what she said next. 'She's at Harriet and Miles's – number two three six.'

Martin nodded, gave a wave and walked off into the night.

'What the hell was that about?' Joel said.

Evie shrugged, panting rapidly, and went back inside.

Joel stayed where he was, hypnotised by the rain bouncing off the lid of the recycling bin, until he pulled away suddenly. 'Oh my God,' he called out after Evie, slamming the front door shut. 'They're having an affair.'

'Maybe.' Evie paused, thinking about Ros.

The more Joel thought about it, the more convinced he became that their au pair was having an affair with one of their friend's husbands. Did he like the idea, or didn't he? What did it mean? On the one hand it was tacky, verging on cliché, but clichés became reality far less than people supposed. And there was something about Martin's face . . . on the whole, he decided, it was a good thing. They were the sort of people who had the sort of au pair who had affairs. When people found out about it, it would lend Evie and him a sort of erotic vibrancy.

'What are we going to do?'

'About what?' Evie was back in the doorway again, gulping something clear out of a tumbler.

'About knowing,' Joel said, automatically taking the tumbler from her hands, pouring the contents into a cocktail glass and returning it to her. It was amazing, he thought, watching her take a gulp from the new glass – without comment – how you could substitute a glass and the scene was immediately transformed from edgy desperation to mellow, sophisticated domesticity.

'Nothing,' she panted. 'Because we don't know – for sure.'

'Nothing?'

'What is it we know, Joel?'

'Well, it was pretty bloody obvious.' He paused, his lips shaking with excitement. 'It has to mean something.'

'It will do – to the Grangers, and their marriage, and their children. Ros is my friend, Joel. Shit – I'm meant to be meeting her first thing tomorrow morning to finalise stall plans. Have you got any idea how that feels?'

Joel wasn't listening.

The Grangers and the future of the Grangers weren't that interesting to him. 'Are you going to say anything?'

'I want to speak to Martina first. Tonight. God,' she broke off and drew breath, 'are we going to have to – I don't know – fire her or something? Get another au pair?'

'Tory says Kurds make good au pairs,' Joel mumbled. Then, 'But . . . Martin.'

'Martin – what?'

'Why choose Martin? I mean, if you're going to go to the effort of having an affair, why choose that?' Joel concluded, outraged at the memory of Martin.

'Well, Martina isn't the one having the affair because Martina isn't married.' Evie let out a strangled, 'Joel . . .'

'What?'

Evie was staring at him, her eyes bulging, one hand grasping her throat.

'D'you think she's actually in love with him?' Joel started to chuckle. 'Martin and Martina.'

'Martin and Martina – what? Joel . . .'

'They sound like prototypes.'

Evie's eyes slid away from him. The kitchen and its contents were blurring over. The only thing she could make out with any real clarity was the bag of peas – which had by now probably defrosted – lying on the bench. 'The peas,' she gasped.

'Yeah.' Joel went over to the fridge and filled a glass with ice from the machine.

'Joel, I can't get my breath – some sort of panic attack.'

Joel stared blankly at her. Evie looked strange, as though she was about to pass out or something.

'Joel . . .'

'What?'

It seemed to Evie suddenly essential that the peas were put back in the freezer. If that didn't happen . . . . 'The peas,' she yelped.

'Evie, I'm getting there.' He poured some Jack Daniels over the ice, took a sip, and the next minute Evie was yelling at him.

'If you don't put the peas back in the fucking freezer, I'm divorcing you.'

He turned and stared at her, the Jack Daniels still raised to his lips.

She meant it.

If he didn't put the peas back in the fucking freezer, she was divorcing him.

She was swaying on the spot, her mouth open.

The next minute Evie blacked out and went crashing to the floor.

# 41

Martin rang on the doorbell to No. 236, noting with interest the security camera trained on him from the corner of the porch. He smiled up at it, then peered through the diamond-patterned glass panel in the front door.

From inside the house he heard laughter. It was Martina's laughter; he recognised it from the countless times he'd made her laugh. The thought of the television making her laugh in that way made him profoundly jealous. He rang the doorbell again and this time the laughter stopped.

Martina answered the door, a relaxed, low-level smile on her face that anticipated the return of Harriet and Miles. Her face changed when she saw Martin standing there. It didn't drop; it just changed.

Martin wasn't Harriet and Miles.

'What do you want?' she whispered, angry with him for being so offensively out of context. 'What are you doing here?'

'You weren't answering my calls.'

'I forgot to charge my phone.'

He nodded, aware that his mouth was open as he stared at her, dressed in leggings, her Will Smith T-shirt and an absurd pair of slippers that made her look as if she was wearing a pair of rabbits on her feet. 'I thought maybe you weren't answering on purpose.'

'I wouldn't do that,' she said, still angry.

He believed her.

She never said anything she didn't mean.

She looked over his shoulder, distracted by someone passing in the street behind. Then she folded her arms across herself. 'I'm working.'

'I didn't know you were working.'

'I didn't know you needed to know when I was working.'

He smiled. 'Neither did I.'

'So, how did you know where I was?'

'Can I come in?'

'No. How did you know where I was?'

'I asked your employers.'

'Shit.' Her breath smelt faintly of what seemed to be her staple diet – stock cubes crumbled into boiling water. 'You've got to go.'

She was terrified of Harriet and Miles Burgess returning home and finding him standing on their doorstep. Plus, right then all she wanted to do was go back inside, sit on the sofa and finish watching *Men in Black*.

He nodded slowly in agreement. It was the first time he'd stopped to think all day. He'd been trying her phone on and off since about eleven o'clock that morning. By seven, he was falling to pieces in the toilets on the second floor of their building in Canary Wharf and realising that whatever line he'd been messing around near for the past nine months, he'd now crossed it. Two months ago, if pushed, he could have stopped it all, but he knew now that he'd gone beyond that point – far enough beyond it to knock on Evie and Joel's front door and ask them the whereabouts of their au pair.

He'd been amazed when Martina actually turned up that first time, at the Hilton near Tower Bridge.

They'd arranged to meet at the bar, even though he'd already checked in to Room 212. He'd decided to spend the night there anyway – whether Martina turned up or not; whether she stayed or not.

She'd walked into the cream and grey bar at the Hilton looking younger than he remembered from the countless baby-sits and brief encounters – and as if she was there for a job interview. The overall effect was one of neatness, but without the restraint or prudishness that usually comes with neatness because her neatness was born of pride. The tightly tied scarf that would have irritated him on just about every other woman he knew, left him feeling protective towards her.

For a long time he talked and she listened, laughing politely and taking the sort of sips from her Coca-Cola that a person takes when they've spent a lifetime having to make things last.

After a while, aware that he himself was becoming drunk, he even began to doubt whether she'd understood his invit-ation. Until she leant suddenly forwards, put her glass down carefully on the table and looked up at him. 'I think you are a good man.'

Was this what she'd been trying to work out for the past couple of hours? What was it he'd done or said that could possibly have made her reach that conclusion?

She relaxed as soon as she said this – and started to talk.

She talked about herself without making it sound like she was talking about herself. Her mother was a doctor – an ear, nose and throat specialist – who had once competed in the Winter Olympics. She was vague about her father and Martin thought he caught a whiff of something criminal. The person she was closest to was her grandmother, who'd brought up her and her two brothers – she told her grandmother everything.

Chocolate rice pudding, tarot cards and fishing made her happy. One of their first weekends away would be spent fishing in the River Tweed, but he didn't know that then.

They went upstairs shortly after she'd informed him he was a good man.

Once upstairs, she was more interested in the interior of Room 212 – and the view, which wasn't great because they'd been virtually fully booked when he made the reservation – but she didn't comment on any of it. She just wandered calmly round in a way that made it impossible to know what she was thinking. When he got to know her better, he came to recognise these poised silences for what they were – Martina pausing before she made her mind up about something.

He was happy watching her pad round Room 212 – she'd insisted on taking her shoes off in the passage outside before coming into the room – in the sort of flesh-coloured stockings he remembered his mother wearing. The blue jumper she had on had been darned on the left elbow.

He took champagne out of the minibar and persuaded her to take a glass.

By the time they got round to making love, he wasn't even sure he wanted to or needed to.

'You never did this before,' she said afterwards, getting out of bed, tidying the pillows and duvets and getting back in again, lying next to him.

He had done this before, but didn't contradict her.

She seemed much more self-assured after making love, which had surprised him. Still the same strange mixture of urbane and naive, but without the nerves.

'Me – I do this before.' She sighed. 'A teacher, at college.' When he didn't respond to this – unsure whether he believed her or not – she said, 'Do you feel guilty?'

'I don't know what I feel.' He rolled up onto his elbow. 'But I wanted this to happen. Have you got to get back – tonight?'

She sat up. 'You want me to leave?' It was the first time her voice had betrayed anything close to an emotion.

'No, no. I want you to stay. I just wasn't sure what you'd said to . . .' He tried to remember the name of the family Martina was working for.

'They think I'm with my cousin.'

'You've got a cousin here?'

Martina nodded. 'She works for a family in Maida Vale who have very expensive shoes.'

Martin laughed. This was the sort of thing Toby would say, but the shoes clearly meant something to Martina.

Later on, one Saturday night, he showed up at the house in Maida Vale, uninvited. They ended up making love on the sofa – something that made Martina furious with him afterwards.

'And the family you work for – they're okay?'

'They're quite good.'

What did that mean? After a while he said, 'You're hungry? You want to order something?'

She shook her head.

As he got to know her better, he realised that she rarely ate.

'You go now,' she said, standing on the doorstep to No. 236.

He nodded. Then leant forward suddenly into the porch light and gave her a hard, angry kiss. 'I can't go on like this.' He hadn't meant to say that; he didn't want to frighten her, but couldn't stop himself. He had a sudden overwhelming feeling that time was running out. 'Let's go away. Tonight. Now. Marrakech. We don't need to tell anyone – we can just go.' He could hear how impossible it sounded – as he was saying it.

She watched him, her face unreadable.

Marrakech receded; he collapsed in on himself. 'I can't go on like this,' he said again.

He turned to go, and she didn't stop him.

*JUNE*

# 42

On June 15, the day of the PRC street party, the sun rose on Prendergast Road. It rose quickly, as though it had been given a tip-off about the day's events and was keen to illuminate fully as many of them as possible, and so – skipping dawn – by seven o'clock was already letting out a flat white heat that soon evaporated the last of the night's secretions.

A lone runner pounded up the street in an unrelenting, unforgiving, highly reflective white Lycra – a mobile blind spot that had already caused an uninsured Toyota to crash into a motorcyclist – which she'd bought from the local Triathlon shop. There wasn't a convex or concave curve the white Lycra stretched over that couldn't put its existence down to muscle and bone. Barely anything on Ros's body shook as the soles of her feet hit the pavement.

David, the Down's syndrome boy at No. 8, was out in the front garden hugging his loquat tree, about to start singing. Out the corner of her eye, Ros saw him wave, but she didn't wave back. She made a mental note to speak to his parents and ensure that David was kept inside during the street party.

Then she turned up the volume on her iPod and started

to build up speed for the home stretch – the final two hundred metres of the five-kilometre run she did three times a week.

Today was *her* day.

She wasn't going to think about St Anthony's today – either the Parents' Evening on Monday or the appeal hearing on Wednesday. She was going to enjoy today.

She ran past Evie's front garden. The olive tree, she noted, had been replaced by a fig. Evie's curtains were still shut.

Harriet's were open. Casper was sitting alone in a haze of blue light from the television, laughing.

Ros's breathing was becoming laboured now and her lungs felt as though they were riddled with cracks, but she kept up the pace – even managing to draw level with a black cab that was making its way up Prendergast Road and now slowing down.

Her mother, Lauren, had driven up from Dorset on Thursday to help with Toby and Lola. She'd insisted, and there was no point putting her off. She was brilliant with Toby – who followed her everywhere – but Ros didn't know if she was up to Lauren right then and Lauren was the sort of person you had to feel up to, even if she was your mother. When she'd gone downstairs at 5.15 that morning, Lauren had been sitting at the kitchen table reading yesterday's newspaper. Ros had left her with the balloon pump and instructions to make a start on the box of pink and black Carpe Diem balloons.

She came to a halt outside No. 188, arms and legs shaking, and cut out her iPod just as the black cab pulled in at the kerb. Her new breathing technique had enabled her to knock three minutes off her best time.

Panting, she watched Martin get out, pay the driver and amble, preoccupied, round the front of the cab – surprised to see his wife standing outside their house. The taxi pulled away. Martin turned and watched it go, still able to make out the school photo of the driver's daughter tacked to the dashboard.

When the taxi had gone, the morning fell silent again, and Ros and Martin stayed where they were, waiting.

Martin looked around him as if he'd been dropped at the wrong address, and Ros's hand wrapped itself round the base of her throat, in an attempt to level out her breathing.

She realised – as they carried on standing there in the early morning sunshine not speaking – that she was surprised to see him. He'd said he was coming home for the party; he'd been expected, she just hadn't anticipated him actually showing up.

Martin was staring at her, under the sway of a peculiar desire to ask Ros if she'd seen Ros anywhere.

Made uncomfortable by his stare, Ros checked her pedometer then clipped it back into the band round her arm.

He gave her a quick, empty smile and the next minute – absurdly – they kissed each other once on the cheek, like colleagues who used to work together, meeting unexpectedly and discovering that they lived in the same neighbourhood.

Up close – albeit briefly – Ros smelt smoke on Martin and the scent of bed linen she hadn't washed, and that they hadn't slept in together.

They let their hands drop, embarrassed.

Ros flicked some hair out of her eye in an unhabitually feminine way.

Martin had a pair of sunglasses in his hands she didn't remember buying him – and that he wouldn't have bought himself. Martin never bought anything for himself.

'You want to come in?' she said at last, as he put the sunglasses on then took them off again.

Sighing, he followed her to the front door, watched her put the keys in the lock then followed her into the house.

They went into the kitchen, which was full of Carpe Diem balloons – and Lauren.

It was the first time Lauren had seen Martin this visit.

'How's it going?' he said. He'd always found his mother-in-law hard work; this morning he could barely look at her.

'It's going fine, Martin.' She paused before smiling.

'They're for the street party,' Ros put in, noting Martin's confusion as he took in the balloons, which she pushed through carefully to get to the kettle.

The balloon Lauren had just finished blowing up shot out of her hand, and all three of them watched it land, deflated, back on the table.

'She was up at five,' Lauren said, for no apparent reason, nodding her head pointedly at Ros.

Martin wasn't sure how he was meant to respond to this so remained silent.

Ros, pouring the tea, was trying to remember how long ago it was that their life had fallen into this pattern of Martin staying in a friend's empty flat in Old Street during the week, and coming home at weekends, because of the case.

To start with, the thought of the weekends spent together had got her through the weeks. Now, it was the thought of the weeks alone that got her through the weekends.

'D'you want tea, Mum?' she asked.

'Leave it there – I'm coming to get myself some toast,' Lauren said, shunting her chair back and wading carefully through the balloons. She stood by the sink, looking out at the back garden.

'Well, look at that,' she said to herself the next minute.

'What am I meant to be looking at?' Ros asked, blowing on her tea.

'That ivy hanging over the wall there – it's full of pigeons; full of them,' Lauren said, sounding pleased.

'It's the berries, I suppose.'

'Of course it's the berries,' her mother replied, sharp but not impatient. 'I've just never seen so many in one place.'

Martin stayed where he was, watching the two women contemplate the pigeons. They looked like mother and daughter – something he'd never felt about them before in all the years since he first met Ros; he just couldn't work out what it was he had to do with either of them.

Lauren had her own life down in Dorset and, although she was often up in London for talks, conferences or exhibitions, she rarely arranged to meet up with them. They didn't see her at all in the first two years of Toby's life because Lauren – as Ros explained when challenged – didn't particularly like babies. Babies were one thing, at least, that Ros could do better than her mother. Toby started to see a lot more of her once he turned two, and he stayed down in Dorset with her for two weeks when Lola was born. Now Lauren was Toby's favourite person. She sent him a letter every week and always included something she'd found on the beach. It was acknowledged, within the family, that Lauren and Toby had bonded.

Down in Dorset they could be busy together all afternoon, especially in the greenhouse or out in the vegetable patch. Toby loved helping in the seedbeds, crouching low with his hands in the mud, and Lauren and him mumbling to themselves. Then Lauren would stand up and stretch, check the position of the sun in the sky and shake her head, laughing. 'Listen to us – like a couple of old women twittering on.'

Toby would grin back at her, pleased. He liked the idea of being a twittering old woman if it meant crouching in the mud with the sun on your back being allowed to talk to yourself without interruption.

Ros was terrified of her mother and that had never changed over the years. Apart from a couple of requests for money in the early years, which Lauren had always been obliging about and always made clear were gifts, not loans, Ros made very few demands on her. She shared the good news with her and remained silent about any bad.

'Why don't you go take a shower? I'll sort the children,' Lauren said in the soft Canadian accent she'd never lost, while drawing a packet of cigarettes out of her back pocket.

Ros nodded and turned to Martin. 'You want to come up and take a shower?'

Martin, too full of horror at the prospect of having to share a shower with his wife to reply, let his mouth fall loosely open – something which had started to give him a double chin in the last six months or so.

'Okay – well, I'll go on up,' Ros said at last. 'They're delivering the stalls in the next forty-five minutes. I'd better get on.'

Martin nodded, amazed that Ros didn't comment on the fact that her mother had just drawn a crumpled packet of cigarettes out of her jeans pocket and was now proceeding to light one.

Martin couldn't believe it.

Ros had gone up without a word and left her mother smoking in their kitchen.

Nobody was allowed to smoke inside No. 188 Prendergast Road; nobody was allowed to even smell of smoke inside No. 188 Prendergast Road. Those who did were sent into the garden.

And here was Lauren, smoking in their kitchen and flicking the ash into the sink.

God, he wasn't even allowed to dream about smoking a cigarette. 'D'you want an ashtray for that?' he said, bitterly, as she tapped another sprinkling of ash into the sink.

'You don't have an ashtray,' Lauren said, without turning round.

'You're right – we don't have an ashtray. Because nobody in the house smokes,' he tried not to yell.

'That's right,' she agreed.

'Look, Lauren . . .' At last she turned round. Was that a smile on her face – ever so slight? Was Lauren *smiling* at him? 'I don't know what arrangement you've come to with Ros about this, but I—'

'You what?' she cut in. 'You really think the nicotine from this cigarette's going to cause more damage to this family than you are? *I don't think so.*'

She exhaled deeply and turned away to pour herself a cup of tea, which she did with a steady hand.

Martin was transfixed by the steady hand – he couldn't have done a steady hand after saying something like that.

She stood with her cup of tea in one hand and cigarette in the other, staring out through the window again – without the enjoyment of before when she'd seen all the pigeons in the ivy. 'Why did you ever do it? You should never have done it.'

She kept her back turned to him as she said it.

Martin stared at her shoulder blades, which were pronounced, like Ros's. Did she know? Had Ros found out about Martina? Had Ros told Lauren?

At last she turned round. 'You've never made any effort to make this marriage work.'

She didn't know about Martina.

'I can't help it,' Martin said. It didn't feel wrong saying it; he didn't even feel particularly sorry. It suddenly occurred to him that he'd as good as told Lauren he was going – so why didn't he? He hadn't taken his jacket off or even put his bags down. He was ready to go. So what if he just went? What if he didn't go upstairs and take a shower. What if he just turned round and walked out of the kitchen, down the corridor and out of the house?

'This is your life,' Lauren insisted quietly, but with just the right tone of command.

'Well, I don't want it,' Martin said with an overwhelming sense of relief, beaming triumphantly at his mother-in-law, without a hint of malignancy. 'I don't want it.'

'I've always hated you Martin,' she said.

Ignoring this – it was only to be expected, and was no surprise – he continued to smile happily at her, and was on the verge of leaving when he heard somebody padding into the kitchen. Turning round, he saw his son standing there. He'd forgotten about the children.

'You're home,' Toby observed flatly, staring at his father then past him. 'Balloons.'

'Hey there, Tobes,' Martin said, lumpish, in his strained, fake-father voice, which sounded even more strained than usual right then because of the exchange between Lauren and him. 'How's school been?' Every time he had contact with his son, he came out with a cliché along these lines.

Toby made the sort of response he often made when he didn't like the turn a conversation took, or felt that a question was too direct and therefore, to him, confrontational: he quoted a sentence – or sometimes up to an entire paragraph – from a current reading book.

Right then, he said, 'Danger lurks behind every tree. God bless you, my child.'

Martin nodded as knowingly as he could, and smiled, aware that he was still poised to leave.

Toby didn't smile back.

'Mum's crying,' he announced.

Lauren put her cigarette down and stared at Martin.

Toby hadn't meant it as a challenge, but the way Lauren was looking at him was turning it into one.

This was the moment; this was it.

He was standing between a woman he'd never particularly liked, in a kitchen he'd never particularly liked, with a son he didn't know how to love. Upstairs there was a

296

woman he didn't love, crying. None of it had to matter any more because he could just walk out. All he had to do was put one foot in front of the other and head for the front door.

If he didn't – if he went upstairs now instead – he might never leave; this moment might never happen again and he couldn't carry on standing here for ever.

He turned away from Lauren and his son and started to walk. He got as far as the fridge when the doorbell rang – and stopped.

Lauren pushed past him and went to answer it.

He thought – absurdly – that it might be Martina.

It was the lorry delivering the scaffolding and awnings for the stall.

He heard Lauren talking to them, giving detailed instructions, aware that he was alone in the kitchen with his son. He turned to face Toby, who picked up a balloon, which popped mystifyingly almost as soon as he touched it.

Without knowing exactly how or why, Martin realised suddenly that the moment had passed.

He brushed his hand gently over his son's head and went upstairs.

# 43

Martina was going home – two months earlier than origin-
ally intended. Joel could hear her on the other side of the
bedroom wall, packing her things with Aggie, who was devas-
tated.

He and Evie had sat up waiting for her the night Martin
had called round. When she'd finally appeared, around
midnight, Evie had been far more sympathetic than she'd
anticipated, and Joel far more angry than he'd anticipated.
This wasn't something they had since talked about, but both
of them were aware of it.

Martina had cried that night – a lot – and Evie had held
her, and the two women had sat there holding each other
on the sofa, locked in a female complicity that Joel just
hadn't been able to fathom. Since that night of tears, hugs
and retribution, Martina had gained a strange ascendancy
over him. He often caught Evie and her laughing together
in a way they never had before, and couldn't shake the
feeling – every time he heard them – that they were laughing
about him.

Martina had confessed to Evie that she was scared of
Martin, who she'd been trying to leave anyway because she

thought he was becoming obsessive. Evie had become very hung up on this notion of Martin being obsessive, and of helping Martina to escape. Evie's mother, Cassandra, had been brought down from St Helen's where she was enjoying the early throes of a second marriage, in order to drive Martina to the airport while the street party was in full swing. Joel couldn't quite see the point in all this secrecy – it was hardly like they'd had to take out a restraining order on Martin or anything.

At least Martina's departure back to her boringly stable post-communist home town meant he could start sourcing the kind of au pair – as it became clear speaking to his agent, Tory – you were meant to have: Kurdish, Chinese (so your children would become fluent in time for the Chinese world takeover), or at the very least Chechen.

Martina – like the Barcelona chair he'd bought a couple of years ago that they were now filling hotel lobbies with – had been a dead-end acquisition. There was something pitiful about having a Slovak au pair – even a Slovak who was having an affair.

His career was flat at the moment, so he had time to think about these things. Tory was dragging her expensive heels over the retrospective of his work he'd been talking up for the past year, and now it looked as though it might not happen at all. He'd been harder hit by this piece of news than he'd ever anticipated. In fact, a mighty worm had set up camp inside him, and it was of the mighty worm's increasing opinion that if he hadn't put so much energy into Evie and Evie's career over the past three years, maybe his own energy reserves would be more intact. Resentment wasn't something Joel had ever really felt before, so he was having trouble even putting a name to it.

He finished getting dressed and was about to go downstairs

when the door to their bedroom opened and Aggie walked in, holding Martina's phone.

'Watch this.'

'What is it?'

Aggie giggled and sat down on the bed. 'It's the pig film – Martina said I could have the pig film.'

Martina appeared briefly in the bedroom doorway. 'Maybe you want to make a copy for Aggie – put it on your computer.'

'Put it on your computer,' Aggie said.

'But what is it?'

'It's starting now – watch,' Aggie commanded, excited.

'This is the pig film?'

On the tiny screen, he watched a boy of about ten in a red hat push his face up close, grinning. In the background there was a loud cheering. The boy turned round, away from the camera. He ran jerkily away from it across a yard covered in partially melted snow towards an indistinct group of people who had a cement wall and drainpipe behind them.

The boy came grinning back across the yard, followed by similarly dressed children – an old woman in the background gesticulating and waving something in the air that was, Joel soon realised, a knife. Then all the people were left behind and the only thing on screen was two gloved hands holding – briefly – a bloodied pig's head with its eyes shut, before the head was dropped into the snow and what looked like a game of football started. The film ended.

A vague sense of outrage started to creep over him at the thought of their non-Kurdish au pair showing Aggie home-made films of her relatives playing football with a freshly sawn-off pig's head.

Then he had an idea. *The* idea.

'You want me to make a copy of this so you can watch it on the computer?'

Aggie nodded, and skipped back into Martina's room.

Joel started to download the clip then sent it to Tory. As he unplugged the lead from Martina's phone, a message came up: five missed calls. Half curious, he took a closer look. They were all from Martin. He'd phoned her five times in the past hour.

Through the open window, he could hear the diesel engine of a taxi making its way up Prendergast Road. Martina's phone started suddenly ringing. Startled, Joel nearly dropped it as Martina appeared again in the bedroom door.

'It's Martin,' he said blankly, handing her the phone.

He watched her check the screen then switch it off.

The next minute his phone started to ring. Martina gave him a quick look. They were both having the same thought – Martin.

'Hello?'

'Joel?' Tory barked. 'I need to talk business – that film you just sent.'

'Film?' Joel tried to concentrate.

'The pig film – just now – I was online.'

'The . . . . Oh, yeah.' Joel turned his back on Martina.

'Joel, are you with me?'

'Yeah, I'm with you . . . I didn't think you'd get it till Monday. So, what d'you think?'

'Well . . . I more than liked it, Joel.'

'You did?'

Tory hadn't more than liked anything he'd done in years.

'It was just so . . . so fucking eloquent,' she carried on.

Now she had his full attention. Fucking eloquent – he'd thought so.

'Where did you film it?'

Joel had given this some thought. 'The Balkans.'

'When were you in the Balkans?'

'I was there in Nineteen ninety-eight – remember?'

Tory didn't. 'Of course. Of course,' she said again. 'Have you got a title for it?'

'No.'

'Well, you need to think of a title. We'll talk. If we get this right, Joel, I'm seriously thinking about the Turner Prize. I mean, what you've done here, it turns its back on gimmickry – it's just so raw. I'm shutting up now. We'll talk . . .'

He was raw – he was turning his back on gimmickry – the Turner Prize . . .

# 44

Margery was back at No. 22 following Leicestershire Council's decision to remove her bungalow's old windows and replace them with uPVC double glazing, rendering her home temporarily uninhabitable. This was how she put it to Robert, knowing it would provoke – as it promptly did – an invitation to come and stay with them. Which was why, on the morning of the 12 June, she came to be standing at the bay window looking through Kate and Robert's single glazing at Kate as she turned into the gate at No. 22 with two Tesco carrier bags.

It didn't occur to Margery to go and open the door. She stayed where she was, listening to her daughter-in-law turn the key in the lock, and only turned round when Kate poked her head into the room to see how Flo and Findlay were doing.

Both her and Margery watched Flo try to pick up a plastic cube that rattled, her hands wide open, distended as she tried to grasp the object, concentrating so hard she was letting out a succession of rasping sounds. 'She'll be crawling soon,' Margery observed. 'You'll have to get a playpen.'

'Where's Findlay?' Kate asked, ignoring this.

'Upstairs.' Margery couldn't be any more specific than this because she hadn't actually been upstairs. She'd been too busy down here watching Kate's friend Evie and her husband start to construct the stalls.

'Isn't Robert up yet?' Kate said.

'Haven't heard a peep from him – must be fast asleep still.'

Kate stared at her then backed out of the room with the shopping.

A few seconds later, Margery heard her banging about in the kitchen. 'When's your mother getting here?' she called out.

'In about twenty minutes – she just rang. Listen, it's a help-yourself breakfast this morning. I've got to get out and start on the stalls.'

Margery smiled flatly at her reflection in the window. Since when wasn't it a help-yourself breakfast in this house?

She went through to the kitchen, walking through the shafts of dust that the sunlight illuminated.

Kate was in the study, irritably folding away the sofa bed.

'I was getting to that,' Margery said defensively.

'Margery, it's fine.' With a grunt, Kate let go of the handle and the bed base dropped into place inside the sofa. 'It's Robert's job.'

Without commenting on this, Margery started to pick up her stray belongings – the nightdress case Robert had made her in home economics, the pink plastic hairbrush. Wincing with the effort, Margery knelt down and pushed the small suitcase she'd bought in the ASDA luggage sale under the armchair. 'There,' she said, getting unsteadily to her feet again. 'Tidy enough for you now?'

'Margery . . .'

'I would of done the bed if you'd given me a chance.'

'It's not your job, it's Robert's,' Kate said again, trying not to lose patience.

304

The next minute she was banging around in the kitchen in an attempt to wake up Robert. Margery knew exactly what she was doing – Kate was far more spiteful than she gave herself credit for.

Margery remained poised in the study doorway, feeling stranded. She often felt stranded at No. 22 Prendergast Road, and as a consequence spent a lot of time hovering in doorways. Something Kate had commented on to Robert, saying that all his mother did was hang constantly in doorways. Most people moved between rooms in a house, but not Margery. Margery moved between doorways.

She held onto the doorframe as the bout of vertigo passed. These were now happening on a regular basis and were probably – Edith pointed out – the precursor to a stroke. A fortnight ago it had happened after her weekly ASDA trip as she was getting off the mobility bus with her shopping at the end of the estate. The bus doors had opened onto a thick black roadside puddle, the sun had been shining, and in the distance she'd heard the sounds of horses making their way from the stables up the road towards the fields near the bypass. She'd looked up at the sound, then the next minute felt herself falling. She'd come to almost instantly – as two of the passengers and the driver got to her.

She could smell mud from the verge she was lying face down across, the bottom half of her legs were wet, she hurt everywhere, one of the bags her shopping had been in was flapping near her face and the vacuum-pack bag of carrot batons had exploded when she'd landed on top of it. The bus driver was saying to her, 'Come on love, let's get you onto your feet.' There were hands all over her – all of them old – a face she recognised came briefly into view, but she couldn't move. She just lay there sobbing, her mouth full of grass and mud.

'D'you mind?'

Margery opened her eyes, trying to get her bearings. She couldn't have blacked out because she was still standing upright, but she couldn't for the life of her remember where she was. The walls around her were painted a funny colour, there was a sweet sickly smell in the air, and a rack opposite full of coats that she had no memory of ever having worn.

'Margery?'

She concentrated hard on the face in front of her. It was Kate. Kate was married to Robert. Robert lived in a house in London.

'D'you mind giving this to Flo?'

Margery stared blankly at the puddle of baby rice in the Peter Rabbit bowl and carried on staring at it as the bowl was transferred from Kate's hands to hers. 'Where are you going?' she said, hoping she didn't sound helpless.

'Upstairs – to check on Findlay and wake up Robert.'

'It's Saturday,' Margery protested.

Ignoring this, Kate jogged upstairs, leaving Margery stranded in the study doorway, staring at the bowl of baby rice.

*One teaspoon to be taken at bedtime.* Margery's mind automatically read out the words painted round the side of the dish then she went off in search of Flo. Where was Flo? She turned round and checked the study, but there was no sign of her there. Next, she went into the kitchen – then the lounge.

She perched slowly on the edge of the sofa and leant forward with the spoon, but Flo just turned her head away. Margery managed to get the next mouthful in, but that was dribbled back out and, as she leant forward to scoop it off the carpet, she felt another rush of vertigo. Afraid, she sat still, waiting for it to pass, then started to slowly, methodically eat Flo's baby rice.

I'm going to have a stroke, she thought, sucking the red plastic spoon. I'm going to die.

She looked up, the spoon in her mouth, as a car pulled up outside.

Kate's mother, Beatrice, had arrived.

'Look,' Findlay said as Kate went into his room – pointing to his radiator, which was crawling with Lego men.

He'd Sellotaped the green magnetic strips from his Geomag kit to the back of all his Lego people and stuck them to the radiator, turning it into an overcrowded rock-face that was being erroneously scaled on Findlay's orders. In the past fort-night, Findlay had become obsessed with all things magnetic.

'That's fantastic, Finn.'

Crouched in front of the radiator, he rubbed his chin on his knee. 'You don't mean it.'

'Finn, I do,' she insisted. 'I think what you've done with your Lego people is fantastic.'

'I know,' he agreed, semi-appeased, then pulled a Lego fireman off the radiator and started to fly him through the air.

Kate went into their room. 'Robert?'

A sigh and the sound of the bed sheets moving as the body under them turned.

She moved slowly over to the bed, the room bright with the broken bars of sunlight making their way through the blinds.

'I've got a migraine.'

Robert looked awful, but then he looked awful all the time at the moment.

'Well, do you think you can get up?'

Next door, in the throes of a game with his newly magnetic Lego men, Findlay let out the sort of triumphant shout that signified a cruel triumph.

307

'I don't know – are people with migraine meant to get up?'

That was unpleasantly said, but then most of their attempts at communication lately – verbal, non-verbal and even the silences – had become unpleasant. She felt that every time he opened his mouth or touched her at the moment, it was to inflict pain.

Then it came to her, driving through sunlight and slow traffic one afternoon that, without either of them being aware of it, their marriage had been up against some huge, lumbering adversary for some time now; one they were meant to join forces against and fight together. She wasn't entirely sure what the adversary was – it was too endless and indistinct to identify. It could be their children, their mortgage lender, the education system, their parents, their friends, TV, London, the twenty-first century . . . or a combination of all these things. It wasn't clear. What was clear was that they'd subconsciously decided to face the adversary alone – not together – and that Kate had won her fight, without meaning to, while Robert had lost his, also without meaning to.

Was one survivor in a marriage enough to keep a marriage going?

Ros would have said 'yes', but Kate never thought to ask her. Firstly, because she presumed this wasn't something the Grangers had any experience of and, secondly, because Ros and she weren't really on speaking terms since Ros had put in her offer on the Beulah Hill house. Despite the fact that Mr Jackson had since decided to take the house off the market . . . .

Harriet would have given a despotically optimistic 'yes' – despite what Kate had witnessed in their kitchen on the night of the last PRC meeting.

But then, Staying Married was all part of Harriet's Plan, and if Staying Married was an Applied Art, she intended to excel in it.

Robert was staring at a corner of radiator where rust was bleeding through the chipped paintwork. Kate thought about sitting down on the edge of the bed, but knew she couldn't bear to be that close to him. There was an overwhelming smell of unwashed bed linen, unwashed hair and bad dreams in the room.

Kate stayed where she was and looked out of the window instead.

Outside, on the street, Evie and Joel and Ros were starting to set up the stalls. Soon she'd have to go down there and help them.

'You've got to resolve this Jerome thing,' she said absently.

Robert laughed. 'What?'

'I said, you've got to resolve this Jerome thing.'

He laughed again. 'Kate – I've got migraine.'

'I know.' She stayed by the window with her back to him. 'You said you were going to speak to the head.'

'I spoke to the head,' he said after a while.

Kate turned round. 'Why didn't you say?'

'She told me to pray for Jerome.'

The blinds started to rattle lightly and Kate lifted her head instinctively to catch the morning breeze coming through the open window.

'Les told me that the LA are currently investigating her for fraudulent activity.'

'What sort of fraudulent activity?' Kate asked, semi-interested.

'Using school funds to launch her career as a prophetess – there are posters of her on the sides of buses. Have you got any idea how much an advertising campaign like that costs? Simba, who'd eat glue if she told him to, reckons she's got enough followers to fill a small arena. The prophetess has got a disciplinary hearing and is threatening to sue the LA.'

'For what?'

'I don't know – business damages? Ellington's on the verge of special measures and they want her to go quietly. So she's putting together a package that includes a six-figure sum and full pension benefits.'

Robert didn't sound like a man with a migraine as he said this.

'You've got to get out,' Kate said, more harshly than she'd intended. When he didn't respond to this, she added, 'And right now you've got to get up – you've got to, Robert. I can't do today on my own – your mum's downstairs, my mum's on her way and we've got this street party.'

Robert groaned and pulled the duvet up over his head.

'And we've got to talk about the house.'

'Shit – please don't bring up the house thing now,' Robert mumbled from beneath the duvet.

'Well, there's never a right time to bring up the house thing.'

A car pulled up on the street outside and, downstairs, Margery was yelling something.

Kate left the bedroom and went out into the hallway. 'What's that?'

'I said, your mum's here.'

Kate went downstairs past Margery, who was hovering in the lounge doorway with the red plastic spoon in her hand, and got to the front door just as Beatrice was about to ring it.

'Good God,' Beatrice said, her eyes running all over her daughter. 'What have they been doing to you?'

'I know – I know,' Kate said, resisting the urge to burst into tears.

Mother and daughter hugged.

'Margery,' Beatrice said, in her usual irately enthusiastic way.

Margery and Beatrice didn't hug – primarily because Margery, who tended to only hug people she actually liked, was too busy eyeing her suspiciously to even contemplate moving from the lounge doorway. She was fairly certain Beatrice had had liposuction done in the past six months.

Beatrice pushed past her – noting the red teaspoon in Margery's hand – in search of Flo and, with a cry of delight, found her poised, juddering on her limbs, on the rug in the lounge. 'Oh, Kate – she's trying to crawl – you never said.'

Kate smiled, uninterested, as Flo was scooped up by Beatrice and placed professionally on her hip.

'She's been doing that for weeks now,' Margery put in.

'Where's Finn?' Beatrice asked.

'Upstairs. How was the journey?' Kate asked her.

'Traffic wasn't too bad. How's it all going – with the house?'

'No one's put an offer in yet.'

'They will.'

'I told them they don't want anyone putting an offer in till they've found somewhere to go.'

'I thought you had.' Beatrice turned to her daughter.

'It fell through. The vendor took it off the market.'

'Well, this is London,' Beatrice said expansively, rubbing noses with Flo. 'Plenty of housing stock. And I suppose you could always take a short-term let or something if somebody wanted this and you had to move out.'

'They can't rent,' Margery cried out, 'it'll cost a fortune. There's four of them,' she added, pointlessly. 'And what about all their furniture?'

'Storage,' Beatrice said. 'Margery – there's no need to panic.'

'But storage costs a fortune. And Robert's got enough on his plate without worrying about where you're all going to be living.'

'Where is Robert?' Beatrice asked.

'Upstairs in bed – exhausted,' Margery said.

'Migraine,' Kate put in.

'Exhausted,' Margery said again.

'Has there been any resolution with that boy?'

'What d'you think, Mum? The school's going onto special measures – nobody cares.' She sighed. 'I said I'd help put up the stalls.'

'Well, off you go – we're fine here,' Beatrice said confidently.

Flo started to cry, and Beatrice walked over to the window with her and watched Kate disappear up the street.

'I suppose we should go and start to get the cakes ready for the stall,' Beatrice said after a while, peering through the window. 'They've got a lovely day for it.'

Margery joined her. 'Um,' she agreed irritably.

'I'm glad you're here,' Beatrice said suddenly. 'There was something I wanted to talk to you about.'

Margery waited, interested.

'They're going through it at the moment, aren't they?'

'Who?'

Beatrice hesitated. 'Well – Kate and Robert.' Why was conversation with Margery like only being able to find reverse in a car backed up against a wall.

Margery didn't say anything.

'What with the house and everything . . . the incident with Robert – I think they've "done" their London stint, don't you? It's time for some fresh air and more metres-square of real estate for their money, or who knows what might happen . . .' Beatrice finished ominously as a van towing the council's recycling centre drove slowly past the window. It had been booked by Ros and was handing out information on composters as well as a limited number of hessian 'Bags for Life'. Ros was part of a local campaign to make their postcode the first plastic-bag-free-zone in the UK.

312

'East Leeke,' Margery said. 'There's a house for sale in East Leeke that would be perfect for them.'

Ignoring this, Beatrice said, 'Okehampton School's looking for a deputy head at the moment. I'm chair of governors there. Robert would be ideal . . .'

Margery stared blankly at her, trying to grasp what she was saying. London was bad for Robert – she didn't need Beatrice to tell her that. But at least while they were still in London, there was the possibility that, when they left, which was now looking more and more inevitable – they would move to East Leeke. If they moved to Okehampton, they'd never come to East Leeke, and Margery would die alone.

Beatrice's voice carried on. 'D'you think there's any way I could persuade him to apply? Or should I let Kate do that?'

Margery remained silent, lost in her own thoughts. Fate threw things at you that were either fair or unfair. You reacted against them and got lucky – or unlucky. It had never occurred to Margery to attempt to control fate; to activate it. Margery was going to die alone – and Beatrice wasn't.

Beatrice remained by the window holding Flo, who was now dropping off to sleep, waiting for Margery to respond to what she'd just said, while wondering if she'd even understood – whether she wasn't, after all, senile. 'Margery . . .'

Margery was staring straight past her, her eyes fixed on the house opposite. 'She's still there – look.'

Beatrice followed her gaze. There was a woman in a Disneyland Paris T-shirt standing at an upstairs window, holding a sign: Pleese help 02081312263

'She was there last time,' Margery said.

'Last time?'

'Last time I was here. She was holding the sign then as well.'

'What did you do?'

Margery hesitated. 'Nothing.'

Beatrice swung round. 'Nothing?'

Margery shook her head.

'Did you go over and knock? Have you tried ringing the number? Here.' Beatrice passed Flo gently to Margery, found her bag and came back with her mobile.

The woman remained motionless in the upstairs window of No. 21 as Beatrice stood in the downstairs window of No. 22 and rang the number.

'Don't,' Margery said suddenly. 'It might be a trap.'

'What sort of trap? The woman clearly needs help . . .' Beatrice broke off. 'It's ringing.'

'Kate says it's a brothel.'

Beatrice stared at her. 'Hello? Hello, I'm phoning from Prendergast Road in London. Hello? A woman gave us this number. From London – yes. It doesn't matter who I am – a woman gave us this number. I think she needs help. I don't know – it's difficult to tell. She's got dark hair and . . . Prendergast Road. She's inside a house on Prendergast Road. Wait – there may be more than one – we're in south London; southeast London, and . . .' Beatrice stared at her phone. 'They rang off.'

'Who were they?'

'No idea – foreign. Sounded Eastern European, maybe Russian. I don't know.' Beatrice looked up at the woman again. 'She's pregnant. Look at the line of her T-shirt.'

Margery was just about to look when the silver BMW pulled up on the pavement opposite and the woman disappeared from the upstairs window. The same man and woman as before got out.

'Nice car,' Margery said pointedly, watching it pull up outside the house – as though the neighbours' BMW somehow reflected well on Robert.

Beatrice stared at her. It was difficult to know how to respond to these irrelevant and misjudged comments Margery made, other than to put them down to something medical. 'I'm going over there,' she said.

'You can't.' Margery was horrified. 'You can't,' she said again, but by then Beatrice was at the front door and the next minute Margery was watching her cross the road and start talking to the Lithuanian woman.

They talked for about two minutes. The Lithuanian was nodding and smiling. Then Beatrice made her way back over to No. 22 as the man and woman disappeared inside No. 21.

'She said the girl's a cousin of hers. Her English wasn't great, but she seemed to insinuate the girl was simple in the head or something.'

'Oh,' Margery said, relieved.

'I didn't like her,' Beatrice announced. 'And I didn't believe her either. Did you notice the bag she was carrying? There was a ph indicator inside and swabs for taking blood tests.' Beatrice paused. 'Those are the sorts of things a midwife paying a house visit would carry.'

'A midwife?' Margery said in disbelief. 'I had her down as a Lithuanian prostitute – although she could probably pass as an air hostess. The landlord at the Fox and Hounds has a girlfriend who looks just like her – and she's Lithuanian.'

Beatrice turned to her. 'Margery . . .'

Margery felt herself start to go dizzy as small black sunspots exploded in front of her eyes. 'I think I'm going to have a stroke.'

# 45

Upstairs in No. 236, Casper was steering his remote control Raptor vehicle backwards and forwards across the floor under the bed while Miles tried to get dressed. Miles was a man who not only felt comfortable wearing a suit; he actually preferred wearing a suit to anything else. Monday to Friday, Miles got dressed in under ten minutes while at the weekend he came down to breakfast in the old three-quarter-length swimming trunks and oversized T-shirt he wore to bed – and was often still wandering around in them at midday. He found a safety net of sorts in sourcing his entire 'casual' wardrobe from one label – it was Harriet who set him on this track – and for a lot of years, his steadfast casual label had been Hackett. But then a few weeks ago, while visiting a development of new-builds that Lennox Thompson were selling, he'd noticed that most of the builders on the site were wearing Hackett. There had been a man laying bricks in the exact same outfit he'd barbecued monkfish kebabs in the Sunday before.

So now he was in a post-Hackett, pre-anything-else casual-wear limbo land. Sighing, he got slowly dressed in an old pair of jeans to the continual electronic snarl of Casper's Raptor.

'Be careful on the walls there, Cas,' he said, as the back-flipping Raptor left two faint tyre tracks just above the skirting board.

'Cas' was Miles's take on his son's full name, which he didn't like. He wasn't entirely convinced by 'Cas' – neither was Casper, for that matter – but they were both going along with it because the intention was right.

He tried to keep his voice level, aware that he got snappy easily at the moment. In fact, ever since a fortnight ago, when Mr Jackson took No. 8 Beulah Hill off the market. He hadn't said anything to Harriet, but he'd been thinking of buying it.

'What was there before buildings and roads and trains?' Casper asked suddenly.

Miles sat down on the edge of the unmade bed. 'Well . . . there was forest.'

'But were there people?'

'Not very many, but there were people, yes.'

'Where did they live?'

'They lived in caves in the forest.'

'Did the caves have doors?'

'No – they were just caves.' Miles pulled a pair of socks on.

'So how did they stop the burglars coming in?'

'Well, there weren't any burglars, there were just lots and lots of beasties.'

'So how did they stop the beasties from coming in?'

'Fire. They were terrified of fire.'

'Why?'

Miles thought about this. In fact, Casper was the only person who made him think about anything. 'Well, they were kind of racing each other, the men and the beasties – to see who would come up with fire first – only they didn't know it was a race.'

Miles had been touched, lately, by the way Casper came

to find him. At the weekend, he actively sought him out, and the nights Miles was home late, Harriet just couldn't get him to sleep.

'Dad?'

'Um?'

'Can you imagine if the beasties won the race?'

'Nope.'

'I can.' Casper paused. 'I don't like my packed lunch.' Then he started the Raptor up again, sending it out of the bedroom and down the stairs.

Miles got up and was about to start making the bed when he noticed the hard yellowish patch on the sheet on his side. He stared at it.

He must have come in his sleep again last night.

It was the same dream every night. An alley . . . in the dark . . . rain . . . Jessica Palmer dressed in the grey pinstripe suit she had that looked so good with the yellow blouse under it . . . pressed against a wet wall. She was covered in bruises, cut up, her clothes torn. She'd been seriously roughed up and he couldn't work out whether it was him who'd done it to her or somebody else and he'd got to her just in time. In fact, she was so badly roughed up it was as though she'd only just got to her feet again. Her right cheek was completely swollen, her lips were doubled in size and her right eye was almost closed.

He went to get a sponge from the bathroom to clean off the stain, sponging it down as best he could before making the bed and following Casper downstairs.

Downstairs, Harriet and her mother were sitting at the kitchen table, so alike from behind that he couldn't tell the difference.

Harriet's mother, Caroline, had arrived a fortnight ago – ostensibly to help with Phoebe, who was going through a bad patch at nights, but really to look after Miles who was,

Harriet had clearly indicated to Caroline, going through his own bad patch.

It wasn't until Caroline arrived and Miles saw her in action that he realised just how much Harriet had inherited her mother's tendency to treat him like a child. In their eyes, he was playing up at the moment; suffering from a lack of attention following Phoebe's birth. Every time Caroline called out, 'Tea time, boys,' he felt a surge of rage. Or when him and Casper were talking and he pushed Casper to argue his case, Caroline would scold them both waggishly with, 'Stop the fighting now, boys.'

She had moved tea time forward so that they all ate together with the children, which not only meant they had time in the evening to watch even more TV than usual, but that he didn't get his first proper drink of the day until eight o'clock.

The other night they had all been sitting round the table when Casper had said suddenly, 'Where did Grandma Burgess go?'

There'd been a pause. The women had looked unusually incapable of answering this. So Miles had stepped in with, 'She's in the sky.'

'What's she doing up there?'

'Sleeping.'

'How did her bed get up there?'

'Well . . .' Miles had thought about this, pushing his fork around his plate of kiddie food. What had possessed Caroline to cook dino burgers for all of them? 'She doesn't need a bed because . . . because just before going up in the sky you turn to dust.'

'How d'you turn to dust?'

'Casper, eat up,' Caroline put in, starting to panic.

Miles could hear it in her voice. 'Well,' he said, 'they burn you.'

'They burn you?' Casper looked horrified.

Caroline and Harriet looked horrified.

'But if they burn me that would hurt so much. I don't want to go up in the sky.'

'Well, you won't – not for a long, long time.'

Then, not only to distract Casper, but also himself – he was, he realised, close to tears – he'd changed the subject, turning to Harriet again and saying, 'Have you got any idea why Martin Granger would call round here at eleven o'clock at night?'

'Martin Granger?'

'Uh-huh.'

'Martin Granger – Ros's husband?' Harriet had said again, slower and more heavily this time.

'I was running through last month's CCTV footage and there he was – must have been about four weeks ago.' He didn't mention how struck he'd been by the expression on Martin's face.

'At eleven o'clock.'

'At eleven o'clock,' he confirmed.

'I don't think I've ever answered the door to Martin Granger.'

'Neither have I.'

'So who did? Wait a minute – it wasn't the night we went to The Phoenix, was it?'

They'd stared at each other.

Caroline had stared at them staring at each other.

'Martina,' he'd said, interested.

'Martina,' Harriet had echoed, worried.

That had been last night.

Now, he ambled over to the bench, extracted two slices of breads from the debris, and put them in the toaster. While these two pieces were toasting, he pulled out another two pieces and ate them, his eyes flickering over the newspaper in front of him:

ANGRY CHEF KILLS LOVER, CUTS HER UP IN PUB KITCHEN AND PUTS REMAINS IN WHEELIE BIN . . .

Half-interested, he read through the piece, shaking some orange peel from the last paragraph.

'Did you see it?' Harriet asked.

She must have been watching him.

He quoted the article he'd been reading. 'Angry chef kills lover, puts her in pub kitchen—'

'No,' Harriet cut in quickly, 'Not that – the house.'

Miles picked up the newspaper. 'What is this?'

'Mum's – she brought it with her. Go to the Property section.'

Miles flicked through – WOMAN DRIVES CAR INTO DISUSED QUARRY WITH DEAD HUSBAND BESIDE HER. He started to read again, fascinated by the idea that there were still people out there – most of them in Buckinghamshire by the looks of things – who quite literally loved each other to death.

'Not there – the back,' Harriet's voice commanded as he read how Mrs Milbank had driven the car over the edge of a quarry with her dead husband beside her – Harold Milbank, aged 52, had died of a heart attack forty-eight hours previously.

He gave up trying to read the article and turned to the Property section. Harriet was standing beside him. He couldn't be sure, but it felt like she was making a point of rubbing against him. She'd been, he noticed, a lot more physically demonstrable since the arrival of Caroline, who had clearly been lecturing her daughter on her lackadaisical attitude towards her wifely duties. Harriet had taken her mother's advice to heart – as she always did – and was attempting to be more proactive in that area, but there was nothing inherent about it and, as a consequence, this renewed effort had the adverse effect on Miles. The other night, as Harriet rolled onto her back – on Caroline's orders – he couldn't even get it up, while later, in his dreams, he raped Jessica Palmer down the alley in torrential rain again.

He couldn't bear the thought of the mother/daughter exchange that would have taken place when he'd gone to work the next day. Caroline probably already had the pot of Viagra to hand. For all he knew, they could have been crushing it up and adding it to his food for days now.

Marriage mattered a lot to Caroline, especially her daughter's – which had, in her opinion, been far too long coming.

She knew all about the death of the libido, the exhaustion, but – as she told Harriet time and time again – there was no point explaining all this to a man who was no longer counting the days, or even the weeks, but the months since he'd last had sex.

'If nothing else, you could at least, you know go down there and . . . before nodding off,' Caroline had pointed out over coffee the other morning while Phoebe was feeding.

At which point Harriet had completely flown off the handle at her, letting out a stream of nonsensical outrage, finally culminating in an explosive, 'Why would I start that now?' Which sent Phoebe into hysterics.

Caroline, incredulous, had said, 'You mean you've *never* given Miles a blow job?'

'For Christ's sake, I've never given anyone a blow job.'

'But you're thirty-nine!'

It was worse than Caroline – taking call after call in her Buckinghamshire kitchen from a sobbing Harriet – had ever imagined. Well, it was all Charles's fault for over-educating her like he did: ruining her, in Caroline's opinion. No wonder it had taken her so long to get married.

'Keeper's Cottage,' Harriet said softly to Miles, leaning over to point out the picture of an eighteenth-century cottage

322

semi-masked in an abundance of flora and fauna. 'Look – I never realised they had a paddock as well. That's the cottage I've dreamt of living in since . . . since forever.'

'But it's in Little Widdrington,' Miles said, trying to imagine himself holed up with Harriet in an eighteenth-century cottage in the middle of some woods in the middle of Buckinghamshire – and shrinking from the idea. What would be the chances of spotting Jessica Palmer from behind the lead mullion windows of Keeper's Cottage in Little Widdrington? Nil. Nada. Zero. Zilch. Fortunately, Harriet couldn't see his face.

Unfortunately, Caroline could.

He looked quickly away.

'And Mum says the Fishers were thinking of selling their estate agency,' Harriet carried on, bringing the whole package together and presenting it to Miles.

'Would you seriously contemplate moving to Little Widdrington?'

There was nothing, as far as Harriet could see, that needed contemplating. Casper not getting into St Anthony's . . . Keeper's Cottage *and* the Fisher Estate Agency coming onto the market . . . it was fate. The planets had aligned. 'I've always dreamt of living in Keeper's Cottage,' Harriet said again. 'I can't believe it's actually for sale.'

'It's only the second time it's been on the market since we moved to Little Widdrington,' Caroline put in.

'And look at the price,' Harriet said, speeding up, allowing herself to get excited now. 'Look at the price, Miles – we'd reduce our mortgage by half. And the garden – the garden, for the children.'

'The Fishers want a quick sale on their business – they've bought land in Spain they want to build on.'

'They've still got the original flagstones downstairs,' Harriet said.

His eyes scanned the ad. 'How d'you know about the flagstones? It doesn't say anything about flagstones here.'

'Mum went to have a look.'

'You've been to see it?' Miles said, turning to Caroline, who was pretending to wash up. 'What – like a viewing?' He was aware, as he said it, that his tone wasn't pleasant, but didn't care.

'Oh, Miles – just imagine it,' Harriet gushed, giving in to her ecstasy.

They were closing in on him – had been closing in on him for goodness knows how long – and he hadn't seen it coming. The relocation to Little Widdrington was being presented to him as a *fait accompli*. There was no escape. He was being sucked into the black tunnel that was Little Widdrington. If he didn't do something they were going to bring him to closure on this – right here, now, on a Saturday morning over a couple of slices of burnt toast.

Yellow blouses, yellow roses . . . all receding; barely visible now at the end of the tunnel.

Caroline and Harriet were staring at him, worried, as if they were about to bind and gag him right then and there and start driving to Little Widdrington with him in the boot.

# 46

Inside No. 283 Prendergast Road, Jessica stood banging on Ellie's door.

'Ellie – open up! Ellie!'

There was no sound coming from inside Ellie's room.

'Mum!' Arthur called out from somewhere.

'Just a minute.'

'There's something wrong with Ninja Action Man's eyes . . . Mum.'

'Just a minute, Arthur.'

Jessica pushed open the bedroom door.

Since Ellie's GCSE exam leave started last month, she'd barely spoken to her. Something was wrong – more wrong than usual – and Jessica didn't know how much more of it she could stand.

Ellie rolled slowly over, blinking in the light and air coming into the room through the open door. She stared at Jessica then rolled back over.

The smell of dope in the room was overwhelming – made worse by the fact that the windows and curtains remained permanently closed. The dope fumes had in fact permeated the entire maisonnette – as she'd kissed Arthur goodbye at nursery the other morning, his hair had smelt of dope. The only two suits she possessed came back from the dry-cleaner's still smelling of it. As soon as she opened the downstairs door, she smelt it. And she'd only found out on Wednesday when she called in to check on Ellie at lunchtime that her supplier was the girl from the florist's downstairs. She'd found them both on the sofa smoking and watching a documentary about Papua New Guinea. The erroneous copies of *CHAT* that kept turning up in the maisonette came from the same source.

The dope smoking had intensified since exam leave started and now Jessica, worried every second of every day, called in as often as she could to check on Ellie. Nobody ever came to the house and Ellie never seemed to go out – other than when she had a shift at Film Nite. Occasionally she might be out of the house the whole afternoon, returning at dusk with mud on her shoes. She said she went to the park.

Jessica wasn't sleeping at night and by two in the afternoon could barely keep her eyes open at work. She'd fallen asleep in the car after a viewing on Thursday, and most nights now she fell asleep for forty minutes beside Arthur on his bed – after settling him.

She was smoking as much nicotine as Ellie was dope, and on Friday she'd had a complaint from nursery staff who'd overheard Arthur saying 'fuck' – which was highly probable given that 'fuck' was pretty much the only word Ellie used when she did bother to talk to her.

She crossed Ellie's room and opened the curtains and the window.

'Why are you doing that?'

'It stinks in here – I've got to get some air in.'

'God, what's that?' Ellie groaned as the smell of barbecue filled the room.

'The street party.'

'Street party? Have they only just found out we won the war or something? I'm going to puke.'

'So – puke,' Jessica said, breathing in the dope-free barbecue fumes.

Behind her Ellie rolled off the bed and made for the bathroom. Outside, the road curved and went downhill, so she couldn't see any signs of the street party from the bedroom window. She'd left messages with Evie, offering to help on any stalls they were short of help on, but Evie hadn't got back to her. She didn't feel like going, but Arthur wanted to. Casper Burgess had told him that they were doing face painting.

'Maybe we could look for some new clothes for you,' she said, turning round as Ellie walked, swaying, back into the room. 'Boutique have got a stall – we could have a poke.'

A sudden memory cut through the morning – of her mother, Linda, saying exactly the same thing to her, and of her giving the exact same response as Ellie was about to give.

Ellie collapsed back onto the bed. 'I don't want any new clothes.'

'We need to start looking – as of September you'll be able to wear your own clothes to school and you haven't got many.'

'Mum, when are you coming?' Arthur called out.

Jessica moved towards the door. 'D'you want me to run a bath or something?' she said, as lightly as she could. 'I've ironed your jeans.' As she spoke, her mind filled with the image of Ellie, Arthur and her moving happily among the stalls – Arthur getting his face painted, Ellie choosing a couple of tops. She allowed herself to become aware of the day outside, the brilliant June day whose airy, wide-flowing breeze brought round stretches of human noise that seemed to Jessica to come from another world.

'Ellie, what's going on? You have to tell me what's going on.'

'Nothing,' Ellie yelled back. 'Nothing's going on so just fuck off.'

Jessica slammed Ellie's bedroom door shut and went

downstairs, glancing into the kitchen where there was a lot of milk on the floor. 'Arthur?'

'I was hungry. I was trying to put it on some cocoa pops then it fell on the floor because of the lid.'

'It's okay – I'll sort it out later.'

Arthur was kneeling at the coffee table with Burke the Transformer in one hand and Ninja Action Man in the other. The lab goggles he wore all the time were over his eyes.

He didn't look up when Jessica sat down on the sofa, folded her arms and put her head on her knees. He carried on staring down at his right foot, resting his chin on his knee and hooking his hands under his toes. 'Mum,' he said tentatively, without looking at her, 'Mum – can you sort out Ninja's eyes?'

Jessica looked slowly up at him, her eyes bloodshot, blank.

He watched her scratch her forehead and attempt to smile.

'Sure I can,' she said with an effort.

He passed her Ninja Action Man and watched in silence as she pulled off the head and pushed her fingers inside until his eyes clicked into place then put the head back on and handed it to him.

'It works,' he said, pleased, moving the switch at the back so that the eyes clicked suspiciously from side to side.

The sound of drums beating somewhere close by started up. This couldn't go on. She needed to talk to somebody about Ellie and the only person she could think of right then was Robert Hunter. She stood up.

'Are we going to the street party?' Arthur asked, hopeful but not excited.

'Not just yet – I need to see Findlay's dad about something first.'

Arthur didn't comment on this. 'Then can I get my face painted?'

'What d'you want it painted as?'

'Burke.'

# 47

Outside, the street party was in full swing and Jessica had to get through it to get to No. 22.

The first stall was the Ghanaian drummer's; as he carried on unpacking drums from the back of the Nissan parked by the stall, children were gathering round the ones already lined up, tentatively beating on them. As she passed, Jessica heard him explain the meaning of the symbols down the side of the drum and tell a teenager how the goatskin had been stretched and treated.

'Can we do the drums?' Arthur asked.

'Later – we'll do them later.'

'My face, I want my face painted,' he said as they passed Harriet's Natural Nappy Co. stall. A turquoise and white butterfly was painted across Harriet's face and Aggie McRae was having her face done.

'Later,' Jessica responded, pulling on his arms and trying not to lose patience.

She probed the crowd for Robert, but couldn't see him anywhere – then noticed Miles, talking to Joel McRae, too late.

Behind her, a patter of drums started up.

Miles had seen her.

\*

Joel was pushing Ingrid backwards and forwards in the buggy, trying to get her to sleep.

'Aggie – drums!' he called out. 'D'you want to see them? They'd be great for her motor coordination skills,' he said to Miles, starting to sway on the spot, suddenly taken with the idea of getting Aggie drum lessons. Most people's kids took recorder or piano or something. Imagine saying to people, 'Aggie does drums.'

'She's dyspraxic,' he explained proudly to Miles, adding, 'developmental coordination disorder. Apparently it affects four times as many boys as girls, so Aggie – she's really rare.'

His eyes flickered quickly over Miles's pudgy face to see if he could detect anything close to envy. Interest – he was sure there was interest. Well, that was good: interest was the first step on the road to envy. He felt buoyed up. He was only just 'coming out' about Aggie and the whole dyspraxia thing, but had already noted that it went down well. His agent, Tory, had been positively intrigued – even murmured something about getting her son, Jed, tested.

'We had no idea,' he carried on to Miles. 'I mean, we noticed she was sort of clumsy, bumping into stuff, unable to judge distances, didn't take to riding her bike, temper tantrums (Miles here let out a short laugh that momentarily confused Joel), rough and aggressive with her sister, Ingrid . . . but we just thought: that's toddlers. Then it carried on and Evie took her to see someone and they put a name to it. It was a huge relief to us,' he insisted, 'really huge.' And Aggie really was flourishing under all the attention from occupational therapists, speech and language therapists . . . her tantrums were getting worse, but then – she was a girl. 'Dyspraxia is a real problem for kids with a high IQ.' He paused, but this didn't elicit any comment. Oh, God, it was tragic, he thought, his eyes sliding quickly over Miles who had gone all static on him. Did he take his tongue out at the weekend or something?

Miles hadn't said a word yet.

'They've got a dyspraxia unit at St Anthony's, which is where Aggie's going.'

At last, Miles turned to look at him. 'St Anthony's?'

Joel nodded. 'What about yours?'

He waited, but Miles just turned away in order to stare vacantly about him again. 'We're thinking of moving to Buckinghamshire,' Miles said, abruptly.

'God, I'm sorry,' Joel said, offering his condolences.

'Yeah.' Miles paused, his attention caught suddenly by Jessica Palmer. 'Little Widdrington – the village my wife grew up in.'

'God, I'm sorry,' Joel said again.

Miles didn't respond; he was too busy watching Jessica, who was virtually running down the street towards him.

She's come for me, he thought, his face looking briefly – to the few onlookers there were in the vicinity – beatific. He ignored the fact that she was pulling Arthur along behind her and that Arthur looked frightened and kept tripping up.

'Robert,' she said, coming to a halt by the stall. 'You haven't seen Robert, have you? Robert Hunter?' Ignoring Miles, she appealed to Joel, who was staring at her, horrified.

Jessica cast her eyes self-consciously over herself – the leggings with the white bleach spots on and the oversize T-shirt with a map of Lake Como on it that Joe and Lenny had brought back from their Italian Lakes trip.

'I think we might be moving to Buckinghamshire,' Miles said to her.

She stared back at him.

Joel stared at him.

'Mum,' Arthur said, tugging on her arm. 'When are we going to get our faces painted?'

'In a minute. I've got to go,' Jessica said to Miles. 'I'm looking for Robert.'

'Wait – Jessica – I dream about you,' he whispered urgently. 'And it's the same dream; it's the same dream every time. It has to mean something,' he said.

'I've got to go.'

'It has to mean something,' Miles insisted, trying not to raise his voice.

Jessica moved on down the street.

'It has to mean something,' he said suddenly to Joel, who was trying to push Ingrid away, towards the drums. 'What if I'm in love with her?'

Joel, realising Miles wasn't going to go away, lowered his voice to a whisper. 'She was wearing leggings . . .'

'I know – I can't stop thinking about her.'

'You can't stop thinking about fucking her. In the dream, you're fucking her, right?'

'Right. Yeah, but how did you . . .' Miles broke off, watching breathless as Jessica disappeared.

Jessica continued to push through the crowds of people, fumes from the industrial-sized barbecue filling the air – past parents busy applying sunscreen to offspring in buggies with Carpe Diem balloons tied to the handles, while trying to keep an eye on their running, tripping, lurching, already heat-addled older children, who had become their animal or superhero familiars at the hands of Harriet and her mother.

These people were enjoying themselves – why couldn't she be like them, just for once?

The Southwark Council recycling unit had a queue of people outside hoping there were still enough 'Bags for Life' left.

She passed Ros, in full control of the Carpe Diem stall.

'Does Arthur want a balloon?' Ros asked, handing the mute, watchful Arthur one of the pink and black Carpe Diem balloons.

Arthur accepted the balloon in silence, and couldn't take his eyes off it.

Ros paused, waiting for Jessica to comment on the balloon, but all Jessica said was, 'Have you seen Robert?'

'Robert?'

'Robert Hunter.'

'Oh. I think Kate said he had a migraine or something – she's just over there, next to the Boutique stall.'

Jessica moved on towards Kate's cake stall, which was opposite the allotment stall run by Letitia Parry, chair of the Allotment Committee. In fact, the Parrys had two stalls – one advertising the allotments, which was also selling allotment produce and taking deposits from people who wanted to add their names to the waiting list, and one covered in banners swaying precariously in the hot wind that read *Save Our Allotments – Say No to Mobile Phone Mast*. The allotments were under threat – from T-Mobile. People on their mobiles walked sheepishly past, glared at by a group of Goths from the Nunhead Cemetery Preservation Society, who'd agreed to help man the stall because Nunhead Cemetery had also been targeted by T-Mobile as a potential phone-mast site.

Letitia was handing out *Say No to Mobile Phone Mast* leaflets, getting people to sign the petition and talking rapidly in incomplete sentences, her tongue licking frantically at her lower lip. 'He'll end up with leukemia if that mast goes up,' she barked at Jessica as she passed, while reminding her husband, Giles, of the price of the vegetables for sale, and talking intimately to Labour Councillor Derek Stokes – who was shifting uncomfortably from foot to foot.

Derek was sweating – sweating intensely. He always found this first flush of summer weather, when women started to remove their outer layers, difficult. Standing there, talking to Letitia, managing with an effort to keep his huge walrus eyes riveted on the network of fine, purple veins that had broken out over her face and looked, in places, as if they might break free altogether – he felt as though he was drowning, quite literally drowning, in a sea of breasts. He was intoxicated and had to put a lot of effort into stopping his eyes from sliding over Letitia, whose body, swollen with the heat, was beginning to bulge in peculiar places.

Fortunately for him, she broke off just then to remind Giles – completely cutting across a young couple trying to buy early tomatoes – that he needed to take his blood-pressure medication.

Giles, in a sudden panic, dropped the money the young couple had given him and ended up taking double the recommended dose.

The next minute Jessica found herself and Arthur herded along with other parents and children in front of the allotment stall. They were being grouped for a press photograph.

'I just need to get through,' she said, but nobody moved.

Next to her, Giles Parry – Letitia's husband – started to hallucinate. It seemed to him that all the children were levitating, either out of their buggies or off the ground, and flying away. 'The children,' he said weakly to Letitia, who was busy giving her best to the camera as the photographer from *Southwark News* asked them to regroup one last time.

'Okay,' she called out, 'say bananas.'

'BANANAS,' Jessica automatically found herself joining in.

Letitia let out a cheer that was taken up in a confused way by everybody nearby, and that completely drowned out Giles's second attempt to point out that all the children were floating away into the sky. 'The children,' he said again.

Letitia's rabble-rousing monologue – primarily for the benefit of Derek Stokes, who'd gone a funny colour, she couldn't help noticing – about how this was only the start of the fight, washed pleasantly over people as slowly, unanimously, they decided they'd done their bit and took it upon themselves to disperse; already distracted by the slow, rhythmic beat coming from further up the street where the Ghanaian drummer was now playing.

Above the sound of the drums rose the clear, high-pitched wailing of David at No. 8, whose parents had ignored Ros's request to keep their son indoors. He stood in his favourite spot, his arms encircling the trunk of the loquat tree, singing happily.

The singing was affecting the older children who'd started to run round in circles in the middle of the road between the line of stalls, yelling excitedly to each other, under the impression they'd run into the middle of a complicated game with rules nobody was going to explain to them.

A boy with a pink and black Carpe Diem balloon tied to his head galloped down through the stalls.

Jessica made her way through the children to where Margery was hovering between the Boutique stall and Kate's cake stall, manned by Kate and Beatrice. Flo was in her pushchair, her face and dress covered in chocolate saliva.

'Finn!' Arthur yelled happily, catching sight of him under the table where what remained of the cakes were laid out.

He squatted down next to him. Today was going wrong and soon he was going to shut down – like Burke. He could make the whole world fall suddenly silent when he decided to shut down, and then the silence became something he could crawl into.

'I'm looking for Robert,' Jessica said to Margery.

'Robert? He's got a migraine – he's in the house.'

Inside No. 22, Robert – lying in bed, still, semi-conscious – heard the drums.

For a moment he thought he had somehow – miraculously – undertaken a journey he'd always dreamt of taking; a journey whose destination had been on the tip of his tongue for as long as he could remember, but that he'd never quite been able to articulate. Then he opened his eyes.

It struck him forcibly, for the first time, that he really had no idea how he came to be lying on this bed, in this bedroom, in this house, in this valley in south London. He'd grown up with the knowledge that the whole is greater than the sum total of its parts, but no matter how much he looked back on all the parts – and lately he'd been doing this frequently, minutely – the mathematics of his current situation were implausible: there was no whole.

He listened to the wind brushing through the branches of the rowan tree outside the bedroom window – now in full leaf – and the drums, louder, carried on the same wind that was blowing through the tree, and tried to decide whether he still had a migraine or not.

He'd been on the verge of getting up earlier – just after Kate left the room a second time – but then everyone forgot about him and in the silence that followed the exodus from the house, he fell into a much deeper sleep than the one he'd been tossing and turning in since 6.00 a.m. He had no idea what the time was now, but the house was still empty. He let his eyes close again, the sun falling warmly across his shoulders and chest, until he became aware of the front door bell ringing.

He waited, hoping it would go away.

It didn't.

With an effort, he put on the T-shirt and shorts he'd taken off the night before and made his way slowly downstairs.

He opened the front door.

There was Jessica Palmer waiting outside, under the sunflowers.

It struck him forcibly, as they stared at each other, that he couldn't think of anybody else he'd rather see right then.

'Ellie,' she said.

336

'Ellie – right.' Robert hesitated, peering – confused – at the activity in the street beyond them and the continual stream of people ambling past the gate. 'Come in – come in.'

Jessica stepped into the hallway, her eyes trying to adjust to the light as Robert shut the front door behind her.

She felt suddenly cold.

'Tell me,' Robert said, trying to lead her through to the kitchen.

Jessica stayed where she was so that they were standing with their backs against the walls of the narrow turn-of-the-century hallway. She was exhausted. What was she doing? Why had she come here? She didn't know this man. Then she found herself talking. 'I can't do it any more – I can't spend any more time in that flat with her or I'm going to kill her. I'm going to kill Ellie.'

She made a move towards the front door, but he caught her by the shoulder. 'Jessica . . .'

That was all it took. The next minute she was leaning against him, her hands over her face, pressed into his chest. The relief of being held, of being accepted and held by another human being after the past five years was almost too much. She'd got by on so little for so long, this would have been enough.

'I should have phoned. I've been wanting to phone you – about Ellie.'

'You have?' Jessica stood back, for a moment afraid.

'She sent me a note – a love letter, I suppose.'

'Ellie?'

Robert paused, watched Jessica accept this as she did everything – rapidly – whether she wanted to or not.

'My God, Robert. I should have seen that coming a long time ago. Why didn't I?'

'I should have phoned you about it.'

'Have you got the letter?'

He turned automatically to go and get it.

'No . . . wait. Leave it.' Jessica paused. 'When did she send it?'

'The week before exam leave started.'

She collapsed against the Hunters' hall wall. 'That's it. Have you contacted her, at all?'

He shook his head.

'Will you talk to her now?'

'Ellie?'

Jessica nodded.

'Is that a good idea?'

'Right now, it's the only idea I've got.'

The next minute, Robert was picking through the pile of shoes by the coat rack until he found his old tennis trainers and started to put them on, having trouble with the laces, which had been knotted since last summer. 'Fuck these shoes,' he said, suddenly furious.

'Here,' Jessica said, crouching next to him and unlacing one of the shoes.

She handed it back to him and he put it on in silence as she picked up the other one and unlaced that.

The next minute he stood up.

'I don't want to make any trouble for you,' she said.

He pulled her up. 'I don't care if you do.'


They stood in the kitchen at No. 283 Prendergast Road as a scream rippled suddenly through the layers of noise coming from outside.

'Ellie!' Jessica called out.

She went through to the lounge.

Behind her, in the kitchen, Robert stood staring at the puddle of milk, now rancid, on the kitchen floor. He heard Jessica run upstairs, then run back down again.

'Something's wrong,' she said from the doorway.

'Where's Ellie?'

'I don't know.'

'Has she gone out?'

'She doesn't go out – she never goes anywhere.'

'Maybe she went to Keisha's.'

'She's not talking to Keisha.'

'Did she have to go to work?'

Jessica shook her head irritably. 'Not today. Something's wrong,' she said again, staring at him.

He tried to take hold of her, but she pushed him gently to one side and went running back into the lounge-diner.

Now she knew what was wrong.

There it was – Ellie's Walkman on the coffee table. Ellie's Walkman never left her room. There was a note beside it:
... *to Arthur*

'She's gone, Robert – she's gone.'

'What d'you mean, gone?'

'I don't know, I mean gone, just gone. We've got to find her, we've got to.'

Robert didn't say anything. He was thinking about a conversation he'd had with Kate some time ago. It was at Easter – she said she'd seen Ellie up in the woods near the allotments and thought she was taking drugs up there.

'I think I know where she might be ...'

# 48

The rhythmic beating from the Ghanaian drummer's stall followed Robert and Jessica back down Prendergast Road. Jessica stood getting jostled on the pavement by No. 22 as Robert went over to the cake stall to talk to Kate.

'Robert? When did you get up?'

'Someone's gone missing,' he said.

'What's going on?' Beatrice asked.

'Ellie Palmer,' he said to Kate.

'Oh,' Beatrice said, trying to fathom the significance of Ellie Palmer and the fact that she had gone missing – and why it suddenly had something to do with them.

'Ellie Palmer? How d'you know?'

'Her mother doesn't know where she is,' Robert said coldly.

'She's probably just gone out and forgotten to say where. You must have done that when you were sixteen.'

'I don't think he ever did – no,' Margery said.

'Of course not,' Kate responded, without turning to look at Margery, who was standing beside her on the stall. She turned back to Robert. 'What's it got to do with us?'

Robert didn't respond to this. 'I'm taking the car.'

'Has Jessica even tried phoning people Ellie might be with?' Kate persisted.

'I'm taking the car.'

'The car?'

'Jessica's car's at the garage.'

'Why d'you need the car?'

'Because I think Ellie might be up at the allotments – you said you used to see her up there sometimes; in the woods.'

'Once. I saw her up there once.'

'I've got a feeling . . .'

'About Ellie Palmer? What has any of this got to do with us – and why the sudden need to start driving round the environs of south London on – on a whim,' she hissed.

'Jessica doesn't have whims,' Robert said, automatically.

'Do I know a Jessica?' Beatrice put in, still confused.

'You might have met her . . .' Kate said, unconvinced and uninterested. 'Robert—'

'Everything okay?' It was Jessica, who'd been watching them and approached unnoticed, her eyes on Robert – desperate.

Kate turned round, furious. 'I don't want you to go,' she said to Robert.

Robert stopped.

Jessica stopped; Margery and Beatrice stopped as well, even though nobody had been moving in the first place.

'That's absurd,' he said quietly.

'Why?' Kate said helplessly, accusingly. 'Why not just phone around?'

'Jessica's already tried that,' Robert said, trying to keep the anger out of his voice.

Jessica remained silent.

'You said you sometimes saw her up at the woods.'

'So why doesn't she go up to the woods and look for her?' She turned to Jessica. 'She's your daughter.'

'My car's being serviced,' Jessica explained again.

341

'Okay, we've wasted enough time.' Robert made to leave.

'I thought you had a migraine.'

'I did have a migraine – this morning.'

'He was exhausted,' Margery said, repeating her earlier theory.

'And after all, you would know – wouldn't you?' Kate said loudly, wildly, rounding on Margery. 'Because you spend so much bloody time here, you might as well just go ahead and move in.'

'Well, I can't help it,' Margery said, shocked. 'I can't help it if somebody on Leicestershire Council decided to replace all the windows in my bungalow with double glazing.'

'Only somebody on Leicestershire Council didn't, did they, Margery?' Kate shouted.

'Kate . . .'

Robert tried to take hold of her elbow, but where only seconds before she'd been desperate for his touch, now she shook him off.

'Kate . . . ,' Beatrice echoed.

'I phoned Leicestershire Council.'

Margery stared at her, horrified.

'They said they had no plans in the foreseeable future to put double glazing in your bungalow or any of the other bungalows on the estate.'

Robert stared at Kate for a few seconds more, then turned to Margery. 'Mum?'

'Edith,' Margery said after a while. 'They came for Edith.'

'Who came?' Robert asked.

'They came for Edith – they took all her cash, cards, chequebook, savings books. They came for her, Robert,' she said, tearful, appealing to him.

'I thought Edith was in hospital having a hip replacement done.'

'Luke – her son, Luke – found her on the sitting-room floor. Her hand was still round the TV remote. She must have been holding it when she went to answer the door.' Margery was breathless, alternately panting and whimpering. 'She *is* in hospital – but I didn't tell you the truth, Robert.'

'Mum, it's okay.'

'It's not okay – they're murdering old folk in their homes in East Leeke; they're smashing windows – setting fire to cars. I've been too terrified to leave the house – been living off *Take A Break* magazines, corned beef, baked beans . . .' She broke off. 'The National Express coach I got down here was the first time I slept properly in weeks.'

Robert stood gently rubbing the tops of her arms. 'Why didn't you just say?'

'I don't know.'

Robert turned to Kate. 'And what on earth possessed you to phone Leicestershire Council?'

'For fuck's sake, Robert,' Kate exploded.

'I can't stand all this dishonesty—'

'Dishonesty? Your mother lies; I expose those lies – and I'm the dishonest one?'

'You are dishonest – not the only one, but you are dishonest,' Margery said, disappearing past them across the road and into the house.

'Jessica,' Robert called out.

'I've got to go – I'll be fine.'

'I'll be there, just give me a minute.'

'I'll start to walk.'

'I'll catch you up – wait.' He went over to Margery who was emerging from the house, a piece of paper in her hand.

It was the St Anthony's letter.

Standing under the sunflowers, Margery watched him read

343

it through, but felt none of the triumph she'd anticipated feeling – just a bitter sort of fear. She even tried to grab it off him, but he turned away.

When he'd finished, he gave her a look that was unreadable, then crossed the street again and pushed the letter into Kate's hands.

'I want you to keep an eye on Arthur – I'll phone.'

Kate nodded, stared down at the letter then across the street at Margery, who was still standing beneath the sunflowers outside No. 22.

Beatrice, stunned, didn't say anything.

Margery turned and went back indoors, then drifted through to the garden, the sound of the drums reaching her over the house, distinct in the quieting afternoon.

Ivan, who now walked with a slight but permanent limp, was watching her. Staring at the flowering purple of an unloved hebe near her shoulders, she let out an isolated sob, put her hand to her mouth then went back indoors.

The front door had been left open and there was somebody standing there, but she couldn't see who it was because she had the sun – now making its way down the other side of the sky – in her face.

'What you doing in there all alone, Margery?'

It was Mr Hamilton.

He knew her name.

He knew she was alone.

He'd come for her.

Like they came for Edith.

Why had she told Robert Edith was in hospital having her hip replacement operation done? Why had she told him she was having double glazing put in the bungalow?

She collapsed against the hall wall to the sound of the drums outside.

'Everything all right?'

'I think I'm having a stroke,' Margery said, for the second time that day, as Mr Hamilton entered the house and Margery, unsure whether she'd screamed or not as she started to fall, blacked out.

# 49

Arthur Palmer crawled out from underneath the cake stall.

'Where's my mum gone?' he said.

Kate was about to respond when Ros appeared wearing one of the pink and black Carpe Diem T-shirts.

'Have you seen Martin anywhere?'

Kate shook her head.

Ros looked around her, trying not to panic. 'We need to talk – about Beulah Hill.'

Kate was about to respond when a black car drove, screeching, round the corner and stopped by the cake stall.

Three men got out and went straight to the door of No. 21.

The woman Margery thought was Lithuanian answered, and when she saw the three men standing there, tried to shut the door again, but they were already in the house, the last one knocking the woman to the ground.

It wasn't until she sat up again that Ros and Kate noticed her arms were covered in blood.

She got slowly to her feet and stared out at the street party, dazed, before disappearing back into the house without bothering to close the front door.

Kate was only vaguely aware of Ros beside her, phoning the police.

Without people realising it, the afternoon had gone silent.

Stunned, people at the lower end of Prendergast Road listened attentively to the screams and shouts coming from inside No. 21 because they weren't sure what else to do. A shot was fired.

The shot changed everything. People were no longer stunned; they started to run, instinctively. Only Kate and Ros stayed where they were, ignoring Beatrice who had Flo over her shoulder now while pulling Findlay after her towards the house.

A man ran out of the house and down the street. Kate couldn't tell whether it was one of the men from the car or not.

Another man ran out a minute later, but was shot at from inside the house and fell onto his side near the pavement where the plastic crates she'd been storing her cakes in were stacked.

Another shot was fired inside the house.

It was as though Kate and Ros were waiting for something – they didn't know what.

The next minute the woman in the Disneyland Paris T-shirt walked, barefoot, out of the house, her legs and some of the T-shirt covered in blood. At first Kate thought she must have been shot at, but then saw that she was carrying something in her arms, intermittently talking to it and looking about her at the balloons from Ros's stall, cut loose, drifting up into the sky. Six heavily pregnant women walked out of the house behind her, squinting up at the sunlight.

'She's got a baby,' Ros said.

There was the sound of sirens, in the distance, drawing closer. Then a police riot van turned into Prendergast Road. The sirens cut out then started again, making Kate jump.

Then they stopped, and the street was suddenly full of police.

# 50

Robert drove up Lordship Lane and through the village before crossing the South Circular and turning onto the old toll road that led up to the allotments.

Jessica stared blankly out through the open window, her elbow balanced, her hair whipping across her cheek so that she had to hold it back behind her head. They drove past courts full of people playing tennis, overhung by horse chestnuts already in full leaf, and two teenagers out flirting while walking a golden retriever. Jessica felt as though she was being bombarded by normality, but then what did she know? One of the tennis players could have spent last Sunday burying a wife who'd died of cancer for all she knew.

'She left the Walkman for Arthur,' she said, breaking the silence, as a motorcycle overtook them and they turned left up the hill.

'Is that a good thing or a bad thing?' Robert asked.

'A bad thing. The Walkman was Peter's.'

'How old was Ellie when Peter died?'

'She'd just turned thirteen.'

'That's a shitty age to lose anyone, let alone a parent.'

'And she was very much Peter's daughter. Arthur was

three, and the logistics of childcare – without Peter – kind of numbed me in the beginning. Then I went through this phase of crying all the time – if somebody walked into me in the street or if I spilt stuff in the kitchen, I'd be mopping it up, sobbing. After that I made a real effort not to cry until after the kids were in bed. I went to grief counselling but it never felt right. Maybe it works for some people, but to me it felt like everybody had these lives they didn't want – me included – that they were being forced to talk about. I'm sorry,' she said, starting to throb with a familiar anger.

'It's Ellie – I'm sick of it – she's gone through me and out the other side. I'm frightened of her.'

'We're all frightened of our children,' Robert said.

Semi-ripe hedges lined the road until they passed the entrance to the golf club, the sun bouncing off the cars in the car park. Then the hedge started again.

Robert stopped the car. The heat had bought a lot of people up to the allotments. As the dust where they'd parked rose and resettled, he turned to her. 'Jessica . . .'

She fell, sobbing suddenly, against his chest, grabbing a handful of his T-shirt and pulling on it.

Robert sat staring through the dust on the windscreen, automatically stroking her hair then kissing the top of her head without thinking – locked in the moment.

A man appeared in the door to the Nissen hut, which was open, and stood drinking a cup of tea, staring at them. 'You can't park there,' he said after a while.

Jessica sat up, wiping at her eyes and sniffing.

Robert turned off the engine and got out of the car. 'We're looking for someone.' He ducked his head quickly into the car to check on Jessica. 'You okay?'

She nodded, slivers of sunlight reflected from Robert's watch darting over her face.

'D'you have an allotment?' the man asked, eyeing them both, unconvinced.

'That one over there – you can see the red roof from the playhouse.'

'Ah.' The man relaxed slightly, and carried on drinking his tea.

'Have you seen a young girl – tall, skinny, about sixteen, blondeish? She comes up here sometimes.'

'We've got a lot of people up here today,' he said, pleased.

Jessica got out of the car, her hand over her eyes to block out the sun, scanning the allotments and the fringes of the wood. 'She's not up here,' she said quietly to herself. Then, louder, starting to panic. 'She's not here.'

With Robert beside her, she turned instinctively towards the wood and into a warm wind carrying the smell of fennel and wild garlic with it.

They started to walk.

'Hey – you can't park here,' the man called out after them. 'You can't just leave your car here.'

Jessica and Robert disappeared into the woods.

They walked in silence, their eyes scanning the woodland to either side – mostly beech, silver birch, elm, some dense holly and the occasional towering oak. They stopped, shaken, when three bikes passed them, the riders calling out to each other, excited. Robert was sure the last rider was Jerome, but maybe it was just the unbearable tautness of the afternoon – he'd only seen him from behind. They waited for the silence to settle again and once it had, started to call out, 'Ellie – Ellie.' They didn't know why they hadn't called out her name earlier. They waited, but heard nothing, and after a while started to walk again – Robert slipping on flint and chalk sticking up from the path.

He thought he might have been here once before – when

they'd first got the allotment; he'd come in with Findlay to pick blackberries and build him a bracken camp.

'Ellie!' they called out at the same time, stopping again.

They could hear the road again, louder now. They were nearly at the Crystal Palace edge of the woods.

The world was still out there and, as soon as Jessica heard it, time came rushing at her from all sides as it struck her suddenly that it was running out.

This hadn't happened when she'd been in the car with Peter, driving down Park Lane. He'd been talking about whether or not to open a business account and she hadn't been listening; she had been watching the fairground lights through the skeleton trees in Hyde Park thinking how much she'd like to be sitting in one of the carriages of the big wheel right then, surrounded by freezing night air. She turned to Peter to try to convey something of this, knowing she wouldn't be able to, but wanting to try – when they'd been hit. There was a crack as Peter's arm swung out unnaturally, and another crack as his wristwatch hit the windscreen. Then nothing.

This time it was different. This time, she was being given some sort of forewarning. 'ELLIE,' she screamed into the trees. There was the sound of animals that had nothing to do with them running through last year's bracken – but other than that nothing. 'She's not here,' she said helplessly to Robert.

As soon as Jessica said this, Robert became aware of just how convinced he was that Ellie was in the woods.

'Come on – let's carry on up here,' he said, starting up a smaller track, heavily covered in undergrowth.

But Jessica stayed where she was.

'Come on,' he said again, as gently as he could.

A woodpecker started up on a tree nearby.

Jessica was no longer standing still; she was virtually

motionless. The breeze had died down and not even her hair was moving.

Robert took a few steps along the overgrown track towards a holly bush, crushing dead leaves and wild garlic underfoot until the smell was overwhelming – when suddenly the three boys on bikes came crashing over the rise. It *was* Jerome.

The excitement had gone. Jerome and the others were curled over their bikes, riding with intent – until they saw Robert standing in the middle of the track.

As soon as he saw them, he knew.

Jerome – wearing Manchester United colours – dropped his bike suddenly, nearly falling off it, the back wheel spinning wildly.

His right hand, in a fingerless leather glove, clutched the handlebar still, preventing the whole bike from lying on the ground.

'Up there, sir,' he said to Robert, his eyes wide, breathless as the other boys skidded to a halt in the leaves behind him. The 'sir' was absurd, but no longer a taunt.

'Show me,' Robert said.

Jerome shook his head and picked up his bike.

'I need you to show me where. You two – you know the allotments?'

The other boys nodded.

'I want you to go and find someone – tell them what you saw. Tell them,' he said, before breaking into a run up the track, not even checking to see whether Jessica was following him.

He ran as hard as he could, slipping over the stones in the path. Jerome, who'd ridden ahead, was parked on the brow of the hill.

Robert stopped to get his breath back then stood up and started to run again. The tree in the dell just over the brow of the hill was an oak.

A black and white converse trainer hung from a broken-off stump and Ellie Palmer was hanging from the first branch – on an orange scarf, her hands grasped round it, her legs thrashing as if she was treading water, the tree creaking in the way it did during a storm.

Robert was aware of shouting something but he didn't know what as he ran into the dell and got hold of Ellie's legs, yelling at her to stop kicking.

Her knees were on a level with his shoulders and he had to press her lower legs against his chest to get her to stop kicking, but he wasn't holding enough of her for her to balance – not that she knew or her body knew that she needed to balance – so she fell forward over his head then flipped backwards.

Robert reached up as high as he could, trying to reach her thighs so that he could support as much of her body as possible.

'A blade – I need a blade,' he yelled into Ellie's jeans, unable to turn round and not even knowing whether Jerome was still there or not.

What felt like ages passed before he heard the sound of footsteps slipping towards him.

'Penknife,' Jerome said, throwing it to him, before vomiting over the trunk of the tree and Ellie's converse trainer.

'I need you to climb up and cut the scarf on the branch. Just cut the scarf . . .'

The smell of Jerome's vomit, rising immediately, was making him gag. And Ellie was kicking repetitively against his groin.

A deep-throated scream rang out from the brow of the hill.

Jerome, who was wiping his mouth, jumped.

'Ignore it – just ignore it,' Robert commanded. 'Climb the tree and cut the rope.'

Jerome burst into tears.

'Just climb the fucking tree,' Robert yelled, kicking the penknife back through the dead leaves towards him.

Ellie wasn't jerking now so much as thrashing; he needed to hold her higher, but was terrified of her falling onto the rope again.

Jerome, sobbing, slipped twice in his own vomit then got a foothold – and the next minute was hauling himself up onto the branch.

Robert couldn't see him any more.

Jessica was there and was trying to hold Ellie as well, yelling incoherently at her as though she didn't recognise her any more; only the pain she was causing her.

The next minute Ellie, Robert and Jessica collapsed into the undergrowth, Robert rolling away onto his back so that he saw Jerome crouched along the tree branch, staring down at him, the sun bright behind him.

A couple of his tears fell onto Robert's face.

From the brow of the hill the other two boys watched from astride their bicycles. They didn't come down.

They turned their heads at the sound of others in the wood, and watched as a golden retriever ran past them and down into the dell.

# 51

It was late afternoon. Joel was standing in the kitchen at No. 112, staring out through the window at Aggie crouched on the lawn with a magnifying glass.

He opened the back door calling out, 'Aggie?'

'I'm finding worms,' she shouted back.

'Where's mum?'

Aggie stared at him, then put the magnifying glass to her face again, catching the sun and temporarily blinding him. 'I'm finding worms,' she said again, the worms gaining a definite ascendancy over the idea of a lost parent.

Joel was about to go out into the garden when he heard a sound in the house behind him. He made his way into the hallway and there was Martin Granger standing at the bottom of the stairs, his hand on the banister, looking helpless and exhausted.

'What the fuck are you doing in my house?'

'I'm sorry. I was upstairs – Martina's room. Where is she?'

'She's gone,' Joel said.

'Gone? Gone where?'

'To the airport.'

'She's gone home?'

'We thought it was best.'

'Did she want to go?'

'Martin – she's gone.' Joel paused. 'So, what now?' He was genuinely curious.

'I don't know,' Martin said blankly, walking towards the front door as somebody started ringing on the bell. He automatically opened it – and there was Ros.

Martin stood poised awkwardly on the doorstep, staring at his wife, his body so full of its intention to leave No. 112 that it felt as if he might lose his balance altogether and fall onto Ros.

'Martin?' she said. 'I've been looking for you.' She stood staring at him. Then, her voice breaking at last. 'Evie?'

'Evie?' he said, wondering what on earth she was talking about.

'Tell me it wasn't Evie.'

'No . . .' He shook his head. 'No – of course not.'

'Of course not?' She stared at him.

'Martina. She's gone,' he added, aware that he was crying.

Joel turned away from Martin and Ros, framed in the doorway, and went into the garden. He made his way past Aggie, still crouched in what was left of their lawn, towards the garden office – and went inside.

There was Evie.

Sitting at her desk, doing something he hadn't seen her do in a long time, and that was sitting up straight, shoulders still slightly hunched forward, after finishing a line of cocaine. The face looking at him was bright, shining, the breath a little quicker than usual. There was a pile of dresses on the floor behind her, cut to shreds.

'Look at her,' she said excited, full of joy.

Joel followed her gaze, unsure what it was that Evie was looking at. It could have been one of two things – their daughter, visible beyond the office window through the bamboo, or the Evie doll on the desk in front of her. Joel didn't know.

'Oh – Evie,' he said, and started to cry.

'No, Joel,' she said, jumping to her feet, her voice full of a genuine concern. 'Oh, no – you mustn't cry. It's fine; everything's fine.'

He collapsed against her as she started to frantically rub at his back, staring happily out of the window at Aggie on her knees in the grass, one hand holding her hair back so it didn't get in the way, the other holding the magnifying glass.

Inside No. 22, Margery was being slowly helped to her feet by Mr Hamilton from next door.

She stood up as straight as she could, hurting everywhere, and her first thought was that she'd been raped. She quickly checked her clothing, which was intact, and Mr Hamilton's face, which was creased with concern, nothing more. He must have somehow managed to restrain himself and not given into his urges, which – according to the leaflet that local BNP canvasser Nick Land had given her – was uncontrollable in Jamaican men.

'I called an ambulance,' he said.

'Why did you do that?' Margery felt suddenly vulnerable, helpless and close to tears.

'Margery,' Mr Hamilton said gently, 'you were out cold for like ten minutes. That's not good.'

Through the open front door she could see the ambulance parked outside – the second ambulance on Prendergast Road that day. The gate was creaking on its hinges and a girl with bright ginger hair pulled back in a bunch was standing in the doorway. The hallway was suddenly full of people.

Gripping tightly onto Mr Hamilton's arms, she shut her eyes and tried to wish everybody away, but then Mr Hamilton was trying to calm her down, telling her he'd come with her. Edith went in an ambulance and she was still in hospital. They took Doreen away and she never came back. And look at what happened to Tom. The point was, not to let them take you.

Margery started to struggle then suddenly felt herself flop. Somebody was talking, incoherently, and she wished they'd shut up – until she realised, surprised, that the incoherent babble was coming from her own mouth.

The next thing she knew, she was being lifted through the air and everything was receding. Every now and then Mr Hamilton's face came into view, replaced by the girl with ginger hair and a man with short grey hair. She tried to grab hold of Mr Hamilton's arm – there was something extremely important they weren't aware of. It wasn't her they should be taking: there was a man lying in the bath upstairs bleeding to death. It was him they wanted; he needed urgent medical attention because he'd tried to kill himself. They'd got the wrong person. He was in the house still. Upstairs. They had to go back inside. Why hadn't anybody told them about Tom? If they didn't stop and turn round right now, it would be too late . . . why wouldn't anybody listen?

# 52

'Are you her father?' the consultant said to Robert, his eyes picking out bits of the forest on his clothing – the mud on his shirt, the ripped cuffs, the drying beads of blood across the back of his hand, the buds stuck to his trouser legs; unsure, almost distrustful.

Robert let out a thin, inappropriate laugh before he could stop himself. 'Her teacher.'

This didn't really explain anything.

'You have to stay,' Jessica said to him, when the consultant had gone.

'For a bit,' Robert agreed.

Jessica nodded.

'I'll go and get us a drink,' he said.

'But you'll come back?'

He gave her a brief nod, then left the room they'd wheeled Ellie into.

When he'd gone, Jessica leant forward, pulled the hair away from Ellie's forehead and made herself look at the red, black and indigo swelling round her neck.

She wondered if she'd ever move beyond this moment, if she'd ever be able to look at her daughter and not see her jerking below the tree – the orange scarf vivid against the perspective of evergreen leaves and bark. She wondered how much of Ellie and herself had really made it out of the woods. Lying her head on the pillow, she breathed in the hospital laundry and Ellie's breath – which smelt of painkillers and death – and thought of all the unanticipated horrors that love could give birth to.

Robert went to the vending machine in the corridor, and waited for the two cans to be dispensed. He hurt all over, particularly around his groin and abdomen where Ellie had been kicking at him. Along from the vending machine, there were two policemen in bulletproof vests posted on the door of a room. A nurse emerged. The eyes of the policeman sitting down on his chair trailed after her as she disappeared down the corridor, stared briefly at Robert as he opened his can of Coke, then sank back to the marbled lino on the floor of the corridor. The other policeman was standing by the window, in a block of sunshine, his head tilted back and his eyes shut.

Robert turned towards the corridor's open windows, which were emitting the slow, late-afternoon sounds of the outside world. Down below there was a courtyard that had never been intended by the original architects, but that had become a courtyard by default – through decades of extensive expansion. The flagstones seemed a long way down and looked as old as the chapel that lay enclosed and forgotten. The courtyard wasn't sought out by anyone and the winter-flowering cherry behind the chapel flowered for nobody but itself. Now it was in full leaf and, although all the blossom had fallen, some of it was still visible on the flagstones.

He had been here before.

The wards behind him used to be maternity wards. This was where Findlay had been born. He'd spent a lot of time by this window. Flo had been born here as well, but in the new Jubilee wing where they'd moved all the ante- and postnatal wards.

He turned round and checked through the open doors to the ward behind him, to see if he could remember which bed he'd visited Kate in after Findlay was born, but all he saw was an elderly woman, sitting in the chair by her bed, a crocheted blanket held round her shoulders, staring back at him, waiting.

He smiled at her, but she didn't smile back.

Her world was full of too many people she didn't recognise and, anyway, she was too busy waiting.

Robert turned away, sad. There was somebody walking down the corridor towards him.

Jessica.

She came and stood next to him, resting the side of her face against the chipped metal window frame.

He passed her the can of Coke he was holding.

'How is she?' he said at last.

'Asleep. I feel like I need a sleep myself – for about a hundred years or something. I don't understand it. At the beginning there's so much love it's almost inhuman.' She picked at a loose flake of paint on the window frame. 'You know what I'm talking about – you're a parent. Their first words, first steps . . . the joy's so . . . so immense you think it'll carry them – and yourself – through everything; but it doesn't because even then – when you're bent over, walking backwards across a garden lawn and their fat little vibrating legs are blundering and buckling after you, the unimaginable is already casting its shadow, mingling with your shadow and their shadow right there on the grass in high summer . . . right there, already.' She turned to him suddenly. 'She thinks she's in love with you.'

'Love,' Robert said, vaguely.

361

Jessica nodded, frowning, then took hold of his hand. The pressure of her hand was so natural, so uncalculated – it made him feel as if he was five years old again.

They stood holding hands, staring down into the court-yard.

After a while, he turned away from her towards the ward where the old woman was sitting. 'She's gone,' he said, bewildered. 'There was a woman sitting there waiting and now she's gone.'

Further down the corridor, the lift doors chimed open and an orderly pushed a bed out, swinging it left and up the corridor towards them and Robert recognised his mother lying on the bed – and Mr Hamilton walking beside her.

Margery was a long way away in a tunnel full of countless pairs of eyes all staring at her, aware of just how strong her desire for life and everything in it was. Along with most of her now-elderly peers, she knew that the real cruelty of old age was that enlightenment comes too late. In the face of mortality – when the fact that you only live once becomes inescapable – you're finally able to see, not right from wrong, but what matters from what doesn't. This impotent wisdom is what keeps you company throughout your final days – when there are more hours in a single day than any sane person would know what to do with.

There was only one pair of eyes left in the tunnel now and they were staring at her, not unkindly.

She recognised those eyes.

They were Robert's eyes, she thought to herself, unsurprised.

Here was Robert – he'd listen. She had something import-ant to tell him, but couldn't think what it was.

She remembered walking out with her mother once when she was very small. They'd gone out to buy wool and she had been wearing a new pair of shoes, which were red with a strap across – and they'd stopped to talk to an old man her mother knew, but she was too busy staring at her new shoes to really follow their conversation. Then she'd looked up, instinctively, to find the old man staring down at her with large wet eyes and her mother had jerked sharply on her arm to say thank you for the warm sixpence the man was pressing into her tiny hands and even though he was giving her something it felt like he wanted something from her and the next minute he'd shaken his head and said, 'I'd do it all again, I really would,' and a strange sigh had escaped her mother's lungs.

Why was it that she could barely remember her mother's face when the old man's was clear as day?

Was this what she'd meant to tell Robert?

No. She remembered now. She'd meant to tell him that it had been a day like today – the day he was conceived . . . she'd had the afternoon off from the electronics factory she worked in and had made up a picnic in brown paper bags for Tom and her.

They'd gone down to the river near the old bridge.

She could still remember how the picnic of sandwiches, boiled eggs and oranges looked on the grass; the broken shell from the eggs and the peel from the oranges on the brown paper. They'd sat watching the river in silence, content, holding hands. She was nearly thirty; he was nearly fifty. They'd known each other for over twenty years, and Tom was the reason she'd never left home.

She'd had boyfriends, but nothing serious. She put up with her mother and everybody else in the house treating her like an unmarried drudge, and she put up with it because of Tom. There were things nobody but she knew about Tom and, despite what they said about her afterwards, Tom and her only ever did it once – that afternoon after their picnic down near the old bridge. Because, as Tom so lucidly put it, it had been far too long coming.

Only he felt so bad about it afterwards, when they got home, that he ran himself a bath, got into it and opened up a couple of his arteries. The waste of it. So much waste . . . it got you mad thinking about it, and what might have been. Laughter might be for other people, but she'd known love . . . love had been hers.

That's what she wanted to tell Robert . . . because there were things children had a right to know.

*SIX MONTHS LATER . . .*

# Epilogue

As Lenny, Jessica and Ellie left the foyer of the Empire, snow was starting to fall on Leicester Square. It fell on the fair – bright, loud and crowded this near to Christmas – and Shakespeare's stony cape and garters. It fell on the women's hair, and the shoulders of their coats as they stared about them, temporarily bewildered, unsure they wanted to find themselves here. The snow got heavier, collecting on lashes and settling on lips before melting in a deceptively intimate gesture.

'Well,' Ellie said at last, 'it wasn't *The Sound of Music*.'

'It wasn't,' Lenny agreed, laughing.

They'd been to see a matinée of a documentary on Iraq that one of the Walking Wounded soldiers had been in.

'How many times have you seen it now?' Jessica asked.

'Seven.' Lenny smiled at her and shivered. 'I'm heading home.'

'You don't want anything to eat?' Jessica said. 'We thought we might get something.'

Lenny shook her head, 'I'd better get going before they start cancelling trains or closing down all the stations.'

Ellie and her hugged, Ellie holding on briefly but tightly

to Lenny – whom she'd spent two months with over the summer. They'd always been close, but now they were virtually inseparable. If it wasn't for Joe and Lenny, Jessica wasn't sure any of them would have made it through the summer. But Joe and Lenny had been there, and they had made it through, and now the summer felt like a long time ago. Especially now.

'Keep me updated on *The Nuclear Years* – and give Arthur a big kiss from me.' She waved at them both, then disappeared in the direction of Piccadilly.

Jessica and Ellie hesitated, nursing feelings of temporary bereavement, before disappearing into the unfamiliar faces themselves – in the opposite direction, towards Charing Cross.

'You want to get something to eat?' Jessica said, taking her daughter in sideways. They'd already decided they would eat after the film, but Jessica felt the need – after Lenny's departure – to run it past her again, wanting Ellie to accept some of the responsibility for the rest of the evening.

'Um,' Ellie agreed, distracted by the focus required to navigate the crowds.

Their relationship lacked the fundamental robustness of Lenny and Ellie's, which was able to withstand all sorts of cuts and abrasions. Jessica and Ellie were fragile together – especially since the summer – which had given rise to a deliberateness and lack of spontaneity between them.

Jessica led the way down a tiled alley between the tube station and Wyndham's Theatre, to a mahogany furnished bar run by Albanians.

They got the table in the window that Jessica had her mind set on, and sat looking through the reflection of themselves at the alley outside, whose edges were already piling up with snow, pricked by drips from the network of drainpipes crossing the alley's walls. The last time she had eaten there was with Peter, but she wasn't going to tell Ellie this.

'I met Martin – the guy in the film – over the summer,'
Ellie said.

'You did?' Jessica looked up at her daughter then back
down at the menu.

Ellie nodded at herself in the window.

'It was really weird – this room full of people who'd all
killed someone.' She paused. 'Lenny told me she killed five
people – five Argentinians – in the Falklands.'

'Did you ask her or did she volunteer this information?'

'I asked her.'

'Why did you want to know?'

'I don't know – I just can't imagine killing someone, can
you?'

'I don't know . . .' Jessica thought about this for a moment
then turned her mind to food again. She was hungry.

A waiter appeared.

'Have you made your mind up?' Jessica asked her.

'Oh . . .' Ellie's eyes scanned the menu. She frowned.

Jessica waited.

'Soup – I'll take the soup.'

Jessica nodded without comment, 'And I'll take the mackerel pâté followed by the chicken.'

'And for you – main?' The waiter turned back to Ellie,
who shook her head, suddenly shy.

'No main?'

Ellie shook her head again, blushing this time.

'Maybe you change your mind?'

'No,' Ellie mumbled, 'just soup.'

The waiter, sighing, left the table.

The food had been navigated. Jessica felt herself relax.

'So – how did the meeting go today?'

'Good, really good. They definitely want me to co-write
a first draft.' She paused. 'I think I'm still in shock – I went
into the meeting thinking I'd completely blow it.'

'You've got to stop being so negative – it really pisses me off.'

Jessica shrugged. 'Turns out one of the producers was a big fan of *How to Survive a Nuclear War* in the eighties.'

'See . . .'

'God knows how I'm going to find the time.'

'You'll find the time,' Ellie said.

Jessica smiled at her, unconvinced. 'The optimism of youth,' she said gently, aware that this hadn't exactly been one of Ellie's traits to date, but then she'd changed so much in the past three months. 'We'll see.'

'No – you'll make it work,' Ellie insisted with genuine aggression. 'This is a huge opportunity for you. What's so scary about getting a bit of recognition at last?'

'I'm not scared . . .'

'You're scared – you think you prefer the comfy clothes of despondency and despair because you've worn them in so they fit better.' Ellie paused, angry. The candle flame, which had been flickering wildly, managed to achieve a semi-upright position. 'Well they don't fit – you've outworn them. It's time for something new.'

'It is?' For a moment Jessica almost dared to believe her.

'I'm not being mean . . .'

'I know you're not.' Jessica pushed a trail of pepper round the table's surface with her forefinger and didn't look up.

'And I was really proud of . . .' Ellie's voice trailed off, her attention fixed suddenly on something passing in the snow outside. A man, shoulders hunched in a way that let the world know he was cold. 'Oh, my God—' She pushed round their table and ran through the door as the waiter arrived with their starters, his eyes following Ellie.

'Mr Hunter! Mr Hunter!'

Jessica sat with the mackerel pâté between her elbows, staring through the window at Ellie and Robert Hunter, Ellie jumping up and down in the snow, trying to keep warm, Robert huddled in his own world – caught out by Ellie; embarrassed.

He'd been found when he didn't want to be and Ellie was too full of a strange euphoria in presenting herself to him – virtually dancing in the snow – to either notice or care.

She was proving to him that she was alive – more alive than any of them had ever anticipated her being – and taunting him by dancing in the snow outside Wyndham's Theatre, aware of his eyes on her, her mother's eyes on her, and maybe even the waiter's, whose name she'd never know.

Then Ellie gestured towards Jessica in the window and Robert turned – and they waved.

They waved quickly – instinctively – happy that there was a pane of glass between them. Jessica didn't stand up, she remained seated, her nostrils full of mackerel pâté and candle wax. Robert remained standing in the snow, a despondent smile on his face, growing more desperate by the second. He had to go. He needed to go. If he couldn't extract himself politely – soon – he was going to start running, and his footprints would soon be covered by the fast-falling snow. It occurred to Jessica that, if he did that, they might never find him again – despite having his address, which was now No. 4 Beulah Hill. If he ran, she'd be left with a handful of chance encounters in Tesco on a Saturday morning, which was pretty much all she'd had since the hospital in July.

She was surprised to find herself standing up.

When – exactly – had she got to her feet?

And there was Ellie, who'd stopped dancing and was now pulling Robert forcibly by the arm towards the bar entrance.

They walked through the door, their hair wet with snow, Ellie's eyes shining, Robert looking alarmed – like a trophy she'd been hunting for a long time; one that had shown up when least expected, and was now being hauled in from the cold.

Ellie led Robert to their table.

Jessica and he smiled awkwardly at each other, and Robert must have been holding his breath as he smiled because he exhaled suddenly.

Ellie remained poised near her recently vacated chair, full of a sense of potential in the situation that the two adults either didn't see or were choosing to ignore. Which propelled them headlong into the realm of deathly small talk because every time they opened their mouths to speak they were only too overwhelmingly aware of what it was they weren't about to say. This meeting was precisely the one they'd been avoiding.

'I've been hearing all about St Paul's,' Robert said with an effort.

'Yeah, that's really working out – well, Ellie tells me it is, anyway,' Jessica said, resorting to speaking about Ellie in the third person – something that was sure to antagonise her – because Robert was making her nervous.

'And I hear you're writing a TV show,' he carried on, blindly.

'Hardly a show – a documentary.'

'Don't worry about her,' Ellie put in, growing in self-confidence by the second, 'She's pathologically self-effacing.'

Robert surreptitiously took in Jessica again.

'It's only in development at the moment – it might never happen.'

'They approached her – asked her to do it because of *How to Survive a Nuclear War*.'

'How to survive a nuclear war?' Robert turned to her.

Jessica batted her hand quickly in the air. 'A book I wrote. In the eighties.'

'Precisely,' Ellie said. 'The eighties were seminal nuclear years.'

Ellie's voice had an edge to it now. She didn't understand what was going on.

372

This moment had to amount to something. Robert had appeared in the snow outside; she'd brought him in – it had to amount to something. People just didn't appear in the middle of – what was now – a snowstorm, for no reason at all. Ellie wasn't sure what it was exactly she was expecting or wanted – something explosive – but there weren't any explosions and she was too young to see that she wasn't the only one who had survived the woods that summer. Robert and Jessica had survived them as well, only they were already halfway through their lives while Ellie had the rest of hers still to come.

'Anyway – you've been made deputy head at Ellington,' Jessica carried on.

'I have.'

'And how's Margery?'

'Margery?' Robert wasn't used to people asking about his mother. 'She's good – unbelievably good, actually. She's got Mr Hamilton staying with her in East Leeke at the moment.'

'Mr Hamilton?'

Robert nodded. 'He thinks East Leeke's paradise on earth.'

The waiter reappeared. 'Should I lay another place?'

'No – no,' Robert said loudly – too loudly. 'I've got to go.'

'Stay . . .' Ellie pleaded.

'I can't.' He shook his head.

'You can.'

Robert's eyes flicked quickly over to Jessica.

'I can't,' he said again.

'But – you can't just go.'

'I've got to get home,' Robert said, glancing at his watch, 'and I'm late.'

'You can't go,' Ellie insisted.

'It's fine,' Jessica cut in, unsure who she was reassuring – Ellie, Robert, or herself.

They stood by their table and watched him leave, walking out into heavy snow and pulling his collar up.

He didn't glance back at the bar.

'That's it?' Ellie said, collapsing in front of the cold soup. 'You didn't say anything—'

'We talked,' Jessica responded.

'That wasn't talk – that was crap. He turns up out the blue and – nothing.'

'Well . . .'

'He's in love with you.'

'Ellie . . .' Jessica laughed.

'He is – I know he is – it's just so obvious.'

Jessica stared at her. 'Maybe,' she conceded, more to calm Ellie down than anything. 'Sometimes the love is there, but—'

'But what?'

'But, it doesn't quite amount to what it should.'

'But it has to happen – if it's there, it should just happen. No, don't give me that sardonic smile-of-experience. Life's short.'

'Life is short,' Jessica agreed, vaguely.

'So you should just say what you mean to say – do what you mean to do.'

'Ellie, it doesn't work like that; nothing works like that.' Jessica felt tearful.

'Then make it work.'

Jessica stood up suddenly and left the bar. She heard something hit the ground and thought she might have knocked her chair over as she left, but didn't turn back to see, running instead out into the snow – barely able to see anything through it, and soaked through in minutes.

The alley was empty.

She followed it onto St Martin's Lane, the theatre foyers full of interval crowds – and watched a drunken woman with tinsel in her hair collapse happily onto the steps of the ENO.

374

There was no sign of Robert.

She turned back down the alley, avoiding an excited group of Japanese students, feeling suddenly disconnected from everybody around her. Maybe she'd had her time in this city; maybe it was time to leave.

Then she heard her name being called out, and saw Robert standing, finishing a cigarette under the wrought-iron and glass awning running down the side of the theatre, the white and brown glazed bricks shining out behind the silhouette of his coat. He looked younger right then than Ellie.

She walked straight up to him until she was standing under the awning, close but not touching.

'You didn't go . . .'

He shook his head and dropped the cigarette into the bank of snow at his feet.

Here – in the snow – in the alley – all the awkwardness had gone.

They held hands loosely.

'It's good to see you – it's really good to see you,' he said. 'We'll see each other again?'

She nodded then they pulled away.

She watched him disappear into the traffic on St Martin's Lane. Before disappearing, he turned back twice and waved. After a while, she walked back slowly to the bar.

Ellie had started on her soup.

'I didn't see him – he must have gone,' Jessica said to her.

Just after midnight, Jessica went downstairs to get herself a glass of water and stood drinking it, looking out at the moonlight in the garden as the wind made its way through it – half wishing to go with it to wherever it went, while the other part of her was happy to stand behind glass and watch it pass through.

As she watched – the dachshund puppy that Joe and

Lenny had bought her for her last birthday panting expectantly at this unanticipated appearance, she had a sudden memory of standing in the kitchen at No. 6 Pollards Close on a night just like this.

She'd stood drinking water, looking out at the Laing garden, which had been subject to quite a few of Linda's not-so-successful whims.

Jessica had gone back upstairs and there was Joe, standing at the hall window.

He'd heard her on the stairs and turned and smiled.

She'd gone and stood next to him at the window, unable to see – other than the night – what it was he'd been looking at.

After a while, he'd said, 'It's good to have the world to yourself for while.'

Jessica had agreed.

Then he'd said, 'I'm looking at forest – nothing but forest as far as the eye can see.'

Jessica tried, but couldn't see this.

Then a train had passed through the night – probably freight – along the tracks at the top of the close, and this had broken the moment and she'd gone to bed.

Now the wind and moonlight were playing tricks on her and the garden was overgrown anyway, but for a moment – when she looked out of the window – she saw nothing but trees as far as the eye could see, and the world was new and belonged to her.

# Acknowledgements

This book – simply – would never have reached its final state without the tirelessly honest input of my agent, Clare Alexander.

A huge 'thank you' also to the boundless enthusiasm, support and laughter-in-all-the-right-places of Clare Hey and the rest of you (you know who you are!) at HarperCollins.

If you enjoyed *The Rise and Fall of a Domestic Diva*, read on for a taster of Sarah May's acclaimed novel *The Rise and Fall of the Queen of Suburbia* . . .

Ever wondered what your neighbours *really* get up to behind closed doors?

Welcome to paradise: Pollards Close, Littlehaven, where the women are happy and the men go out to work. Here the UK's lowest crime rate goes hand in hand with the highest suicide rate; international politics is about as relevant as inter-galactic war and you'll need anti-depressants before entering the nuclear fallout shelter. Follow Linda Palmer, queen of suburbia, on an unforgettable descent through hysteria, adul-tery, aerobics and gazpacho into the black heart of suburbia, during a decade that taste forgot.

*The Rise and Fall of the Queen of Suburbia* is a darkly comic portrait of families, marriage, underage and overage sex, fake fur and black forest gateaux.

'Sarah May has a wonderfully observant eye for detail'
*Independent*

'A truly witty page-turner, both moving and utterly hilarious' Helen Lederer

# 9 DECEMBER 1983

**8**

It had been snowing in Littlehaven for what seemed like forty days and forty nights, and everyone over four feet tall was tired of having to keep Christmas tree lights on all day long so that flickering neon could counteract a numb and unanimous sense of foreboding. The real world and snow didn't go.

Then on 9 December, which was a Friday, it stopped.

Inside No. 8 Pollards Close the heating was pumping and the blinds in the master bedroom were still on tilt. Linda Palmer was naked, bent over the open drawer of her vanity unit. When she straightened up, a pair of clean bikini briefs in her hand, she was able to see not only herself, but the reflection of the TV screen and Selina Scott's face just left of her hips, at pussy-level.

She put the bikinis on and turned the TV off. Since the show's first airing in January she had done Diana Moran's workout faithfully every morning, but now they were nearly at the end of the calendar year, her body had clocked up over eighty hours of workout since then and the Green Goddess just didn't do it for her any more. The Green Goddess was for people who wanted to be like Linda Palmer, so what did she want with the Green Goddess when she already *was* Linda Palmer.

She turned back to the vanity unit, changed the Barry Manilow cassette in the stereo for a Bruce Springsteen compilation, then climbed onto the mail-order exercise bike she'd had long enough for the rubber stoppers on the legs to leave imprints in the carpet. With the switch on *dead flat* she started to pedal. If she didn't do twenty minutes before the aerobics class, sweat formed on the back of her pink and grey striped leotard, and at the end of class Dominique Saunders would ask her if she was okay; tell her she looked tired.

A slow track came on, something about Vietnam, and she switched to *gradient*. She was just getting into the uphill rhythm when the phoned started to ring. After counting six rings, she flicked the switch from *gradient* to *dead flat* to *off*, and dismounted.

'Is that you, Joe? Joe?'

'Hello? Mrs Palmer?'

'Joe – is that you?'

'Mrs Palmer?'

The voice sounded foreign, and she didn't feel like being spoken to by a foreign-sounding voice right then. 'Who is this?'

'Mrs Palmer, it's Mrs Klusczynski.'

'Who?'

'Jessica's advanced physics teacher.'

Linda backed away from the vanity unit, put the phone on the floor and jammed the receiver between her right ear and shoulder. The only word she caught the foreign voice saying was 'advanced'. 'Listen, if you're trying to sell me anything . . .'

'It's Mrs Klusczynski, from Jessica's school.'

'. . . anything at all, I'm just not . . .' she stopped herself.

A long time ago, she had trained herself to keep the unfamiliar in the background, and this is what she did now. The foreign woman faded out and all she could hear was Bruce, still singing about Vietnam, and she couldn't work out if he'd actually been or not or whether this even mattered. Maybe she was just missing the point. 'It's who?'

'M-r-s  K-l-u-s-c-z-y-n-s-k-i,' the foreign woman yelled down the phone.

Linda held the receiver away for a moment as forty years of Poland in exile made its way through the barricade of redneck vocals on the stereo. She had a sudden image of a woman who wore cardigans and the sort of slip-on shoes that were more prescription than high-street, emerging from one of the two-bedroom terraces at the top of Pollards Close with her severely epileptic son. 'Wait. Mrs Klusczynski, top-of-the-Close Mrs Klusczynski?'

'That's right. I'm also your daughter's advanced physics teacher here at school.'

'Her physics teacher. Right. I knew that. Sorry. I'm with you now.'

Looking at her alarm clock, she saw that there was less than an hour to go before class. The phone line fell in a coil between her breasts as she got back onto the bike. 'I'm with you now,' she said again, sideways through the receiver as she started to pedal.

'Mrs Palmer, are you still there?'

'I'm here.' She flicked the switch to *gradient*, and breathed out hard.

'I'm afraid there's a problem with Jessica.'

'A problem?'

'It's an interesting problem.'

Linda had never found problems interesting and didn't like the fact that Mrs Klushwhatever was enjoying this

384

conversation more than she was. 'Yes?' she said harshly, switching from *gradient* to *gradient: steep*.

'She refuses to complete – no – even to look at the module on nuclear physics, which is a compulsory part of the A Level examination.'

'What d'you mean "refuses"?'

'I mean she walked out of my classroom just now on ethical grounds.'

Mrs Klusczynski paused. She sounded pleased and this confused Linda, who had begun to swing her head slightly in an attempt to regulate her breathing. 'You're sure?' She couldn't imagine Jessica walking out of class.

'I'm sure. It's never happened to me before.'

This was too intimate – more of a confession than a comment. Linda arched her back and tried to relax her shoulders.

'But the school said to put her in for early-entry A Level Physics. They said she was a straight "A" – no doubt.' Linda was having trouble finding enough oxygen to speak, think and cycle at the same time.

'There is no doubt. All we have to do is get her to overcome her reaction to "nuclear" in the syllabus. I respect it. I respect Jessica and her decision,' Mrs Klusczynski added, 'but she doesn't fully understand the physics of it. Once she understands the physics, or begins to understand, she will be able to see – or she will be a lot closer to seeing, anyway, that it's not the physics that are corrupt.'

Linda became suddenly, acutely aware of her thigh muscles.

'. . . She can't study physics and turn a blind eye to the splitting of the atom. That's not wanting to know the whole truth . . . that's fanaticism –' Mrs Klusczynski said, carried away, '– and ignorance.' The art block was being refurbished and they were holding art classes in the science block this term.

She reached out for the plastic cup full of mixing water that Miss West had been using during the last period and drank it like coffee. 'I urge you and your husband to talk to her.'

'We'll talk,' Linda said, with a hungry intake of breath.

'Tell her – tell her not to throw her strength away on morality; that's not the path for Jessica. Tell her –'

'If she does the work she's meant to do on this . . . this . . . module, she'll still be in line for an 'A'?' Linda cut in, breathless, thinking about the number of times she'd told Dominique Saunders and others that Jessica was going to get an 'A' in A Level Physics – and Mathematics – at the age of fifteen. Trevor Jameson at the *County Times* was going to run a whole feature on her when she did – and here was some foreign woman whose garage wasn't even an integral part of her house talking to her about nuclear bombs; about Jessica and nuclear bombs. Why was this all anyone ever talked about any more? She lunged forward as her lungs collapsed, her entire weight on the edge of the saddle . . . fuck the bomb.

'Mrs Palmer? So . . . you'll talk to Jessica, Mrs Palmer?' Mrs Klusczynski no longer sounded convinced. 'I had to give her a detention, I'm afraid. Whatever I think of what she did, I have to make it clear to the rest of the class that walking out in the middle of a lesson is unacceptable behaviour, and . . .'

'You gave her a detention?'

'Don't worry, an hour's supervision in the special needs room is all it really amounts to.'

'Tonight?'

'Tonight, yes, between four and five.'

'But I'm having a dinner party tonight. The Niemans are coming to dinner, and . . . Jesus, that's enough.' She flicked the switch down and changed gear, at last finding some sort of karma between the balls of her feet and the pedals. 'Jessica was meant to be helping with the canapés . . .'

# 16

Mrs Klusczynski put the phone down, pulling a tissue out of her cardigan sleeve and wiping her mouth, which was tingling. She had phoned Mrs Palmer to talk to her about her daughter, and Mrs Palmer was having sex. She was sure of it. She looked at her watch – it was ten a.m. – and carried on dabbing at her mouth. There had been music in the background as well. Mrs Palmer had taken a phone call concerning her only child while having sex to music. She stared at the tissue, which was stained black – why was that? – then through the windows in their chipped, cream-painted metal frames. Standing up on the rungs of the stool, she could see the entire school playing field. It had stopped snowing.

**8**

Linda pressed the phone against her chest and rested her chin on it as she recalled what it was she had been trying to remember about Mrs Klusczynski, who lived at No. 16. It had happened the summer they moved in. Mrs Klusczynski had been to meet the local-authority bus that used to drop off her son, who was prone to, on average, seven fits an hour, and Linda was watching mother and son walk back up the street, when it happened: Peter had one of his fits and collapsed onto tarmac that was melting in the heat. She remembered Joe, who was coming home early from work, leaving the car in the middle of the road and breaking into a run – she'd never seen Joe run before. He took off his suit jacket and put it under Peter Klusczynski's head, and she watched from behind the blinds in the lounge as he carried the boy indoors, into their kitchen, sat him at the old dining-room table – the one they used to have before the glass-topped one – and gave him water to drink. Mrs Klusczynski hovered at the front door in a canary yellow sundress and Linda stayed in the lounge because she didn't know what to say to her. At that moment she didn't understand Joe bringing the boy into their house like that.

'You all right?' she heard Joe say.

'Peter?' Mrs Klusczynski's voice came through the front door.

Afterwards Joe walked mother and son up the street. Linda saw him and the Polish woman talking together and the car still parked in the middle of the road with the door open. For a moment, the world felt as if it had suddenly emptied and she was the only one standing there, watching, only there was nothing left to watch, and someone somewhere was laughing at her.

**4**

By the end of the aerobics class, Dominique Saunders' leotard was wet and the 'D' pendant on her necklace was stuck to her collarbone. She crouched down at the side of the hall where some orange plastic chairs were stacked, rocking back on the heels of her Reeboks while trying to regulate her breathing and not worry about the fact that Linda Palmer still wasn't sweating.

Mrs Kline from No. 10 sat slumped beneath the Union Jack the Guides used for church parade, in a well-worn peach and turquoise tracksuit. The sort of tracksuit you put on, Dominique thought, to gorge and cry in. The sort of tracksuit she didn't possess; not even as a secret. Mrs Kline was sitting with her legs stretched out across the brown carpet tiles that covered the floor of the Methodist Church hall, wiping sweat off her forehead and studying the palm of her hand.

Dominique wondered what had made Mrs Kline, who weighed sixteen stone and who had done the class barefoot, decide to take up aerobics. She didn't strike her as the sort of woman losing weight meant anything to.

Linda knelt down next to her, her blonde perm letting off

hairdresser-fresh aromas, and they watched as Mrs Kline put a pair of summer sandals on over some socks. It took her a while to get to her feet and when she did she walked unevenly towards where Dominique and Linda were sitting. Dominique realised, too late, that she was coming to speak to them, and that she should have said something before now anyway, given that they were all neighbours.

'Haven't seen you here before,' Dominique said.

'No. Well.' Mrs Kline smiled shyly.

'Thought you'd come along and give us a try-out?'

'Well. Yes.'

'Well. Great.' Dominique hung back on her heels.

'Well,' Mrs Kline said, clutching the empty carrier-bag her sandals had been in. 'Bye.'

'What was she thinking of coming here?' Linda said, realising that the story of Mrs Kline at Izzy's aerobics class – that she could try out first on Joe when he got home – would go well with the gazpacho tonight. 'Does somebody who's murdered her husband and buried him at the end of the garden have the right to come to an aerobics class?'

'That's only rumour,' Dominique said.

'Well, I thought we were going to have to resuscitate her after the high kicks and that's not fair on Izzy – having someone in the class she might have to administer first aid to.'

They watched the Reverend Macaulay talking to Izzy as she stacked the blue aerobics mats away.

'What's he doing?' Linda said.

'Telling her about the design for the new stained-glass window behind the altar.'

'How d'you know that?'

'There was something in the local paper about it.'

'But how d'you know that's what they're talking about?'

'That piece of paper he's showing her.' Dominique watched

Izzy in her rainbow-coloured head and wrist bands, smiling at the Reverend Macaulay.

'Is stained glass something she's into?' Linda asked.

Dominique shrugged. Mrs Kline was more of a problem for her. As much of a problem as the rapport between Izzy and the Reverend Macaulay and their mutual interest in stained glass was to Linda. Things that didn't fit; things that broke up the rhythm they lived their lives to. 'Right. That's me. Everything.'

'You off?' Linda asked.

'Mick's taking me out to lunch.'

Linda didn't want to think about lunch – she'd been on a liquid shake diet for the past fortnight. 'Where's he taking you?'

'Gatwick Manor – and the snow's stopped so we might actually make it.'

'The snow's stopped?' Linda said, then called out, 'See you tonight,' as Dominique left the church hall in her new sheepskin hat. 'Around seven thirty. Don't forget.'

Through the windscreen of her two-seater green Triumph that was an anniversary gift from Mick, Dominique saw Mrs Kline, in sandals, waiting at the bus stop, which was banked in grey slush. She slowed down, trying to imagine Mrs Kline in the seat next to her with her empty carrier-bag and having to talk to her for the ten minutes it would take them to reach Pollards Close.

Mrs Kline watched the green Triumph pass, not bothering to back away from the kerb when the car's acceleration sprayed the pavement with more slush as it sped up again.

Dominique told herself that Mrs Kline probably had shopping to do or friends to meet for lunch, but she knew this wasn't true: Valerie Kline had an armchair lunch every day in front of *Dr Kildare* repeats. She'd seen her through the windows of No. 10 with her legs rolled up under her, a plate of food balanced on the arm of the chair and Richard Chamberlain on the screen.

She'd probably watched the series as a teenager when it first came out, Dominique thought, suddenly able to see – clearly – an immaculate room with antique rugs and cut flowers that somebody had been taught how to arrange, and an overweight girl sitting in it, alone with Dr Kildare. And into this room walked a young man . . . or rather arrangements had been made for a young man to walk into this room and turn the overweight, lonely young girl into Mrs Kline.

Five years into the marriage, Mr Kline had bought No. 10 Pollards Close, a four-bedroom executive house on Phase III of the Greenfields development, and moved Mrs Kline and their adopted son into it. Then he left for work one morning and never came back. He hadn't been seen since, and nobody in Pollards Close really remembered him. Dominique had heard rumours during waxes at Sinead's that Mrs Kline waited a fortnight before informing the police. Without really knowing why, she had a sense that the marriage had been brutal. She thought about Valerie Kline at aerobics that morning in her peach and turquoise tracksuit, and the way she looked standing at the bus stop in socks and sandals with an empty carrier-bag in her hands. Then she thought about the table in the bay window that Mick always booked when he took her to Gatwick Manor because it overlooked the gardens. She couldn't have lived Valerie Kline's life; she couldn't have lived a single second of life as Valerie Kline.